THE GRAY BLADE

LAST OF THE HOLY HOUND TRILOGY

M.N.M. Abbott

ISBN: 978-0-989-7008-2-5

ACKNOWLEGEMENTS

A very special thanks to all those who live to see others smile and who also share my love for adventure. Read on and see what else my land of magic has in store this time around. Thank you family, friends, and everyone else who helped me to get this far with my dreams.

As far as specifics go, I want to thank David for making this second installation possible. Then I have a very big thank you for Lynda and "Cally." If it weren't for you two I would have been lost at the very start.

Thank you all.

God Bless!

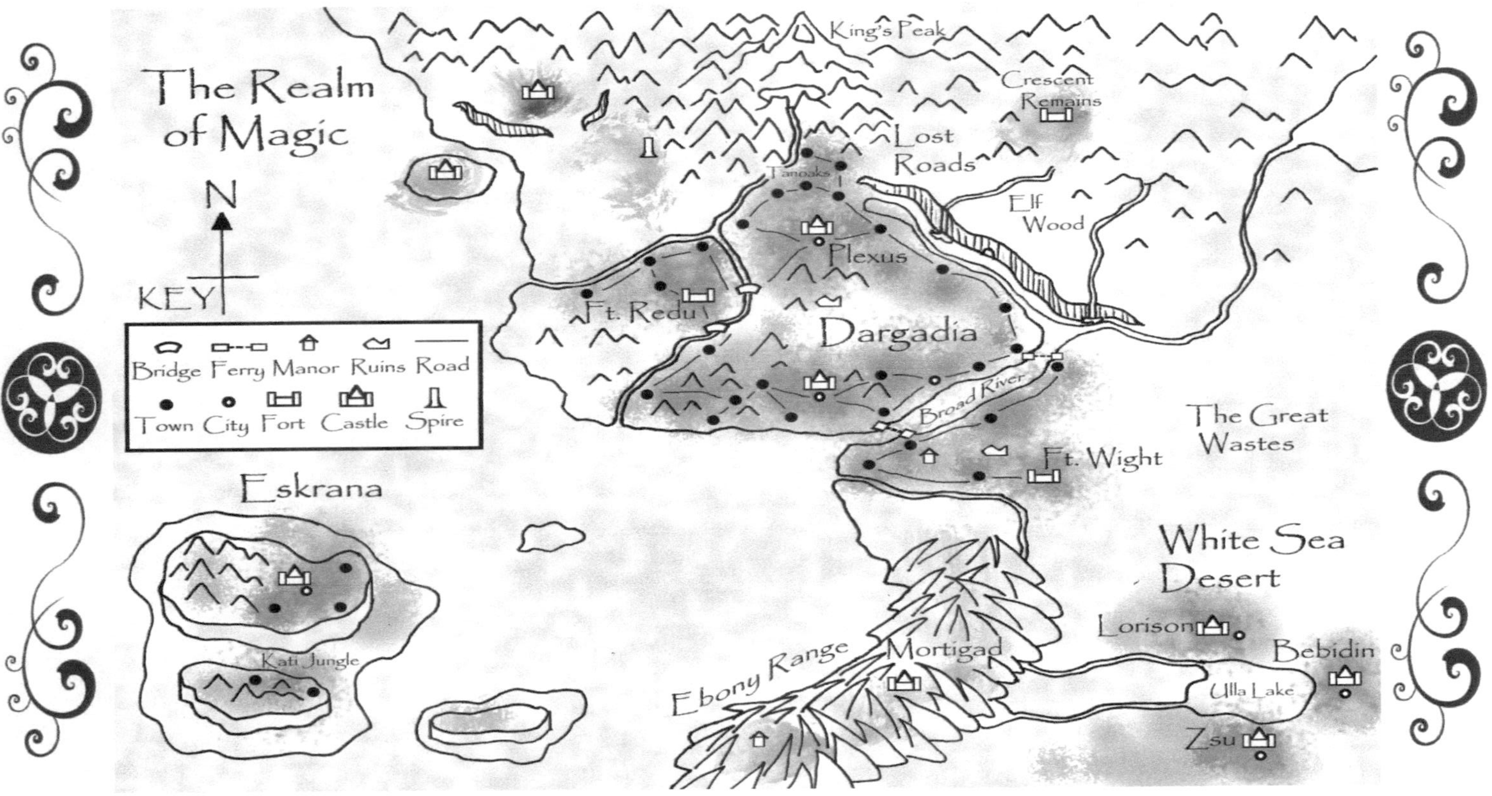

The Realm of Magic
N
KEY
Bridge Ferry Manor Ruins Road
Town City Fort Castle Spire
King's Peak
Crescent Remains
Lost Roads
Elf Wood
Tanoaks
Plexus
Ft. Redu
Dargadia
Broad River
The Great Wastes
Ft. Wight
White Sea Desert
Eskrana
Kati Jungle
Ebony Range
Mortigad
Lorison
Bebidin
Ulla Lake
Zsu

INTRODUCTION

Sir Oryn Reynard Conrad ran. His unnatural strength helped him to go as fast as his urgency demanded. The search took him far from the river and into the wind that carried smells from the town he had visited not so long ago. These pungent odors of chemicals and fumes were foreign to him, the same as most everything else from the realm of logic. If he were to find Adwen, he was sure to find her here.

The world he found himself in was so real that he had to remind himself at least once that this was all a powerful magical illusion, a manifestation within the Mirror of Lies. It had transported him here when he leaped after her. She was pushed into the deceptive glass. Oryn clenched his small fangs at the thought, as the one who sent her to this prison was also inside the illusionary world. Sycan, the White-Eyed Demon, was every bit as vile as the ancient texts in the Order described.

Oryn had become strong, but as much as he wanted to make the monster pay for torturing Adwen, he was too weak. His strength was sapped, as hers was the source for much of his. Jack and Alex were weakened in the same way. It was good that they stayed behind, he thought. If he could not pull Adwen free from the mirror, perhaps they could find help on the outside.

As the sun began to set he was determined to find her and bring her back. It was his duty. He had called her back from beyond death into her immortal form only to lose her again to this wretched spell. She was weak, wounded, and he was certain something else was wrong with her. Sycan had to have done more than just torture her and force the images of her family's demise into her mind. No matter what it was, he had to find her, and quickly. There would be no rest for him until he knew she was safe.

When the lights of the valley town were in sight from atop a hill, the supernatural warrior ran with more determination. Avoiding open streets, where humans would see him running faster than a racehorse, would soon be difficult. That kind of attention was not desirable. Once he reached the outskirts of the little city, the rescue would become much more methodical and covert. Sycan was surely in town as well.

Chapter 1
IT'S A WONDERFUL LIE

When the first set of car headlights flashed across the sidewalk, Oryn was already disguised. The magical garments he had earned from proving himself as Adwen's servant could shift seamlessly into whatever pleased him. To blend in, he melted away the sash, arm guards and other unusual accoutrements to don a black hoody and slacks with green scrawling designs. No matter what he wore, the colors stayed the same. As the car passed him, Oryn slicked back his brown bangs and donned the hood, continuing onward.

The street was dark. Infrequent cars and lamp posts illuminated patches of the neighborhood, but it did not matter. Oryn's green eyes could see perfectly in the gloom, and they glowed like embers. His ears were pricked for signs of danger. Thinking about it reminded him that his long pointed ears needed to be disguised as well. At a whim, both tips shrank down to a normal shape, and he also shrank his fangs. Remembering those minor details was becoming easier, while the quests as a Holy Hound were becoming all the more strange and hazardous.

Every so often, Oryn sniffed for her scent. Time and again, the same stinks and nose-burning odors bombarded him. There wasn't so much as a trace of the smell he was seeking. It was disheartening, though the search had to continue. Around him were more buildings with shops, signaling the beginnings of the downtown plazas. Would she be here somewhere?

That's when Oryn stopped dead. He knew exactly where to look.

The creature in human form checked for witnesses before leaping to the roof of the closest brick structure. Almost immediately his nose smelled the dirty river. Darting straight for the park, he felt the wind whip at his body, adding to the anticipation. His heart hammered as his feet touched the solid rooftops, rapidly carrying him across town. Keeping to the shadows, his sprint went unnoticed until he reached the bridge. The final landmark before the green hills and playgrounds forced him to slow to a brisk stroll. He had not found Adwen yet, so blowing his cover was still not a good idea.

The darkened green was hemmed in by towering pines and maples. Only a handful of lamps stood lit. From the point that Oryn reached the park, and all of the way to its center, he sniffed and sniffed to no avail. Feeling defeated, the warrior sighed. Frustration was expressed by the hardness with which he strode to a bench, awash in fluorescent light from overhead. Plopping himself down with a hard thump, he glowered. Clenching his jaw, the warrior mulled over everything he knew about Adwen and this strange world. There had to be something he had forgotten. There must be a clue as to where to find her in this dreaded maze of technology and ignorance.

Soon his contemplations ground to a halt at the sound of footsteps and rattling chains. Listening carefully, there were voices belonging to several young men. As they drew closer, a small rumbling growl reverberated in his throat. He smelled trouble melding with the stink of this city.

The pack of delinquents chuckled and chattered like curious hyenas. Six in all, they snickered and sized up the trespasser on the bench.

One young man approached Oryn, trying to get a good look at his downturned face. The hood made it impossible. To get his attention, he smiled and prompted, "Yo, G. You got the time? What's got you in the playground at night?"

Being discreet, Oryn sniffed to get a sense of how many were surrounding him.

When the stranger said nothing, one of the lesser hoodlums came up from behind and swiftly pulled back the hood, messing Oryn's hair. This was followed by a series of whoops and jeers. They knew the man was irritated when he slowly glanced over one shoulder at the culprit.

Then Oryn locked eyes with the ringleader, glaring angrily.

This did not impress the young man, who merely smiled. He let out a low whistle. "Those are some kickin' contacts you got. How about you let me borrow them?"

It did not matter that Oryn was unfamiliar with what contacts were. He understood that the riffraff was referring to his glowing eyes. This was a threat.

The lack of a reaction made the punk leery. He gave his friends behind the bench a look, telling them to prepare for resistance. "Okay, G. If you won't give up the contacts, I can settle for that bangin' hoody. The art on it is sick. What do you say?"

Softly, with a tone of defiance, Oryn murmured, "No."

Some of them were entertained and gibbered to each other while the leader's smile disappeared. Reaching for his back pocket, he drew out a folded device. With the push of a small button, out flicked a razor-sharp blade.

"Let's try it again. I'll explain it to you better. Take off the hoody, and you can walk out of my park. Do it."

In answer, Oryn narrowed his eyes and made their glow intensify.

At once, the cronies pounced. Two grabbed the warrior's arms as a third came, reaching out with a chain to restrain him by the neck.

Oryn's hands moved with an unnatural quickness, taking hold of the pair by the fronts of their jackets. He pulled hard, wrenching them over the bench headfirst into the cold cement as a groaning heap. When the chain came around his throat, he grabbed it and pulled again. At the same time, he raised an elbow, bringing the assailant's face into the rock-hard joint.

Nose broken, the young man fell away, gasping in agony.

While two more attacked, the leader saw how deftly the man was picking off his gang. Dropping the blade, he reached under his sweater for another weapon stowed behind the button of his breaches.

After punching one man in the gut and backhanding the other, Oryn pulled a knife from the back pocket of a fallen hoodlum. He pressed the latch the same menacing way that the leader had then glared dangerously along the muzzle of a .44-caliber pistol.

Afraid, the gang leader held the handgun sideways, pointing it and shouting. "Drop that knife, home boy. The party is over. Do you hear me? Drop that knife! Do you wanna die? Huh? Do you wanna cap in you?"

Oryn didn't pay the gun any mind. Locking eyes with the street punk, he played with the blade, expressing a fraction of his skill. He had seen a gun before and even seen one fired. Preparing to strike, he reversed his grip on the weapon, intent on frightening the young man into fleeing.

Just as the punk realized the stranger was going to come at him, he pulled the trigger. As he did, he fell silent and stared. The stranger did not fall.

Although Oryn had seen a gun fired before, he had never been hit by one. In an instant he heard the concussive sound and felt as though he had been punched in the chest. Surprised by the force, he gazed a moment at the young man's look of horror. Glancing down, there was a gaping wound as if something the size of a fist had ripped through. Blood was splattered all over the bench behind, the metallic smell wafting to his nose. For his first time being shot, Oryn concluded that he did not like it in the slightest.

A thundering sound rumbled in his throat. Snarling loudly, he looked back up at the punk who was beginning to shake. Then he took a deep breath and roared. The deafening sound filled the park, blotting out everything else. He continued to roar while the young man stumbled back before scrambling away into the night with some of his gang following.

Stopping to seethe, Oryn heard someone call from another corner of the park near the road.

"Hey, you! Are you all right? An ambulance is coming!"

A pair of patrolling police officers had heard the gunshot. The uniformed men hopped and skidded down a steep hill as bright lights flashed atop their car.

Oryn growled again. He didn't have time for cops.

Tossing the knife aside, the warrior bolted, vanishing in the shadows. He ran fast, coming to a tiny neighborhood before finding a bridge that crossed back to the other side of the river. It was so late that he saw no cars, so he ran to the opposing bank as quickly as he dared. Oryn carried the pace, leaping over a fence into a quiet factory yard, weaving between towering buildings and machinery.

On the other side of the property, he jumped the fence and ran a few blocks further, finally stopping on a darkened street corner. The pain had gone, and he examined how his body had healed. Touching his chest, the wound was completely gone, the magical garments having also been repaired.

Oryn heaved a sigh. If he had still been human, that gun would have been the death of him. Yet again, there was a sense of relief at being what he had become. Mortal weapons were hardly anything to worry about.

Sounds of police sirens reached his heightened senses, making him glance about. It seemed he needed a hiding place, not to mention a change of attire. Some distance away was an establishment with bright windows that smelled of food and drink. Making his way for it, he shifted his clothing into his personal favorite disguise: an expensive-looking black suit with a green vest and tie. He brushed away some of the remaining dried blood from his front and back. Once satisfied, the warrior slipped inside, escaping the wailing of distant sirens.

The bar counter looked the quietest, as most of the seats were empty. The majority of the patrons were gathered around a bright screen, screaming and jeering at images of men with helmets, grappling over an oblong brown ball. Sitting at the dim counter, he refused to watch because of their boisterous ruckus.

He was seated only a moment before a cheery waitress approached, in the middle of mixing a drink. She wore a shirt partially torn down the front – no doubt to expose part of her chest, making her more of an attraction to the bar.

"Hello, sir. My name is Rachel. What can I get you tonight?"

Not knowing whether she was like the barmaids of the magical world, Oryn used his best judgment in responding. "No, nothing thank you. I need a moment to think."

She blushed as she heard him speak. His accent was impossible to place, but it sounded distinctly European. Smiling, the girl replied, "Okay. Let me know if you change your mind."

As she stepped aside to keep working, the mirror on the wall caught Oryn's eye. A menagerie of liquors stood on the shelf there, but his refection made him stare. He had completely forgotten one of his personal flaws: How he felt about himself was directly shown by his reflection in any mirror-like surface. Gazing back at him was his beastly self, dark brown fur, fangs and all.

Suddenly this choice of seating didn't suit him. Getting up, he went to a more secluded table with high-backed benches that separated the tables from each other.

An older man close by looked up at the mirror just in time to catch a glimpse of the image. Blinking hard, he stole a glance at the stranger in the suit and back again. Grimacing at his empty cup, it seemed time to call it a night.

Relaxing back onto the springy seat, Oryn frowned. This search was not going well. The only thing he had managed to do so far was to get into trouble. Now he had become lost. Adwen had taken him on very short visits to this world. He had almost no experience in navigating it, let alone in finding his missing leader. Feeling more defeated than before, he propped an elbow on the table, resting his head in his hand, staring at the wooden surface.

Another waitress came to his table, and he smelled the human odor before she arrived. Ignoring her presence, he waited as she announced herself.

"Hello. My name is Shari, and I'm going to be your waitress tonight."

Sitting upright to respond, he didn't realize the name was familiar, along with the voice. The moment he made eye contact with the young brunette, Oryn nearly did a double take. It was her.

Shari watched his striking green eyes widen at seeing her. While he stared, she blushed, feeling awkward in the uncomfortable lull. Clearing her throat, she held a pen and pad. "Can I get you anything?"

The more Oryn gazed at her blue eyes, the more he knew it was Adwen, and that she did not recognize him. Calming down, he struggled to think of how to go about this. He had never seen her before she had become a magical being. The white and gold hair was gone, her skin was fair and not copper tan. The look about her was meek. The magic of the Mirror of

Lies had even changed her scent to that of a normal girl. She looked so different; she was so human.

At last, he murmured, "I have no way to pay."

Still blushing because of how intently he stared, Shari fidgeted and offered, "Water is free."

Thinking about it, he nodded.

Nodding in reply, she smiled and left.

When she was gone, he tore his eyes away from her with some difficulty. This was not what he was prepared for. If she was being deceived by magic then he would have to find a means of making her remember. It crossed his mind that perhaps this form of Adwen could be a deception of the mirror in his mind, a sort of trap or distraction.

Shari soon returned with a tall glass of water and ice. The cubes chimed inside melodically while she smiled. "I'll be taking care of other customers if you need anything."

"Thank you," he managed to say, catching another glimpse of her eyes. They did not glow as he remembered, but something in them was unmistakable.

His fingers felt the condensation on the outside of the glass. It was freezing cold. Playing with the texture, Oryn considered a few ideas of how to get Adwen's attention. She was inside that human visage somewhere. Perhaps, he thought, he could try to call her like he had when her spirit was departed. Oryn closed his eyes, mustering his feelings for her. Building up the sensation, focusing it, he prepared to call out her name in his mind.

Shari was busy in the back getting a set of platters for another order. The way the man in the suit had looked at her was intriguing, as she usually wasn't stared at by anyone. Mostly she went ignored. It was the other girls who were sized up or asked for phone numbers. Forgetting the awkwardness of the episode, she took up a set of plates, covered in steamy, greasy food bound for bloated customers.

Using her shoulder, she pushed through the squeaky, swinging saloon-style doors into the serving floor of the pub. Shari passed the table with the young gentleman, making sure she didn't as much as glance. Balancing plates while walking by unperceptive guests was hazardous. Each body or chair was a potential obstacle. She was nearly there, and the obese couple knew she had their order. As she approached, smiling, Shari set the first plate down and was about to serve the second when a word crossed her mind.

The instant she registered it, she forgot it, but a sharp pain struck her chest. It was a sharp stabbing pain that took her breath away. She gasped and buckled.

Across the pub, Oryn heard a crash and quickly looked around to find Shari at another table. She had dropped a hot plate of food on a woman in the exact second he had called her name. Also because of their link, though it was weakened, he felt the pain that had struck her heart. This was undoubtedly Adwen disguised by the mirror.

Shari completely forgot the mysterious pain that had come from nowhere as she was beset with yet another problem. The couple at the table was enraged.

"I'm so sorry, ma'am. Let me get some napkins. I don't know what happened."

Despite her best efforts, the woman was inconsolable. "You think this is funny? I want to see a manager! I want the manager right now!"

As if on cue, the manager arrived. The man graciously poured out apologies before steering Shari aside while others started to stare.

"Go in the back," he hissed. "Get your things, and wait for your last check in the mail. Get out."

Dipping her head, she darted out of his sight. Her hands shook as she clocked out, grabbed her purse and coat from the locker, and scurried out the front door.

Oryn watched her flee before casually standing to leave. He was not about to let her vanish. Losing her so many times in succession was depressing.

Out in the cool air, he found her walking toward a signpost by a bench. Watching her sit there, he felt some remorse for putting her through the trouble, but it was not real. He had to show her what was.

She shuddered. Sitting at the bus stop with her things, Shari couldn't hold back the tears. Weeping, she tried to catch her breath. The job was terrible anyhow, she told herself. The thought of quitting had been on her mind for weeks. As for apartment rent, she would figure something out.

Then she heard a set of polished shoes on the pavement beside her. Realizing somebody else was outside, drying her face became the next problem. But once she saw it was the foreign gentleman, shock made her cheeks go redder than the rest of her damp face. She quickly looked down the other end of the street, thoroughly embarrassed to be seen this vulnerable. The sleeve of her coat worked well for mopping herself up in a hurry.

Standing beside the bench with his hands folded behind him, Oryn pondered: How to remind a close companion, who does not know she is one, of who they really are? This was like a riddle. He almost scoffed. Adwen was always speaking in riddles.

"I am sorry your night is not progressing well," he said to break the silence.

Refusing to look up, Shari faked a laugh. "I've had worse, but thanks."

Oryn rolled his eyes. How right she was.

"Where will you go from here?"

She shrugged. "Back to my apartment, I guess. I have nothing better to do for now. Tomorrow I'm unemployed. Maybe I'll even go through the trouble of getting benefits while I job hunt."

Trying very hard to keep up with the terminology of this place, Oryn pretended to understand. "Perhaps."

Stealing a small glance, she asked, "Where are you from?"

Oryn paused. "It is difficult to describe."

"Oh." Shari got the sense that he didn't want to talk about it.

Hoping to draw her attention to familiarity, he said, "You look very much like someone I know."

Beginning to feel vulnerable in a more physical way, Shari looked along the street with more anxiety. Something in this man's behavior let on that he was more interested in her than she was comfortable with. Not only that, but they were alone outside. The bus was nowhere to be seen. Was it late?

He smelled the fear right away. Wary that she saw him as a threat, he changed tactics. "I do not intend to frighten. My aim is to console."

Shari's guard was still up. Pulling out her cellphone, the time clearly showed that the bus was late. Then she saw what day it was and realized her mistake. The bus wasn't scheduled for another two hours. Finding herself trapped in the dark with an overly interested male at night was not her favorite thing. Some girls fantasized about that, but she certainly did not. Things weren't going to improve by sitting on a bench, so she got up and started walking home.

To be polite and dismiss the man, Shari nodded as she passed. "Thanks for trying to help. I'm better off on my own."

Oryn's heart wrenched. He was losing her.

Walking off with the bag on one shoulder, she called, "Good night."

Allowing her to go, her words cut into him. Better off on her own? Was this the mirror's taunting him? He had made a mistake before this mess, having told her she was better off alone, because no one could ever be good enough to deserve her. He was dead set on denying himself of her affections. Having hurt her before with such a statement, it was coming back to haunt him. Taking into account all of Jack's speeches, Oryn realized just how much more she needed him than he deserved her. Eager for a second chance and to accomplish his quest in bringing back the Heir, the warrior turned to confront her.

Oryn called, "Adwen, wait."

A similar pain struck Shari's heart, though not as severe as before. Stopping dead, she looked back at the strange man. His expression was pleading at first, a far cry from the stoic one he had maintained prior. Then, as she felt afraid, his look became worried.

Oryn knew he had made a mistake. No one but her closer friends in this world knew that name.

Accusingly, she asked, "Where did you hear that name? Who are you?"

Before he could say another word she ran. About to pursue, he called again, "Wait!"

Flashing red and blue lights appeared behind him atop a police cruiser. The driver inside made the car whoop once, letting Oryn know he was of interest. When the cop pulled up and rolled down the window, he growled.

The cop raised an eyebrow. "Hey, buddy. Can we talk to you for a minute?"

Angry at the intrusion, Oryn had had enough of playing coy. Jumping up and bounding off of the hood of the car, leaving a large dent, he leaped onto another rooftop. Next, he dropped down and ran along a street that paralleled Adwen/Shari's route. He followed for several blocks, looking for an opportune location.

Shari kept running, even when she did not hear footsteps behind her. Most streets were dark, making safety seem much farther away than the next block. There would be no stopping, but she needed to catch her breath. This night just kept getting worse and worse.

Arriving on the main street, she felt more secure with plenty of light. Slowing to a walk, and regaining some breath, she knew she was a long way from her apartment. There were one or two more bus stops that were actually on schedule for the night. Reaching into her bag as she continued, her fingers searched for the transit pamphlet. It was wrinkled up somewhere in the seemingly limitless folds of the purse.

A strong hand grabbed her coat and pulled her into the darkness of an alley. She screamed and tried to resist, starting to search her bag for a different item.

Oryn felt terrible for causing her distress. He tried to talk some sense into her. "Forgive me, and please be calm. I must speak with you."

That was when Shari found what she was looking for. A loud crackling met their ears, and she swiftly jammed the Taser into the stranger's ribs. But when he was struck, she was even more startled to hear him yelp like a large dog and see his eyes flash bright in the dark. It was hard to see, but his clothes also furled around his body like smoke, reminding her of snakes. Even more frightened by the anomaly, she screamed again, dashing away down the next street.

The warrior didn't know what had hit him, but he was

stunned and collapsed. It had completely exposed him. His armor and medieval traveling garments were back, as well as his long ear tips and fangs. Quivering on the chemical-stained ground, he watched helplessly as she disappeared from sight.

Oryn released a soft whine. Then he gathered his thoughts and became determined. Getting to his feet and shaking off the last of the odd weapon's effects, the warrior resumed his pursuit.

The next street was much darker. Using his sensitive nose, he sniffed and sniffed, tracking the frightened girl. Tall trees and benches ran along the side of a small park. No lamp posts covered this place. It must have been out of sheer panic that she had run this way to escape him. As much as it pained him to make her feel this way, he had little choice. She had to be made to remember. All of life in both worlds depended on it.

Then another scent came to him, and he froze. Sniffing again, he knew there was no mistake. The hair on his neck stood, and his teeth clenched.

"Good evening, Conrad."

Whirling around, Oryn summoned his six foot sword into his grasp, snarling at the bench holding Sycan.

Wearing a red suit and white tie with black spots, it matched his eyes almost perfectly. For the moment he was not sporting his wine-red leathers made of human skin. Now he looked as if he could blend in with this world, aside from his bleach-white eyes.

Inclining his head, the demon chided, "Really? You must be joking. We both know that with Adwen in her current condition, you don't stand a chance. Put that thing away before you hurt yourself."

Practically shaking with rage, Oryn declined. Using animal speech, he snarled, "What do you want, snake?"

Unperturbed, Sycan rolled his eyes. "Come now. Name calling is beneath you. Contrary to what you might think, I am here to appeal to your better nature."

The angry Holy Hound growled. Sycan inclined an eyebrow. "Do you or do you not want what is best for her?"

Keeping a firm hold on his magical blade, Oryn ignored the baited question, turning away to follow Adwen's trail.

Sycan called out with a serious tone, "It would be a pity if you broke her in the process of trying to free her from this place."

The statement made Oryn stop cold. Fangs bared, he rumbled angrily, knowing the demon was trying to manipulate him. There was no telling what was a lie and what was true. Unable to ignore the fact that he needed clues to the mystery of the mirror, Oryn waited for further information.

A smile spread across Sycan's pale face. "If you wish to help her, put that away and I will tell you what you need to know."

After struggling with the concept, he dismissed the weapon, turned around to deal with the ancient fiend and spat, "Out with it."

Rising from the bench, he strolled closer. "This place in the mirror is a magical construct based upon Adwen's most unobtainable innermost desire. She wishes to be home, happy and free of all things magical. She wishes she never had discovered her lineage. This world is normal, with minor pitfalls and regular struggles for common folk. That is what she wishes to return to. Though she is not happy at the moment, she is indeed happier."

Oryn glared as the demon began to circle him, continuing to elaborate.

"The thing is, that her heart, the core of her being, is fractured. She is fragile, like a glass ornament. Stress it much more, and it may shatter. Each time she comes close to remembering the truth, Adwen breaks a little bit more. Think on this: Even if you do manage to make her remember, what awaits her on the outside will destroy her."

"That won't happen," Oryn snarled.

"Don't be so sure. If you've tried, then you've felt the pain it's caused." They locked eyes, and Sycan stood before him, looking serious. "The truth is that this is the one place where she can be happy. You and I both know she deserves better than the pain and loneliness of reality. If you want that, then risking her existence by trying to reclaim her is contradictory. Give her a chance. Let her go."

Staring down the demon, Oryn said, "She deserves better

than this place."

"Like what?"

"The truth."

Sycan rolled his eyes. "How original. Fine then. I tried my best to reason with you. If this is your choice, then I propose a game." Summoning a wicked green clock made of bones and wire, he showed the time was midnight.

Oryn's glare deepened, shifting between the monster and the floating omen.

"I give you twelve hours to free Adwen from her lie. Making her remember is not enough. You must make her want something more than what the mirror holds. If you cannot, I will kill you. Then I will have a little more fun. I want to know what happens when a heart of gold breaks. Do you know what will happen to her then? I'm positively dying to find out."

In a flash, Oryn snarled and darted off into the night, racing against the clock.

Again, Sycan smiled to himself. "This is going to be beautiful."

Shari was so scared she wanted to cry, but the pain in her lungs from running so far made it impossible. There was nothing to explain what she had witnessed in the alley. There was also no way to explain how that man had caught up with her. It was miles later when she staggered to a curb. She had arrived at the bus stop on the far side of town. With any luck, the next ride would come in a few minutes.

Looking around, she tried to spot any sign of the strange man. There was nothing but her and the trees amid the sleepy downtown neighborhood.

A loud wailing came from her bag. Jumping and almost screaming, she realized it was her phone. A wild '80s rock song blared louder when she pulled it out. Reading the caller ID tag brought some comfort. It was her mother. She sat on the nearby bench to take the call.

Oryn stood by to wait between the trees behind where she sat. He arrived just as the phone went off and now listened as she talked through the device held to her ear. It didn't take long for him to realize whom she was speaking with.

"Hey, Mom. How are you?"

(I'm good. How was work?)

Shari puffed. "It was the same as usual. Can't wait to look for a better job"

(You better not quit working there. Learn some coping skills. Not every place is going to be heaven on earth.)

Feeling guilty for being dishonest, she replied, "I'm not quitting, mom. Give me some slack. I need a chance to figure things out."

The more Oryn listened to the conversation, the more he became remorseful. This was like watching her speak to the dead. There was really no one there to have words with. Adwen's family was gone, never to return. He had seen men mad with grief converse with corpses. This was somehow much worse. It was hard to decide which was crueler: the truth, or the morbidity of the mirror's vile lie.

"It's all right. Don't worry. I'm fine. We can have lunch or something next weekend. Just have a nice night and get some sleep."

(I'm supposed to worry. I'm your mother, remember? I love you and good night.)

Shari smiled. "Love you, too. Good night, mom."

Pressing the power button concluded the call. The time showed the next bus would arrive shortly. As she stowed the phone in a pocket, Shari had the feeling of eyes on her. First she paused, then took out the Taser, keeping it in plain sight. A moment later, Shari knew the man was just behind, watching from the shadows. She found she was too afraid and too tired to run. Instead, she sat rigidly like a tightly coiled spring.

Oryn was saddened. She was so close, yet so far out of reach.

"If you come near me I'll zap you again."

He had no intentions of doing so, though it had nothing to do with her weapon.

Shaking like a leaf, she glowered, "What do you want?"

Solemnly, he replied, "To protect you."

A soreness was in her chest. Massaging at it didn't make it go away. Nevertheless, her attention was with the relentless stalker.

"I am here to help."

"Help me? I don't even know you. Just stay away."

"I cannot."

"I don't believe you."

Oryn paused, struggling to find a way around her fears.

When Shari heard the silence, she got the sense that he was unhappy. Out of curiosity, she asked, "Why do you want to help me?"

Choosing his words carefully, he knew the slightest slip could set him back.

"You have lost something. I must help you get it back."

Shari almost laughed. "I don't want my stupid job back."

"Not that," Oryn replied. "There's something else."

"What then?"

Another pause came before he answered, "Me."

The same pain swelled inside Shari's chest, but this time it lasted a long while. She squeezed the Taser tight, using it to deal with the discomfort.

That was when Oryn realized the real reason her heart was fractured. He had done it. The torture Sycan had put her through was only the cause for its worsening. He, not the demon, had broken Adwen's heart.

For reasons she couldn't understand, his voice seemed familiar. He didn't say anything else, and the pain subsided. "How did you know the name you called me?"

More regretful than ever, he answered, "That is your name."

She wanted to believe him, but was afraid to. "Who are you?"

Oryn didn't know how to tell her. Surely, his name would cause more harm. To spare her, he was tactful.

"I am one who serves at your side. There are others. They are waiting for you."

This seemed absurd, but Shari was beginning to believe him. "Why are they waiting for me?"

"Because you are the first of us."

Alarmed, Shari didn't know what to think. "I'm ... what?"

Oryn looked at his hands, wondering if he dared to do

what he was planning. It could work, or it could send her running again. As long as it did not hurt her, it was worth a try.

"If you wish, I can show you. I only ask that you not be afraid."

Wondering what he could mean, Shari's mind was a mess of confusion. Already scared, there didn't seem to be a way to be more so. Looking over into the trees, she spotted the man standing amid the branches.

Once he knew she could see him, Oryn let his true form emerge. His body swelled, elongated, thickened, and his face became blackened jaws with coarse fur. All of this changed in seconds until he was towering eight feet tall.

Shari gasped and looked away, shaking in horror. Covering her mouth, she struggled to keep from screaming. Tears streamed down as she shuddered.

It may not have hurt her to see him, but it pained him very much to see her reaction. His ears folded while he watched her try not to cry. He couldn't give up on her, but he could not put her through this any longer.

After a short while of being near panic, Shari got hold of herself and opened her eyes. "What are you?" He quietly stepped out of the dark beside her in his human disguise, making her give a small start and gasp.

Oryn couldn't look at her. Staring at the black pavement, he murmured, "I ... shall be in the park, if you have need of me. I'll not bother you further."

Stunned, she watched the creature that looked like a man walk across the street at the approach of the coming bus. By the time she boarded the roaring machine and looked out the window, she saw his outline fade into the night.

Chapter 2
JOB HUNTING

Cars rolled past the patio where cigarette junkies got their fix. Everyone else in the brick building indulged in dark brown perfection in a cup. Some sipped it hot, and others preferred chilled slushes, but coffee was coffee. Modern rock drowned out the din of orders and many conversations. Some patrons had laptops, taking advantage of the Wi-Fi.

Sleep had not come easily to Shari. The past night's happenings lingered with her every second since first approaching that stranger. She was in the shop beside one of the big windows overlooking the busy street, reading a wide-open newspaper. As she skimmed the help-wanted ads, the sound of his voice pervaded her mind. Try as she might to look for a new job, she couldn't focus. Sighing heavily, she took another sip of her java. Maybe it all had been a dream.

Returning her attention to the paper, she saw the side of the sheet was being pushed down by the head of a walking cane. Taking a second to look at the head, it was a steel depiction of a chimera, flowing out from the top in a trinity of horns, fangs and jaws. She looked up to see its owner, a man in a blood-red suit.

The man smiled, adjusting his sunglasses in a gesture that expressed apologies and salutations. Taking back his cane, he fondled the fearsome figurehead.

Leery, Shari greeted, "Good morning."

"Good morning. I couldn't help but notice, you are looking for work."

"Yeah, um. I'm not having much luck."

Taking a moment to watch her, he chuckled. "I could help you there. My name is Mircea. I'm a businessman."

As he reached to shake her hand, she felt a twinge of fear, but cautiously accepted the gesture. "My name is Shari."

He tilted his head genteelly. "My company has been established in the states for a while and is beginning to make good progress. Is there any chance that you might consider working in a different location?"

Her answer was no, but instead she murmured, "Uh ..."

Readjusting his spotted tie, Mircea chuckled again. "There is no rush in your decision. I'll just keep an eye on you and get back in touch. Sleep on it."

"What does your company do?"

"Not to boast, but it does a lot. We do innovations. Our focus is the future of technologies in every kind of production. We need smart, strong, trustworthy employees for our tasks."

Shari swallowed another sip of coffee to mask her unease. "Thanks. I'll think about it."

He nodded in appreciation then said, "Oh! I almost forgot to ask. I'm in town trying to find an old associate. He's been avoiding me recently, and it's very important that I find him."

"What does he look like?"

Mircea stared for a moment. "He gave you a run of trouble the other night."

A chill went down Shari's spine.

"Do you know where he's hiding out?"

Instinctively, Shari didn't want to tell. Something about him was terribly wrong, though she didn't know what. Recomposing herself as she had suddenly forgotten to breathe, she cleared her throat, which was turning dry.

"I'm not a hundred percent sure. He took off, and I didn't see where he went."

"Ah. That's too bad. Oh well. He's bound to turn up sooner or later." Mircea took out a business card and handed it to her. "I'll be in touch."

Examining the card as he left the shop, she noticed a red ring with a line through the center, like a calligraphy depiction of a cat's eye. No print was to be found on either side; there was only the logo. Tossing the card in a nearby trash can, Shari knew it was pointless to keep scanning the classifieds. There was something else she needed to do.

High up in an oak tree, Oryn sat back in the crook of two boughs, resting his eyes. He had not slept. The hours rolled by, and he knew time was short. If she didn't come to find him, he may have to break his word and seek her out.

Overhead were many leaves, chattering with the wind. Down below were tall bushes beside the steady river. Few frequenters of the park lingered in this area. His nose told him so. This meant that being bothered was highly unlikely.

His mind normally would have been busy, pondering strategies. He had none. His heart wasn't in it. He had created this mess; there did not appear to be a way out of it. If he was going to lose her, nothing he could say or do was of use. Oryn was a warrior, a knight. This dilemma was beyond him.

When he got a whiff of her scent, his eyes snapped open wide.

One side of the park was closed off with police tape, so Shari had to enter another way. Avoiding the apparent crime-scene investigation, the rest of the city landmark was open to travelers. Walking through the playground, looking for anything unusual, the strange man was not to be found. Taking her search elsewhere, she began to browse the dense greens along the river's edge.

She pondered what she was going to do if she found him. First she would warn him that he was being hunted. Next she would see if anything about this person was familiar, besides his voice. She didn't know him, but somehow did. It was confusing. Maybe she should go back to reading the paper and making phone calls.

The grass underfoot was wet with dew that the sun had not dried. It soaked the tops of her tennis shoes, making her wish she had worn something different. Biting her lip, Shari searched the brush. Eventually, she found him and froze.

He stood on the other side of a natural screen. His piercing gaze startled her at first, but she quickly got over the shock. The stranger came closer, and she could see his ears came to long points, like an elf. His clothes were anything but ordinary, with a broad waist sash and several pieces of black armor. The pair of boots he wore didn't make a sound in his approach.

When he came closer, Shari nervously took a step back.

Oryn instantly stopped, not wanting to frighten her.

Now that she found him, Shari's mind was blank.

Gently, he murmured, "Thank you for coming."

"I'm sorry. I don't even know why I'm here."

He frowned. "What made you come?"

"It's your voice. I can't get it out of my head. Your voice is familiar. I don't know why."

Relief washed over Oryn. She apparently wanted to remember him.

"Why do I know you?"

"We've traveled to many places. You are the one who leads us."

A little pain pierced her chest, but it wasn't bad.

"The journey we set out on cannot continue without you."

"These places we've traveled are different from this, aren't they?"

Oryn nodded.

Shari paused before becoming frustrated. "This is insane. I can't believe any of this."

It was Oryn's turn to be confused. "Then why seek me out if that is so?"

She heaved a sigh. "It's this guy. He came by and said he was looking for you." Seeing his glare meant he understood. "I don't know what he wants, but I don't think it's good."

"Keep away from him," Oryn warned. "Nothing good ever comes from that wretch."

A voice called, "Again, with the name calling. You are so rude."

Oryn's eyes snapped to the fiend walking across the green and Shari turned, surprised at having been followed.

The red suit and tie smoked as if they were smoldering until they changed into Sycan's leather armor with spiked shoulders. When the pair of sunglasses evaporated, revealing his eyes, the sight made the girl's skin crawl.

"Shari!" he said, smiling. "That was a fair deception you played. The problem is that I knew you would go looking for this animal. Thank you for helping me find him more quickly. Why don't you go back to your job search? This creature won't be bothering you any longer."

Oryn stepped forward, shielding her from the demon and snarled, "Go back to the pit that spawned you, filth."

For a moment, Shari thought she understood the sounds he made.

"Names don't become us, little warrior," Sycan mocked. "Time's up. Say your good-byes to the young lady. She has other places to be."

Oryn warned her, "No matter what you see, stay back."

A glimmer appeared in the warrior's other hand an instant before a massive sword materialized. The weapon shocked the girl, but before its wielder leaped into action, she saw a symbol by the base of the blade. It looked floral and painfully familiar.

A storm of images flashed through her mind and were gone again.

Grasping her head, she thought she was going insane. As Oryn lunged for the villain, sounds and smells of blood and fire came and went. All the while in these intense visions, his voice was there, too.

Sycan laughed at the warrior and dodged the large blade. Punching the weapon as it knifed for his chest, he redirected its course for a pine tree. The blade stuck fast, and the look of outrage on Oryn's face made the demon smile.

"Aw, look, Conrad. She's trying to remember for you."

He did not need to look. Oryn could feel it. The magical link was regaining its strength. Sneering and giving the sword a hard twist, splinters exploded, and the sword came free. To resume the fight, he swung hard for Sycan's laughing face, only to miss again. The demon continued to toy with him as if he were a child. After swinging and missing several more times, Oryn lashed out again, but Sycan had summoned a weapon of his own.

Billowing shadows unfurled from his hands, turning into a black, raw, tarnished blade. It was several times broader than Oryn's Greatsword, looking as if it were fashioned from a weathered piece of darkness straight from the void. Six white spikes protruded along the opposite side from the cutting edge, resembling the teeth of a fallen dragon. They were stained by centuries of bloodletting.

Gazing back at the knight-turned-Holy Hound, Sycan's smile became a monstrous grin. The white around his eyes faded to black in a fit of glee. When he spoke, it sounded like many voices at once.

"The blood of your ancient predecessor is on my blade, Conrad. I'll add yours to my collection in a moment."

When the evil sword brushed Oryn's aside like nothing, the warrior barely brought his back up in time. As the hit connected, it sent Oryn tumbling backward across the grass.

As Oryn worked fast to recover, Shari's mind cleared enough for her to see what was happening. Every few seconds, more visions of carnage and wondrous scenery bombarded her mind, but the state of the familiar stranger kept her lucid. It looked as if he were going to lose this fight. She did not want him to.

Sycan struck Oryn's upheld blade again, again and again. Each time the warrior staggered back, absorbing the force, but unable to retaliate. When Sycan struck another time, it was much harder, and his opponent's defensive strength faltered and failed.

Oryn's sword, the Rose Thorne, was knocked loose from his hands, and its master was sliced diagonally across the ribs and belly.

Shari screamed as he yelped, hardly realizing she could feel a portion of his pain. Cupping her hands to her mouth to stifle cries, she watched helplessly as he fell back, landing flat on the lawn.

Face contorted by pain and sheer determination, Oryn held an arm around his torso, valiantly crawling to reclaim his sword. It was inches from reach when he was grabbed by the back of his jacket and lobbed into the base of a nearby oak. More anguish coursed through him, some of it passing over to Shari.

Kicking at the turf, Oryn struggled to sit upright against the tree. Blood poured from the wound, drenching his clothes and armor. He clenched his fangs, sneering at the demon.

Standing proudly over the warrior, the monster looked down his nose, smirking. "At the least, I expected another name to be tossed at me. No matter. Sticks and stones. They should have included swords."

While Sycan savored the moment, Shari couldn't stop staring at the bright green eyes of the warrior. Those brilliant eyes became even more familiar, and she wanted to know why. Her psyche reamed itself, searching for the answer to the question:

Who was this stranger who was about to die for her?

The mental images ground to a screeching halt. A single moment played before her mind. Those eyes were gazing at her, glazed with tears. He was cradling her in his arms. She had been dead seconds before, and he stared at her then with the only tears he had ever shed. His tears of joy had been for her.

Her eyes became wide, and she whispered breathlessly, "Oryn."

Sycan casually cracked his neck to and fro. Hefting his monstrous weapon up, he aimed for the knight's racing heart.

"Good-bye."

A mass hit the demon from the side, bowling him over and sending him tumbling.

Using his immense dark powers, Sycan landed on his feet. Turning around, he smiled at the young girl.

"Now, Shari, it is not polite to interrupt."

The world around them began to blur. Figures of police officers rushing to the scene of the battle shattered like glass, one by one. Like exploding figurines, parts of the illusionary world fragmented, sending sparkling sprays of light and dark in all directions.

Standing over Oryn, she clenched her fists. Her whole body started to crack, light shining out from every fissure. Growling, her blue eyes glowed, boring into Sycan's.

Staring him down, she rumbled. "I am Adwen."

Chapter 3
NO REST FOR THE WICKED

"Oryn! No, you idiot!"

Jack ran toward the broad mirror designed to imitate a spider crouched over its web. Being an inch under five and a half feet tall no longer affected Jack's speed, as his supernatural strength empowered him to bound down to the bottom of the dreary cavern.

Lying by the shiny, silver frame was the unconscious Marine, Alexander Greeves. The knock he had taken over the head should have killed him, but his body was becoming much like Jack's and the knight's. Examining the extent of the damage, Jack determined that Alex was alive, with a small bump and a splotch of blood staining his blond hair. Once he had turned over on the limestone, he started to come round, groaning inaudibly.

When his baby-blue eyes were open, Jack sat him up and showed him a hand. "How many fingers do you see?" Blinking to steady his sight, Alex gave him a cynical look. "One."

Jack heaved a sigh of relief. "Thought he broke you, Jarhead."

"Who hit me?"

"Sycan got you again," Jack explained, helping Alex to his feet. "After that he pushed Adwen into the mirror and went with her."

"What? How?"

Jack waved before the Marine's eyes. "Maybe you are broken. Magic, you dummy. This is the Mirror of Lies that Adwen and Oryn told us about back at the sky king's palace. You know? Where you got your weapon to officially join the team?"

The golden shortsword shaped similar to an eagle feather had fallen from Alex's waist when he was knocked out. He reclaimed it and put it back where it belonged. Feeling the knot on the back of his scalp, he asked, "Where did Oryn go?"

Folding his arms, Jack stared blankly, waiting for him to come to the answer on his own.

Alex glared at the insulting expression. A second passed, and he glanced sidelong at the mirror. Eyes widening, he murmured, "Oh."

"He just went inside a few seconds ago."

Suddenly, the surface of the mirror rippled with black rings like water. Sycan emerged and pounced, knocking them to the ground.

Before the pair could respond, he bounded away through the cavern passage, laughing maniacally. The sound echoed endlessly in the bowels of the cave.

Turning over on the ground, looking after the fiend, both warriors gaped in shock. The sound was dying down as they exchanged looks of confusion. Next, they gasped and shielded the backs of their heads as the giant mirror exploded with a mighty crash. Shards and slivers showered them, but they were lucky not to be cut.

On the ground where the mirror used to be, in the midst of the bent and broken frame, stood Oryn. The first thing Oryn did was check his wound. It was gone, and not a spot of blood could be found. Anything that had affected their bodies within the mirror had disappeared with the false reality it contained. Noticing Adwen standing close by, gazing out into the dark recesses of the cave, he stopped checking himself, and waited to see if she was all right.

The first thing she felt was the cold, dank air. It was very still, not unlike the feeling within herself. Inside, an indescribable emptiness resurfaced. It was the same as before she had entered the false world. Her blue eyes were dim from weakness. The dark circles beneath them were back. Her tan skin was flushed. Even a gray shade had appeared in her white and gold armor, dulling the shine. Emptiness weighed on Adwen, just as the lapping waves of grief found her heart again. It steadily rose, drowning everything else.

Jack and Alex silently got to their feet, watching her turn around with the same air of suspense as Oryn felt. The knight was unaware he was holding his breath. Watching her face him and give an empty look, he hung his head in shame.

A high-pitched dog cry broke the silence, and Adwen threw her arms around Oryn, burying her face in his chest.

Her sobbing was what they heard next. Getting past the surprise, he didn't hesitate to hold her shuddering form, before frowning and resting his cheek atop her white hair. For a time, they stood together, her in tears and he returning her embrace, wishing he could take back all the pain, but knowing he could not.

Bright sunshine made colossal trees covered in life glow. The three large Griffins found the Holy Hounds in a clearing, where the jungle canopy let them through to pick them up. Astride the feathered beasts, Adwen shared a mount with Oryn, while Jack and Alex flew on either side. During the flight from the tropical island, no one spoke. Powerful gusts would have made communication difficult, but mostly they were weary.

Among them, the one who did not have a mind empty of

thoughts was Jack Towers. When he was a cop he was always keeping track of his surroundings. He treated his role in the team no differently. Already having a knack at studying individuals, his ability to read open thoughts served him well. Whatever was at the forefront of a nearby being's mind, he could hear in his own.

There were a few exceptions. Alex usually did not have strong, or "loud" thoughts, as Jack called them. It took a single glance to know the Marine was cold. The newest warrior did not have his magical garments yet. This meant that whatever clothes he owned were at the mercy of his inevitable transformations into a massive creature with claws and a tail. At the moment, the Marine was shirtless, shivering in his shredded peasant trousers.

Steering his feathered companion to go closer, Jack smiled and shouted over the roaring wind. "Hold on, Jarhead. We can get a pair of new-issue uniforms in the city."

Alex scoffed and tried to disguise a smile but failed. "Don't you have anything better to do than mess with me?"

"Yeah," he admitted, "but everybody's quiet. I don't hear anything. Brain surveillance is only good if you're gathering data."

"Weird."

Seeing him glance at Adwen with the knight, Jack picked up on a moment of uncertainty in his friend's thoughts. "What's bothering you?"

Alex kept part of the explanation buried. "Don't you feel that?"

The childish look faded from Jack's face. "I know. I'm keeping an eye on her."

"I don't know if it's the animal part of me developing, but something about her has me edgy."

Beneath him, the Griffin chortled, "Me and my flock sense the same."

"Why do you think we're anxious?" Alex asked.

"Give me some time to work that out," Jack urged. "I'm magic now, but not that magical. I need a chance to listen. When she starts thinking louder thoughts, I'll let you know. Until then, go back to shivering."

Alex rolled his eyes and did exactly that.

Together, they covered many leagues over water until they reached the main island with the gargantuan plateau. Returning to the capital city, the aftermath of the battle lay everywhere.

Hundreds of adobe homes were destroyed; roads and shops were reduced to rubble. Even more casualties of the demon assault littered the ruins. Mourners and soldiers of the dark-skinned civilization worked hard to begin the recovery. The return of the four Holy Hounds brought relief, though not celebration in the light of what lay before them. The heat of day made corpses of both man and Griffin decay rapidly, filling the decimated hub of the kingdom with the smell of death.

On their approach to the damaged yet standing palace, the king's adviser was waiting for them. Isla approached, eager to see the state of things. When the team slid down from the Griffons' shoulders, Isla stepped closer and spoke in his thick accent.

"I cannot say how glad I am to see you all again. The king asked that I wait for your return, no matter how long — ." He stopped in mid-sentence at seeing Adwen. The injuries did not look serious, but she looked ill.

She noticed the pause and returned his stare with a baleful one. At first she thought to greet him but instead she looked away.

"Lady Adwen?" He turned his attention to the knight at her side. "What has happened?"

"Much," he answered.

Isla took the hint and left the topic alone. "Come inside. Come. King Zulo must know that you are living."

As they were leaving the plaza, Jack and Alex bid their Griffin mounts farewell. Within the grand palace, the only indicator that there had been an assault was the occasional broken vase or mirror. Some rubble had fallen from the roof, but things were far better here than in the city.

Adwen could smell the sadness of everyone nearby. Keeping her mind blank was the better alternative to being totally present. That would be anguish. All of the death would trigger thoughts she would rather not have. Her family had been eradicated. Whatever she did, she could not afford to become emotionally involved, or risk more pain.

Her bare feet and Alex's padded in the midst of boots and a pair of sandals, creating a dreary percussion on their way to the king's chambers. Reaching their destination, they found the door had been ripped from its frame. Inside was the king's vast bed. Beside it were king Zulo and his queen, grieving over the body of their son, dressed as a warrior for burial. He would later be taken to a pyre, but custom demanded that he be mourned properly for a time.

"King Zulo, I have brought Lady Adwen and her warriors."

The large, muscular king touched his head with that of his wife before standing to meet them. He stepped methodically toward them, shell-shocked by recent events.

"Thank you for all you have done," he greeted in his deep voice. "My son passed at the start of the attack. He was brave for his people."

Adwen's eyes threatened to tear up, downcast in remorse. "I'm sorry."

The strong voice of the king soothed, "No, Lady Adwen. You could not have saved him. Now he is passed on and out of harm. His memory is of honor and courage. There could be nothing better under the circumstances." When she furtively glanced up, he saw how she looked and frowned. "Lady? What have you suffered?"

She could not stop the tears this time. Unable to utter a word for fear of breaking down completely, Adwen stood still, letting the drops fall on the ground.

Oryn stood as close as possible without touching her. As much as he wanted to hold her as he had before, this was neither the time nor place. Adwen was an emissary for the Light Spirits. He could not openly show affection anywhere; he was a servant.

Addressing the knight, the king was firm: "Take her to a room for rest. All of my guards are tending to the people. Stay as a watch over her and never leave her side."

No one could have stopped Oryn from doing so in the first place. Nodding sharply, he replied, "As you wish, King Zulo."

Isla directed the group to follow, leading them to a nearby wing of the palace meant for esteemed guests. The sleeping quarters were spacious. Jack and Alex received rooms to themselves across the large hall from where Adwen was escorted. A large veranda looking out to sea greeted them, and a cool breeze brought in fresh air from across the waves. Isla left to attend to other duties, allowing Oryn to stand guard.

Adwen let them shepherd her to the lovely room, but she was unmoved by the view. Any other day she would have gazed, contented by the sight. She felt as though she were the only one there, even though it was not true. Ignoring the knight's presence beside her, she padded across the room to the bedside. Usually broad window sills served best for sleeping. For now, the cradling comfort of a pillow and sheets was more appealing.

Watching her settle into the folds of the fine linens, Oryn seated himself on an empty dresser by the door. He could see everything from this location, but having her in the center of his line of vision was his primary intent. It did not take too long for her to fall asleep.

Hours passed during his vigil. As she slept, he hardly took his eyes off her. It was not just that he had feelings for her. This time, a nagging sense of unrest urged him to be an astute guard. Memories of how dawn's first light no longer danced on her skin to heal her were disturbing. In their flight back, the sun had hardly mended her wounds. Scratches with her silver blood glistened, lingering far longer than normal.

She appeared to be resting well, serving as some comfort to

Oryn. There was little to do now. Investigating her new maladies would have to be done later. For now, Adwen needed peace and quiet. Sitting back atop the dresser, finally closing his own eyes for sleep, Oryn drifted off as daylight outside lingered into the afternoon. Oryn was tired and just beginning to notice. For the time being it was safe enough to grant himself a little rest as well.

Oryn drifted into a dream and was mildly aware of the fact. The details sharpened, forming the silent guest lounge where King Zulo had once taken Adwen, Toth and himself some weeks ago. Flames licked the air along white marble walls, illuminating the space. Out the broad open windows was solid black, where there should have been sea and sky. The room was cut off from the world, isolated in the eerie dream.

Across the way, beyond the collection of chairs, stood the three stair steps to the elevated side of the room. At the center atop the stairs stood the tall, narrow golden frame of the Mirror of Truth. Only the looker could see what was within, a reflection of their truest inner identity, no more and no less. To anyone observing, there was only a normal reflection. Seeing Adwen in front of the glass staring into its depths, he was surprised and concerned. Going to her, the closer he got, the darker the room became.

By the time he was at her side, there was only him, Adwen and the reflective surface. Nevertheless, his attention remained on her. Standing just behind, he looked at the glass. He saw her sad, mournful composure. Whatever she was seeing did not make her feel better. The circles on her face were darker, and the light in her eyes was barely noticeable. After a few seconds of observing, Oryn concluded it was time to intervene with her misery. To end it, he gently touched her shoulder.

When she moved, her image in the mirror did not mimic her movements. It remained stark, staring as she slowly turned her head to face him. As she did, Oryn felt a chill. Seeing her face, his heart hammered madly. Horror filled him while she gazed back with eyes as red as rubies, drilling into him. The whites around her irises faded to black like the room, spreading to the rest of her body like a wicked virus.

Oryn awoke with a gasp. It was nighttime, and he still was within the cool room on the far side of the palace. All was still, including Adwen in the bed.

Calming himself, he detected the scent belonging to Jack, indicating his presence. Breathing a steady sigh and settling back against the wall, he watched Adwen sleep, uttering no sound.

Watching Adwen from the doorway with folded arms, Jack's mahogany eyes glinted as he grimaced. "I think your dream is right."

Oryn frowned.

Adwen heard Jack's voice and woke but did not stir. Sorrow kept her mind clear of thoughts, making Jack none the wiser to her listening. Nothing they said impacted her. She did not care and could not. Her heart was numb.

"There has to be something we can do. What happened in the mirror?"

Oryn rumbled softly, "There's nothing to tell."

Jack wasn't going to give up so easily. "How about another question: What did Sycan do to her in the mirror?"

"Nothing. Anything he did was to me. He left her alone."

Jack turned to give a glare. "Like I said, what did he do to her?"

Frowning back, Oryn rumbled in his animal speech, "She did not know me. The mirror had tricked her into thinking she was her old self from before."

After receiving the answer, Jack was thoughtful. "If the mirror was like a spell, then it must have been broken by you or her from the inside. I'm sure that she broke it by wanting to remember who you are."

A sick feeling was in the pit of Oryn's stomach. "I fear her desire to kill Sycan was what broke the mirror."

Jack shook his head. "No, that can't be it. Did you sense any anger from her when the mirror's spell was breaking?"

Thinking back to when she was standing over him, Oryn could not recall anything similar. Conceding to the pestering cop's point, he admitted, "Her desire was to protect me once her memory returned. She was only beginning to remember the demon's handiwork."

"That's good. Then it seems to me that Sycan was just horsing around. Whatever he has done to her occurred before going into the mirror. That leaves to question: What did he do?"

A bitter frown formed on Oryn's face. "Something worse than death."

"Going back the Order in Dargadia is not a good option," Jack said. "The elders can't be allowed to see her in this state. What do you think we should do now?"

Looking back to Adwen in the sheets, he rumbled, "I am open to suggestion."

Both studied her motionless form, pondering separately. Their thinking was put to an end when the wind brought in a smell different than that of salty spray. It smelled of dirt and dander. Adwen smelled it as well. Only she recognized the scent.

Jack and Oryn dashed out to the veranda, peering from atop the palace watchtowers. They thought they glimpsed wings but could not be certain.

Adwen warned from her side of the open landing, "Harpies."

Both warriors stopped to stare. Neither had heard her join them. Jack had never seen Harpies before, but Oryn knew what they were, having battled a few at her side some time ago. Oryn turned to Jack and growled, "Fetch Alexander."

"No," Adwen commanded. "The four moons are coming out, and one of them will be full, as always. Let him change in his room. The three of us are more than enough to handle these beings." She leaped up high, taking hold of a decorative wall facet, ready to climb to the rooftop. Taking care of some pesky invaders temporarily alleviated her from internal anguish. It was a welcome distraction. Stopping to look over one shoulder, she saw that her warriors were still standing on the ground level. "If you're still open to suggestion, how about giving me a hand?"

Jack and Oryn exchanged abashed expressions before following.

The three crept up to a tall stone statue of a Griffin and carefully looked over the back of it to see how many enemies had arrived. Their chests and torsos were that of men, while the rest of their anatomy was of a powerful bird of prey. Armed with spears and knives, the beasts wore loin cloths decorated with primitive adornments. More than twenty of these eagle-headed warriors folded their wings as they landed silently on the roof of the palace. Their talons and hands barely made a sound.

Watching them all craning and bobbing their heads, Adwen felt strong gusts toss her golden bangs and white hair as she whispered, "Jack? Are you able to pick up anything from them? What do they want?"

More wind tussled his short black hair and the red patch of strands on his brow. He wet his lips, sorting through the mess of different thoughts. "They are curious. It seems like they are here to investigate. I can't figure out why."

Oryn glowered. "They're scouts."

"It's weird that they would come at night," Adwen said. "Their vision isn't suited well for this lighting. If they are scouts, we can't afford the chance that they are preparing for an attack. The populace cannot handle anymore. We have to get rid of them."

"Many will likely flee at the onset. We cannot stop them all."

"It doesn't matter," Adwen said. "Those that fly away will know that the city is protected. So long as we make a clear point to these scouts, the chance of an attack will dissipate. Are you ready?"

Oryn frowned but nodded, as did Jack, summoning his daggers.

Adwen growled and transformed, retaining her armor as she became a tall, white hound warrior. Flexing her clawed hands, she sized up the flock, staring along her muzzle. Pale moonlight made the golden emblem on her brow glisten. Coiling up, she leaped high through the air, landing on all fours in the thick of the winged invaders.

Some were bowled over, and a few took flight. Adwen bit into arms and legs, tossing startled Harpy bodies aside. Those that retaliated never landed a strike with their bone knives. She was too fast. Her claws and bladed hand guards countered, dealing deadly blows in fractions of a second.

Blood splattered her white coat and pristine armor, but the light in her body turned the filth to dust, blown away by the wind. As the fight continued, more blood hit her fur and disappeared an instant later.

Jack decimated his opponents. Changing into his hound form to combat them, his burly body bore a thick coat of black and white fur in the likeness of a Siberian husky. His curled tail flicked and swished while he bounded and stabbed at the much weaker creatures.

Oryn's sword was even more deadly. It cleaved in half those that did not take wing. None were a match or posed a threat. To the Holy Hounds, these beings were just a nuisance. Moments into the one-sided fight, the flock's survivors took to the air. Most of the Harpies were maimed but able to fly off and report the failure of their mission. Squawks and trills accompanied them on their way.

While the last of the avian warriors fled, Adwen stood and barked to Jack, "Even though they're retreating, I want you to check and see if any more are in the city."

Adwen froze as a sharp spearhead sliced the side of her neck. A droplet of silver blood trickled down. Pain from the minor scrape registered in her mind, suddenly infuriating her. The anger grew quickly and fiercely, like a match dropped in a vat of fuel. A burning sensation lit up, coursing along every limb and out to her extremities. The air danced about her body as she turned to face the unfortunate Harpy that had dared to attack her.

The Harpy's wing was damaged, grounding him. As he could not flee, he chose to take a stand. Pulling out his bone dagger, the bird warrior stared along his raptor beak with scarlet eyes.

Adwen snarled, baring sharp fangs. The armor she wore began to melt, warp and tarnish. Leaping with jaws open wide, she sunk her sharp fangs into the Harpy's torso, throwing him aside.

Jack stood in shock, staring as if she had gone out of control.

Oryn's eyes widened in alarm as the once pearly armor on her body crumbled and disappeared.

Mauling the bird creature, Adwen was lost to a world colored red. The rage in her was overpowering. Even when her victim was dead, it did not sate the bloodlust. Casting the carcass farther out, she went after it, ready to rip it to shreds with her claws. As she bore down on the mangled mess of feathers, flesh and bone, Oryn headed her off. He dismissed his sword and stood as a barrier between her and the body. Determined to end the rampage, he watched her charging closer and shouted in an effort to bring her to.

"Adwen!"

She stopped and stood over him, snarling. When he did not move, she roared an unearthly sound in his face.

Oryn stood his ground. While she seethed and growled, his harsh expression became unsettled. Her eyes were still blue, but a red light flashed in them. Worse yet, the golden mark on her head was fading. When it disappeared entirely, Oryn realized that the blood from the Harpy was not turning to dust on her fur. Black and red smears, splotches and streaks covered her from head to foot. Adwen's wrinkled muzzle was drenched with it.

After a moment of snarling and growling at Oryn, the red cleared from her vision. Her body felt weak, drained. She slowly changed into her elf-like form, lowering her gaze to the bloody roof tiles. A terrible numbness haunted her as she realized what she had done. That was the moment she realized her powers were gone.

The knight gaped, horrified. Adwen's sweet face was still covered in blood. She refused to lift her gaze. The golden hair that had been her bangs was now as pale as the rest on her head.

Tasting the Harpy blood in her mouth and smelling it made her feel shame, almost as much as she felt from the way Oryn was staring. Saying nothing, Adwen turned to the south side of the palace roof and leaped down to the city streets. When she landed, she changed into her hound self again. This time, her form was not humanoid. In the absence of her light powers, she had the form of a massive white dog. She did not give a care to the alteration of her true self and continued to run through the city, away from Oryn's looks.

While Oryn stared after the direction Adwen had fled, Jack came alongside to stare as well. The hulking black and white hound whined, "Did you feel that?"

Oryn did not respond. Looking to see if the knight was stunned or just ignoring him, Jack added, "I'm going to get Alex. Find Adwen so she can open a portal and get us out of here. We'll find you as soon as possible."

Into the evening, Alex lay awake on the bed in his private guest quarters. When the room grew dark, it dawned on him that he could see in the gloom perfectly, almost as if it were a cloudy day. Then again, he had been able to see when they ventured into Mortigad to rescue Adwen from Sycan's clutches. Only now was it becoming clear how quickly even his human body was changing. He did not like it, yet he did not hate it either.

It had been less than two weeks since he was locked away on the fifth floor of a county jail. The charge was murder; which degree did not matter.

Ever since he arrived in the magical world, he had been experiencing things he never had imagined. On top of the prospect of magic or becoming something more or less than human, the experiences he was having originated from hauntings of his past. At first, forgotten memories of the war returned, fresh as the breeze from the open window. Then, memories he had purposefully buried began to rear their ugly heads. Though Alex had been warned, it did not seem possible that he could ever be forced to face the frigid fact that his wife, his love, was dead. That horrible truth was locked away, deep down with any feelings for himself in the loss.

Until Adwen reached into his heart the other day and ripped down his mental barriers, the Marine had not confronted the loss. In one fell swoop, she smashed his internal defenses from the pain, laying him bare to his own torment. Staring at the ceiling, self-loathing knotted his stomach. When the police had arrived that night to answer a call, he was instantly taken into custody, later to be accused of her murder. Ever since finding her with his own knife in her heart, Alex had cut himself off from his feelings, inadvertently leading everyone to think he was cold as stone.

He was a hero from the war, dishonored by the accusations of murdering his wife. The looks and threats from his brother-in-law had made no impact. Alex could not recall what was said. It took weeks for him to shield himself from thoughts having to do with her death. Now those wounds were reopened, weeping with ill feelings.

Alexander Greeves hated this pain. He would not be feeling it now if it were not for Adwen. She was responsible for this anguish. Who did she think she was to interfere with his personal affairs? His heart and mind were his own business, no one else's. As far as he was concerned, this breaking of his mental defenses was a betrayal.

When his light-blue eyes began to glow brighter, the Marine felt his heart beat faster. Heat filled his body, and he knew a full moon was rising. The robes given to him were going to handle the change better than anything else available. They were roomy, held to his body by a loosely tied sash. These clothes did not need to be removed, thankfully.

Alex turned over to sit on the bedside, breathing a heavy sigh. As he did, a cold pang struck his chest. It was gone right way, but it left behind a haunting chill. He felt weaker. The sudden sensation frightened him. According to his animal instincts, something terrible had just happened. It was a moment before he considered that the source could be Adwen. A resounding roar came from outside, and he knew it was her.

Getting up to see what was going on, the full moon appeared in the sky, stopping him in his tracks. Staggering and falling to his knees, muscles constricted and bulged. Bones elongated, letting the blood-laden tissues extend even further, filling in his shifting frame. He grasped his aching head, as lengthening claws drove into his scalp, which was quickly becoming part of a thick, yellow pelt.

As the warrior began to howl, Jack opened the door. The more powerful Holy Hound was in his smaller shape. At seeing Alex in mid-transformation, he winced, trying to ignore the loud crackling of joints. Unfortunately, his acute hearing made it impossible. When it finally ended and the hound warrior was on all fours panting, Jack told him, "I definitely do not miss that."

Alex heard the comment but ignored it. "What's happening? Where's Adwen?"

Jack shook his head. "I wish I could answer either of those questions. Come on. We need to find her and Oryn."

Adwen's paws padded down bleak streets, claws scraping cobbled stones. With the warmth of her light powers gone, she felt even colder than before. Smells of dead yet to be uncovered filled her nose, dulling the metallic odor of blood matting her coat. Shame flooded her as she wandered. This was not supposed to be possible. The Light Spirits were supposed to shield her from darkness.

In that moment she felt completely alone. Arriving in the plaza by the fountain, sounds of burbling and splashing drew her closer. Though the top was smashed, water spilled down into the shallow pool, rippling with the light of the four moons.

Adwen went up to the edge. First she lapped at the cool contents before gingerly stepping in. For a time she stood in the clear waters, drinking the spring. No longer thirsty, she drank merely to feel something cleaner within herself.

From a darkened alley, Oryn rounded the corner and found her. When he came out into the open she did not react, continuing to lap at the pool. Cautiously approaching Adwen and the broken fountain, her shoulder was little more than hip high. Taking a moment to study the scene, the sight of blood on her pure white fur saddened him.

At last he entered, and water quickly bogged down his boots. By her side he knelt, slowly reached for one of her paws. His handling was gentle in taking it up, washing away the filth with handfuls from the fountain. She stopped drinking and avoided eye contact. This did not bother the knight. He continued to rinse Adwen's coat.

Alex and Jack came running along Oryn's scent trail. Both stopped to gape at the sight of Adwen. The change to her true form confounded them. Eventually Jack gestured for Alex to wait and went closer.

At the edge, he crouched down, looking at her downcast eyes. Jack spoke firmly, determined that she listen. "We have to leave." He allowed a few seconds of silence, soaking in the thoughts coming from her and the knight. After establishing the situation, Jack frowned.

"I know those Light Spirits, or whatever you call them, are still telling you where to go. Trying to suppress the directions they're giving you won't help. You and I both know it's time to move. Stop feeling sorry for yourself."

A growl rumbled in Adwen's throat as her ears folded back. When she pulled her paw free from Oryn's grasp, her eyes closed. Jack was right. An energy source indicating a light gate made itself known. The instinct to seek it out became stronger, providing the initiative to leave the pleasant waters behind. She stepped out then bounded through more devastated districts of the Eskrani city.

The three warriors followed her through several blocks of rubble. Eventually, a glowing sphere as large as a palace doorway materialized, hovering in mid-air. Ripples of light coursed across the surface as if it were water. No one, including Adwen, knew what could be waiting on the other side. As this portal was not in a hidden location, they assumed it was a gateway to the none-magical world, not a neighboring kingdom. Immersing themselves in the ball of light, the four travelers vanished from the land of Eskrana.

Smells of dead leaves struck them along with a dramatic drop in humidity. Strong odors of algae hinted that a river was close by. These particular scents were familiar for Oryn. It was much like the place he had landed when he entered the Mirror of Lies.

Alex gasped as he materialized beside the others, his hulking beast form rapidly shrinking to human. No full moon hung in this night sky. A few seconds later his bare feet were struggling to support him, the swiftness of the change having made him dizzy. The feeling passed soon enough for the Marine to follow the others.

Though Adwen led the way, the emptiness flooded her mind once more. It fogged every thought, dulling feelings and stifling senses. If not for the heavy weight of sadness, she would have realized this location was familiar. After quietly plodding along, head hung low, the wind changed. A sea of smells struck her in the face. Instant recognition made her stop dead, nearly making her stagger.

Oryn, Jack and Alex watched in surprise as Adwen froze in place, long ears erect. Before Oryn could begin to ask her why, the white hound bolted ahead, leaving them in her wake.

They ran after her. Rushing through the trees, bushes dispersed and then disappeared within the park grounds. In moments they were at the edge of a large area isolated by yards of police tape. From behind the yellow border, the three observed Adwen in the midst of a crime scene and did not go any farther. Grim expressions washed over their faces while they stood watch from a distance.

She could smell them. Their blood was everywhere, soaking patches of earth. None had survived; Adwen already knew that the victims had not lived. Her heart ached, and her head seemed to hum with an overload of emotions. Scents belonging to her brother and sister were the first she smelled. She mourned them immediately, until she saw blood coating a nearby pine. Her father had died there. The knowledge made her ill. A flash of the implanted memory surfaced, confirming the obvious. Then she found the last plot of soiled earth. The blood of her mother had leached into the dirt, soaking down deep. Copper smells from the stain were so strong she tasted them on her tongue.

Overcome, the white hound splattered with red lay beside the place where her mother breathed her last. While in this body she could not shed tears, though she could cry. Instead of sobs, she vocalized low, drawn-out moans coupled sharp whimpers.

The warriors standing by listened to the soft howls. Alex distanced himself from the sounds of grief, keeping them from waking his own.

Oryn had glimpsed the memories implanted in her mind before. He wanted to be angry. This evil against Adwen and her kin was unspeakable. Rather than direct his wrath at the demons, he refused to divert his thoughts from her. Oryn chose to lament.

Jack took on the anger that Oryn had shrugged. The sight made him clench his fangs, mahogany eyes glowing hot in the dark. Something had to be done about this. The demons responsible needed to pay.

A sound from up the hill caught their ears, making their thoughts cease. A flashlight came on, waving down at the police tape.

The man pointing it trudged along and called out, "Hey? Who's down there?"

Oryn's green eyes brightened as he growled dangerously.

At the same time, Jack saw the uniform of a sheriff's deputy. Once the stranger was near enough for his mind to sense intent, he was put at ease. As Oryn was about to defend Adwen, Jack held him back with a hand, earning a very threatening glance.

"Don't bother," Jack whispered. "He won't hurt her."

Another deadly growl came from the knight, "You had better be right."

The unsuspecting deputy continued to follow the moaning sounds, growing wary as this seemed less and less like a prank. By the time he reached the yellow tape his light fell on a very large white dog, lying in the leaves. Curious and surprised, he stared for a moment. Then he realized the dog was crying.

"Hey?" The deputy gently called. "What are you doing here?"

Adwen ignored him and continued to whimper and moan. The deputy wanted to investigate, but he was not supposed to enter the crime scene. After thinking it over, he rolled his eyes and disobeyed, pushing up on the plastic strip to let himself through. Going a few steps closer, red splatters all over the animal were startling and made him stop to reconsider the situation. The bloody dog still cried, leading him to discard any fears. It looked injured.

As the deputy cautiously approached, Adwen silenced. His human scent flooded her nose, interfering with the odors that were so distressing. She lay still on the cold ground, refusing to respond.

"Hey? What's the matter? What happened to you?"

A louder whine issued from the white dog.

This whole scenario was so odd, the deputy thought. As he wondered why the animal was lying here in the park crying, he realized what the answer must be and frowned. The idea tugged at his heartstrings.

He shushed, touching the side of her neck with his knuckles. "It's alright, pup. It's okay. You knew these people, didn't you?" He shook his head, ruefully. "This shouldn't have happened, I know. But you can't stay. There's nothing here. You need to find your home, pup. Isn't there somewhere for you to go? Where's your safe place?"

An idea occurred to Adwen when he asked the question. Her look brightened slightly. Lifting her head to glance balefully at the deputy, she watched his sad expression turn to intrigue at seeing her glowing eyes. He was right; she could not stay here, but now she knew where to go.

Hidden by deep shadows, the three warriors watched Adwen

bound away into the trees. They dashed after her, finding the scent in order to keep from losing her entirely. After they left the park behind and entered the dense forest, seeing the white Holy Hound was impossible. When they burst from the foliage, hot on her trail, the river was just ahead. Adwen had plunged in, swimming across for the other bank.

Panting heavily, Alex tried to ignore the pain in his bare feet. "Where does she think she's going?"

She was too far away for Jack to read her thoughts, but light flickered in his eyes as he worked out the answer. "I know where. This way. There's a bridge."

Alex sighed in distress and braced himself for more pain. More than ever, he wanted a new pair of shoes – anything to dull the sharp pebbles and sticks. He strained to move as fast as the others up an embankment onto a paved highway. It took them through the valley by the river.

Taking the lead, Jack sprinted down the road with Alex and Oryn. As they traveled swiftly, only a few minutes passed before they came to the gravel turnoff for a distant trailhead. Flying past the hiking markers and billboards, hard dirt and roots replaced the loose rocks. The hiking route narrowed and abruptly rose and fell, closely following the river below. Blasting wind beat back at their faces and chests as if to hinder their progress. Their strength defied the rough terrain and howling gales, carrying them farther along the mountainside.

Both the knight and the Marine couldn't help but notice Jack's pace quickening. He knew this location from some time ago. Up ahead was where he had made his marriage proposal to Ashley. There was another thing that occurred that day that cast a shadow over the happy memory.

Thick trees enclosed a small clearing. It was empty until the three came skidding to a stop. They didn't see any sign of Adwen, but before any of them could remark, Oryn was first to catch her scent. He nodded toward the river through the brush, reclaiming the head of their small pack. The short charge ended at the edge of a high cliff overlooking the river chasm.

Adwen was there, in her woman form, staring down at the blackened opposing bank, masked in the shadow of a mountain ridge. As she stared, her thoughts lingered on the day she was pushed from that very place. Because her body was never found, it was believed she had drowned, and that she had jumped.

Wind whistled in their ears. Taking a determined step forward, Oryn called to her.

"Adwen."

"The end is near," she murmured.

Her warriors tensed, not entirely sure what she meant.

Adwen went on, "It has become a circle. For me, this place was the beginning. Over a year ago, Sycan came and pushed me from this exact spot. I fell from the falls into the magical world for the first time. He meant to kill me." After a pause she whispered into the wind, "If only ..."

While Alex and Jack were disturbed, Oryn's jaw clenched. He took another step closer to her side.

To their dismay, Adwen silently fell forward and out into space, plummeting for the black, thundering current.

Oryn snarled out of surprise, diving after her immediately. Jack grabbed Alex by the front of his robes, knowing he would fall behind if he did not. They both hollered in fright at the rush of falling so far, though Jack's voice was muddled with a shrill howl. Just as the two friends plunged into the deep waters, Oryn breached the surface for air.

He tried again to find Adwen, searching all around. Right away he realized she was underwater. After diving again he glimpsed her drifting along passively with the current. He had seen Adwen swim alone some nights and knew she could hold her breath for long durations. When asked, she had said the feeling of weightlessness soothed her. Regardless, this was not a pond or lake.

The thought of unforgiving rocks in approaching rapids spurred him into action, swimming after her silhouette in the darkness. Hard, determined strokes brought him near enough to reach out and touch her hand. He grabbed hold of her wrist just in time for the hazardous part of the river. White clouds of bubbles were blinding as he quickly brought her close, using his body as a shield. Wrapping her in his arms, he held her head tightly to his chest, intent on not letting her strike a single stone.

Above the surface and just behind, Jack discovered Alex's difficulty with swimming, never mind that his water-laden robes weighed him down. Jack dived under a short way, transformed and swam back up from under the struggling warrior, saving him from choking on more white water. Alex coughed and sputtered, panting for breath. Wiping his eyes, he heard Jack whine loudly, "Get ready to hold your breath again, Jarhead. Here comes the big one."

"What?"

The Holy Hounds hurtled toward the roaring falls and plummeted over, then plunged into the depths. Thick white bubbles almost completely hid the light of a magical portal as they passed through. On the other side was a much calmer current. It was easier to swim, and Jack took Alex up for a breath.

The Marine had been ill-prepared and had swallowed a substantial amount of water. Coughing violently, Alex hacked and gasped, clinging to Jack's magical garments and thick coat of fur. The sky was black with clouds, blocking the moonlight and letting him remain as a man. Adwen and Oryn were getting to their feet on solid ground by the time they also reached the riverbank. Jack's paws and clawed hands supported himself and the Marine on his back. For a while, he hung his muzzle low, panting for air. When they noticed the eerie silence, both looked up together at Adwen and Oryn's backs.

All four studied a solitary cloaked figure standing atop the hill, watching them.

When the stranger reached up to pull back his hood, Oryn took a swift step between him and Adwen, snarling, eyes blazing in anticipation of a fight.

Within the black cloak, dark tresses tumbled onto broad shoulders. Ageless eyes locked onto Oryn's deadly glare, studying the familiar things he saw in it. A second later the wrathful look melted into surprise at seeing elegant, pointed ears.

Jack saw the stranger's pointed ears also but did not understand the relevance until he sensed Oryn's shock. This was an elf, and fewer than five elves still existed in this region of the magical world, showing themselves only to a select number of individuals meant for a great destiny.

Adwen stepped past Oryn to look the ancient being in the eye.

The elf slightly dipped his head, saying, "I am glad at your return, Adwen."

She hesitantly replied, "Hello, Healer."

As Oryn did a double take at their familiar greetings, their host beckoned with an open hand. "Come with me."

Chapter 4
BACK TO THE START

Storm clouds continued to blanket the sky. The forest on Dargadia's western-most border was thick with towering trees, their leaves rustling in the gathering wind. Branches waved rapidly, seeming to urge the small company to hurry. This storm would be harsh.

"Hey," Jack called to the elf. "Your name isn't really Healer, is it?" He was attempting to hear the thoughts of their guide but found nothing. Instead he only heard the verbal response to his question.

The elf was patient. He knew the woods so well that he did not need a torch to light the way in the dark. "We may speak once within the sanctuary."

Reaching a meadow, the sky suddenly filled with an apparition. In seconds the mass solidified as a gigantic tree. Numerous candles and glowing hearths flickered, lighting the windows on every tier. Its roots took up the whole of the clearing, gripping the earth like one hand grasping another.

Oryn murmured breathlessly, "An elf sanctuary."

"The last sanctuary," the elf corrected. "Come."

A door trimmed in protective gold with inlaid runes was the only way inside, and the elf ceremoniously opened it wide for his guests to enter. Closing it again, the magical landmark vanished completely.

A short entry hall opened up to a bright, warm lounge. Many chairs, cushions and stools were strategically set throughout. None belonged to a matching set, yet all were inviting and offered service to a different sort of guest. Lightning flashed from a round window, a hint to how close they had come to being caught in the ensuing downpour.

Waving a hand over the collection, the elf insisted, "Sit where you may, please."

"I call dibs on that one." Jack had been eyeing a plump,

green chair and brushed Alex aside to reach it. The others, including the elf, stared abashed as he slumped heavily into the luxurious furnishing and sighed happily.

Adwen claimed a springy footstool, and Oryn promptly sat in the center of the sofa just behind. It did not matter where she chose; he would remain at her side.

Meanwhile, Alex was indecisive until a chair caught his attention. It had carved wormwood arms and legs, and looked nearly as soft as Jack's. It was in a nearby corner, close enough to not seem aloof from the meeting that was about to take place.

With his guests seated, the elf sat in a royal blue high-backed chair carved from cherry wood. His posture was perfect, as a king would sit in a throne. Once comfortable, his attention was on Adwen. Taking in the tormented look hidden deep within her eyes, he saddened.

"I have been watching your progress for some time. Much of your experiences are known to me, but one thing eludes me, and I am sorry that I must be selfish enough to ask: What has become of your friend and my nephew? Where has he gone?"

Adwen blinked in confusion. Then she knew who he meant and was stunned at first. Deciding that she was not so surprised, she couldn't help but smile a little. "Toth is King Lorvan's new adviser and guard. They're together in the Order's fortress."

The elf smiled and sighed. "I thank you. My visions would only show me your whereabouts and wellbeing. When he no longer came into my sight, I feared the worst."

As he was distracted with Adwen, Jack made a second attempt to read the elf's mind. He heard nothing but kept listening.

Then the richly colored eyes of the elf shifted to glance his way. Jack's mind was assaulted by images of those drilling eyes, staring him down. An intense pressure filled his head as if it was caught in a vice and someone was cranking it closed. Gripping the arms of the soft chair, Jack squirmed, clenching his jaw. He tried to figure out how to resist, but what resistance he put up the elf brought down like a house of cards.

Adwen, Oryn and Alex heard him gasp and turned to see him in agony, making dog whimpers.

Glaring angrily, the elf spoke in an annoyed tone. "It is rude to enter the mind of another without permission, Jack Towers. Keep your urge to pry in check."

In between gasps for air, Jack winced and tried to laugh off the pain. "Sorry. I didn't mean to. It just happens. I don't know how to turn it off."

A single word came from the elf. It echoed in Jack's mind, sending him reeling from the force. <Learn.>

It stopped at once, and the warrior relaxed. Bodily harm he could tolerate, but the psychic shock he received was not something he ever wanted to experience again. His ability to read minds, for the moment, had stopped. The mental attack left him sapped to the point that he didn't need to fear accidentally offending the elf a second time. Blinking at the soreness behind his eyes, he puffed and muttered to himself. "Wow."

As if nothing had happened, the elf returned to the prior conversation. "He is where he should be. Greatness is in his lineage; same as yours."

Emotions choked Adwen at the thought of family ties.

The elf was sympathetic. "When you were last in this room you had questions I could not answer. Now I have answers for you, as it is time you hear them.

"While in the dark lands of Mortigad, you were beset by Sycan. Before the final blow was struck, I saw what was done. A sliver from the crown of Guillot was used upon you to break your will. If it had contained anything other than those memories, you would have been able to resist. But because it was of those dearest to your heart, the fragment of darkness became a part of you."

The three warriors froze and Adwen shuddered, lowering her gaze to the crimson carpet. Tears swelled and fell, patting the ground.

As the elf went quiet, wearing a mournful look, Oryn asked for more answers on Adwen's behalf.

"How may this sliver be removed?"

The elf's gaze pierced into his, and he looked back unflinching, knowing he was being searched inside and out to see if he deserved the response.

Satisfied, he shook his head in reply. "It is no longer possible. As I said, the fragment of shadow has melded with her; it is one with her."

Jack joined in, eager to get answers as well. "Is that why her powers are gone?"

Having already searched this warrior thoroughly, he arched an eyebrow, causing him to brace for psychic bombardment. The reaction pleased the elf.

"No, but it did lead to the loss of much of her powers. Not all of her power was rooted in the light she carried. She may still change shapes and perform feats impossible to mortals. The divine and all-seeing Light Spirits granted her a portion of their power to wield on their behalf. Two other gifts were taken: Her hood of concealment and fist weapons were stripped as well. And before you ask again, it is because she took a life purely in anger. That was forbidden to her. Before the darkness polluted her essence, it would not have been possible."

Jack's brow furrowed. "Essence?"

"Adwen is not of the living worlds," he elaborated. "Her bones are not bone. Her flesh is not flesh, and her blood is not blood. She is a spirit in solid form, residing in a living skin. When Adwen's first life came to an end, it was planned to be so. A body of living flesh has limits and contains equal amounts of both light and darkness. In order to hold the power to defeat her ultimate enemies, she would need to be a pure vessel capable of containing the power. If any of you were to have that much power inside, it would slowly destroy you. Your ability to regenerate could not keep up with the strain of containing such vast amounts of energy. A body comprised of spirit essence can hold almost limitless power."

Leaning forward, Jack was hopeful. "So, even if we can't pull the darkness out, she can still get her powers back, right?"

They waited with baited breath for the reply.

Pondering whether this was a truth they needed to hear, the elf finally said, "Yes, she may. It will not be easy."

"We just need possible," Alex murmured from the corner.

The elf did not look at him, but nodded. "Indeed, it is possible. Although, as long as there is darkness within Adwen, she cannot reach her full potential. She must if there is to be hope for any of us at the hour of the darkening time."

Now that her tears were under control, Adwen raised her

head, curious. "What is the darkening time? This isn't the first time I've heard about it."

The elf paused, then said, "You shall know when it comes."

Dread itched at the backs of their necks, forcing the Holy Hounds to be wary of their surroundings.

"Be calm." Their host reassured. "They are combing the woods for you, but their ilk are incapable of finding this place. You are safe from all harm outside."

"They can't get in?" Jack asked quizzically, glancing out the window from his seat. Forms more solid that shadows shifted and stalked under the sheets of rain.

"They can march through the meadow for an eternity and will never see or touch this sanctuary."

Adwen gaped at the window, eyes widening in horror. "He's out there."

The elf stood and casually blocked her view to the outside. "Listen closely, Lady Adwen. On the morrow you shall take your warriors through a portal I have watched over through the centuries. It will take you all to the world without magic. There you must remain until you have reclaimed your light."

He grew more serious. "Above all, until that day, you must not fight." Sensing Oryn about to interject, the elf cast a brief and hard glance to silence him. "Keep hate and rage from overcoming you. Rely on these three companions, as that is a part of their purpose. You have aided them. It is time they did to you in kind."

She nodded.

For the first time that evening, the elf showed a flicker of a smile. "Come. It is time for you to rest. I must give guidance to your warriors now."

As Adwen was about to depart down the adjacent hall for a room, the elf called out, "And, Lady Adwen?"

She looked back, wondering what he might say.

A small smile warmed his flawless face. "No more climbing out my windows."

Adwen nearly laughed, dipping her head, smiling. She would not do so again.

The sound of a door closing down the hall let them know she was gone, cuing the elf to return to business.

Oryn was going to say something but soon forgot it. As the elf turned back to look at each of them, a harsh expression was set on his face. His razor sharp stare cut into them all, demanding full attention. He was angry with each warrior, as he had seen what they had done in the past and partly what was to come.

At last, the fiery eyes settled on the knight. "You, Sir Oryn. You are the last of the house of Conrad." Frowning, he grilled him. "Best you watch your tongue while speaking to Adwen from now on. The demon General Guillot and Sycan may have done their worst, but you made it all the easier when you broke her heart."

He stared back, regrets spilling over. His jaw clenched hard, and his green eyes blazed from the storm of emotions.

The elf shook his head and added, "I've never witnessed such gutless fear of sentiment. You are learning, I admit, but you must learn quicker on the affairs of the heart if you are to save Adwen this time."

Jack interrupted, "Hold up. What are you talking about? Save her this time? What's going on?"

The elf's eyes never left the knight. "This infection of Adwen's is far from benign. It is a viral sickness that works at this very moment to consume her."

Alex did not like the sound of this. "What happens if it does?"

Staring down the knight even more intensely, he explained, "Sir Oryn has had a glimpse of what will become of her."

His heart skipped a beat, and horror washed over him.

"If you all fail to save her, Lady Adwen will cease to be the Heir of Darien the Master Knight. She will become one with the darkness and unable to be restored."

Jack blurted out, "She's turning into a demon? Are you serious?"

Looking to the alarmed warrior, he studied him. "If that were to occur, your bonds to her would be severed. You each would be restored to the state you were in upon being marked."

Jack turned white as a sheet, but Alex failed to understand. "What?"

"Two of you were whole and physically well in the moment of marking. Sir Jack was not. His body was failing, succumbing to a mortal wound. If Adwen were to become fallen, you all would return to being mortal men, and Sir Jack would regain his wound. He would not live long after that."

A quiet fell over the room. Once the facts completely settled in Jack's mind, he slouched back, overwhelmed. "Crap."

"But you are not without tools. In the event that darkness takes hold, your weapons can halt the process and give Adwen the chance to regain control. They will not harm her. They were made by her predecessor."

"You are he, aren't you?" Oryn asked the elf.

Caught unawares, he looked down at the emerald-eyed warrior.

"You are the elf prince who gave Darien life."

The elf said nothing and was unreadable.

"Your name is Arianwyn, last elf king of the Northern Wood."

Breathing a long sigh, he replied, "Sir Oryn Reynard Conrad, Son of Sedro Conrad, descendant of Keegan Jaeger Conrad, Right Hand to Darien the Master Knight."

Jack and Alex stared drop-jawed. They knew just enough to know this was extraordinary. They had never heard this before.

Oryn had, and he frowned. "I do not claim to be as worthy as my ancestor, Your Eminence."

The elf king softened. "You were bloated with pride once. It poisoned your thoughts in every way. I see none now; you have become self-loathing. That must end. You only see your true form as your reflection in the mirror as you think of yourself as an animal, a ruthless, savage beast. Even in this form you would see that appearance as a reflection."

Oryn looked away, ashamed that it was true. There was also nothing the elf could say to make him think otherwise.

"It is difficult at times to forgive oneself. If you cannot forgive yourself, tell me, what use will you be to her?"

His green eyes snapped back up to glare in return for the hard point.

Arianwyn was not perturbed. "Adwen has needed a stalwart knight. Now she needs kindness. Without it she is lost.

Consider this before you set out tomorrow."

Jack cleared his throat and asked, "Excuse me, your highness? If his job is to fix her heart, what do I do?"

"Regardless of what I say, you are likely to do what you please."

The elf obviously knew his habits. "Point taken, and I'm sorry, but I have a lot at stake in this."

"We all have a great stake in the outcome of your new quest. Provide what you may when it is needed. The light chose each of you for a reason. Who you are is what is needed for Adwen to succeed. Trust in that if nothing else. Who you are is the answer to the question of what to do; be who you are and no more."

Jack nodded. "Thank you, your highness."

"Now is the time for the both of you to claim a room for the night."

Alex stared as Jack and Oryn quickly realized the elf king wanted to speak with their third counterpart alone.

"Sir Oryn, if you wish, you may watch over Adwen. A chair is beside the door just within. Jack, do not cause trouble, or consequences shall be severe. Take a room to yourself."

Both stood and quietly bowed before making their way along the next hall.

After the sound of two doors opening and closing, Arianwyn slowly strode closer to Alex. Their gazes were locked as stags' horns in a battle, shifting and jostling for an advantage. What Alex had seen done to Jack did not frighten him. The elf king gracefully sat across from him, speaking fathoms of voiceless words with a look. He did not like this warrior in the slightest.

Alex eventually felt the elf break through something in his mind. He sensed his thoughts being frisked for anything dangerous or worth noting. The search was short-lived, and Arianwyn frowned.

His tone was dark. "You have built strong walls about you. I've just found the opening Adwen created in them. Walls will not protect you from your fear. She warned you that her warriors must face their fears as part of their trials. You shirked yours, until it was forced upon you."

Alex had worn a placid expression through the evening. It

now warped slowly into a look of defiance. "My business is my own. Neither of you has the right to manipulate my personal life. If I'm a warrior, then what I think and feel have nothing to do with the mission."

Arianwyn scowled. "Until you were collected by Lady Adwen, this was true. More than ever, it is critical that you do combat with yourself and emerge at peace."

The same angry look lingered on Alex's face.

"Very well. There was something that went unsaid while the others were listening. To you, I give the first key for Adwen's restoration. The links that bind the three of you to her grant her power over you. Now she is so weakened that her being draws directly from each of you, like a sinking raft, tied to three docks on shore.

"She is not a living being. Adwen is spirit. Through combined efforts, the pure and impure churning inside her can be stabilized, preventing further growth of the darkness. For the moment she is unstable; neither the Adwen you know nor the thing trying to break free has control."

Alex thought over the information but stood his ground, unwilling to give in.

"To clarify: If the three of you feel sorrow, she will surely be sorrowful. Feel joy, and her heart will lighten. But feel anger, she will too, and the darkness shall grow. You have the power to save or condemn Adwen. You must make a choice. To be apart from this is to abandon her. There is no alternative. Her fate as well as Sir Jack's rests within your hands."

This new information made Alex think twice. Confused, he frowned. "Why are you telling me all this? Why not Oryn or Jack?"

"Because," the elf king replied, "they can do so without this knowledge. It is you who is the deciding factor. If not for you and your viciously bitter thoughts, the two warriors alone could restore her. To grant her back the power to destroy demons, you must face your own."

When he could see the warrior still resisting, he shook his head. "How can you be so callous? For the pain she brought back upon you, you would begrudge her? She is not herself; otherwise Adwen would not have done this to you. Would you be so prideful of your pain that you would have her and those around her suffer as a penance?"

"No."

Arianwyn glared dangerously. "Do not insult me with deception. I have had my fill of your contempt. Claim your room for the night. I dismiss you."

Alex was taken aback. He had not thought he was lying. Getting to his feet, he bowed as the others did before and found his way down the hall. The scents of Adwen, Oryn and Jack alerted him to which rooms were occupied. Opening a door, he became Jack's neighbor.

The bed was made with linen and fur blankets. Lying cross the soft layers, nestling his head on a down pillow, he pondered. All of the elf's warnings circled his mind like a flock of birds at a roost. Did he really have to try to feel for or even forgive Adwen? Then another question came: Was he capable of letting go of the anger?

Rain fell into the night, the tiny percussions striking the forest outside. The musical beats drummed for hours. Through the dark into dawn, Alex lay awake, interrogating himself to no avail. He did not sleep at all.

Chapter 5
CONTEMPT

Jack woke early. Breathing in deeply and yawning, smells from the elf and his herbal collections filled the room. Wondering if the others were up, he rolled out of bed stretching and cracking his stiff neck. When he got to the door and opened it, he thought he would go bother Alex and see what the elf had said to him.

Waiting on the other side was Arianwyn, staring down with an accusing expression. He raised an eyebrow, letting on that he knew what Jack had been thinking.

Frozen in the doorway, Jack was wary. <Can't blame me, can you?>

The elf looked sardonic and replied using his own telepathy. <I do, very much. Leave the soldier be. See to Sir Oryn and Adwen in their quarters instead.>

Realizing he was safe for now, Jack shrugged. "Whatever you say." Arianwyn left for other parts of the sanctuary just as Jack knocked on Adwen's door. No answer came, so he knocked again.

An irritated growl reverberated on the other side. Jack opened the door.

Inside, he found Oryn beside the door in a wooden chair, glaring. Jack could not stop his refreshed psychic mind from reading the knight's thoughts. His annoyance was that the noise had woken Adwen.

Gritting his teeth, revealing small fangs, he apologized. "Sorry about that. The king asked me to check on you."

"Consider us checked upon. What is it?"

Adwen was rubbing her eyes and rousing herself from bed as Jack explained, "I'm pretty sure it's time. He was waiting outside my door when I got up. Hey, Adwen?"

"Yeah?"

Jack raised a curious eyebrow and whispered in case the elf was close by. "Can this king see the future or something?"

She rolled her eyes. "Yes, Jack. He can see the future. Mostly he sees the present and the past, though. The future is tricky for him. He wrote the texts about me that were given to the four kings."

In an attempt to make her laugh, Jack asked, "Do you think I made a good impression?"

Instead he received two very cynical looks and an awkward silence. That was close enough, so he left the door open and went down the hall to the lounge. Both shook their heads.

The room with many odd chairs was not empty when he got there. Alex was on the sofa, drinking something dark and steamy. Once Jack smelled the rich, brown aroma, he craved coffee. Sitting beside him, he sniffed loudly and exclaimed, "What in the world have you got there?"

Alex stared straight ahead and replied as he prepared to take another sip. "Elf Breakfast Tea."

Their royal host came around a magical corner concealed on the far side of the lounge, carrying a platter with three more cups. Jack closed his eyes, nose in the air, sniffing repeatedly at the hypnotic brew. A soft growl of contentment vibrated in his throat. Getting ahold of himself, he stopped sniffing and salivating by the time the elf set the platter on the short table.

Passing one, Arianwyn said, "I believe you prefer darker brews. It is not 'coffee,' but it should suffice."

"Thank you, your highness." Tasting it, Jack smiled. "This is amazing."

"You are welcome, Sir Jack."

After taking a bigger gulp, he asked, "Can we take some with us?"

Arianwyn smiled.

At last, Adwen and Oryn joined them, sitting in chairs near the others.

"Now that you are gathered, I must tell you a little more. The gateway will take you to a city. Once there, the darkness will be hard-pressed to attack in force. They will eventually find you, but their presence is weaker there. Remain within the outer limits, no farther. But over time, their attempts to harm you will increase. Take too long to accomplish your goals, and they can take you all. Time is on no one's side."

After eyeing the drinks and deciding he did not want any, Oryn spoke. "If they are too weak, why would they waste effort in attacking?"

The elf turned to Adwen. "They seek to provoke you into combat. The demons know you are vulnerable and that any sort of threat is potentially enough to harm you further. Rage is what they want to awaken. Do not let them. Rage will give way to hate, and that will be your undoing. Allow your warriors to defend you, and still your heart. Resist the anger with all your might."

She nodded. "I'll do my best."

Smiling kindly, he replied. "I know."

Jack slurped loudly at the last of the tea beside him.

"Sir Jack?"

Instantly on edge, he nearly dropped the cup onto the now two empty ones on the platter. "Yes, your highness?"

Pleased again by Jack's apparent fear of retribution, the elf king smiled. "I trust you shall put great effort into this endeavor?"

"Absolutely." Setting the third finished drink down, he licked his lips. They tasted strongly of the wondrous tea.

"Good. Then the time has come." Arianwyn strode to a bare wall and grasped at an invisible handle. Opening a magical passage, everything beyond was empty space. The dark was so complete that Adwen and none of her warriors could see any definition within.

Adwen and Oryn were first to enter, followed by a hushed Alex. Lost in thought, he did not care about the strangeness of the eerie black emptiness. Jack stepped in after them and turned back to have a last word.

"Thank you for everything, your highness."

"The pleasure was mine."

Wetting his lips, he asked, "How can I learn to control my mind reading and block things out?"

Smiling coolly, he replied, "Do you truly wish to learn how?"

"Yes."

Continuing to smile, he began to close the door.

"Wait! Tell me how to make it stop!"

The king issued his final word before shutting them in. "It will come to you."

All was silence in the dark.

Then Jack opened his mouth somewhere beside the others. "You've got to be kidding me."

Adwen sighed and muttered, "Jack, shut up."

Exasperated, he went on. "Really? He could have given me something better than, oh it'll come to you. Have a nice life."

Oryn snapped, "Stop talking for once!"

There was more silence.

A light materialized before them, reaching around the edges of a new door. Oryn approached, took the handle and opened the door into the sunshine.

They were each blinded as they exited, looking about to get their bearings. The four found themselves on the bottom floor of a vacated apartment building. Dust coated the floor and hung from corners like webs. It was noon wherever they were, a few hours ahead of what they were accustomed.

Jack scoffed at the filthy place then turned back to reexamine the mysterious room. It was gone, along with the door. An empty wall stood at their backs.

"So now what?" Alex asked. "Should we stay here?"

Before Oryn could answer, Jack shook his head. "No way. We need to go where there aren't any people to bother us."

Adwen, Oryn and Alex stared as he turned around and elaborated.

"If you haven't forgotten already, you're wanted for murder and escaping prison."

"Jail," Alex corrected.

"And Oryn here doesn't play well with others. The last thing we need is a cop questioning him. You would come across as suspicious and get us all chased around town."

He growled and sneered.

"My point exactly."

Adwen asked, "What about Alexander?"

"Like I said, he needs to keep a low profile."

"How's he supposed to do that in medieval robes?"

They stared at the blond Marine a moment, and Jack scratched his head. "You know, he might get us shot at in a black neighborhood dressed like that."

Alex rolled his eyes.

"I can start by getting Jarhead new clothes."

Oryn was not impressed. "From where shall you steal them?"

"Do you know what size I wear?"

Jack barked in aggravation. "Too many questions! Just trust me for once. Everybody stay here until I get back."

The knight grabbed him by the back of his jacket, forcing him to stop.

"I doubt it would be safe for any of us to travel alone, even for petty errands."

Looking back, controlled frustration made Jack's mahogany eyes shine. "Petty errands?" His tone became ice cold. "Cut me some slack, Cujo. This is not a joke. You're good at fighting. I am too, but I'm better than you at other things. Let me do what I do best and establish a chance for this mission. Am I scout material or not?"

Thinking it over, Oryn released his grip. "Hurry."

"All right then. I'll be back in an hour or so." He said as he stepped out the open door to the city street. "Don't do anything I wouldn't do."

"That must be a short list," Alex said.

Adwen nodded.

Jack discovered on his own how to make himself appear more human. The pointed ears and fangs shrank to unassuming lengths, as his enchanted clothes also bent to his will. Forming his attire to the local fashion, a black and blue hoody, roomy slacks and boots took shape on his body. To ensure he blended in, he made his scruffy black hair even messier, roughly brushing it around. With street clothes and bedhead under control, the next goal was finding cash.

Stealing needed to be avoided. If they were to stay in or near a city, stealing clothes from locals would risk getting caught later. It was not necessary for Jack to steal, in the technical sense. He could get his hands on enough money to take care of essentials. It was a matter of finding the opportunity.

The perfect opportunity presented itself after an hour or

so of walking among regular Joes and street women of the downtown. Seeing a few signs pointing to local landmarks, Jack determined that he was in Chicago. A laugh escaped him. If only he were on vacation. At the end of the next block, he stopped. His mind had been abuzz with nearby people's thoughts, but a new kind of voice found its way into his mental ear. Like radar, Jack detected the mind of a gambler.

In a narrow alley across the street, three punks used a battered shipping box as a makeshift table. Behind it stood two big bruisers, watching over their friend, who sat on an upturned bucket, shuffling a deck of heavily worn playing cards. Jack made a beeline for them, casually jaywalking to their setup.

Watching him come closer, the burly thugs looked him up and down. Their card playing companion was curious. Then he wet his lips, thinking that he had found a new sucker.

"Hey, got time for a round?"

The punk huffed in response. "Sure, if you're not a cop?"

He used to be, Jack thought. Gesturing his own clothes and pointing at his colorful hair, he chuckled, "Come on! Tell me a better joke, dude."

Laughing as well, the player smiled. "It's not poker, man. You got to find the queen."

"Even better. Should take less of our time away from bigger things, huh?"

Before Jack could sit opposite, the punk held up a hand, "Hold on. How much you got on ya?"

Reaching into the pouch on his hoody, Jack summoned one of the twin daggers. Pulling out the golden blade etched in runes, he laid it on the table. Light glistened on the razor-sharp edge.

One of the bruisers whistled in response.

Unsettled, the punk shook his head. "No way, man. That thing is hot. It's got to be stolen. I'm no idiot. I get caught hawking that, and I'm looking at time."

Jack rolled his eyes. "Look, I just got into town. I need quick cash, and I'll bet you can find a buddy to fence this for way more than what you have in your pocket. What do you say?"

It was a very enticing offer. His gaze shifted, and he shuffled the cards more slowly as he considered the options. Studying Jack again, he said, "I got nine-hundred on me."

Pretending to consider as well, Jack knew he really had double that amount. It didn't matter. A few seconds later, he smiled and nodded. "Let's play."

Jack took back his weapon, stuffing it into the pouch before making it disappear. Now was not the time to frighten off the hustlers with magic tricks.

The man set the deck aside and revealed the queen of hearts, ace of clubs and a joker. "Now I have a story." Beginning to shuffle in rapid fashion, he said, "This pretty lady and her man got into an argument. Her man beat her bloody, and she ran away." Setting the three face-down cards out in a row, he asked, "Where did she hide?"

A second was all it took for Jack to read his thoughts. Flipping up the left card, the queen of hearts rocked from side to side on its warped backing.

"You're quick," he admitted. Taking them and shuffling again, the punk continued the story.

"With the pretty lady gone, her man called in a ho. The pretty lady found out and went to buy a gun to do the deed." Setting out the cards, he asked, "Where did she get her gun?"

Jack waited a moment before flipping over the middle card. The queen of hearts rocked on her curled backing a second time.

The two goons stared the stranger down. Waiting, they wanted to know if their friend was going to lose nine-hundred dollars in a single blow.

Alarmed, the punk looked Jack in the eye, thinking hard on how to go about the final round. He couldn't afford to let him win the cash.

"All right, it's cool. You got to find her one more time."

He shuffled the three cards more elaborately, telling the end of the story as he did so. "When that pretty lady came home, the ho was gone. He was a liar, so she shot him in the face."

With finality, he smacked the cards down hard on the box.

"Now where did she hide his stinking corpse?"

They stared at each other for what felt like an hour. Eventually, the punk smiled broadly. Reaching for the cards, thinking he had won, he chuckled, "No guess, huh? Better luck next time."

In the blink of an eye, Jack had hold of the hustler's wrist. The goons prepared to pounce if there were any sudden moves. Watching the stranger holding their friend's wrist, they were unsure what was going on.

Frowning, Jack slowly reached out and pulled a hidden card from the punk's sleeve. Brandishing the queen of hearts, he glowered, "Nice try, player."

In shock, the punk spat, "You aren't getting nothing."

Leaning forward so that only he would hear, Jack whispered threateningly, "I know where you hid the body, Jason Lewis Benson."

The eyes of the punk bulged, and he almost gasped for breath.

"Give me the nine-hundred or the man is going to pay a visit real soon."

Adwen, Oryn and Alex waited an hour. Then two hours passed. Four hours went by until they began to wonder if Jack was going to return before dark.

Leaning in the frame of the open front door, looking much more like a human wearing street clothes, Oryn stood guard. He used his keen sight to scan up and down the street of towering apartment buildings. While studying the local residences, some stared upon passing, confused by the stranger staying in the condemned establishment. The unfriendly look he wore made them all the more eager to say nothing, kind or otherwise. That suited him just fine.

"Where is he?" Oryn glowered.

"He'll be back," Adwen murmured from a corner, sitting against the filthy wall. "We would know if he was in trouble."

"Yes, but it does not explain his prolonged absence."

Alex had thought a long while about where Jack might have gone and came to a few conclusions. "If he did get hold of some money, he said he was going to get me clothes. What if he went into a mall?"

Adwen sighed. "Oh, boy."

Oryn rolled his eyes in agreement. He knew what a mall was.

"Either way, I know he'll be back soon."

No one spoke for a while. They only listened to the sounds of car engines, pedestrians on the sidewalk and the wind whipping betwixt the structures.

"If he wastes all this time," Alex grumbled, "and brings back something that looks stupid or is too small, I'll try knocking him out myself."

"Cut it out," Adwen snapped.

Alex glared back. Then he thought of the elf's warnings and tried to get her to calm down. His and Oryn's negative moods were affecting her. "I know he's probably going to come through with whatever he's doing, but it's Jack. He makes it easy to think the worst of him. Trash talking on him passes the time."

Adwen frowned and looked away, staring off at the other side of the empty space. She felt cold and rubbed her arms to warm them as she sat. "Whatever."

Trying again to set her mind right, he added, "So that you know, thinking about something other than what's bothering you doesn't help at first." He pondered over how he got past the aftermath of his tragedy. "Doing things makes it easier to move forward. It starts the process."

Disgust in her voice, she growled and spat, "Don't talk to me about my problems. I'm dealing with them just fine."

Alex struggled to keep his own anger restrained. "Take it easy. I just want to help."

"Help? How?" She turned back to sneer. "Come talk to me about moving on once you figure it out yourself. Do I look like a pathetic little child to you? Keep your sympathy to yourself, where it belongs, you weak-willed maggot."

Alex stared speechless. His drill sergeant had called him that hundreds of times in basic training. It used to make his blood boil; it still did.

From the doorway, Oryn forgot the street to give Adwen an uneasy look. This behavior was completely unlike her.

Temper flaring, Alex muttered, "Roger that."

The sound of quick footsteps outside announced Jack's

arrival. As he came up the stairs, Oryn moved aside, and Jack raised a hand, magically summoning one of the items he purchased. He pressed it firmly to his irritated companion's chest.

Oryn received the forcefully given gift as he continued into the room. Upon examining it, he saw the image of a happy puppy eating the same biscuits that were within the package. The knight growled and eyed Jack dangerously.

"Sorry I took so long. Had to find a few more things." Jack summoned a small stack of clothes and a pair of running shoes, handing them to Alex. "I had a pretty good idea that you wear a size twelve-and-a-half shoe, extra-large shirt and have a thirty-four inch waist. Enjoy. It took forever to pick them out."

The sheer accuracy was so confounding that it made the Marine completely forget about the argument. "What? How do you know my sizes?"

Jack folded his arms, raised an eyebrow and stared, waiting for him to realize the answer on his own.

This annoyed Alex. A moment later, Alex felt stupid and sighed. "You read my mind before you went out the door."

Using an exaggerated condescending tone, Jack smiled. "Very good! Go in the other room to try them on."

Taking the brand new polo shirt and slacks, he did as asked. A minute later, Alex returned in the blue and brown ensemble. The clothing fit, but something didn't feel to his taste. Standing before Jack, Adwen and Oryn, he asked, "Does this seem odd to anyone else?"

Jack smiled proudly as Adwen finally smiled for the first time in days. If she were in a better mood, she would have laughed.

Oryn was first to comment. Brow furrowed in confusion, he asked, "Why do your arms, chest and hips appear to be emphasized by the clothing?"

The smile Adwen wore threatened to crack.

Alex's voice rose up in dismay. "Jack? Where did you buy these?"

"The shoes came from some local store. The shirt and pants are Amber-something and Finch."

"You mean Fitch?"

"Yeah, that's right."

Adwen put a palm to her head, shaking it in astonishment.

There was not enough curiosity in Oryn to ask what the relevance was. "Before we waste more time on deciding how his attire is flawed, I suggest we move out."

As they left for the streets and started heading north, Jack asked, "Hey? Where did the doggy treats go?"

Glowering, the knight replied, "The nearest waste bin."

"Aw! I was going to try those."

Alex had not seen them. "You bought dog treats, too? How much money did you throw away on junk?"

In answer, Jack summoned up a detailed map. "Not everything was for fun. Got this from a visitor's center. It should help us find a hangout."

"For once, you impress," Oryn admitted, reaching to take it and study the layout of the city around them."

The attempt was not quick enough, as Jack pulled the map book to one side. "Leave it to me. I've got this. Just do what you do without causing a scene and let me take care of navigating."

"You'll get us lost," Alex groaned.

Jack chuckled, getting their bearings with the map. "No more than you would."

Traveling the city on foot was easier with the help of Jack and his map, though the network of streets was so vast it was daunting. Oryn was in awe of the size of the buildings, but his mind was mostly with Adwen. He sensed tangled emotions in her. The outburst made him all the more alert to her state. He was not sure, but he thought she could be succumbing to the infection.

Beside him on the sidewalk, she ignored the sights, sounds and intense smells. A chill seeped deep through her limbs and chest, no matter how much she wrapped her arms about herself for warmth. Her heart ached with feelings of bitter loss applying almost constant pressure as if to crush it. Along with the city distractions, she distanced herself from the warriors who walked alongside.

Busy with leading the others, Jack was well aware of Adwen's thoughts. He pretended to be ignorant, hoping not to upset her by being openly concerned. She was delicate. The slightest thing could make her snap. He did not want to be the one who drove her over the edge.

Jack put on another act of carefree enthusiasm. As they reached the center of the city, he said, "All right. Now that we are here, it's time to decide where to go. Any place of interest is four miles in either direction." Seeing Oryn by Adwen, watching her with a worried expression, he called out, "Hey, Cujo! Come take a look. There are a few places where we could stay. I think the forest northwest of our location is the best bet. What do you say?"

The knight took a step closer to look for himself. Nodding, he agreed. "That appears to be the best place within the city."

Then Jack turned his attention to Alex. At the moment, he was fixated on a crack in the pavement. His mental barriers were as thick as ever, leading Jack to think that something was bothering him.

Clearing his throat, Jack prompted, "Hey, Blondie? Feel all right about staying in a couple acres of forest? It seems big enough on the map to avoid locals."

"What's good for you is good enough for me."

Raising an eyebrow, he inclined his head. "What's eating you?"

Alex was annoyed. "Don't worry about it. Let's just go."

Giving a suspicious look, he replied, "All right then."

The four made their way west, no longer uttering a word. Jack felt the unhealthy tension, hoping against his instincts that told him it was building toward a breaking point. As the sun set and dusk fell on them, lights from hundreds of sources gave life to the city. Shadows transformed streets into dark pathways, which they walked in search of their destination.

On a particularly quiet block with few street lamps, Jack's mind heard distant plotting thoughts. He was on edge, and soon Oryn's sixth sense made him alert as well.

Up ahead in the dark, two big men exited an alley and stood in their way.

The Holy Hounds did not go any further down the street once they spotted the threatening men. Turning to go back, three more came strolling up from behind. These individuals Jack recognized right away. He quietly swore to himself for not realizing this might happen. To keep a safe distance between

them and Adwen, he went to meet them, leaving Alex and Oryn to protect her.

Acting casual, Jack smiled. "Hey, how are you boys doing? How about we go out for some drinks. We'll put it on my tab."

"Shut your mouth, man," the punk yelled. "First you cheat me. Then you blackmail me. Now you have the brass to mock me? You are one stupid dude."

Jack dropped the act and became reasonable. "Okay. What do you need from me? If we make a fair deal, everybody can have a nice night. So what do you want?"

The punk sneered, "How did you know my name, dog? Why did you say you know where I hid the body? Give me answers."

Trying to read his mind was difficult. The only thoughts in the young man were on the consequences if he did not like Jack's response. He made his best guess as to how to reply.

"I have a few friends who called me in for work. They said to pay you a visit and to rattle your chain. They knew it would get a rise out of you if I knew your name. It's not a secret that you tell the same story over and over with the cards. They said to tell you I knew the answers if you decided to go back on the bet. It was a joke."

The punk studied Jack for a long while. Taking a deep breath, he took out a pistol and pointed it for Jack's head. Flicking the safety off, he sneered, "You're lying."

Seeing the gun, Oryn growled and went to stand by Jack in order to intimidate the thugs. Alex took a step after him but thought twice. Someone had to be with Adwen. Taking a glance at her, he could see something in her eyes that made him nervous. He wasn't sure, but he thought he saw a flash of red.

Adwen could smell the thugs threatening Jack. She did not like them. Most of all, she sensed the darkness in their hearts. They had done terrible things, staining their souls in a patchwork of black and crimson. The scent of evil began to stir something within her core, and she no longer felt cold. She felt searing heat.

"Hey, tell your buddy to back off. This is none of his business."

Jack blocked Oryn's path, putting up a hand to keep him from bearing down on the thugs. The situation was volatile already without his help. "Hold up, Cujo. It's okay. Don't do anything crazy."

Oryn growled, and it sounded like rolling thunder. "I've dealt with their kind."

Abashed, the punk nearly laughed. "Hey, are you growling at me?"

Oryn's emerald eyes glowed hot, locked onto the man aiming the gun. "Put your weapon away or I shall take it from you."

All three villains shifted nervously. "Hey, man. What's up with his eyes?"

To the men, Jack reassured, "It's some funky contacts." Then to Oryn, he growled quietly, "Stop. You're making it worse."

Far behind them, Alex was becoming unsettled by what was happening to Adwen. Wisps of steam rose from her, and heat radiated from where she stood. He knew he had to do something. Avoiding touching her, he murmured, "Don't worry. Oryn and Jack have it under control."

Glaring at him, she spat, "Don't talk to me, maggot!"

As she looked past him again to the confrontation, Alex clenched his jaw and balled up his fists, observing the way she sized up the thugs. His blood boiled the same as hers.

Jack continued to stave off the potential for a shooting. No matter how much the punk wanted to get at him, they were becoming more and more afraid of Oryn, who was not shy about showing off his inhuman attributes. So long as he could keep the gun from being fired, it was possible the men could change their minds and leave.

"Everybody needs to calm down," Jack said. "No one needs to get hurt. This is just a conversation about how I knew his name and how much money I need to compensate with."

After aiming for Oryn, the barrel turned back to Jack's forehead. Anxiety and anger caused the punk to shout, "Shut your face! Give me my money back! I want every dollar in my pocket right now!"

Jack was about to explain how it was not possible, as he

had spent quite a sum. That was when his heart skipped a beat and instincts drove him to look at Adwen. Her eyes were bright red as patches of her blouse began to char, turning black and burning away. When she leaned forward and began to charge, Jack saw Alex step aside to let her pass. The two warriors locked eyes for a moment. The Marine was stone cold with indifference.

Thinking fast, Jack ran to intercept her.

Adwen pounced, knocking him to the ground, and they slid several feet. He tried to get hold of her, but she was too fast. Using her sharp nails, she slashed his face, making him yelp.

Oryn whirled around and gaped in shock.

Terrified by Adwen's dark visage, the two thugs took out their guns and fired at her.

A few bullets struck her in the chest and arms. She roared, changing into a raging white dog before bounding across the street into a blackened alley, snarling.

Oryn yelled and quickly gave chase. "Adwen, no!"

Wiping the droplets of blood from the scratches on his cheek, Jack angrily picked himself up. Ignoring the stares from the street criminals, he snapped at Alex, "Come on! We need to fix this!"

The Marine was unreadable but followed as they ran after Adwen.

Chasing her through dark corners and in front of screeching, honking cars, Oryn never let her out of his sight for long. Each time he came close to catching up, she darted through another narrow alley. Oryn leaped to the rooftops, keeping up with her just below.

When the next street opened up, unfortunate bystanders were in her path. A pair of adolescent girls across the way saw her coming and screamed.

Adwen roared and leaped for them with jaws open wide.

Oryn dived down, knocking Adwen to the ground, and they tumbled in a flurry of snapping fangs and hair. The girls ran to safety as he kept grappling to control Adwen. She leaped from his grip, and he got to his feet.

She crouched low, growling and snarling, bright red eyes

following his every move. As she stalked him, Oryn held his hands up in preparation should she pounce. Circling closer, she snarled louder and louder. To Oryn's horror, wicked black spikes sprouted from her back, lengthening into deadly barbs as long as his arm. Her body smoked and began to grow. Adwen's rage fed the horrible changes, warping her dog features into a monstrous beast.

Her shoulder was as high as his head when she lunged for him. From his training as a werewolf slayer, he was ready. Oryn sidestepped just in time, then snared her around the neck.

Adwen roared in outrage, jumping, rolling and flailing roughly to shake him off. She smashed him into the side of a brick building, loosening his grip, then ran farther into the city.

He staggered and relentlessly pursued. They couldn't afford to let her reach any defenseless humans on the streets.

She ran and ran, huffing and growling. The claws on her feet became curved spikes, scraping at stone while she sped along. Gouges were left behind, leaving a trail for Oryn to follow. Sensing the warrior coming from behind, Adwen used her strength and dagger-like claws to race up the side of a towering building. Reaching the top, she waited, pacing and gnashing her teeth, watching the edge where he would surely appear.

It was more difficult for Oryn to scale the height with such speed. When he arrived, she was at the other side of the structure, having anticipated him. Hopping off the roof ledge, the knight called to her through the powerful wind gusts.

"Adwen? Adwen, fight it. Fight this. Keep it from controlling you."

Suddenly standing still, she bared her fangs and rumbled.

For a moment, Oryn thought she might be trying to regain control. He was proved wrong when she lunged. He barely avoided her enormous teeth and got hold of her neck once more. She did the same as before, jumping, rolling and shaking madly to remove him. He did not let go, no matter how many times her immense weight crushed him to the rooftop. Just as Jack and Alex climbed up over the ledge, Adwen's wild fit sent them careening off and out into space.

They were very high up when they began to fall. A bright

and busy intersection was rushing up to meet them, and she kept trying vainly to bite at Oryn. Repeatedly she snapped her head to the side, trying to reach him with her spear-like teeth.

Oryn held on, watching her eyes, which had turned ruby red. With all his might, he wanted them to turn blue again and not look at him with such blood lust. He wanted Adwen to wake up.

The enormous creature she had become crashed onto the hood of a cab, smashing and rocking the vehicle violently. Adwen's jaws found the knight's leg and snapped shut.

He snarled as he was shaken mercilessly and lobbed into another car parked across the street. Dozens of pedestrians gasped and screamed. Oryn staggered to his feet, resisting the pain in his leg, never taking his eyes off of Adwen. The stares of bystanders did not matter.

Locals began pulling out cameras, snapping pictures and recording video just when Adwen tried to finish what was started on the roof. She moved for the kill, and Oryn dodged her once more, her head smashing through a car's passenger door. He grabbed hold of her ear and clung to her neck. Shouting at the pain of his injury as she pulled free and started to flail, Oryn could see no end to this struggle.

Far overhead, the others leaped to join him on the ground. To help slow her down, Jack threw a dagger straight for Adwen's back.

In the instant that the blade sank in up to the hilt, her rear end collapsed. Adwen roared in pain. Then she cried out again in infernal rage, the sound building and becoming so loud that it nearly deafened the crowd watching the battle. When they began to cover their ears, all of the cell phones, electrical systems and machines flashed, sparked, then exploded from the surge of energy Adwen radiated. Eight city blocks went dark as electronic devices and their sources of power were destroyed.

Adwen began to howl again when Jack and Alex came down, landing between the spikes in her back and burying their blades in her flesh. She collapsed under them, unable to move. Their weapons held her still, immobile in the street.

Surprised by the sudden quiet, Oryn looked back to find the others pinning her down. Jack nodded to him, communicating that he could let go. Oryn released his hold and limped to the place where her jaws lay on the road. She was growling, watching him come closer. Only her eyes could move in the magical paralysis. Adwen's rumbling did not deter him as he crouched down, laying one hand on her muzzle and the other atop her head. She continued to snarl, unfazed by his gentle touch and the urgent expression he wore.

Oryn whispered, "Adwen, wake up. You must hear me. Stop this before it is too late."

Her snarls became louder as a response.

Desperate to save her, he urged, "Please, Adwen, look at me. Don't look at my face; look at my eyes. Look at me." Adwen's raging red eyes followed his, staring ravenously. A few moments passed until her growling ceased. The spikes on her began to recede. Her body shrank. In shock, Jack pulled out one of his daggers, and Alex stepped away with his short sword, observing her transforming back.

As Adwen's eyes turned from red to blue, she was almost her regular size and whimpered, "Oryn?" Her ears hung low, and she began to cry in short, sharp whines.

Oryn felt relief once she was no longer monstrous. He pulled out Jack's second dagger, releasing her from the magical binding. He studied her face while she sat up, shifting into her woman form. Her skin had become gray, eyes dim and the circles beneath them as dark as ever. She looked sickly and pale. Then she began to sob.

When Jack came and took back his weapon, Oryn placed his hands on her shoulders, looking into her face. "Adwen, listen to me. You're not alone. We are here to protect you. You mustn't be afraid."

The people in the streets were beginning to lose their fear. It was very dark, but their human vision could discern the Holy Hounds out in the gloom. Some inched closer as Jack growled to keep them from hearing too much. "Oryn, we need to leave. The police will be here in seconds."

Oryn asked, "Adwen, are you able to stand?"

She only cringed and sobbed harder, unwilling to move or respond.

The sound of sirens echoed in the distance.

Jack growled louder, "Come on!"

Out of options, Oryn scooped her up in his arms, quickly limping after Jack and Alex. He was able to overcome the pain and began to run as well, using shadows for cover. They made their way west, determined to seek refuge in the woods marked on the map.

Stopping only once to check their location, it was less than an hour before they found the forest. At night the forest was very dark. Bike riding and hiking trails were few, with no lamplight to reveal the group to strangers, and no one lingered here after nightfall. Following the rise and fall of the land, they approached a small cave. It blocked out the wind, and all four of them could hide just within from any prying eyes.

Oryn took her into the cave's confines. She had passed out on the way, and he wanted to let her rest. While he tended to her, Jack and Alex waited around the corner in the open air.

Both warriors were silent. Leaves rustled in the trees and crunched under Jack's feet while he paced to and fro.

Alex stared at the ground, head empty of thoughts or feelings. Minutes passed, and nothing was said. Now that the horrible ordeal of stopping Adwen's rampage was over, he turned to Jack.

"Now what?"

Jack's fist swung faster than Alex was capable of seeing. It hit him square in the jaw, knocking him to the ground with a mighty crack.

He gasped, stunned while his head felt like a spinning top. The forest began to stop whirling around him when he heard a dangerous growl.

"Do you understand what you've done?"

Dazed, the Marine tried to force his battered brain to function. "What?"

Outraged, Jack shouted, "Do you have any idea how many people you almost got killed? It's amazing that none of those civilians was seriously hurt!"

Irritated by the commotion outside, Oryn emerged while Alex was righting himself. "Let her rest, you fools. What is this about?"

Jack turned to face Oryn, frowning bitterly. "I don't really know. Why don't you ask him?"

Studying the Marine with a firm look, Oryn was unsure

what he might hear. "What is the meaning of this?"

Touching his jaw to see if it had broken, he stood and returned the knight's stare, equally aggravated. "I have nothing to say to you."

Oryn's eyes narrowed and glowed brighter.

Knowing he was not going to cooperate, Jack spoke: "When Adwen tried to attack the guys in the street, he let her go past him. He didn't even think of trying to stop her or even care what would happen."

Taking another limping step closer to the stoic Marine, Oryn scowled. "Does he speak the truth?"

A long silence hung between them.

Frowning, he replied at last, "So what if it is?"

It took all of Oryn's self-restraint to keep from attacking. Keeping control of himself, he grilled the warrior before him.

"You nearly caused the deaths of many innocents. What's worse, you willingly allowed harm to come to her. This did not happen without a reason. Tell me, what reason could you possibly have to hold such contempt for Adwen?"

Alex stood amid their piercing gazes, defiant and silent.

Even angrier, Oryn sneered, "Why would you do this to her?"

A rippling chill coursed through them, halting their exchange. They felt weakened. At once, they looked back to see Adwen come out of the shelter, walking toward them.

The skin on her face and neck was white like bone, same as the now wispy strands of hair on her head. It was thin like spider silk and floated about her shoulders regardless of how the wind moved. Her armor was black, covered in scarlet runes. Taking the place of her smooth feet were inhuman talons, biting into the soil on each step. The white around Adwen's ruby-red eyes turned pitch black while they wandered over the three warriors as they stared in horror. Coolly, she strode closer, flexing both hands that were now hardened with fingers like spider's legs, ending in razor sharp claws.

Wide-eyed, Oryn took a step toward her. "Adwen."

Closing her eyes and cracking her neck from side to side, she then smiled and locked onto his frightened face. Her voice was sonorous, a compound of multiple voices that spoke at once.

"Hello, knight. Why so afraid?"

Jack coughed, leaving a bit of blood on his lips. He and Alex both looked in shock as a spot on his abdomen began to darken with blood from an open wound. Jack grabbed at it to stymie the flow. It was no use, and the stain grew in diameter.

Adwen cocked her head at them. "Aw, that's too bad. I guess he'll just have to sit this next one out."

Oryn quickly took her by the shoulders and pleaded, "Adwen, no! Stop this!"

With the flick of her wrist, she knocked him aside. "Don't touch me! I am not yours to command, fool. Besides, in a moment you will be human again. Does that not please you?"

Jack and Oryn's enchanted clothing began to fray in places, the colors muting, while the magic they held began to wither.

Wiping the blood from his mouth, Jack called to her. "Adwen, I know you're in there and you can hear me. You have a job to do, a responsibility. The Light Spirits haven't left you!" He coughed again, and more blood splattered from his mouth.

She chortled wickedly. "I am Adwen, pathetic whelp. I hear you and, I have to tell you there are not any Light Spirits with me. I don't need them anymore. I ... am ... free."

Going to stand before a speechless Alex, she smiled, stroking his cheek with a deadly claw. "I thank you, Alex. If not for you, I would still be bound by those bonds to your souls."

Oryn growled and spoke simultaneously, his body becoming more human with each second. "Adwen, leave him alone! Speak to me! Listen to me!"

Whirling around, she shrieked, "I have heard enough of you to last a hundred lifetimes! Was it not you who broke the heart that was offered so openly? The time has passed for things as trivial as love! Wallow in your sorrows. It is more than you deserve."

Defiant of the lies, Oryn shook his head and glowered. "Never."

She huffed and sneered. "Pathetic."

While Jack began to sway and turn pale, she stepped aside, raising her arms to the night. "I smell the demons who come to entice me! Come! Let us fight once more! Complete my breaking away from the fools who follow the Light!"

Near twenty man-sized demons covered in a sickening rainbow of colors scrambled out of the trees, rushing for her and the others. They shrieked and wailed in excitement, ready to make her part of their darkness.

She laughed, took a driving step and leaped high into the air, ready to come down and slash the demons to pieces.

But Oryn, with what remained of his supernatural strengths, lunged to intercept her, summoning his long blade.

Adwen did not care. She grinned and was about to use her claws to slit his throat.

With an almighty thrust, he caught her in the chest, driving her back. Continuing through the strike, Oryn pinned her to the ground. He held her there, the magic of his sword keeping her still.

Jack and Alex blocked the demons known as Clowns from reaching Adwen. They came close, but not enough to touch either Oryn or Adwen.

As Jack killed demons with swift swipes, the effort wore him down. He killed a few of the fiends, but his vision began to swim, and his head spun from the loss of blood. Though he struggled to fight on, he collapsed, unable to get up again, daggers lying by his sides.

Alex saw him fall. "Jack! Get up!"

His friend did not move or make a sound. It was down to him to kill the last three demons alone. The first jumped at his face, and he cut it in half, dodging the remains. The final two scurried for his feet, but had their heads severed instead. With the monsters melting into purple muck, the Marine turned to survey the scene.

He panted from the effort, gasping and gaping at Jack's fallen body, face down in the dirt. Looking to Oryn, holding his sword that had her impaled into the ground, his heart sunk. Going closer, he saw where the blade met her armor and flesh. Instead of silver trickles, purple demon's blood hissed and burned on contact. When he saw the blood, he saw something else in his mind.

As Oryn knelt over her, Alex relived his darkest moment for the third time. He had been downstairs in the kitchen, cleaning up a mess he had made. When he got a strange feeling, he wondered what his wife was doing.

He remembered calling her name. "Emily?"

When he went to look in their room, she was there, bathed in her own blood. The same machete that had saved his life and his platoon members in war was through her heart, same as Oryn's through Adwen's. The pain he had felt was enough to kill him. The desperation for it to not be real had threatened to drive him insane.

King Arianwyn's words seemed to ring in his ears. How can you be so callous? For the pain she brought back upon you, you would begrudge her now? Would you be so prideful of your pain that you would have her and those around her suffer as a penance?

Oryn stared deep into Adwen's red eyes, hoping against all hope that some glimmer of her would resurface.

"Let me go," she hissed through jagged teeth. "You're killing me. That's not what you want, is it? Is this because you would rather have me dead than reject you?"

"No," Oryn said defiantly, gazing longingly from where he gripped his sword with both hands.

She sneered, "You lie."

"Not to you."

Going to her side, Alex stood over them, watching as she looked back.

"I'm sorry."

Adwen's face twisted into a nasty scowl. "You aren't sorry for anything, soldier."

Her evil words cut him. That was what was said to him when he rescued his platoon, but at the price of killing a young boy who had explosives. This time, what she said did nothing to anger him.

Sadness filled his words. "I did this to you. When you made me face the truth of my wife's death, I couldn't handle it. I hated you for it. She was everything to me; the one good thing in my life. Without her my life was nothing ... until you found me."

He knelt at her side, bowing his head in shame as she continued to scowl.

"Emily is gone. Nothing can change that. What I've done

to you is just as terrible and unfair. You don't deserve this. I should have done this as soon as we got you out of that mirror."

Looking into Adwen's eyes, he asked, "Please. Forgive me."

Adwen appeared disgusted. Then a moment passed and she seemed confounded. Beginning to understand, she blinked and studied his look. As soon as she wore an expression of remorse, every inch of her glowed white, and she screamed in pain. Her cry split the night and finally died down with the glow of her body.

As her face became redefined, her skin returned to the color of caramel, her garments a white shirt, black vest and a simple gray skirt. Lastly, her bright blue eyes glowed and became almost completely dim, vacant and staring out into nothingness. As they closed, her form slackened and relaxed, lying still.

Once they realized she was not in danger of being retaken by darkness, Oryn made his sword vanish. Her body had become whole, and the blade had left no marks.

The color slowly returned to Oryn's clothing as it mended, and they heard Jack coughing beside them. Their companion gingerly got up, plodded over and looked at Adwen for himself. Sighing deeply while all three watched her sleep, Jack patted Alex's shoulder.

"Good job, Jarhead. Good job."

Chapter 6
FOR EMILY

In the first morning light, they were awake. Jack knelt where Adwen sat in the little cave, waving a hand before her eyes. Her look was vacant and distant. She would periodically blink, but responded to nothing. He tried snapping his fingers – to no effect.

"Is she even awake?"

"Yes, Jarhead, she's definitely awake. The weird part is that her eyes don't even dilate. It's like the lights are on and nobody is home. This is something like a coma." He snapped his fingers closer to her eyes a few more times.

Oryn batted Jack's hand away. "Enough of that."

He frowned but did not protest. "This is really strange. She's gone blank."

Alex blurted out, "She's stabilized."

Both gave him curious looks.

"The elf king mentioned this. We had to stabilize her first."

"Well," Jack asked, "what did he say to do next?"

"He didn't say anything about what comes after that."

Oryn and Jack huffed in irritated disappointment.

"When did she wake up?"

Jack turned to Oryn for the answer. "Well? You were up first."

He watched her a while, thinking. "It seems strange. I asked her to, and her eyes opened not long after that."

"Try something else then. Ask her to talk."

In a kind tone, Oryn murmured, "Please, speak to me."

Adwen blinked and did nothing.

Before Oryn could feel too defeated, Jack encouraged him. "That's okay. That was a longshot. Try asking her to stand up."

To her, he whispered, "Please, stand."

She blinked. Then a small shudder came over her. The next thing they knew, Adwen did what he asked. She slowly stood.

Jack patted a very pleased Oryn on the shoulder. "Yes! This is progress. Let me try."

He gestured to go ahead.

"Please, sit down."

They waited a moment, and she didn't as much as blink.

Then Oryn tried. "Please, sit down."

Adwen blinked, shuddered and then gradually sat back down.

Rubbing his chin, Jack mused, "Very interesting. She's not just doing what you say. It's your voice she reacts to. Have you tried calling her back, like when she crossed over?"

Oryn sighed heavily. "Yes. She only blinked."

"Okay. I think I know what to do."

"Let's have it then."

"So, what if she's responding to your voice because it's familiar and important to her? That would mean that if we find the right thing to stimulate her with, she might come to. It would have to be something positive, of course; something that made her very happy."

To Jack's and Alex's shock, Oryn leaned in and kissed Adwen directly on the lips. When he finally pulled away, they waited to see if it did anything.

There was no visible change to her state.

Oryn frowned, and Jack patted his shoulder. "Nice try, buddy. But how many times have you done that?"

Brow furrowed, he replied, "I see."

"She's not familiar with you doing that. Let's keep it simple. I think we all need a field trip."

"A field what?"

Alex translated, "It's an outing."

Oryn shook his head. "There are those who might recognize us from last night's disaster. I would not think it wise to risk taking Adwen into public view, for her sake."

Jack countered him. "For her sake, we need to learn what we need to do to make her come back. Sitting in a little hole won't accomplish that."

Jack was right, and the fact disappointed Oryn. "Fine. It is agreed. First you must scout the area and see if there is any risk of us attracting attention."

Giving a salute, Jack smiled. "Consider it done. Be ready when I get back, Jarhead. We are going to the Chicago Zoo."

Alex's stomach bottomed out. Until this point he hadn't realized where they were. "Excuse me? What city is this?"

Laughing, Jack said, "Chicago! Didn't you notice how windy it was? Is something wrong?"

Keeping his head clear to avoid Jack prying, Alex replied, "I just didn't know. I'd like to give the zoo a try."

Jack was unaware of the deception. "Glad you would. Stand watch while I'm out, would ya?"

With Jack gone, Alex went to the mouth of the cave, leaving Oryn to sit alongside Adwen near the back. The fact that they were in Chicago gave him cause for worry. This was where his brother-in-law, Kyle, lived. He knew that Kyle never had liked him and that Kyle believed that Alex was responsible for Emily's death. It would be unfortunate if they crossed paths with Adwen in such a bad way.

An odd sound distracted Alex from his watch. A crunching at the back of the cave got his attention. When he looked back, he was surprised.

Munching curiously on a dog biscuit, Oryn considered the taste before swallowing. It was dry but not entirely awful. Noticing the warrior staring from the entrance, he sneered, "Make mention of this, and you shall pay."

"No problem," he said and looked back out into the forest.

The following two hours before Jack returned were uneventful. Alex thought no more of Kyle, and Oryn ate no more of the treats, dismissing the small bag for a later date. When Jack arrived, he led them out along a trail to the streets. Alex gave his sword to Jack for safekeeping, and Adwen followed at Oryn's requests, walking alongside wherever they went.

On the side of the road, Jack smiled and pointed east. "The zoo is that way about eight miles." Then he summoned up a disposable phone and began to dial. "I don't think anybody here would like to walk that far, so how about calling a cab?"

Alex was going to protest but stopped himself. The odds of a cab driver recognizing him were quite low, so he did not interrupt.

Happily, Jack instructed the cab service on where to pick them up and concluded the call. "That's that. You ever been in a car before, Cujo?"

"Yes, I have."

"Good. Then this should be easy. Just don't say anything unless you have to."

Ten minutes later, a yellow minivan came to park on their side of the road. Jack opened the doors for his companions, helping guide Adwen to sit between Oryn and Alex. Jack took the front passenger seat, and they were driven back toward the city.

The driver was a stout man who smelled as most humans did: sweat and oils. Being in a confined space such as a car bottled up the odors, and this particular man was in desperate need of deodorant. His breath was not much better. The Holy Hounds' noses detected every last rancid molecule.

"Where we headed?" the driver asked.

Jack resisted the need to gag and disguised his discomfort well. "The zoo. How many minutes is it to drive?" He wanted to know how much longer he had to endure the odors.

"It's fifteen minutes if you get good traffic. I can get there in ten."

"Excellent."

"You don't sound like you're from here," he remarked. "From the West Coast?"

"On a getaway vacation with my friends."

"Oh." Looking back at the others through the mirror, he smiled. "It's good to see a bunch of young people having some clean fun for a change. Kids these days usually get into nothing but trouble."

Jack restrained a laugh.

Taking a second look at Alex, the man frowned. "Do I know you? I've seen you someplace."

Looking back through the mirror, he replied, "I doubt it."

The cab driver was thoughtful.

Jack furtively exchanged glances with his friend.

For the remainder of the ride, the driver left the blond man alone. Instead he brought up another topic. "You picked a bad time to visit. A bomb of some kind went off in the middle of the city last night."

"No kidding," Jack played off. "Was anybody hurt?"

"Amazingly, no. They think it was an electromagnetic pulse. Anything electrical within four square blocks got fried! Lots of people were taking pictures and things, but none of the stuff made it through the blast. Even the underground generators blew. The survivors in the middle of it all were talking crazy about monsters falling from the sky."

"That's pretty crazy."

"There's never been testing on the effects of that kind of bomb on the human mind. Chances are that the energy made them hallucinate."

After stealing another glance at the others, Jack commented. "Well, we won't be going anywhere near that part of Chicago, right?"

"I'm driving a block or so around that mess. Almost there."

Five minutes later, the cab pulled alongside the curb before the zoo entrance.

"That's thirty-five fifty."

Jack was becoming more skilled with concealing the summoning of his things. Taking a wallet from a nonexistent pocket where the man could not see, he paid him forty. "Keep the change. Have a nice day."

They began to climb out, and the man replied, "Thanks, pal."

Before Alex could close the door, the driver looked back and said, "Hey! I remember who you are!" Alex froze and stared with the door handle in his grasp.

Pointing a finger, he grinned. "You're that new linebacker for the Ducks!"

Relief washed over Alex as he smiled back.

"Hope your A.C.L. gets better soon."

"Thank you. Take care of yourself, too." With that, he closed the cab door and rejoined his company.

Jack laughed at him. "I knew that guy didn't really recognize you! Come on, Jarhead. Let's get moving."

They went through the walkways that wound about the many exhibits. It was early still, and few other visitors were wandering about, enjoying the captive creatures. Jack hoped that perhaps Adwen's love of animals would get her to respond to the sights and sounds, as she had to Oryn's voice. Where they entered the gazelles' enclosure was the first reason to stop. Having been to zoos before, Jack and Alex were having a strange new experience. This time, they could hear and understand anything the beasts said. Mostly the herd animals bantered amongst themselves about gossip while chewing on grass. They were boring, so the group went north toward to the monkey exhibit.

A domineering howler monkey grunted at Alex. What none of the humans could hear was that the creature was laughing. "Ha! More men in tight clothes! Look at this one! I can't get enough of this."

Jack called out to the animal, "Yeah, doesn't he look charming in them?"

In shock the monkey nearly fell from the limb and squawked. "What? You can hear what I'm saying? What kind of human are you?"

Before he could cause more trouble, Oryn grabbed Jack by the back of his hoody. They dragged him away as the beasts became excited, causing a ruckus and following as far as their enclosure would allow, whooping and calling after them.

Jack laughed at Alex's expense all the way to the polar bears' location. When they got there, the huge creature was taking a swim. Oryn marveled at seeing a white bear for the first time.

Coming up below them, the bear sniffed and stared. "You're not humans. What are you doing here?"

"Hey," Jack greeted, leaning on the rail. "We're taking our friend here for a walk. Trying to help her heal."

The polar bear sniffed again, curious. "She seems nice to me. Don't take her to the giraffes. Those are a bunch of rude hunks of meat." With that he dived back underwater.

"Thanks for the tip."

Oryn steered Adwen clear of the creatures with extraordinarily long necks once Alex identified them as giraffes. Jack, however, went right up to the fence. One was there, eating leaves from a high tree.

Jack called out, "What's up?"

Looking down, the giraffe was curious at first. Then he replied, "Give me a break."

"I'm not going to give you a break. I'm here to have some fun. What's with the bad attitude?"

Neither surprised nor bothered by the fact that the man could understand, the indifferent beast began to clean its nose using its tongue while it spoke. "I don't associate with short animals. You least of all, as you're shorter than your peers."

Entertained by the petty insult, Jack laughed. "Hey now! That's uncalled for. Look at me when I'm talking to you."

Turning to graze elsewhere, the giraffe flicked its ropy tail. "Buzz off."

Jack chuckled and returned to his friends. "The bear wasn't kidding."

Oryn shook his head, guiding Adwen farther along the path. They passed the penguins, and Jack had fun antagonizing them. By the time they left, the birds were squawking madly, making almost as big a commotion as the monkeys had. Some onlookers were in shock as keepers appeared, trying to restore calm. Jack was headed for to the seal tank, but Alex and Oryn dragged him away.

They came to the red wolf enclosure. A few of the pack members sunned themselves or lay in the shade, thoroughly bored.

"Hey!" Jack called out. "How you doing today?"

The heads of the pack went up, and their ears perked. Coming closer to see who was speaking to them, they whispered to each other.

"What in the wild world are you supposed to be?" one yowled and yipped. "You're not human, but you don't look like our kind. What do you want?"

Thinking for a moment, he glanced at Adwen's face. It was still blank and unseeing. "My friend here. She needs some cheering up. Could you sing for her?"

The wolf laughed. "Are you serious? This is the first time we've gotten a request. Let me see what the pups think."

"Take your time."

Now completely annoyed, Oryn glowered. "Is it your intention to turn this entire place into a madhouse?"

Jack held up a hand to shush him. "Just wait. You'll see. I've got a feeling zoo wolves live for this sort of thing."

Several wolves took positions in their habitat and began to howl.

When the knight stared in surprise at their potential for harmony, Jack laughed. "I thought it was worth a try. Adwen likes to sing on rare occasions, and these guys enjoy it, too."

They watched her to see if the wolf choir did anything to stir Adwen's consciousness. It did not, but the performance put on by the pack still gave the company some entertainment. When their act was finished, the creatures said farewell and went back to lounging in the sun.

The neighboring bears snoozed when the four passed. Jack did not get the opportunity to rile them up like the other animals. For this, his friends were thankful.

No humans were around when they came to a narrow path between the outer fence and one of the facilities. Everything around them hushed. Coming to a halt, the three braced themselves and looked around. Something was not right.

Out of the shadow of the building, five demons leaped and attacked. Jack summoned up Alex's sword and tossed it to him before bringing back his own weapons. Right away, they killed the first demons to reach them.

Oryn summoned his sword to fight and stole a look at Adwen. Her eyes watched the demons. When he saw a red light starting in them, he swiftly buried her face in his chest, wrapping his arms about her, using the blade to further shield her back. He relied upon the others to kill the fiends, which they did in moments.

When the last one was dead, Jack and Alex panted and stared at each other. "They attacked in the daylight? I didn't see that coming." Jack took Alex's sword back and magically concealed them so the group could continue uninterrupted by security.

They gathered around Oryn as he gingerly pulled back to examine Adwen. The red glow was gone, but her stare was as distant as ever.

"Seeing them nearly turned her," he murmured.

The two at his sides were quiet. When Oryn dismissed his own weapon, Jack nodded to the ponds ahead, "We should leave."

Sighing heavily, the knight agreed.

Making their way to the zoo exit, Jack led them through the gift shop. After the run-in with the demons, their moods were dreary. Adwen followed, as ignorant to their moods as she was to the shiny bobbles and knickknacks. Her clean bare feet shuffled like those of a patient in a medical ward. As the warriors continued forward, her feet stopped moving.

Oryn was first to notice that she was no longer with them. He had only gone a few paces before looking back, watching in amazement as she turned on her own accord to look at an item on a shelf. Going to stand by her, he joined in listening to a tune chiming within a music box. Her eyes were unfocused, but she was undoubtedly attracted by the sound.

Jack and Alex arrived, smiling jubilantly.

Restraining his need to laugh at the top of his lungs, Jack grinned from ear to ear. "Music! I knew I was on the right track with the wolves. Yes, I can work with this."

About to guide her away, Oryn saw what was just behind the shelf and froze in place, stunned. For the longest time, he had gone without ever seeing his face. His reflection showed him as he was, close to human with the exception of the soft glow in his eyes. The sight held him enraptured.

From the shop exit before the gate, Jack called to him. "Hurry up! I know where to take her!" Pausing a moment to look at both of their reflections together, he smiled and led her after the others to hail a cab.

Ten minutes later, they exited the vehicle in front of a store. Upon entering, a seemingly exhaustive collection of CDs covered leaning shelves and racks. Jack scoured the selection, looking for what he thought could be the right sound to get a reaction from Adwen. Gradually he gathered CDs and stacked them beside a headset and scanner.

Alex took a look at what he was picking. Holding up one case, he tapped him on the shoulder. "What do you think you're doing?"

The case he brandished was of a metal band.

"I don't see the problem," Jack shrugged.

Alex set it aside, shaking his head, frowning. "I don't think she's that type of girl. Why aren't you looking up something like classical music or choir music?"

Wearing a dumbfounded look, Jack raised an eyebrow. "You're kidding me, right?" Taking Adwen from under Oryn's protective arm, he held her before him and pointed to her face. "Look at her, Jarhead. She has white hair, a nice tan and black lips. She looks like a rock chick. What's the matter with you?"

Alex opened his mouth to protest but was shushed by the ex-cop.

"Rock?" asked Oryn.

"Yeah," Jack replied. "It's a type of music."

Realization dawned on the knight, and he mused, "She made mention of it and shared rock music with me once."

"There you go, Gomer. You see? Let me work my magic here."

The Marine rolled his eyes, shaking his head.

For hours they lingered in the store, getting strange looks from workers while they presented various albums to Adwen, holding the headset over her ears. It was so large that the contraption would slip off of her head if they were not careful. Most of what they tested caused her to blink and raise her head to listen, but nothing more.

Eventually, while Jack was busy putting Adwen through the rigorous search for the right sound, he helped Oryn satisfy some curiosity. Oryn also had a pair of headphones on by the end of the day. While Jack watched her, he sampled song after song, waiting to see when she would reawaken.

Adwen had not come around before they left at dusk. It did not discourage them. In one day they had learned a lot to help and protect her. They caught a cab to the edge of the forest, returning to their hideaway for sleep. Alex curled up near the entrance across from an excited Jack. He had ideas of what to present to her next.

In the back of the earthy hole, Oryn lay down to rest, holding her close, blocking her from the chilly air outside.

The next day they returned to the music store by cab. Jack

went about monitoring Adwen and Oryn with their head-phones, answering questions as the knight asked them. Oryn had worked his way through almost every category, intent on seeing why Adwen liked this music so much. Eventually he found classical music and was charmed by Beethoven and his piano compositions.

Alex borrowed a few dollars from Jack to get a protein bar from a rack near the register. He was busy with Oryn at the moment. They were safe in the open with humans around, so it seemed allowable to let their guard down. After paying and taking a bite, he saw two young punks investigating Adwen.

Both scoffed and giggled at the way she stood, staring out at nothing. But when Alex came to glare at them, their faces straightened. Though he didn't mean to, his pale blue eyes shined in anger. The eerie sight was more than enough to frighten them into minding their own business.

His expression softened when he turned to check on her. The headphones were askew again, so he repositioned them. Leaning forward, he looked to see if her eyes showed any hint of change. Alex did not find anything. He sighed. As his own eyes took notice of a figure in the far window watching him, he stopped and stared.

At that moment, Jack returned. "Hey, sorry about that. I've got her. Finish eating that bar before I eat it for you."

"Whatever you say," he muttered, watching the figure.

Waiting until Jack was completely distracted with his chore, Alex calmly turned and quietly exited the shop. He knew Kyle was sure to follow.

Alex hiked down the block and kept going. He would keep going until his pursuer caught up with him. By that point, they would be far away from where Adwen could be harmed. Demon or not, it was too much of a risk for her to be around anything related to rage or destruction.

Almost an hour passed, and the sixth sense from his besti-al side confirmed he was being followed. Downtown was far behind him, and the scent of running water reached his sens-es. Eventually he could hear the man taking long strides to catch up. Knowing it was time to take this elsewhere, the Ma-rine turned down a narrow corner leading to the canal. He heard the angry voice of his brother-in-law once he was nearing the other end of the alley.

"Alexander Greeves!"

Alex stopped and slowly turning to face his pursuer. Kyle had come to a halt several yards away, watching carefully. The man inched closer, talking as he did, shuddering with the Adrenaline rush he experienced at seeing him again. Alex held perfectly still, maintaining an alert but unimposing composure.

"I never thought you would have the gall to come here of all places." Kyle quivered, and his voice faltered from the waves of grief. "After what you've done, you don't even have the decency of staying behind bars to face your trial?"

As Kyle stood just out of arm's reach and continued the emotional rant, Jack peered down from one of the rooftops above. It was hard to pick up the man's thoughts from this distance, but he heard everything Kyle said loud and clear.

Spittle flew from behind his teeth with the venomous sentences. "What kind of man are you? I knew something was wrong when we first met. You can put on your uniform and act like a good soldier, but now the whole world knows what you are."

Unafraid and recognizing the pain being unleashed upon him, Alex knew it was very much like his own. Alex murmured, never breaking eye contact, "What am I, Kyle?"

Kyle's face was beat red with rage. "You're a murderer. I know you killed my sister. You killed Emily! Why can't you admit it, coward? Say to me that you killed her!"

Alex softly replied with a heavy heart, "I would never hurt her, Kyle."

To Jack's shock, Kyle took out a high-caliber revolver, aiming shakily for his friend's heart. He tensed and waited, not knowing if he would follow through.

The sight of the gun did not affect Alex. He instinctively knew this would happen. As if the weapon did not exist, he continued to look back at Kyle, balefully.

"You killed her. We all know you killed her. My family is sick of not getting the closure we deserve. You broke our family apart with your bloody, filthy hands. There's nothing in the world that is going to bring her back."

Making no sudden moves, Alex replied, "There's a hole in

your heart. It's big and dark. No matter what you try to fill it with, nothing makes it close. That dark, cold hole pulls you in and takes the warmth out of your life. I see that in you, through your eyes."

Tears began to stream down Kyle's face, soaking spots on his shirt. A couple sobs wracked his body, making the gun shake violently.

"I know each and every one of your family has this hole. You know what it looks like. You see it every day."

Kyle swallowed and tried to steady his aim.

"Look in my eyes, Kyle."

They stared at each other for many tense seconds. The longer Kyle looked at him, the more he saw what was so perfectly described of himself. Kyle found the same pain in Alex's eyes, yet he could not bring himself to put down the gun.

Shaking his head, Kyle sobbed louder, "No. No!" I know you did it!"

"Emily was the center of my world. I lost the will to live when she died. I wanted to die. Each night for a long while after, I wished for death to take me."

Slowly, Alex stepped closer, and Kyle watched in disbelief as he lifted the barrel and placed the muzzle between his eyes. The wind-chilled metal rested tight against his skin. His light blue eye stared back, watching and waiting.

"If you think I could hurt her, do what you came here to do."

The mind and heart of Kyle Bisbee waged war with each other. What he believed and what he wanted to believe tore his consciousness into pieces. Truth and doubt made him sob, fighting to come to a solid conclusion where there was none. Either way, his broken heart would be left standing on a rocky shore of pain. At last he spat and lowered the gun. "I don't want to end your pain."

Jack breathed a sigh of relief overhead.

Alex did as well.

Then Kyle's eyes sparked with renewed rage. "But I won't let you hurt us anymore."

A loud gunshot rang out and echoed throughout the surrounding blocks. Blood flew through the air behind Alex as his body fell, hitting the ground, limp and lifeless. Blood pooled behind his head, a small red bead trailing down from his brow.

Jack watched in shock as Kyle vomited profusely and looked at the gun in his hand as if it were a snake. Panic took over, and Kyle acted quickly.

After throwing the gun as far out into the canal as he could, he returned to drag Alex's large body to the water's edge. He was very heavy. Jack waited. The instant his friend tumbled into the water, he sprang into action, racing down out of view of the would-be-killer. Rushing out to the water once Kyle was gone, Jack ran along the current and dived in after the dark silhouette deep under the surface.

It took forty-five minutes for the wound to close and another hour and a half for Alex to regain consciousness. Alex found himself propped against a wall behind a dumpster, not far from the canal. Beside him was Jack, who was also soaking wet, sitting with his back to the wall, watching the clouds.

"About time you woke up, Jarhead." Alex said nothing, content to stare at his soggy shoes.

"Brother-in-laws. I have to ask, did you know the gun couldn't kill you?"

After thinking a moment, he answered, "It never crossed my mind."

"That bullet sure did."

Again, Alex was quiet.

Jack watched him and considered what had happened. "He lives in Chicago?"

"Yeah."

Scratching the back of his head, Jack sighed. "I'm going to have to find a new hangout for us." He climbed to his feet and helped Alex stand.

Going to the curb, they looked around for a moment before Jack summoned his cell phone to call another cab. While it was still ringing, he said, "Hey, Alex, let's not bring this up to Oryn."

A glad smile came to him. "Thanks."

"Don't mention it. Oh! Yes, I would like a cab for a pickup."

More than almost dark before they arrived at the store to find Oryn and Adwen. Jack waved for them to come outside.

Toting Adwen, Oryn emerged glowering. "What is the meaning of this? You left us alone without a word of warning. Why are the both of you as wet as fish in a net?"

The two exchanged glances, and Jack shrugged. "Dummy here went for a swim."

Oryn's angry look became suspicious. "Never mind. It will be night soon. Let us return to our temporary home."

Taking the cab back to the woods, they concluded their day with no more excitement. Neither Alex nor Jack shared the day's events with anyone.

Chapter 7
NEW TRICKS

"Where do you think you are going?" Oryn stalked after Jack as he was walking away from the cave in the late-morning hours. "We need you and your device to travel back to the shop of songs."

To cover for Alex, Jack stopped and made up an excuse. "If we keep going there without buying anything, the store owners are going to call the cops. Doing what we did there with Adwen two days in a row has them thinking she is our hostage. It's time to find a new music store."

Oryn growled and looked about them in their wooded shelter. He knew the music store was safe. But if Jack was right, returning there time and again would be a grave mistake.

"There are other shops of songs, okay? Other than at the zoo, haven't you been able to trust me?"

He glared. "You have been invaluable."

"I know that hurt to say, but thank you. Coming from you, that is the highest compliment I've ever gotten. Let me keep being invaluable. Protect Adwen. I'll be back in a few hours."

Fighting his urge to argue, the knight forced himself to let Jack go. He went to the cave, rejoining Adwen and Alex.

Jack walked the streets away from any of the places they had already disturbed. The tall buildings and unending traffic surrounded him. Wind gusts brought in smells of the sea and the fishy odors of the piers at the far corners of the city. Only he with his powerful sense of smell could notice at this distance. On his way he asked around for advice on where to listen to rock music. In his inquiry, he was given directions to one place multiple times.

The club known as Scooter's stood proudly near the heart

of the metropolis, close enough to compete for popularity with any other business of its kind. It regularly hosted live bands, with schedules booked a week or so in advance. According to the word on the street, this was exactly what Jack was searching for.

It was almost noon, and the front door was locked. He could see through the shadows inside and spied a young woman. Jack rapped his knuckles rhythmically on the window for her attention. First she ignored him. When he did not leave, she opened the door to see what he wanted.

The brunette had black and silver extensions in her hair. Dressed entirely in black with a dark brown leather jacket, she wore a necklace with a purple robot logo. She frowned and looked Jack over, her bright hazel eyes working to see whether or not he was a waste of her time and breath.

"We're closed. If you need to book a party, call one of our lines and we'll hook you up with the earliest date."

Jack cleared his throat and smiled. "Yes, thank you, but I need to talk with the manager. The owner would be better if they're in."

The woman wore a suspicious look. "What do you want?"

"I would really rather ask whomever's running the show, please."

A hard scowl tugged at the sides of the girl's mouth. "If this is about money, you can take a hike."

She moved to slam the door, but Jack slipped his boot in the way. "It's not about money!"

When she slowly opened the door again, Jack was more careful not to get on her bad side. Her mind was like a steel vault he could not fiddle his way into. Paying close attention, he did not take his second chance lightly.

"Then what is it?"

Heaving a sigh, Jack came clean as she would know if he was lying. She could smell it. "I have an act he needs to see."

She rolled her eyes. "Can't you make an appointment?"

"No, because this is for a short time only. I can't wait a week or even a few days to do this."

Becoming curious, she asked, "What kind of act?"

Finally, Jack cracked into her vault. "Let me talk to the boss and I'll show you, Mia."

Mia's eyes widened, and her pupils became tiny specks.

Alex sat at the mouth of the cave keeping watch, while Oryn dozed with Adwen wrapped in his arms. Even in sleep, he didn't dare to let her go without his protection. The Marine admired and envied the knight in that he still had her. A smile broke his stern face. It also made him feel good to see Oryn hold her like that. The sight brought comfort, as there were few things that revived positive memories in him. Once upon a time, he held Emily like that when they took naps on the couch.

Suddenly his ears pricked at the sound of footfalls in leaves. If he could, Alex would growl to call out. Any human would back off. So he waited until his nose caught the familiar scent, and he relaxed.

Jack came closer, knelt down and grinned. "I've got great news."

Alex looked at him and waited.

To his confusion, Jack pointed a finger at him and laughed loud and hard, waking Oryn from his nap. "We've got a drooler! Oh man, this is priceless."

The Marine didn't understand until a draft chilled the long string of spittle dangling from his chin. Disgusted, he wiped at it but the substance was slimy like that of a real dog. As shocked as he was, he was more embarrassed that Jack had noticed.

Angry to be woken so abruptly, Oryn turned over and snarled. "What is so funny that you could not contain yourself?"

Still pointing, Jack crowed, "I caught Alex drooling like a Neapolitan mastiff!"

While the flustered Marine continued to mop up his face, Oryn turned to Jack and snapped, "If you cannot cease your laughing, I shall have to throw a stick!"

Jack fell quiet and muttered nervously, "You wouldn't."

Then it was time for Alex to laugh.

"Aw, shut up, Pluto."

Oryn's loud bark silenced them both. Getting up, he asked, "Have you not found a song shop?"

A sly look came over him. "I'll do you one better."

While in the cab, Alex constantly checked for dampness around his lips, still alarmed that he had been drooling. Jack snickered quietly at Alex's expense, and Oryn shook his head, his arm tight around Adwen's shoulders. Their destination was a ten-minute drive, but the afternoon traffic slowed them down considerably.

Sunset was upon them when they arrived. Stepping out with Adwen, Oryn turned to Jack, concerned about the time. "It is late to be out. This is a risk."

With everybody out of the cab, their big-mouthed companion was not bothered.

"It's a risk worth taking. Come on in. There's somebody I'd like you to meet."

The four entered through the double door into Scooter's. Inside was a long bar, dance floor, stage and a balcony level, which overlooked the three. Neon illuminated the sign over the bar selection. At night most of the lights would be off, but for now the workers prepared for the evening's events in a fully illuminated club.

Waiting by the bar was a tall blond man with eyes slightly bluer than Alex's. He was lean and dressed in expensive designer clothing. His shoes were a loud shade of highlighter yellow. Upon seeing Jack and the others, he smiled broadly, his eyes sparkling with delight.

"Hey, Jack!" The club owner greeted while shaking his hand. "Glad you made it. This is going to be a busy night."

"I hope so. The more the better." Indicating his friends, Jack said, "This is Oryn, Alex and Adwen. Guys, this is Thomas Lee. He runs the place."

"No, he doesn't," Mia corrected as she joined them. "I run it. He just owns it. It's my responsibility to babysit him and his finances so he doesn't run this place into the ground."

"Sorry, I need to introduce you to Mia, his sister."

Rolling her eyes, Mia smiled as she was used to Jack already. "Don't start too much trouble. I'm having the bouncers standing by just in case there's a riot." Addressing the innocent bystanders, she nodded. "Have a nice night."

Mia left them to go about her business, and Thomas shook his head. "She needs to smile more. I try my best, but she's too serious."

"No kidding. So it's still on for tonight?"

"Oh, yes. Prepped and ready for takeoff."

Brow furrowed and very suspicious, Oryn asked, "Mr. Lee? What is ready exactly?"

"Call me Tom," he smiled. "I think I'm going to let that be a surprise. If you're smart, the three of you can take a table up on the overhead. That's the best view of the stage. It's going to be a blast." Jack felt the frightened stares of the knight and the Marine piercing the back of his head. They didn't know what he was up to and sensed it was not good.

Tom looked at his military-grade watch. "You should go to your table now. It's going to be packed in a few minutes."

Turning to his anxious friends, Jack insisted, "Go ahead. I'll be up there later. Save a seat for me."

Watching them climb the stairs, Tom was concerned about them. "Is the girl all right? She looked a bit freaked out."

Jack frowned. "She just lost her family. We're trying to bring her around. She likes rock music, so I went looking for a place to take her."

At this, Tom smiled. "You found the best place in Chicago."

Guiding Adwen to a chair and having her sit by the railing, Oryn growled. "What does he think he's playing at? Is this a club?"

Alex was surprised. "You know what a club is? Yes. This is a night club."

Sitting close to her, Oryn shook his head. "I gather it is going to be loud and brimming with fools?"

"Like every place. Let's see what he's going to pull off. If it looks bad, we can sneak out."

Forty-five minutes passed, and the building became crowded. Speakers played music loud enough to hear over the din. With drinks dispersed to reaching hands, the influx of laughing and smiling partygoers rose to a fever pitch.

Oryn acted as a bulwark to the crowd's jostling and pushing. As when demons appeared, he used his body as a barrier, sheltering her from all manner of intrusion.

A young man came and saw the great view from the rail. Getting Oryn's attention, he asked, "Excuse me. Can we squeeze in next to you and your girlfriend? We really want to watch from that spot."

Oryn looked back, and his eyes lit up like headlights as he growled loudly. By the time he turned back to Adwen and the stage, the pestering human and his friends were gone.

"You could have just said no," Alex offered, raising his voice over the crowd.

"I did."

To signal the start of the first show, the room dimmed and the stage lights burst on, spotlighting an announcer. People whooped and whistled in anticipation.

"Ladies and gentlemen, we have an announcement. The band that was due to open tonight canceled the other day, and a new act has taken its place. This is a very rare opportunity to see a multitalented performer. I saw some of his skills, and it still has me blown away. First up tonight is an illusionary performance by the Amazing Jack!"

As the audience clapped and a few booed for their own entertainment, Alex and Oryn watched in disbelief as Jack walked out on the stage to take the microphone, dressed in a tuxedo. Unable to put anything past him, they waited to see what was in store this time.

"Thank you." He smiled and strolled to the front of the stage. "This is an illusion act, but if you like, it can be a bit of a standup routine. It all depends on the crowd, and this, I have to say, is a good-looking crowd tonight. Am I right?"

The people clapped, and a single drunk below yelled excessively.

With quiet restored, Jack ran into a problem he had anticipated. The many minds so close to him were buzzing, and it made it difficult for him to think clearly. Rubbing his forehead, he went on.

"Since I'm performing magic tricks, I think I'd like to cater to the ones who don't believe in that type of thing. With that in mind, these sleeves are just too long. I could hide almost anything in them."

To the awe of the crowd, Jack skillfully manipulated his

attire. The magical clothing he wore shifted until he was wearing a vest and a collared white shirt and tie. The people clapped, and he smiled, rubbing his temple, which was throbbing. So many thoughts at once struck him like rocks, giving him a spitting headache. Regardless, Jack pressed on.

He chuckled. "Whoops! Forgot the undershirt." The sleeves of the collared shirt receded, earning more applause.

"If I can be honest, I don't like this look very much. Watch this." Pulling on his tie, he made red pinstripes run down his black vest. "That's better."

More clapping and whistling came, while his friends watched in shock. Oryn was wide-eyed. "What does he think he is doing?"

"He's toying with them," Alex said. "They all think it's an illusion."

Again, a hurricane of minds slammed Jack's. Laughing it off, he told them, "The guys here call me the Amazing Jack. Really, I'm not. I read thoughts."

From the balcony, Alex sighed, "Oh, here we go."

"And tonight I'm going to prove it." Ever since the start, Jack had struggled to single out the streams of thoughts flying at him. It was impossible, but he kept trying. He needed to be able to single out individual minds for the next act to work. Looking over the different faces, the volume suddenly dropped to whispers. Jack focused on a face, and he was relieved to hear only a single mind's thoughts.

Having put himself through so much, Jack's own mind finally formed a defense against bombardment. He thought of what the elf king had said. Shaking his head, Jack could almost laugh. It had come to him.

"Who here likes mind reading?" Scanning the people, he discovered right away who did. "Okay, now who does not? Who doesn't think it exists?"

This question narrowed down his search. Locking onto three men at a table nearby, Jack pointed at one of them and called out, "You, Timothy. How was the game last weekend?"

His friends laughed as Timothy rolled his eyes and nodded. "It was great."

Holding up a finger, Jack replied, "Oh, but you didn't watch the game. You were too busy hanging out with Laura in a hotel by the waterfront."

Timothy stared, dumbfounded, and one of his friends yelled, "What were you doing with my sister?"

The other friend yelled, "What do you mean? He's cheating on my sister!"

As the audience began to laugh, Jack readjusted his tie. "That's awkward."

His companions did not like how the show was turning out. Oryn murmured anxiously, "This is worse than the penguin exhibit."

Waving for calm until the volume died down again, he asked, "Who's next? Who else doesn't think I can read minds?"

Two couples were seated not far away. One of the girls became his next target. "Chelsie. Chelsie, Chelsie; biggest skeptic in the room."

The redhead crossed her arms, eyeing Jack suspiciously. "Guilty as charged. So tell me, big shot. What am I thinking right now?"

"That I should take this microphone and put it where the sun don't shine."

She rolled her eyes dramatically. "That was too easy. How about now?"

Jack smiled toothily. "You think that every good magician is supposed to wear a stuffy hat." He summoned a top hat from his collection of items and placed it on his head, tilting it from side to side for a comfortable fit. It was too big for him.

The girl's jaw dropped, and her friend asked, "Is he right?"

She nodded, mouth hanging open.

The audience clapped again, this time putting Alex and Oryn at ease. There was far less tension in the air. But while the people fell quiet, the drunk on the ground floor became far more belligerent.

The slurring man screamed, "You tell her! Tell her all about it!"

Jack chuckled. "Somebody is having a little too much fun."

"Read my mind," he hollered. "Tell me what I did in the car on the way here."

A bouncer was on the way to drag the man out, but the

crowd was very compact, making it hard to move. When the bouncer was almost within reach of the drunk, Jack's eyes flashed and fixated on the tall glass full of ice and liquor. Before Jack realized what he was doing, he gained access to an energy source he had not tapped into since his last conflict with Sycan.

A violet light that none but he and the Holy Hounds could see formed around the glass. Then the contents flew out, splashing and falling down the drunk man's face.

The room went quiet. Even Jack was shocked.

Oryn whispered, "Oh, no. He's done it."

"What?"

"He's learned to move things."

Getting up and sputtering, the man yelled, "Hey! Did you do that?"

The eyes of the crowd fell to Jack on stage.

Smiling, he laughed. "Hey! Accidents happen."

Then the people gasped as a glass of water floated up off of the same table. The drunk stared at the amazing sight, then sputtered again when the water flew into his face. A bouncer grabbed him from behind, dragging the drunk off so as not to interrupt the show further.

Jack lost his hold on the cup, and it fell back on the table. People began to clap at the removing of the loud man and turned to give applause for the great trick. He shrugged before taking a small bow. Excited to finally acquire the ability he wanted most, it seemed appropriate to take things further.

"For my last trick, I'm going to need a trustworthy person for an inspection."

Without having to be called, Chelsie stood and approached the stage.

Jack shrugged. "I trust you to find anything hokey."

"You bet." The onlooker's laughed.

In his hand before the woman's eyes, Jack summoned out a Frisbee. When the ensuing applause died down, he asked her, "Can you look at this and tell if it's just a normal Frisbee?"

Turning and flipping it, she eventually tried bending it as if to break it in half. Passing it back, she nodded, "Yup. It seems normal to me."

"Okay, thank you. Tell your boyfriend he's lucky."

She smiled broadly on her way to her table, and the audience laughed.

Taking his position in the center of the stage, Jack laid the plastic toy in the palm of his hand, holding the microphone with the other. Gazing at the flat item, he said, "I've never tried this before. Give me a few seconds to get it started."

Everyone, including the Holy Hounds on the upper floor, watched closely.

Taking a deep breath, feeling for the energy, Jack formed his psychic grip around the item. He could detect every surface, even on the underside, which he could not see. First he tried to make it spin. Slowly, it turned an inch and stopped. He made a second attempt with more determination. The plastic slid across his fingers, turning like a dial.

Then, once he had it steady, he lowered his hand, leaving the Frisbee turning in midair. The audience clapped.

It took a lot of focus to keep it free floating. His power wavered, making the Frisbee tilt and bob up and down slightly. Fighting to keep it airborne, Jack sent it drifting low over the heads of the crowd. Louder clapping and cheers made it more challenging, but he welcomed that. The challenge was what pushed him to excel.

Alex clapped as the Frisbee drifted past the loft railing, laughing at the odd spectacle. Even Oryn smiled and shook his head.

Making the Frisbee come back, Jack began to look at it differently. It still floated, but once it returned to the stage, he lunged. A split second later, the taste of plastic was on his tongue, and the hard edge held in his teeth. The people laughed and clapped when he swiftly pulled it from his mouth.

Alex laughed with them, his sides hurting from the fit.

Chuckling, knowing he wasn't going to hear the end of this, Jack waved the Frisbee at the crowd. "Sorry about that. You guys caught me playing fetch with myself. This has been an awesome crowd. You all have an incredible night. Thank you!"

The audience clapped and whistled, and Jack headed backstage. On his way past the bands setting up behind the curtain, Jack tossed the Frisbee in the garbage and returned the top hat he had borrowed to a drummer.

The band member laughed. "You got to show me how to do that."

Jack only smiled, continuing on his way to join his friends.

Coming up the stairs, he was greeted with back slaps and clapping. Sitting beside Alex, he heard Oryn growl.

"What possessed you to do such a thing?"

Before he could come up with an answer, Alex asked, "How much stuff do you actually carry with you?"

"Funny thing," Jack said, smiling. "I bought as much stuff as I could in order to find out how much I could magically carry. As it turns out, about as much as I weigh."

Oryn was surprised by the revelation. "I was unaware of that."

"Well now we know, thanks to me and my tendency to go all out. Also, it has to be something you can hold in your hands. Trash cans and chairs don't count."

Alex buried his head in his hands. "What in the world is wrong with you?"

"I'm going to get some drinks," Jack announced. "And one more thing: If either of you tell Adwen about the Frisbee thing, I will make your life a living hell. Got it?"

While Jack was gone, the first band introduced themselves and commenced to rile up the audience. They played a hard jam. By the time Jack returned, Oryn was surprised to learn he enjoyed this scene. Adwen turned toward the stage, as Oryn soaked in the sounds, finding that he liked the harmony of the instruments and voices.

The more the band jammed, the more Oryn felt alive. The people around them did too. Couples danced below, shaking and jumping to the beat. With all of the flashing lights and distractions, Oryn thought it may have been a trick on his sight, but he thought he could see Adwen's eyes glowing a little brighter than before. Instead of looking to confirm his assumption, he decided to let her be and simply believe she was more alive.

Jack passed Oryn a glass of something. "It's on the house, pal."

Having barely heard him, Oryn spotted the drink and

frowned. "I think I'd rather not ruin this evening by dampening my thoughts."

"You're too uptight. Mellow out. Let me keep an eye on things for a few hours."

The knight gave the cop a deadly look.

"Come on. Do I have to keep asking? Trust me."

Finding the will to do as Jack advised, Oryn tasted the drink. It was sweet, and the alcohol was not overpowering. This led him to think that the concoction was nothing to take too seriously. To Jack's and Alex's amusement, Oryn downed the entire glass as if it were water, and he was thirsty. He brought the glass back down and firmly declared, "This shall be the one and only time I do this for you."

"You're so sweet." Jack smiled. "Thank you."

Alex had a sip from his own drink and asked Oryn, "You sure? Looked like you enjoyed it."

Oryn glared and made his eyes glow.

"Okay, have it your way." For half an hour, they listened to the music, relishing the nightlife. The building was a ship, and the band was its sail, leading everyone on a grand excursion. The drinks had some people swaying and staggering as if they were on the top deck of a ship, buffeted by rolling waves. Some revelers experienced this more than others.

Jack had two or three drinks, same as Alex. Oryn stood by his word and refused any more. About the time the second band emerged, Oryn turned to Jack, and his eyes were slightly glazed.

"Jack, I'm going to ask something of you, and you had better do it."

"What?"

"Make absolutely certain nothing happens to Adwen tonight. If you fail, I will find a way to kill you with my bare hands." A second later, Oryn was face down on the table.

Laughing, the Marine asked, "What did you give him?"

Cocking his head and shrugging, he answered, "A fuzzy-navel."

Both burst out laughing hard at the knight passed out before them.

Chapter 8
BALLAD

Loading Oryn into the cab was as ponderous as seating Adwen — like carrying groceries in human-sized bags. They folded and flopped whenever you thought they might be in a stable position. Making the process worse was the fact that both Alex and Jack were quite drunk. The cab driver thought nothing of it. He had seen worse.

When they reached the forest, dragging Oryn and Adwen out of the cab was easier than putting them in. Jack cradled Adwen in his arms. Her eyes were closed, and for all he knew, she really was asleep. Beside him, Alex carried Oryn's tall body over one shoulder. He was heavy, but the Marine was very strong now. The comatose knight did not hinder Alex's pace down the hiking path.

As the cab left and they were part way into the forest, Alex chuckled. "Remind me again why I'm carrying him instead of her?"

"Because," Jack replied, "if I carried him, his feet would drag across the ground." Alex laughed hard, struggling not to drop the dead weight.

"Cut it out. You've laughed at me enough for one night."

"I haven't laughed this much since my bachelor party."

Jack shook his head. "I can only imagine. You must be that kind of drunk."

While they walked deeper into the woods, Alex's raucous laughter continued. He could not help himself.

"Shut up," Jack chuckled. Then a chill came over him, and he sobered up. Sniffing the air, he said with much more urgency, "Shut up! Put a lid on it. We've got company." The Marine stopped laughing altogether, laying Oryn on the ground. The two grew more alert, and Jack set Adwen down, using Oryn's body as a pillow for her head. They knew he wouldn't mind. With their friends lying together, Jack drew out the weapons, returning the Marine's as well. The sounds of wildlife hushed, signaling the beginning of a vicious attack.

Demons spewed toward them, snapping jaws like bear traps. Alex stabbed a fiend to his right and put a fist into the face of one on his left. He made quick swipes and stabs, killing his enemies at will.

Jack was more lucid than his cohort. He felled twice as many in the same amount of time. What he realized that Alex did not was that they were terribly outnumbered. Coming up with a solution, Jack yelled, "When I tell you to, drop and lie flat on the ground."

"What? Are you kidding?"

"Now!" He cried. "Hit the dirt!"

Taking hold of the twin daggers with his mind, Jack unleashed a whirlwind of razor-edged death. The weapons whistled around him, slicing through the air. At his telekinetic command, the blades twirled and flew around in a widening circle, spinning out enough to keep the demons back. Purple blood flew in arcs about the Holy Hounds. No matter whether the vile things leaped or dived low, Jack' mind tracked their movements, and the blades found them. When no more demons came, Jack released control of the daggers, and they fell close by.

Exhausted, Jack slumped to his knees, panting. "You can start laughing again. It's all clear."

After that scene, Alex lifted his head and could only say, "Wow."

When Oryn awoke the next morning, he found Adwen had been placed in his arms, where he usually kept her. They were in the back of the cave. He was thankful to see that the other two warriors had been reliable enough to return them safely.

Some residue was on the side of his face, and it smelled awful. Wiping at it, he sniffed what rubbed off onto his fingers. Becoming suspicious, he slid out from beneath her and went to confront his companions. Alex was standing watch by the entrance while Jack slept.

The knight put an end to it with a firm kick to his backside. "What happened?" he snarled.

In a stupor, Jack blinked blearily. "Good morning to you, too."

"I ask again, what happened?"

"For starters," he groaned sitting up, "you kicked me and woke me up."

Oryn rumbled impatiently, forcing him to smell the substance on his fingers. "What is this?"

Taking a whiff, Jack replied, "Dirt."

"There is demon blood on my hand. It had been on my face. How did it come to be there, I ask?"

Exchanging glances with Alex, Jack smiled. "We had to carry the two of you back. On the way, we did our jobs and saved your lives."

"Why did you not wake me?"

The Marine chimed in. "You were completely out."

Oryn became more curious than angry. Raising an eyebrow, he considered Jack and his mischievous smile. "We are weakened, and they attacked at night. I am sure they did not intend to let you live. How did you stop them without my help?"

Jack's eyes glowed as he grinned. "Wouldn't you like to know?"

A few minutes later, all four were outside in the sunshine. Oryn stood with Adwen beside Alex, who started to smile as well. The knight did not know what to expect when Jack put some distance between them, summoning his daggers.

Taking a few breathes, Jack warned, "Nobody move. This will take a second."

He closed his eyes, feeling his blades. Letting go, the weapons hung suspended at his sides. Focusing with all his might, Jack sent them whirling around, slashing and spinning in a circle like before. With no enemies to lock onto, his focus wavered, and the blades fell to the ground. Dropping to one knee soon after from the effort, Jack panted, still smiling. A second passed, and he looked up to ask, "Well? What do you think?"

The knight stared unblinkingly. "Impressive."

"It takes a lot out of me," Jack said, gathering up the weapons. "Have you ever seen anybody at the Order who can do things like this?"

"I have trained many men, some of whom were gifted enough to slay vampires and witches. None of them has been able to so much as tip over a blade, let alone swing one with a thought. I have never seen nor heard of anything like this."

Jack chuckled. "That's cool. How about I keep going until I can't keep it up longer?"

A clever glint sparked in Oryn's eyes. "I have a better thought. You can move them swiftly. When it comes to training for any form of combat, if one cannot perform the smallest of actions, the more complex are pointless. It would be best to begin simply."

The next thing Alex knew, his smile had gone, as he was ordered to stand a few yards from Jack, holding up a long stick. Oryn set the challenge of sending out a dagger to strike the stick then return it back to his hand. This seemed easy, but the Marine was hesitant.

Looking at his companion beyond the dried switch, a sinking sensation weighed down the Marine's insides. "Okay, so about how good is your aim?"

Holding one dagger sideways, Jack set his sights on the stick. Closing one eye to see if it would help his focus, it did not appear to. "I've been able to lock onto the demon's tiny brainwaves like radar so that I hardly miss. Right now I'm aiming at a big twig. Then again," he laughed, "a jarhead is holding it. It should be about the same odds of hitting the stick as hitting you."

"Outstanding."

"Hush up, William Tell. I need to concentrate."

The Marine gritted his teeth, waiting.

Jack stared long and hard, gaining a powerful hold of the dagger. Once he thought he was ready, he sent the weapon whirling through the air. In an instant, it passed the stick entirely, spinning before Alex's nose then flying back to its owner.

"Oops," he uttered once the cool handle came in contact with his palm.

Alex was beside himself and shouted in fright and outrage. "Are you serious? That's it; I'm done."

But when he turned to stalk off, Oryn was blocking his path, growling.

"Give me another chance. That was only the first try."

Deciding that he didn't want to tangle with the knight, Alex swallowed his fears and got back into position, holding up the stick. "What happens if I get stabbed?"

Taking aim, Jack replied, "It's a holy weapon, so it'll hurt, but you'll be fine."

This did not soothe his distress.

While in preparation, the same feeling of holding his dagger with his thoughts carried over to the target. With more confidence, he announced, "I think I've got it."

The dagger flew. Along an invisible tether from the blade to the branch, he guided the spinning weapon in an arc. Like a hot knife through butter, the stick was cut a mere inch from Alex's hand and flew away twirling.

Oryn smiled as Jack caught the weapon and began to celebrate, laughing and whooping excitedly. This pupil had begun to show promise at long last.

Alex did not join in the jubilation. He watched the long end tip over and fall, leaving a nub protruding from his grip. "It just occurred to me," Alex said. "What would happen if I were decapitated?"

Falling quiet, Jack was contemplative. "Oh. Well, I haven't a clue."

Tossing aside the short end of the stick, Alex decided that there was no way he was going to continue this game. Turning to go, he came face to face with Oryn. Returning Oryn's frown with a defiant look, Alex shook his head. "Nice try, but you couldn't pay me to keep being his test dummy. You're on your own."

Oryn allowed the unintimidated Marine to take a seat beside Adwen in the grass. Now seemed to be a good time to try something else. He asked Jack, "Out of your absurd collection, what do you have to prop in the crook of this tree?"

The cop considered his magical inventory before summoning and lobbing a wooden baseball bat, which the knight caught and studied.

"It shall do."

Beside Adwen on the turf, Alex shook his head and stole a

look at her. She remained vacant, eyes open and unseeing. He thought it would be nice if she were to come around in time to put a stop to this. Some of the men he had fought alongside in the corps had played stupid games with fire. That had often ended in near disaster.

With the bat secured in the branches, the knight turned and gave his next instruction: "Now, strike the club behind me."

Jack gave an incredulous look. "You're kidding? I know you haven't seen that movie."

Oryn grew impatient. "No senseless remarks. How is this technique of yours to be of use if you cannot strike an opponent without striking your allies? Concentrate."

Lining up his aim, he muttered, "Okay. You asked for it."

The dagger flew at a blinding speed, narrowly passing Oryn to hit the bat and return again. It failed to find Jack's hand, as the tip drove into the back of the knight's upper arm. He snarled at the unpleasant sensations as the others winced.

Alex was glad he had avoided this exercise.

It was a brief moment until Jack made the blade remove itself. Catching it, he wondered what kind of punishment might be forthcoming.

To Jack's and Alex's surprise, the knight merely brushed away the now-dried blood. Intent on carrying on, he was firm in calling out, "Again."

For hours the training continued. Jack overcame a steep learning curve by not letting his weapons touch his friends after the first time. He was instructed through a series of drills, either guiding the daggers to targets or avoiding them all together. Performing somersaults with both blades hovering alongside, he found the effort it took to maintain control was immense.

By evening, Jack was masterfully making the blades hover with the knight and the Marine. His ability to sense enemies was just as useful with his companions. Wherever they were, he could ensure the daggers would not fly, but he also could defend their backs.

Feeling exhausted, Jack held his eyes closed. "It's actually easier to do this when I can't see you."

"Likely the reason is that plain sight would be a distraction." Oryn theorized. "Sensing space and what occupies it seem to be part of the technique. Raise them higher. They are too low to the ground."

Shaking his head and looking at them at last, Jack admitted, "I'm done. That's all I've got. We've been at this all day, and it's time to go to Scooter's."

Glancing at the setting sun, the knight conceded. "Indeed. Your training shall resume on the morrow."

Dismissing his daggers, Jack rolled his eyes. "I doubt it."

In the cab, Jack rubbed at his temples, hoping to massage out the odd soreness. He was so drained by the rigorous exercises that he couldn't even hear the thoughts of their driver. Hopefully they would not be attacked tonight. He was in no way ready to use his telekinetic abilities for a while.

Alex noted how bleary-eyed his friend looked. Leaning forward to Jack's seat, Alex tapped on his shoulder. "You awake?"

"Awake enough." Jack chided. "Don't worry. I can still out -think you."

This got a smile from the Marine. "Roger that."

Oryn had noticed Jack's demeanor as they departed. It satisfied him to know that there would be less trouble-making. Pulling Adwen a little closer on the wide seat, Oryn sighed. She was mischievous at times, but not as much as the cop in their midst.

Arriving downtown, the four got out and entered the establishment. This time they had not beaten the crowd. It was busy, and they had to jostle and wait to get a good table on the balcony again. That location was safer, away from the mass of partygoers. The ground floor was more tightly packed than Oryn would tolerate. Eventually, they commandeered a spot from a group who had failed to guard their chairs while getting drinks.

Sitting down, Jack blinked, struggling to dispel his mental fog. He had gotten used to hearing the murmurs of nearby thoughts. It was like losing the ability to smell during a head cold. Small particles got through, but the rest was blocked out.

"The show's going to start soon, Jarhead. Want anything

from the bar?"

Amused again by his delirium, Alex replied, "Two rounds of Jack and Coke."

"All right then." He caught on and rolled his eyes. "Funny, ha ha. Next time you try to make a joke, ask yourself if anybody else would laugh."

Both chuckled, and he went off to buy the alcohol.

The two friends drank on either side of Oryn, who held Adwen tightly to his side, sharing warmth in the raucous din. Rock bands roared over the heads of many screaming revelers, jumping and smiling. Adwen's attention was drawn toward the source of the sound, same as always. In the past several days of their stay in the city, seeing her respond to music had brought the knight relief. Now he was confused and worried, though he did not voice it; she responded to music but was not wakened from this state. Oryn came to the realization that it would take something more than rock to bring her back. At this thought, he squeezed her a little tighter.

Feeling toasty from the liquor, Jack caught a fragment of Oryn's thoughts. Emptying his next shot to become less sober, his attention went to the band on stage.

"It would be nice to know what part of this is getting her attention," Jack said.

Eyes slightly glazed, Alex shook his head. "You said you could still out-think me, Lil' Pig. It's obviously the melody."

Shooting a warning look, Jack's eyes glowed brighter. "I heard a story downstairs."

"Oh, yeah?"

"Yeah. On a base in Virginia, a memo was sent out to each command. It went into detail on why it is no longer admissible to refer to Marines as jarheads."

"Really?"

"It stated that Marines cannot be called jarheads because it has been scientifically proven that you can put a brain in a jar."

Laughing hard and catching his breath, Alex replied, "That must be what happened to me."

"I think so, Mr. Abby Normal. They just gave you the wrong brain."

In the midst of their rambling, Oryn began to watch and listen to the music. Adwen did appear to respond to melodies, but what did these performances lack that was needed to bring her to consciousness? Watching and listening to the performance of the young man at the front, Oryn let the question circle his thoughts. Just as Jack was going downstairs to the bar, a revolutionary thought struck him like lightning, making his eyes glow as bright as the neon on the walls.

Ordering more shots, Jack failed to notice the knight wading through the throng. The odors of so many bodies masked Oryn's scent completely, making the shorter Holy Hound none the wiser. Gathering the multiple glasses, he returned to the table.

Alex heard the glass land on the table. "Thanks, buddy."

"Where did Cujo wander off to?" He tossed back the first shot.

"No idea. Didn't even see him leave. Weird that he would leave her alone with us. Thought it was impossible to peal him away from her."

"Oh, he probably went to use the can."

Even if he had, Oryn would not have known what a restroom looked like. With some effort, he did find the set backstage. Then he found the band scheduled to play next.

"You got a screw loose, man. It's not easy getting a good gig like this. Competition is intense."

Oryn stared at the band leader, undeterred.

Curious, the guitar player cocked his head, punk hair flopping over one eye. "Is there a reason you want us to do this?"

"Is it critical that I have one? What does it matter?"

Curious about the stranger's confidence, the leader toyed with the prospect. "If we screw this up, it could make us look bad, and no joint likes to bring in bad bands."

Twirling a stick, the drummer asked, "Why don't we let him?"

"Can you do it?" asked the guitarist.

Narrowing his eyes, Oryn replied, "Are you competent with your instrument?"

The leader chuckled at his temerity.

Somewhat drunker than before, Jack stared at Alex, brow furrowed.

Alex stared back, smiling casually.

Almost a minute passed until Jack sat back and gave up. "I can't. What is it?"

"It was ten thousand and forty-two. Want to try again?"

"Forget it. I'm just giving myself a headache."

"I'm starting to worry about Oryn. Where is he?"

Rolling his eyes and rubbing the sides of his head, Jack grumbled, "Really? You think I can sense him in here while I can't even read your pea brain? You've had too much to drink."

Glancing down at the crowd for any sign of the knight, Alex saw only heads of strangers in a sea of shoulders. "I don't see him. Can't even smell him."

"Good luck with that. Not even my nose can. He'll turn up."

"You're right." Then the blond Marine gazed wide-eyed over the crowd.

"What is it?"

"Uh, I found him."

Confused, Jack followed his gaze until he saw the same spectacle. His jaw dropped. "Oh, boy."

The newest band was preparing to play, while the lead singer gave a brief rundown to Oryn on how to properly use a microphone. Before relinquishing it entirely, he turned to the audience and made an announcement.

"How you doing tonight, Chicago!"

The people screamed.

"All right! We have a surprise opener. This is our guest, Oryn, and he's going to cover an awesome hit, Right Here."

There was a series of whistles and claps as onlookers wondered the same thing as the two by the balcony railing: How was this going to sound? Beginning the ballad, the drummer and guitarist set the steady beat, until it was time for Oryn to take part.

At the first subtly sung verse, Oryn's voice struck the notes with immaculate accuracy, making the crowd cheer. He continued into the driving main chorus, ignoring the resounding approval. His only concern was Adwen. He looked to the balcony every so often to see her watching. Her soft blue glowing irises inspired him to sing with even more emotion, as every line was true for what he knew and felt.

He sang on, putting more of himself into the song until he and it were indistinguishable. His voice began to awe the audience as it echoed slightly, as if it was a technical effect. As he reached another mellow lull, Oryn stared up at her blue eyes and softly sang the next verse, sincere with every word.

Adwen's blue eyes were a bit brighter when they blinked, and she beamed.

Seeing her smile made his heart leap for joy. As the tempo rose, his eyes glowed so brightly that the whole room could see the happiness in them. Completing the final chorus, his voice echoed, and a green light that the humans could not see silhouetted his form onstage. Streams of the light leaped from him over their heads with his passionate lyrics. When the end came and he fell silent, the cheers were deafening.

Jack laughed and clapped, amazed at the knight's hidden magical talent. With his own mental energy back to full power, Jack also noticed that he was sober again. The strange magic had forced the alcohol from their blood, disappointing Jack very much.

"Aw, come on. I paid good money to be drunk tonight. Did he make you sober, too, Jarhead?"

Turning for an answer, Jack found Alex staring at Adwen. She was smiling and glancing between them. Not saying a word, the sweet expression on her face clearly showed she was better, yet she was not whole. Her mind was a bundle of emotions rather than thoughts. For now, she was very entertained and thought their abashed looks were quite funny.

Oryn came to join them, while the band carried on the show. Sitting beside her, he received a very excited hug. It was surprising at first, though he shared the embrace a second later. He could tell without Jack's help that she had a childlike mind. At the least, this was a familiar piece of her that he had gotten back tonight.

Later, after returning to the cave, Jack stood watch. Lying down, Oryn was pleasantly surprised to have Adwen sliding herself into his arms, resting her head on his chest. Before closing his eyes, he remained awake, admiring her while she smiled in her sleep. How he had missed that.

Chapter 9
ONE MISTAKE

After a restful sleep, Oryn awoke to find himself alone. Annoyed that the two other warriors had left him behind, he rumbled and got to his feet. Outside the cave showed no sign of Adwen. Jack and Alex, however, were close by, crouching behind a small land formation.

Stomping over to the pair, he growled, "Where is she?"

Jack immediately shushed him.

Smiling, Alex pointed off toward the dirt pathway.

Once crouched alongside them, he was able to see that Adwen was in her white dog form. She was not alone.

She panted excitedly, bounding and whipping her tail while a gaggle of children chased her about. They played as a distressed woman trying to rein them in, shouting to no avail. Adwen was not a threat, but the chaperone was still tense.

"Stop that!" she called out at the ten- and eleven-year-olds. "That's a strange dog! Leave it alone."

But Adwen was far too much fun for them to listen. She licked their faces when they got close and flopped on her back, letting them pounce with their small hands. Panting happily, their laughter was music to her ears.

"Jamie! Lucas! Leave it alone! It's time to get back to the bus!"

A man in a black suit and green vest came to stop beside the woman, watching the spectacle. The woman was surprised at hardly hearing him approach.

"Oh! I'm so sorry they're in your way."

Oryn folded his hands behind his back, casually observing. It pleased him to see her so carefree.

Glancing between the handsome gentleman and the white dog, the woman gasped. "Is this your dog?"

Thinking about it, he replied, "Yes."

Slightly embarrassed, she admitted, "It is very sweet."

Not paying the human any mind, Oryn called out, "Adwen?"

Perking her head up, she quickly bounded to him. Panting with her tongue lolling, she placed her head against his side.

Smiling down at her, he rubbed her ear with his fingertips.

"Well, I hope my little troop of monkeys hasn't given you any trouble. We have to be going now."

Still admiring Adwen, he murmured, "Good day to you."

Ushering the disappointed kids, the woman chastised them for not listening to her earlier. About to take the lead, she stole a look back at the gentleman. He was walking away to the other trailhead. The dog had vanished, and a girl in a blouse and gray skirt was under his arm, walking barefooted by his side.

Having Adwen partially returned was uplifting for the warriors. Jack was determined to spend the day in celebration. To this, Oryn did not object. Together they revisited the zoo, entertaining her with the silly animals, including those that had not forgotten, or in some cases forgiven, Jack for his trouble-making. She never spoke, but her expressions and canine sounds were familiar enough for the others to interpret. The entire time, Adwen smiled.

Once the sun was about to set, they went to the club again. They could not keep her from the dance floor. Through experience, Oryn knew that this was inevitable. Even though it was uncomfortable for him to be in the dense crowd, he refused to leave her alone in the jostling mess. At her side, he watched her dance and felt the same thing that Jack and Alex did on the overhead balcony: She was getting stronger.

The knight smiled, but not at that fact. It was at seeing her so happy. He hoped more of this would come in the future.

Late in the night, the cab that brought them back to the park pulled away, leaving them to walk the unlit path to their hideout. Adwen hung on Oryn's arm as Jack and Alex savored memories they had made.

"What was the matter with you?" Jack asked Oryn. "Why didn't you share the spaghetti with her for lunch? That's an insult in this society!"

Oryn tossed an irritated scowl. "That is highly unlikely."

Alex chuckled. "It was a good try. That would have been like 'Lady and Tramp.'"

Oryn snarled. "What did you call me?"

Both laughed hard, nearly to the brink of tears, while the knight glared, unsure of what was going on. The two warriors carried on, joking and sharing thoughts. As usual, the path was empty even where they trekked off through the brush.

Approaching the hill to where the cave awaited, the four gradually became leery. No insect chirped; all was still. The feeling in the air did not seem right. Jack gave Alex his sword, while Oryn guided Adwen to the opening in the earth. It would be easier to defend from that place.

Jack followed at their backs, and Alex cautiously took the lead. Once they got to the cave, a wave of waiting demons lunged, hissing and screeching.

Knocked to the ground, Alex cried out at the sensations of multiple bites on his arms and legs. Jack's daggers helped to clear them off, but even more demons swarmed from all angles. The Holy Hounds were swiftly surrounded.

The knight and the cop shifted into their true forms, utilizing all of their strength and speed. Fighting hard to buy Alex enough time to get up did not come easy. The Marine activated his own ability to ignore pain so he could reach the safety of the others' deadly reach. Then he fought back with all his might, bleeding profusely.

Fear gripped Adwen, while she helplessly watched, keeping close to her protectors. The sight of the monsters made her quake and whimper, crouching by Oryn's enormous clawed feet.

The green-eyed beast cleaved enemies over and over, making way for more. They were relentless. Waves without pause leaped and cried out in the dark for blood. When Oryn could, he stole a look at Adwen. She returned it with a terrified expression.

A faint red light was in her eyes again, and he barked hurriedly, "Close your eyes! Do not look at them!"

She did as he said without hesitation, cringing at the sounds of violence. Several seconds after his warning, she uncovered them again, sensing something horrible in the distance. A cold chill coursed through her heart at the feeling of something terrible about to occur. Unable to deny the urge, she transformed into the white dog and bounded over the heads of the demons. Adwen outran any that pursued, pressing northward.

Engrossed in combat, Jack's enhanced telepathy let him know the instant she had departed. He struggled to fend for himself and yelped, "She's gone! Oryn! She ran away!"

Startled by the revelation, he yelped as well. "What?"

A new wave of demons spawned from the shadows, rushing in to overwhelm and engulf the weakened warriors.

The lashing of the underbrush added to Adwen's fear. Those sounds coupled with her paws on the dirt and turf made her feel alone. In her current state, her mind was simple, incapable of complex thought, or else she would have been even more anxious about what lay ahead. Already, her keen ears heard screams belonging to children.

When Adwen raced into the open campsite, miles from the other Holy Hounds, her ears drooped and her eyes widened. The same children were here with their parents, or what remained of them. Four Clowns scurried around, clawing the humans unable to see their colorful assailants with their mortal sight.

The children could see them. In their innocence, their pure hearts let their eyes pick out the monsters' silhouettes. When another adult toppled to the dust, the wails and cries escalated.

Adwen rushed in to crouch between the demons and one of the remaining parents. By the time she got in the way, the father figure collapsed. Barking desperately at the fiends was the one thing she could do to keep them away.

One demon cackled and struck her across the muzzle.

She yelped and tumbled across the ground, changing into her woman form. Two boys and a girl nearby cringed, watching her pick herself up. Gashes wept silver from the left side of her face, trailing to her chin. Even more fear gripped her at the sight of the dark creatures stalking her, circling in, gnashing shark-like teeth. Their target was no longer on the panicking humans; Adwen had their undivided attention.

Whimpering as she scurried to the campfire, there was no way out. When her eyes started to turn red, she felt a hot burning sensation and realized something horrible inside was trying to destroy her. Adwen fought with the internal enemy, too frightened to open her eyes and defend herself. A burning chill rippled along her left arm up to her face, causing her to yelp in pain as the skin there blanched and darkened. It threatened to consume her whole, but she tried to resist, even as she felt it reaching toward her heart.

In the last moment, a spark lit in her chest. Her body erupted in light, blasting the enemies away, tumbling end over end through the air. A roar broke out into the night with the blast from her shifting form. The raw energy seemed to hold the everything frozen in time until it receded into lapping pale flames on a tall white creature in black armor.

Breathing deeply, she gazed up into the starry sky, feeling herself manifest. She let the energy dissipate, canceling out the flames cloaking her body. Adwen lowered her gaze to calmly assess the scene. Right away, she spotted the last of the monsters. Part of what she saw was through night vision, another kind of sight also allowed her to see the twisted creature through a large log as if the wood were transparent.

Her blue eyes burned bright in anger. Going to it, she snared the half dead and oozing thing by the neck, snarling into what remained of its face.

"I know you see me, Guillot." She rumbled. "Your one mistake was provoking me by using children."

With that, she crushed the demon, turning it into muck. The plasma residue on her fur smoked and turned to dust, drifting away. Clean of the filth, Adwen checked to see that the survivors were safe. They were in shock and afraid but otherwise well. One or two surviving parents saw her and froze, still frightened and confused.

Bursting through the trees with bloody wounds covering his whole body, Oryn arrived, followed by Jack with Alex on his back. They too were severely injured. The Marine had endured the worst of the damage and was unable to carry himself. The three stared at her by the fire and held their breaths in anticipation.

The knight stepped forward, changing into his more human self. "Adwen?"

Leaving the humans alone, she turned and approached her loyal warriors. When she was closer she stood before them. Seeing that they were alive despite their injuries, she tilted her elegant, gold-marked head and rumbled softly.

"Thank you; each of you."

Jack's gaze faltered, and she saw that he was worried. Lifting her left arm to examine what bothered him so much, she was not surprised to find what had become of the dark shard.

It may not have claimed her, but it had managed to grow, taking hold as a part of her form. The arm of a sliver-formed demon was in the place of her own. Beneath her skin, she could feel that it reached even farther, affecting one of her eyes. The white around her left iris and pupil was darkened like polished onyx in her face, and below it was a small black mark on her cheek.

What she found was unfortunate but better than what almost became of her. Done examining the hardened black surface of her arm and hand, a twinge in her heart ignited a gold glow in the center of her eyes.

Oryn frowned. "What is your command?"

When the vision from her golden heart concluded, a stern expression made her long ears flatten. Growling, she advised, "We have to hurry. This way."

She bounded into the shadows, and the three followed.

Chapter 10
THE CAPTAIN'S CLAN

The portal brought them to the side of the river that flowed along the western edge of Dargadia. Tall pines and monstrous oaks stood, veiling the night sky. It was cloudy. Rain made music on leaves overhead. Quickly getting their bearings in the magical world, their fleeting rest came to an end.

As they ran, it went unsaid that the rain was a blessing. The deluge covered the scent of their blood, so the chance of being followed was slim. Regardless, Adwen, Oryn and Jack remained on guard. There was no telling if a large flying demon, a Dred, might come swooping down.

Alex tried to hold onto his friend but was weak, and the pain of being jostled about sent tremors of anguish throughout his body. The others sensed it.

Trying his best to take loping bounds, Jack growled to Alex, "Hang tight, pal. The Order fortress is a little bit farther."

The Marine's eyes rolled at more pain. "How much farther?"

"We can smell the city through the rain."

Despite extreme discomfort, he felt relief. "Roger that."

Running close to Adwen's side just ahead of them, Oryn growled to her, "I sense no enemies, but I fear that the state of Plexus must have deteriorated. Your absence would have been exploited by the demons."

"I have no doubt of that," she rumbled. The distant blinking of torches on the high walls shone through the downpour as Adwen added, "With me gone, there was an obvious window of opportunity."

"What if an ambush awaits?"

She glanced over, and black mist streamed from her dark eye while the blue iris glowed. "They cannot hide from me.

My strength may be hindered by this infection, but it gives me the ability to see as they do. Our enemies will have to try much harder to lay surprises for us now."

Thunder shook the air in their approach to the colossal gates. Steel grating fifty feet high stood in their path, framing many segments of the cityscape beyond. Wind howled through the gaps, pushing at their soaked chests and faces, tossing their hair, fur and garments. Adwen and Oryn shifted into their more human forms. Flickering torches threatened to be doused by ensuing gusts and gales.

Just as they peered through at the structures of Plexus, a distant voice called from atop the ramparts: "Who goes there? Name yourselves!"

Backing up with the wind tossing her hair wildly, Adwen saw two guards. Knowing the humans could not recognize her in the darkness, she used her enchanted voice to call through the storm.

"I am Adwen the Tame One, Heir to Darien Andredan the Master Knight. I ask that you please open the gate."

There was a pause as the men hesitated and exchanged words. Finally, one replied, "We have orders to refuse to open the gate for any reason. How can we know you are not an imposter?"

Oryn growled, clenching his fangs. But before he could form words to throw at the leery guardsmen, Adwen turned twice as furious. Sensing her rage, he stopped to stare as she snarled. Heat radiated from her, and white flames flashed from the surface of her armor.

Then to the surprise of her warriors, and the shock of the guards, Adwen transformed and lunged for the gate, taking hold of the solid steel segments. With a fraction of the immense strength she possessed, the white Holy Hound roared and lifted it as high as her arms could reach, making the windlasses on the ramparts spin madly.

Oryn and Jack took the nonverbal cue to enter, darting to the other side. Only then did Adwen twirl out from under the weight, simultaneously shifting into her woman shape. The gate slammed behind them, resonating through the streets as loudly as the frequent thunderclaps.

The other warriors gave Adwen a look of concern after her

outburst, worried that perhaps she was being influenced by the dark piece of her anatomy.

Calmer, though still irritated, she acknowledged them by giving an incredulous huff. "I'm fine. There's no time for distractions. Another day we'll stand in the rain to bicker with peons on a wall. Come on." She took brisk strides, ignoring how soaked she and the others had become. It was difficult to smell anything.

As they walked farther into the city, the smells of filth and sweaty human bodies rose, alerting the Holy Hounds. What they saw surprised and angered Adwen beyond words. People and their possessions formed cramped slums. Men, women, children and their faithful beasts of burden tried to hide from the rain, forced to remain close amid the rancid smell of sewage. These were refugees from across the kingdom, survivors of demon assaults.

Adwen's rage compelled her light-footed stroll to turn to a wrathful march. These people had received her promise of sanctuary in the fortress. Even with the Order of knights so close, if demons struck, it would be a massacre. The Council of Elders would have plenty to explain in these early hours.

Ascending the sloping main road, the four came to the large metal and oak gates. For hundreds of years they had been left open. Now they were closed. Standing with the warriors at her back, Adwen did not know what to feel at first. It occurred to her that she was angry, though the emotion suddenly felt distant. Gazing up at the wood and steel, a strange connection became apparent for the first time. The magic imbued into the gates and everything beyond was bonded to her. Adwen had never taken notice of it before. Perhaps, she thought, it was not until now that the Light Spirits let her be aware of it.

Wrath and purpose melded, growing in her chest. Bright blue eyes aglow, Adwen raised her normal hand, and white flames burst to life on her shoulders like a spectral mantle. Like an extension of herself, the gates of the fortress eased open wide, letting in the Holy Hounds and the howling wind.

Into view came the main plaza and its three entrances. Another large gate led into the mustering courtyard, flanked by the archway to the paddock and the doors to the main hall.

Seeing two knights guarding the threshold, staring in alarm, she let her flames dissipate before entering the grounds.

By the time they reached the torchlight, the two guards realized who had arrived, bowing their heads and crossing metal-covered fists over their chests in salute.

"Greetings, Tame One," The higher-ranking guard announced, "The Order is relieved at your return. Word will be sent to the king and the elders of your arrival."

Adwen nodded in acknowledgment. "Allow King Lorvan to rest. Send him word at dawn and let him know I requested the delay. As for the elders, wake them and tell them that I call for a council immediately. It is on an urgent matter."

They saluted again. "At your command, Lady Adwen."

As the two moved to open the door and let the company in, they raised their partisans and shouted. "Be on your guard, Tame One! Behind you!"

Oryn and Jack turned to anticipate an attack, but Adwen sensed no threat. Only she remained calm as she looked back to see two winged figures in robes land yards away, one letting down what appeared to be a hooded man. Watching the visitors, Adwen understood how this ally could go for so long without demons catching him. To her normal eye, he looked no different from any other person, but her dark eye saw nothing at all.

Smiling, Adwen's tone brimmed with relief. "Core. Your timing is still better than mine. Thank you for coming."

The ancient being and his young Gargoyle bodyguards bowed deeply.

"Lady Adwen." He declared, "You asked that I come to this place, and hence no force of nature or spirit could stop me from aiding your cause."

Jack relaxed at recognizing the familiar face, but Oryn and the knights sensed something strange. Once Core stepped into the torchlight, his deathly sallow skin and dark eyes put them on edge.

"Vampire!" A knight hissed. "Why would the Heir trust such a vile creature?"

Adwen was prepared for this reaction. "Core is a Day Walker and was one of the Master Knight's closest advisers in the Great War." When she received silence and stares, she went on: "And because he helped me and Jack on our visit to the dark lands of Mortigad, his loyalty has been tested and proved honorable. Lower your weapons and let him pass."

The entrance creaked open unexpectedly, making everyone turn about in surprise. Core's voice came from within, beyond the enchanted barrier that kept out evil beings. "I am flattered at your gesture, Lady Adwen, but no mortal could hope to keep me from following your command. Thank you for giving me purpose once more."

"How is this possible?" The first knight gasped. "Has the barrier been destroyed?"

"Do not worry," Adwen reassured. "Darien gave him his blood, transforming him into a unique entity similar to a spirit. One of his many titles is He-who-does-not-thirst. Core is not evil."

"Tame One." The Gargoyles came to kneel before her, heads bowed beneath ragged cloth hoods. "With our charge safe in your service, what would you have us do?"

"Go to the ramparts above and rest. Stay out of sight and wait for my call. I have a critical task that only you can do for me."

"As you wish." A rush of air came from the thrust of their wings as they vanished.

Although Adwen's summons of the Elder Council was urgent, there were forty-nine members to roust. Taking a little time to see Alex to a place for rest and recovery, she thought of how to unify and redirect the efforts of the Order. More than ever, the focus of the most powerful force in Dargadia's army had wavered. Adwen aimed to set the path straight again. Once healers came to tend to her friend's wounds, she charted a course for the council hall.

Coming to the mighty doors inlaid with gold, she heard Jack clear his throat.

"No, you cannot come in," she told Jack. "This is a delicate situation."

He replied, rolling his eyes, "If you can't trust me with delicate situations, then why did you ever trust me to go see the undead king?"

Adwen's eyes flashed dangerously. "I didn't have a choice."

"Ouch."

"Unlike then, you have the potential to cause lasting damage with your mouth."

"And unlike then, I have the chance to help. I can control my mind reading completely now and analyze a room loaded with crotchety, old men."

She sized him up, considering the risks.

"Come on," he urged with his most charming smile.

Oryn scowled. "Can you keep open comments under your breath at the least?"

"Why not? You find ways to keep from hitting me. Why wouldn't I be able to keep my trap shut?"

"We have a difference in levels of restraint."

Seconds of silence passed, and she glared at her shorter companion. "If you speak out of line just once, so help me, you're going to regret every syllable."

Jack pressed his lips together, moving his hand across them to pantomime closing a zipper.

Elder guards opened the doors for the three, revealing the vast hall. As they strode ahead with the terrace of benches on their right and an open veranda to the left, the exit soon closed them in. Nearly fifty weathered faces turned to watch Adwen lead the way to the far end of the hall, where the benches curved around, overlooking the seat of the High Elder. The eyes of the Holy Hounds quickly noticed that Mamalis had been replaced by an elder with whom they had little prior dealings. This stony man's predecessor now sat in a small group away from the rest, farthest from the head of the hall. The majority sat behind the new High Elder, scowling, murmuring, and studying the Heir and her warriors.

They were nearly to the front when Jack briefly glanced about and growled subtly, "These guys really don't like you. If your plan was to make peace, I think you're better off finding a new pack of codgers."

Adwen growled, "Duly noted."

Finally standing before the council, a long dragging silence passed. Adwen and the High Elder locked eyes the whole while. The more time went by, the angrier Oryn became as he realized that the old man was not going to greet her and bow.

Instead, the bearded speaker for the Elder Council inclined his head, frowned and announced the start of the meeting.

"Adwen the Tame One has called this council on an urgent matter. The council's ears await your words to be presented."

Giving a slight nod, she acknowledged the formality. Then she scanned them, taking in every detail with both normal and dark sight.

"Thank you, Elder Council, for waking from your soft, clean linens to heed my early-morning call to muster. A dire matter has come to my attention. Some subjects of the king have been denied sanctuary and left to the mercy of the city streets. As I have been able to return at last, it is my wish that each and every refugee, or whoever calls Plexus home, would take shelter in the fortress."

The High Elder cleared his throat and announced, "The council has heard your words and has made its decision to formally deny your request."

Jack frowned, and Oryn rumbled, eyes burning with outrage.

Meanwhile, Adwen was calm.

"The council now has questions as to your recent disappearance."

Adopting an unreadable expression, she replied, "Very well."

One of the other forty-nine elders stood, staring with great intensity. "In your prolonged absence, the fields meant to support everyone through the winter were ravaged. Not even the straw was left untouched by fiery demons. Even if the enemy is routed within a fortnight, a famine such as this is sure to be the end of Dargadia. How do you answer for this travesty?"

A moment rolled by as she pondered. She was hopeful, but no answers were forthcoming. Then her heart warmed, and a soft golden light glimmered in the depths of her eyes. Confidence almost brought on a smile.

"There is a way to weather the famine until crops can be replanted. The answer is hidden among the poor souls out in the rain."

"You sound rather sure of yourself."

At this she was firm in replying, "The answer is always hidden within the people, just as diamonds are hidden in a mountain."

Another elder stood and called to her, "Then let in those who would save the kingdom. The rest are sure to bring sickness and filth with their sheer numbers. A plague added to a famine will end in disaster."

Adwen's patience was beginning to be tested, though she remained cool. "To let in a select few and leave the majority to suffer in the cold would be unjust and set the stage for a rebellion. Saving a few and leaving the rest to die is far worse than opening the gates to them all."

The first elder frowned deeply. "Then none will enter. That is just enough."

Anger made her fists clench into tight balls. For a second, the fortress around them shuddered, and particles of dust fell from high facets and fixtures. Some of the old men murmured or exchanged glances, while Jack and Oryn wondered whether she had been the cause of the tremor.

Wearing a grimace, Adwen stared down the most immovable of elders. "Your ability to reason must be faltering in your old age."

"How dare you!"

She shuddered in anger, sparking white fire on her shoulders as the whole fortress began to shake with even more force. Dust rained on their heads, and the pair of defiant elders quickly sat amid gasps and shouts of fright. Adwen's warriors tried to remain steady while the ground quaked. Her voice was magically magnified, with each tone felt in onlookers' chests.

"You dare to forsake the purpose of the Order for fear and pride? Woe to you and your selfish hearts! Protecting and serving is the reason this place stands, as a monument of hope, courage and resolve. When I came, I looked to find determination or even an ounce of compassion!"

Regaining control of herself, and in turn ending the shaking of the fortress, she added with a scowl, "All I can see is fear, indifference ... and spite."

Jack stared, and Oryn did as well.

Fear swept the council benches when Adwen took on her true form, shoulders lit with white fire. A few recoiled as she held out her clawed right hand, covered in white fur under the jeweled arm guard. She conjured a small golden light in the likeness of a lily. The fluid form turned and flowed into itself and grew upward over her. After many thin streams of light sprung from the center, as vines do when in search of a trellis, the men calmed, enraptured.

Then Adwen's energy tendrils struck at the elders' hearts. Wails of pain and fear erupted in the hall, while Jack and Oryn watched in shock. Guards outside pounded on the doors to no avail, as Adwen would not allow them to open until her work was done. Feeling the grip of her power taking hold at last, she snarled, grabbed her lily of light at its stem and pulled back, extracting the tendril strands.

When she did, more than thirty writhing masses of darkness came out of their human hosts, shrieking madly. The men fell unconscious, and the parasitic Spites stood on four spindly legs, ready to either attack Adwen or return to their former hosts. Jack took care of a few that got close by unleashing his daggers with quick telekinetic strikes. This bought Adwen enough time to make her body glow brightly, and the brilliance reached out, igniting the bloated and vulnerable demons like dry grass. Then Adwen allowed the guards to enter the chamber and see the remains smoldering into dust.

Sixteen elders remained alert, horrified as the humans in armor came to their aid. Confusion made the guards halt and study the scene.

"Elders, Tame One, what has happened to the High Elder and the rest of the council?"

Adwen shifted into her woman form, ignoring the confounded men. "The position of High Elder is to be restored to Elder Mamalis. See to it that all elders remain indoors and those who are not well remain in bed for recovery. In the meantime, I will assume command of all knights within the castle until nightfall, when they shall resume their service under the Elder Council. I bid you good day and good luck. This council meeting is concluded."

The reappointed High Elder called down to her just as she began to depart. "Lady Adwen! What has happened?"

Adwen stopped but didn't face Mamalis. For the first moment since regaining full awareness, she was stricken with grief. Memories threatened to crush her where she stood.

Fending off the feeling, she glanced over her shoulder and answered, "I am now the last of Darien's true bloodline."

The man's jaw slackened as others gasped.

A glimmer of remorse in the old man's face brought some comfort. It was the first sign of compassion she had ever seen from the elders. "We may speak tomorrow. I have work to do."

There were no attempts to prevent her from leaving. The warriors left the Elder Hall behind for the series of cavernous passages. Nothing was said until Adwen's march reached a stairway with a view of the sunrise.

Atop an open landing, Oryn became wary of the situation. "What is the matter that you are not telling us?"

She ignored him and made for the next stairway to the highest level.

Swiftly cutting ahead to block her progress, he wore a stern expression.

Adwen's face had been blank but turned sour in irritation.

He had sensed her pain while in the Elder Hall. It went against his better judgment to say nothing. "Many a time I have quietly watched you lead and not share your knowledge. Often it is that you know little to the ends yourself. Under the circumstances, I am compelled to ask what is happening. You know more than you are willing to tell."

Glancing away to watch the rising sun, it provided a meager distraction from the topic. Adwen was afraid.

They smelled the fear, and Jack stepped in. "We're not just servants; we're your friends. After everything we went through together, don't you think you could lean on us a bit more? Take some of the pressure off of yourself and give us some of the weight."

She looked at him, calculating the statements.

He shrugged. "That's what we are here for, right?"

Shaking her head and heaving a sigh, Adwen began, "Before the sun goes down there are two tasks to complete. That is all I know. The most important of them is to move every man, woman, child and as many livestock as possible onto the fortress grounds. It will be difficult to convince some to leave their city homes, but it needs to happen."

At this, Oryn grimaced. "This is in preparation for an attack?"

"Yes. It feels like something is coming."

"Well," Jack pondered, "how long will the people need to stay in the fortress? If it's just for the night, it shouldn't be a problem."

"I believe the city dwellers can go home the next day. The refugees will have to stay much longer."

Jack raised an eyebrow. "Living in the halls is going to make for a lot of trouble."

"I have the power to make things easier. My connection with the stones of the fortress should let me form temporary living spaces."

"And toilets, I hope."

A tiny smile tugged at her mouth. "Yes. I can make arrangements."

Oryn asked, "And what is the second task appointed to you?"

Nodding to the stairs, she said, "Up that way."

Arriving at the top of the fortress wall, ignoring the powerful gusts, Adwen gazed at the central tower. The spiral stairway was covered by a guttered overhang, decorated by hundreds of stone carvings. Human eyes could hardly make out any detail from this distance, but she and her warriors pondered as they observed her search its surface. Finding what she was looking for, Adwen let out an echoing howl.

Disguised as statues among the rest, the two adolescent Gargoyles took wing, gliding down to them. Their human cloaks were gone, showing their thick, mineral-textured hide. No sooner did their talons touch ground than they bowed deeply.

"Thank you," Adwen nodded. "Please stand."

The spiny female's long, reptilian tail swished as she asked, "How may my brother and I serve you, Heir of Darien?"

"I have a task I could only ask of a Gargoyle." Going to a nearby statue similar to the winged warriors, she gestured for them to follow. "You are the first of your kind to breathe in this place in hundreds of years. Now there will be many once again."

Everyone studied one of the Gargoyle statues, proudly holding a spear and adorned with magnificent armor. "They have slept, listening to the earth through dreams. Wake them by breathing into their mouths. This one shall be your first."

The sister was stunned by Adwen's command, so the brother stepped forward. Taking in a deep breath, he exhaled into the mouth of the sleeping Gargoyle. He moved away. A sound like grinding rock met their ears.

Under a thick layer of stone writhed the ancient being, shifting like a pupa in a cocoon. Finally flexing his vast wings, the shell crumbled away. The ancient Gargoyle let out a mighty roar that shook the air. Black and gray skin on his chest expanded with the next breath the proud being took. Opening bright yellow eyes, he looked down at them, smiled and laughed in merry guffaws.

Oryn and Jack did not know what to make of this, and neither did the young Gargoyles beside them. Adwen was charmed and smiled back.

Twirling the golden spear aside to take a sweeping bow, the creature spoke in the deepest, roughest voice they had ever heard. "The stones have told me in my dreams that you are Adwen the Tame One. I am Captain Slate, leader of the Watchful Mountain Clan. It is an honor and a pleasure to meet you in the waking world at last."

Adwen nodded. "It is good to finally meet you as well, good captain."

Standing tall to study the young ones, he inclined a scaly eyebrow. "Younglings? From the fallen Crystal Mountain Clan? This surely is a surprise."

The pair wondered if they should flee, until Adwen clarified, "They were hatched from untainted eggs so they could wake you when the time was right."

A sly look came over Captain Slate, and his chuckles were sonorous and gravelly. "Is that so? Seeing as they are Gargoyles without a clan or a master, I proclaim before the Light Spirits and the stones that these two hence forth shall be of the Watchful Mountain Clan. May your courage and strength bring honor to the stones!"

Relieved, the siblings bowed and lowered their heads in thanks.

"Now you two must wake the whole clan before dusk." Adwen reminded them. "Those you awaken can help, but work swiftly."

"Aye," Captain Slate agreed. "More than a thousand wait to be pulled from the stones."

"I will meet you here, Captain, when the sun is about to set. Make sure your clan is ready. This is going to be a very long day."

Less than an hour later, the three Holy Hounds stood in the Hall of Knights, surrounded by multitudes of engraved names of deceased warriors from the Order. Before them was Captain Sir Peregrine and each of his lieutenants in formation awaiting instructions. Oryn and the leader of the knights exchanged an unspoken greeting until the captain recognized Jack and wore a calculating expression. It had been a few weeks since the warrior was chained as a punishment in the Ring of Trials.

Jack smiled broadly, clearly recalling being shot at by his men for fun. They missed on purpose, but the memory was still fresh.

Tossing a warning look to Jack, Adwen growled, "Please don't antagonize him."

He shrugged, pretending to be innocent. "What?"

Ignoring him, she addressed the knights: "Today I have returned, and with urgency I implore, knights, you are needed."

They all saluted in unison with metal greaves striking their chest plates. The metallic sound echoed in the cavernous hall.

"I have been able to return to you in the last hour before a battle, a battle which I ask none of you take part in. You are all strong, brave and honorable. I need you all to be ready for the final battle, and that is not tonight. Tonight, you are needed to serve this kingdom and its people as you always have. As we speak, ancient guardians of old awaken, and their wings and spears will tear the shadows to ribbons. This day, you must shepherd the wayward souls from the streets and into the halls."

"Lady Adwen," Sir Peregrine asked, "where will they stay?

We haven't enough beds or food. There is only just enough for my men and the servants."

She smiled softly. "Tonight shall be hard. On the morrow I will take care of the troubles of food and other necessities. Core?"

Oryn, Jack and the captain flinched as a hooded figure in violet appeared out of thin air at her side. Core lowered the hood of his new adviser garments, and sunlight that filtered in touched his face, turning his pale skin to life with color. His eyes went from black to the color of silver, and he dipped his head.

"How may I be of service?"

"Core, this is the captain of the knights, Sir Peregrine."

Nodding to the knight, he smiled. "I have heard your name spoken many times with pride and great respect in this place."

To the stunned human, she continued, "Sir Peregrine, Core is an ancient servant of the Master Knight. He is going to be my adviser. As the people enter, he will record them so that later, more can be done. The first to be brought in must be the refugees. Once they are inside, send for the people of Plexus. Not even the city walls can protect them after nightfall. Have their animals go to the stables."

Sir Peregrine replied, "Once the paddock and stables are full, where shall we send the rest of the beasts?"

Restraining a smile, she answered, "To the gardens if need be."

A knight hidden in formation choked and chuckled. The gardens were the elders' private contemplative walking grounds.

Jack grinned and growled covertly, "Guess where all the goats are going."

She rolled her eyes and carried on: "It is urgent that this be done before sunset, but I do not want panic. Rumor will spread of danger, as the people are not fools. Do not talk of attacks by demons unless it is absolutely necessary to make them move. Keep them calm. The people of the city will be allowed to return to their homes at daybreak. Core shall advise where the city dwellers will stay the night apart from the rest. Go, and let the Light Spirits guide your steps."

While Sir Peregrine ordered his men to muster their

knights to carry out the task, Jack gave him a very childish wave goodbye.

"Jack, you're going with the captain."

Both turned to stare in surprise.

Before either could ask why, she said, "Surely as there is a sky, there will be those too stubborn to leave their homes. Jack can find a way to oust them. He has a way with making people do things against their will or better judgment."

Sir Peregrine saluted and tossed Jack a clever look.

When Jack didn't budge, she thought of more terrible tasks to employ, and he decided this was the best option.

Core cleared his throat for her attention. "Lady Adwen? The king is in the library with his adviser. They have taken notice of the Gargoyles and are unsure what to make of this occurrence."

"Thank you. I had planned to visit the king next."

Adwen and Oryn strode to the heart of the central tower, passing high over the mustering yard where Sir Peregrine's men prepared to set out. Vigorous shouts carried on the wind, excitement in their voices. She hoped that the sound of enthusiasm was a sign that they were ready.

To put her at ease, Oryn said with the confidence, "The captain has great influence. Everything you asked shall come to pass."

"I hope so," she sighed.

"I know so."

A glimmer of a smile crossed her face, and they continued to the Order library. Arriving at the sold oak door, she knocked.

"Enter," called the voice of King Lorvan.

When Adwen willed the door to open, an odd rustling like leaves met their ears. At the end of the room by the window stood Toth, the half-elf. Once his one good eye could see who was entering, he dismissed the ropy vines that were arching over the entrance.

"Oh, stars above! I'm so glad to see the two of you!"

Smiling with relief, King Lorvan stepped out from behind a rack of scrolls holding an open tome. "I would have to agree with our friend, Lady Adwen. It is indeed good to have you here."

Closing the door, she and Oryn watched with unease as the plants recoiled into their respective pots.

"I'm glad you didn't decide to attack us. I still remember the first time I saw what you were capable of with green things. When did you add these to the library?"

Closing the book with finality and a frown, the king replied, "After the first assassination attempt. Your fire bird, Malik, has taken up residence in my personal quarters to be sure no traps are laid for me. Toth has not left my side since a madman disguised as an Elder Guard attempted to cut my throat."

"What happened to him?"

The blond half-elf rubbed his eye patch and chuckled. "There are a few singed book covers and the back window is still in need of replacing."

"Better him and the window than anything else in here," Adwen said.

When they were closer, Toth got a better look at Adwen's appearance and nearly gasped. "What? Stars and moons! What's happened to you?"

While Adwen studied her deadly, slivered left arm, Oryn quietly watched, noting that this time she did not allow grief to well up.

Knowing how she must look, she shook her head. "Too much."

An idea struck Oryn like lightning, and he was urgent. "Toth? Have you found no more knowledge of Guillot?"

Gently taking her hand to examine it more closely, he murmured, "I've found a small collection of texts involving him. Nothing references anything like this. What I can say is that if this is his doing, then we are all in a great deal of trouble."

Frowning, Adwen added, "It was Sycan's work, but he used a sliver taken from the demon general." Toth shook his head. Turning over a dusty book bound in leather, he skipped to a marked page depicting a young girl in a circle and a drawing of General Guillot. Reading the old runes, their friend relayed the information: "It says, roughly, that the demon would use fragments of himself to control others as an extension of himself through a ritual."

Sensing their alarm, he continued, "But that cannot happen unless the ritual is performed before the sliver is implanted.

He also must be present to form the connection. The one person recorded to have suffered this was the twin sister to one of the Master Knight's warriors."

"How was it removed?" Oryn asked.

"Sorry," Toth sighed, showing charred pages. "This was what I was reading when the king was nearly killed."

Adwen became even gloomier.

"I do know from studying that although he cannot make you his puppet, what he can do is potentially worse. If he touches you, then he can make the infection spread beyond your control."

Already aware of this, as the Light Spirits had given her the knowledge, she added, "And even then my warriors could not bring me back from the darkness."

Frustrated that there appeared to be nothing to raise her spirits, Oryn glared at his childhood friend. "Anything you know that could help would be appreciated."

"There is one thing."

Oryn rolled his eyes and sneered out of annoyance that he had to ask.

Brushing aside the contents of the next nearest table, Toth opened another book and flipped to a page near the end. On one side was a drawing of Darien the Master Knight, sword drawn for battle.

When three confused faces stared him down, he pointed happily to the picture again. "The answer is right there!"

King Lorvan massaged his throbbing temple, and Oryn glowered. "Having the Master Knight here would be helpful, but he is gone."

"No. It's his sword! We need the Gray Blade!" Pausing to think a moment, he murmured, "Actually it's Adwen who needs it."

She studied the drawing more intently, while Toth explained: "Darien the Master Knight was powerful and gained that power from three things: curses, his four warriors and the Gray Blade. Without it, he would not have been able to face the Demon Lord Melanin. That is the final piece for winning this war. If we find the sword, the demons could be stopped before the winter frost sets in."

Raising an eyebrow, a hesitant look came over Adwen. "Do

you know where it is?"

Smiling broadly, he replied, "Not the foggiest idea." Seeing that the others were non-plused, their friend added, batting a hand through the air, "I'm not worried. This is a part of the foretelling. Adwen, you are meant to find the sword. Only Darien himself knew where it went, and if it is the one and only thing that can keep you from stopping the demons, then surely you will find it when the time is right. What do you think?"

Unable to look away from the sword on the page, the half-elf's statements rang true. This was a key, but not the only one. No one but she knew that Darien's body was gone, turned to spirit and sealed away in a secret place. The sword was sure to be gone in the same way; lost to the living worlds. She had no clue as to how to obtain it, but again, Toth was right. When the time came, the Light Spirits would guide her.

Shaking off the surreal feeling of looking at the depiction of the blade, Adwen decided it was time that she shared some information of her own. "King Lorvan, it is my assumption that the man who tried to murder you was in fact one of the Elder Guard. Don't worry. I'm sure I've already fixed the problem. More than half of the Elders were hosts to Spites. The parasitic demons are destroyed now, and by tomorrow, those responsible will have their own minds back."

Stern with outrage, the king replied, "And tomorrow I will have strong words to share with them as well."

Toth pondered aloud, "That explains quite a lot."

"Never mind that, Toth," the king shook his head and opened the window. Several Gargoyles swooped past, in search of others to awaken, and he pointed. "What is the meaning of this odd sight? Don't mistake my shock for ill will, but what is all of this about?"

Adwen and Oryn exchanged looks, and she said, "I sense a battle is coming tonight, King Lorvan. The Knights are busy gathering the people into the protection of the fortress. With the Gargoyles at the ready, there is no doubt that the enemy will be routed."

A smile lifted the old man's bearded cheeks. "Do you ever cease to impress, Lady Adwen?"

Blushing, she replied, "I do my best not to disappoint."

"Impossible." He chuckled.

Jack, Sir Peregrine and the rest of the knights worked tirelessly, knowing what was at stake. Droves of refugees filtered into the fortress past the watchful eyes of the unseen Core. As the influx of people neared four thousand, the locals added several hundred to the number. So many animals were brought that the stables did overflow, and the rest were locked in the garden, the only place left. A few of the knights found this amusing. It aided in releasing the growing tension among the ranks in anticipation for the end of the day. Whatever was coming they could not fathom.

Atop the eastern-most wall, staring into the distant forests and mountains, Adwen stood alongside Sir Oryn and Captain Slate. Away from the controlled chaos beneath their feet, the three waited, listening to the whistling of the wind in their ears. Daylight was beginning to wane, and behind them the sun sank lower to the pointed teeth of the horizon. Warm orange and crimson light streaked the clouds overhead, then started to shrink, recoiling from the unfurling of night's wings. In minutes, darkness would fly over and engulf the land.

Core appeared at their heels. "Lady Adwen, the people and their creatures are safe within the walls at last. Captain Sir Peregrine has once more proved his mettle and kept his word. Is there anything else that I might do to serve you, good Lady?"

A weight lifted from Adwen's shoulders at hearing the news. "Thank you, Core. Tell Sir Peregrine I need him and his men to maintain order among the people. The city guard will not be able to do so alone. And no matter what, the knights must not leave the fortress for any reason."

"As you wish, my Lady. And, my Lady..?"

She gave her new friend a curious glance. Core's smile beamed with warmth. "The Light Spirits are with you."

Hearing that lifted her heart, and she smiled back before he vanished.

Oryn did not say it, but he was thankful for the eerie entity's kind words.

In the west, the night began to devour the sunlight. To the

east before the warriors and the Tame One, darkness started to churn and roil. Out from every crevice in the earth and shadows under the green burst forth spiked shapes and waving tendrils. Purple smoke like low-hanging mist slithered toward the city like a tide announcing the coming of a typhoon.

Sneering at the sight, Captain Slate glowered, "They conjure, Lady Adwen."

"I see them," she replied.

Oryn glared at the materializing army and rumbled, eyes aglow. "At your side."

"You're not coming this time."

With a wild look, he pleaded that she take back the statement.

She couldn't look at him. "I need you to stay."

Anger made him growl. "This is no time for sentiment to get in the way of what must be done!"

Watching thousands of demons rising up and howling into the cold air, she heard their wails but paid no mind. "You must, for all our sakes. In the tower library, Toth told you what would happen if I were to come in contact with General Guillot. What he does not know is something far more critical."

Locking eyes with him, fearful of the truth, she said, "I have passed on to the other side before and left this body behind. The first time, the Light Spirits summoned me; the second time it was your voice that called me back." Raising her blackened hand beside her face, she was tearful. "Because of this, I cannot do so again."

Oryn was horrified, and he blanched.

"If I am struck down while this darkness is in me, it will swallow me whole; I will not be able to come back, and the demon will take my place. Do you understand?"

More frightened than before that she intended to fight on the ground with only the Gargoyles for protection, her most devoted warrior cringed at the thought.

"If you die, I cannot be saved," she told him. "Your voice can heal me and keep me from falling on the battlefield. Without that kind of protection, there is no chance; not until I am cleansed of this. Will you stay?"

Clenching small fangs, Oryn whimpered through his teeth.

"If the General appears ..."

"He is not here," she reassured. "He will not be. His presence is far away, building another army for another time. They do not know I am here, and they will not before this is done. Please, Oryn, stay here. For me."

His heart ached at the realization that he had to let her go alone. Fighting the animal instincts he had once conquered, he replied, "I will see to it that you return to this fortress alive." When fear made tears glaze her face, he sighed and nodded. "I shall remain here so long as it is effective."

Adwen wanted very much to lean into him and feel his warmth, but the hour had arrived. Turning to the Gargoyle leader, her voice resonated with resolve.

"Captain?"

"Aye, Lady Adwen?"

"Rally your clan."

"Aye. It will be done." With a few thrusts of his enormous wings, Captain Slate arched over and landed on a pediment, raising his spear at the figures dotting the spiral tower like bees on a hive. "Brothers! Sisters! My clan!"

Earsplitting calls filled the air in answer.

"Behold! In the east! The battle we dreamed of through the stones has come! Ready your claws, grip spears, and raise shields with me once again! Tonight we remind the darkness that free Gargoyles still serve the living!"

To Adwen, he bellowed out, "My clan is at your command, Tame One!"

"On my mark, good captain!"

With a few gestures from Captain Slate, two armored Gargoyles landed at Oryn's sides to protect him during the assault. The rest took wing and swarmed, flying circles around the tower until each one was in formation, ready for the next call. Like mad birds, they flew at blinding speed.

Analyzing the attacking legion, Adwen used her dark eye to clearly see if any more were arriving out of the murk. When the last of them emerged, more than three thousand Wretches, Fellons, Creepers, Frites and a few Dreds gathered ahead. Adwen howled.

Captain Slate roared, thrusting his spear toward the horde, and his Gargoyle clan soared. He soon joined in the charge, riding on zephyrs and gusts.

Adwen and Oryn watched in stillness as the Gargoyle clan bore down on the enemy. One line of the clan formed a V with shields and spears out, carving a rift into the gathering before swooping up, and a second dived down behind to continue the maneuver. Purple muck streamed through the wind like watery ribbons in the wake of the Gargoyles. The gold on their spears and spiked shields cut into the demons again and again.

The captain's clan was effective in cutting down the numbers but only while the demons were clustered together, charging for the fortress walls. As the monsters dispersed, the next threat was the gigantic Dreds and flocks of ravenous Frites.

Knowing it was her turn to join the fray, Adwen fought her urge to give Oryn one last glance. Knowing it would make things harder, she refrained and leaped far out from the wall, barreling toward earth like a meteor. In midair, colliding with an unwary Felon, Adwen transformed in a flash of bright light. Her body cut clean through the demon, shredding it to ash. With the speed she gained through the plummet, she carried it into a wild dash, grazing the demons closest to the walls, making them give chase back into the fields.

Her claws raked the soil, and the angry demons scraped it behind her. For several sweeps through the ranks, the white Holy Hound with black armor gathered the attention of the horde, drawing them to the center of the fray. When she ran out of space to run, the demons surrounded her. Finally she resorted to hand-to-hand combat. Using light in one hand to shred enemies with her claws, her left hand proved to be just as effective. The slivers that made up her arm were not restricted to a single form. Her arm melded and flowed into spiny armor to block enemy blows or extend into piercing spikes for stabbing without mercy. Jumping and twirling in and out of danger, none could touch her.

The Gargoyles had their hands full dealing with Dreds, but this was not their first fight with these monsters. One by one, they slowly picked off the spitting menaces. Frites proved more of an annoyance than a threat. Often, they barely touched the Gargoyle's gold, blessed armor and fell from the sky as filthy rain.

With the demons moving in to try to overwhelm Adwen, she shifted into her woman form, making for better agility. Chasing, lunging and swiping at such a small target caused some to wail in outrage at missing until they fell dead a second later.

Galloping over a hill, three of the remaining demon riders spurred their mounts toward the battle. Seeing Adwen alone made them laugh. Even more amusing was that she did not see them. The leader raised a skeletal hand of blackness, summoning a long, jagged spear.

From the fortress defenses, Oryn saw what was to come. He lunged for the edge of the stone wall until a pair of gold spears slammed down in his way. Unable to reach her in time, he roared.

Adwen heard him, killed another Wretch, then looked to the fortress. When she saw nothing, a split second of confusion came over her before something punched the middle of her back.

She gasped, paused and looked down at the spear, coated in silver essence. Her metallic fluids glistened by the light of the four moons as her knees buckled. Stumbling forward, the long end dug into the dirt, her full weight on the demon weapon. Overhead the Gargoyle captain roared, issuing commands to assist. The din of battle grew dull and distant to Adwen's ears.

For Oryn, the pain felt just as sharp. The instincts in him bonded with a geyser of emotions, forcing his body automatically into its true form. A resonating howl blasted from his jaws across to her. With it came all the magic and feeling he could muster, taking his own strength and sending it straight to Adwen's faltering body.

The surge of familiar strength gave her what she needed. Adwen's sapphire eyes flashed brilliantly, and her black hand grabbed the twisted metal rod. It writhed at her touch, and her will overwhelmed that of its original owner. Ripping it out and standing, she swung the rod back through the air until its end curved and arched into a wrathful scythe.

Throwing the demon riders a deadly glare, she snarled, "It's mine now."

Anger at the pain, as well as desperation for the end of the fight, launched Adwen into a rampage. Renewed support from the Gargoyles protected her from approaching enemies as she vaulted and dived to and fro with her new weapon, rending everything within reach. The rage blinded her to the fact that the riders had fled, so she kept killing every demon she saw until there were none left for her or the Gargoyles to slay.

When there were no more, she spun about, looking, searching and scanning with her dark sight for demons. There were none. They were destroyed or had fled.

Captain Slate landed nimbly behind her with a few of his warriors. "Lady Adwen, the battle is won. Shall we lift you back to the walls?"

Making the scythe disappear for later, Adwen tried to form the words. They never came. Her vision faded, and the captain could not catch her before she fell unconscious. Quickly and gently, the winged guardians bore her back to the fortress and to her companion's arms.

Chapter 11
BEAR OF DARGADIA

Descending shadowed stairs, Sir Oryn Conrad held Adwen close, cradling her tightly. Her head lolled by his cheek with his every step. Descending closer to the third floor, knights' voices resonated along the stone walls to his pointed ears. At the bottom, men who had gathered for their return hushed at his arrival. Sir Peregrine, Jack and Core stood first in line wearing anxious looks.

There Oryn stopped, hushed as the rest held their breath, not knowing what exactly they waited for.

Sir Peregrine took a step and asked, "Brother? Was the battle not won?"

For a moment he glanced at Adwen, then nodded and replied, "The enemy was beaten."

Roars of excitement swept the knights before their captain tried to quell the clamor. "Hush, lads! Shut it. How bad is she hurt, Sir Oryn?"

Knowing immediately that his traveling friend would not like to speak about it, Jack stepped in and answered for him. "She'll recover after some rest. It looks worse than it is. Come on, guys! Let them through! The demons are gone, and Adwen is alive. Everybody here has some place to be and something to do!"

Sir Peregrine plunged an elbow hard into the warrior's ribs. Chuckling at his gasp for air as some departing knights laughed, the captain mocked, "Awe, don't be such a whelp. These are my men to boss about. Don't forget that. And thank you for your hard work today. You've earned my respect, even if you are a silver-tongued scoundrel."

Rubbing the pain away feverishly, Jack made dog whimpers and replied, "Feels like it was better to stay on your bad side!"

Guffaws bounced off the walls in response.

Core gestured for Oryn to follow. "Her quarters are prepared."

Oryn knew where Adwen's room was but allowed the being to guide the way. When she was finally laid on the silk linens, several waiting healers tended to her, and Toth was among them. He had the most experience in treating Adwen's wounds.

Quietly letting himself be brushed aside by his friend and the attentive humans, Oryn drifted into the hall to wait. Resting back against the marble wall, he found the cold touch to be relaxing. Staring vacantly at the floor, he let a numb silence fill his thoughts. This was not the worst to have happened to her, but knowing the truth of how much more delicate her immortality had become left him dazed. One slip, and she could be consumed by a monster from within.

More than ever, he thought, she needed his protection. If not for his healing voice, the battle and her fate would have turned out very differently. When he healed her, his own strength was taken away. It had required a lot to keep her standing. Once that was done, if not for the Gargoyles, he would have been vulnerable. At this thought, he understood: She was wise to have made him remain on the wall. The demons could have picked him off too easily. Perhaps, with practice, this problem might be mitigated for the future.

The flock of healers in white filed past, and Toth came to lay a hand on Oryn's shoulder. Smiling kindly, he comforted, "The infection is making the healing process slower, but by noon tomorrow the wound will be gone. Try to get some sleep yourself. We all need it after today."

Oryn nodded but did not move.

Shaking his head, Toth sighed and added, "Do as you wish."

Plodding footfalls resounded like the ticking of a clock as his friend departed. Oryn was exhausted, but he could not pull himself from the wall by her door. They were safe in the heart of the Order fortress, yet he was driven to stand guard.

Hours passed in silence. Nothing stirred to alert him. An occasional breeze brought interesting scents to sample. Some he knew; others were a mystery. The night dragged on. When he smelled another unique odor that left him stumped, a tight feeling in his chest caused the warrior to forget about odd stinks. The knot in his chest tightened, making it seem hard to breathe. Soon he realized it was Adwen's pain.

Entering her quarters, Oryn was cautious while investigating. In the long walk to the end of the room, Adwen lay still, beads of sweat on her brow. Her eyelids were closed but moved rapidly. The bandages appeared clean, and the wound had not reopened, leaving to question: What was causing such discomfort?

Seeing the darkened left hand flinching, an idea came to him, and he ignored caution by reaching to touch it. A flash of death imagery flitted through his mind's eye, confirming his suspicions. The infection was denying Adwen of peaceful sleep by making her relive scenes of lost loved ones. There was little Oryn could do.

The sounds and gruesome colors were so vivid to Adwen, it was as if she were there. Visions bombarded her, flying by or forcing attention to terrible details. Screams replaced by sickening quiet moments made her heart race. When she could take no more, Adwen woke with a gasp, sitting bolt upright.

It took a moment for her to remember where she was, safe in her private chambers at the Order. Still, the memories rooted in the evil sliver plagued her waking thoughts, drawing tears down her cheeks. Hugging both knees to herself, hanging her head, a sob ripped itself from her quivering lungs. By the second gasp, she smelled Oryn's scent and searched the room.

Fast asleep, her dear friend sat against the wall, facing the bed and open veranda. The sight of him propped by the side of an antique armoire brought back memories, while in a lesser state, of being held close at night when it became dark. It had felt very safe.

Oryn was awoken by something heavy sidling up to his chest. By the time his arm was taken and tugged over a quivering shoulder, he realized Adwen had joined him on the floor, pulling his hand about herself. Oryn closed his eyes again, gently embracing her the way she needed him to, pretending to do so in sleep. When she curled up, sharing warmth with her fearless knight, the shuddering dissipated and the tears slowly dried. For the time being, the nightmares were kept at bay.

Bird chortles and the smell of fire awoke Oryn at dawn. Adwen was no longer in his arms. She stood by the carved stone vista overlooking wide-open fields awash in sunlight. Malik, the phoenix, perched on her hand, relayed what had transpired in her absence in great detail. She listened, nodding, passively digesting the knowledge.

Once Oryn moved to get to his feet, both paused to look and resumed their meeting. It ended by the time he was close enough and awake enough to hear what was said. Malik nodded to Oryn, bowed to Adwen and then took flight to places he did not know.

Remaining just behind her, Oryn asked, "Has your messenger brought good tidings?"

Folding mismatched hands at her back, she stared at the sunrise. "Malik rarely brings tidings more than warnings. This occasion he brought good news along with words of caution. The elders who had been hosts to parasites have recovered enough to ask for a meeting through High Elder Mamalis. According to Malik, they seem more agreeable. As for the warning, I must make a gentle request of you."

"Whatever you ask will be done."

After a slight pause, Adwen said, "A rumor came about last night that Sir Oryn is making aggressive advances on Lady Adwen as if she were a woman of ill fame. That she does not send him away defines her as a whore."

Oryn's hands became fists instantly, and his jaw clenched. He did not dare to speak his thoughts.

"Sir Peregrine and your closer connections in the ranks intercepted it. However, he did see you enter this room at night and not leave it soon after."

"For his vile slander, I would think the punishment was one that involved cleaning up after."

"We are symbols to these people. Our every move is judged; such is society. While in public view, do not occupy this room by night, no matter the reason."

His good intentions and emotions had compromised her goals. Shamed by his poor judgment, he lowered his head and humbly saluted. "At your command."

When he was nearly out the door, she turned and called, "Oryn?"

He paused to look back.

A sad smile came to her as she murmured, "Thank you for not leaving me alone."

For a moment he watched her as he held the door handle in his fingertips. Then Oryn heaved a sigh, smiled and went on his way.

After bowing deeply to Adwen in the Elder Hall, High Elder Mamalis announced, "Lady Adwen, we greet you on this new dawn and thank you for coming to hear our words. Are you prepared to be presented with the testimony of the council?"

Nodding cordially, she replied, "Thank you, High Elder. Please proceed."

The first to stand was the man who had temporarily replaced Mamalis. His face was as firm as before, but his eyes were humble. "Had I known what would become of this council on the arrival of Darien's Heir, I would have shuddered. I myself was blinded by a demon to what is right and just, but it does not change that it was through my own pride that I did not resist its hold. Thank you, Tame One. Thank you for breaking me free from my dark harness."

Saying nothing and giving a kind smile, she waited till the chance to speak was granted back to her.

Another elder stood. "I echo my brother's words in saying that the demon's manipulations could have been fought. If you seek retribution, I offer myself up to what punishment you deem fitting. I was a knight once, as were we all. I have not forgotten duty and the pursuit of honoring others before myself."

Another elder spoke with trembling lips: "My family and friends told me I had gone mad. Bitterly, I cast them out. Tame One, you have given me my life back as well as my will. For that, there is nothing I can repay you with."

The elder who stood next did so with enthusiasm. "To save what little pride we still have for supporting our old bones, let me speak what I think all can agree upon: We were a lot of bickering fools when you first came here. For what was done, we have no right to ask forgiveness. At the least, may we try to make amends?"

This was followed by many nodding heads and pleading faces.

High Elder Mamalis turned to her. "You have heard the council, and they beseech you to give an answer that rings with truth. They await your words."

Taking a moment to use her blessed eye to look into their hearts, Adwen saw sincerity. "It is my judgment that this council is no longer the one that sat here before. I have no retributions. All I ask is that we work together to defeat our enemies and restore the king to his thrown. After that, I command that you consider any debt you owe to be paid in full."

Several men quaked with thankfulness, tears restrained behind iron wills.

Raising her voice proudly in the Elder Hall, Adwen called out, "Elder Council, there is work to do, and the knights are needed. What say you?"

A wave of crimson- and golden-robed men stood, hands folded and eyes bright.

High Elder Mamalis announced, "The Elder Council is thankful for your benevolence. They offer their unquestioning service to you in defense of Dargadia and the Kingdoms of Day."

"Thank you." Adwen nodded. "I have an announcement for the council. The final fourth of Darien's weapons has been made known to me by the Light Spirits. I am to seek it out. They will give the path to me as I tread upon it. Soon, I shall have bound my final warrior and cultivated my strength yet again. Once this council has concluded, my three companions and I are to set out and claim the artifact. Is there anything else that the council would ask of me?"

The High Elder looked to the council, and one stood.

"Go with our blessings, Lady Adwen. Return to us safely."

Jack whistled a tune as he went to reclaim Alex. When Jack discovered that the Marine was not in his room, a servant informed him that Alex was making a final visit to the infirmary. When Jack arrived at the entrance to the infirmary, the head healer Gertrude was thoroughly looking over Alex to see if he was in need of any more salves. The robust woman had the presence of a kind yet strict practitioner. This accounted for why Alex clearly wanted to leave but feared the consequences if he so much as asked to do so.

Leaning in the doorway while Gertrude flipped up Alex's shirt and examined his torso, Jack announced himself. "Hey, Jarhead! I was looking for you! The knights donated a pair of dragon leathers! You're going to love these."

Without looking at the intruder, Gertrude grabbed, pinched and prodded every part of Alex's body that had been an open wound two nights ago. She paid no mind to her patient's discomfort. "Dragon leathers?" she said. Those are expensive! Nobody just gives dragon leather away. Count yourself lucky and get them on before the lads change their minds. Go on, now. You're as fit as a stud." She gave his stomach a merciless smack before letting his shirt down again.

Alex flinched in pain and blushed bright red.

Finally entering to pass the gift of indestructible clothes to his friend, Jack noticed a man covered from head to toe in bruises, cuts and a single burn. Bandages disguised most of the damage, but the sight caught his attention.

"Geez! What happened to that guy?"

Gertrude gave a single, sardonic laugh. "What do you think? Can't you see his jaw is broken on both sides?"

"I can't see his jaw," Alex said.

She shook her head. "Then you don't know the boys very well, do ya? That means they wanted this poor sod to shut his yap. That ought to do it for a few weeks, won't it, you whining sissy?"

The unfortunate knight wheezed and flinched at the pain of breathing.

When the man looked at Jack and realized who he was by the pointed ears and magical garments, he unwittingly let the warrior know the reason for the injuries.

Smiling and licking his lips, Jack pulled over a stool and

leaned in uncomfortably close. Once the human was thoroughly frightened, he asked, "Hey buddy! Heard any good rumors lately? So what happened?"

While folding clean linens, Gertrude said, "According to Sir Peregrine, the lad fell down a very long flight of stairs."

Jack mockingly winced and inhaled through gritted teeth. "Looks like there were a lot of stairs, pal." Pointing to various places very closely with a finger, he remarked. "A stair there. One there. One way over here. And, oh! A couple there. And then a really, really big one way down ..."

"Jack!" Oryn snapped from the door to the infirmary.

Finger suspended horribly close to a tender wound, he glanced back happily and asked, "Yes? What do you need?"

Realizing what he had interrupted, Oryn suddenly felt like walking away. "We are about to depart."

"Aw." To the knight, Jack consoled, "See you later, Boo-bear." Giving a hearty tap as a farewell, Jack left the man to his misery with Miss Gertrude.

Oryn's next most disappointing moment of the day was learning that their destination lay hidden in the Lost Roads. Adwen reassured him that this journey would not be like his past visits. No ambush could be laid that she would not see. This settled him down considerably, though he was determined to stay extra vigilant. Adwen, Oryn and Jack raced at top speed with Alex as a passenger. In an hour they were past Dargadia's northern border. Another hour went by before the company was deep in the heart of what used to be a mighty Elven kingdom.

There was a day when the trees grew in the shape of buildings with seamless hollows, rooms and spiral stairways to the forest canopy. Now it was untamed, as pure magic flowed overhead like crystalline fog that did not hinder the sun's penetration. The energy rippled and moved as if alive. Fairies hid in plain sight. The many roads that were once safe to all were now open to beasts and even more to werewolves and witches. That was how the Lost Roads earned its name; it was lost to the wilds.

"Are we close?" Jack panted once they slowed to a walk.

Wearing breeches and a unique battle harness made of red dragon skin, Alex was healed but still disliked clinging to his friend's back. Two hours of bouncing and getting the wind knocked from him every so often were strenuous.

"Can I get off and walk yet?"

"Yes on both counts," Adwen declared, shifting into her woman form along with Oryn. Jack soon followed suit. "We are very close."

As she gazed around for a sign or marker to an entrance, Jack watched Alex stretching his arms and back.

"What's the matter? Saddle sore? You could go back to the infirmary."

"Why don't you go back instead, Scruff-McGraw?"

Jack rubbed his hands together, grinning. "Oh yes! Then I can help Gertrude take care of the blabber mouth."

Oryn chimed in, "That was the first moment that I found pleasure in seeing you be yourself. What you had in store for the vermin was more torturous than anything I could have provided."

"Good! When we get back you can come watch."

Oryn contemplated the idea. "Perhaps."

"Now we're talking. Let's have some fun, Cujo!"

Before Oryn could agree, Adwen hissed. "Quiet! Listen."

Everyone's ears pricked. The sounds of the forest were the most noticeable. Seconds passed, and they discerned a melody. It was too faint to make out anything more than the rhythm.

Oryn murmured, awestruck, "I've heard tales as a boy of the heartbeat of the elf wood. Until now, I did not give them any credence."

"That's what it sounds like; it's a heartbeat," Alex replied.

"This way. Come on."

Keeping close, the four waded through thick ferns and straddled over moss-coated logs. The rhythmic sound grew a little louder, leading them deeper into the thicket. Treading softly, Adwen got a strange feeling and froze, looking about for signs of trouble.

"What's wrong?" Jack asked.

"I feel some kind of powerful magic. It's strange."

"Any guesses?"

Then Adwen saw the problem. Finally standing up with shoulders sagged, she muttered under her breath. "Uh-oh."

"I don't like 'uh-oh' very much."

Alex was confounded. "What's wrong?"

"Toadstools," Oryn said, glowering.

As the music became clear, tiny imps, fairies and their instruments came to stand on the white mushrooms that were in a vast circle around the travelers. Blowing horns and flutes while others rapped on drums made of acorns covered in mouse hide, the miniature band stood atop every space of the ring.

"What's the deal with toadstools?"

Adwen was calm and a bit disappointed. "This means we're stuck."

"Yeah, right." Jack puffed and started walking. "A bunch of mushrooms! Give me a break. I used to be the mushroom king back when ..."

As he tried to cross, a solid barrier of pure magic struck Jack hard like an electrified fence. Bowled over backward, he yelped and whimpered. "That sucked!"

Smiling and raising an eyebrow, Oryn pointed. "There appears to be a gap on that side. Try it again."

"Not funny."

Alex didn't like the looks of this and knew nothing of the folklore. "What can you tell me about toadstool rings?"

Adwen explained, "They are used by fairies to trap unsuspecting people and take them away to their world. That was the story in the non-magical realm. Here, that could be very different. It's a gateway, like a revolving door; you can't get out until you've gone through."

Massaging his red-marked face, Jack asked, "Then we can come back from the other side?"

"That is the trouble." Oryn frowned. "That is up to the fairies to decide."

"Adwen, make one of your portals to get us back!"

"Darien had that power, but I don't. Or at least not yet anyway. I can use doors he left open in specific places. I just activate them."

"So we are going to wait then?"

"Yup. That's all we can do."

Even more fey folk flitted into the open, joining the circle. Unlike the legends Adwen had heard, the song did not hypnotize. It fed the power of the spell meant to send them elsewhere. Otherwise enjoyable, the tune carried on, growing with the gathering. What appeared to be the whole world's fairy population had arrived. As far as they could see, little figures swayed and sang if they did not have an instrument. Leaves on trees swung with their movements until the forest itself was dancing.

When the sound was near deafening for the Holy Hounds, it stopped, and they were no longer in the woods. Their eyes quickly adjusted to the environment of a grotto.

The only sources of light came from blinking blossoms underfoot. Their lacy petals glowed white and green, illuminating a path. Adwen led her warriors along it, following the flowers. As she walked, each blossom detected her presence, leaning toward her like a face observing a passerby.

Meanwhile, Jack was looking up, trying to find the distant ceiling. "I think I see a crack with daylight."

"It's not," Adwen corrected. "Those are crystals. We are too far underground."

Entering another chamber, clouds of tiny flying lights drifted about in the air. One swooped past, and a few landed on Adwen's hand when she reached out. Examining them, she saw misty figures with light coursing through them and their gossamer wings. The sprites exchanged looks and darted off again, rejoining the swarm.

When Adwen and the others came to a flat stone at the edge of a pond, they stopped and looked around. Then the sprites went to the surface covered in fairy moss and hundreds of lotus flowers. There they hovered at the center.

Suddenly, the flowers closest to the pond brightened, and a soft glow appeared beneath the surface. The centers of the lotuses illuminated, while a shape pushed up silently under the loosely growing plants. Water droplets fell from what seemed to be an intricate white carving that resembled the silhouette of the flora. But as it continued to rise, an enormous deer came with it, fur soaked with foliage clinging to its snowy coat. The single antler on the Guardian's head sat like a crown, and its flanks and legs were plated with iridescent fish scales. A ropy tail like an ox's flicked at the curious sprites, encouraging them to make way. The creature covered in water, moss and lotus flowers turned its luminous green eyes to the travelers.

Awe held them speechless, and Adwen smiled.

The elegant giant took a knee and bowed, the crest leaning far over them, raining green and water drops. Adwen bowed in return.

Long ears flicking, the Guardian greeted them: "Welcome, Adwen Andredan and companions. I am glad you have finally arrived in my realm."

"I'm pleased to meet you. Do you have the weapon Darien left behind?"

The surface of the water broke a second time as a pearly chest came up at the edge where they stood, pushing aside a cluster of plants.

"Indeed, I do. The Light Spirits would have me grant it to you now because time is short. You will be unable to bring the fourth warrior to claim it from me personally."

"Do you know why?"

The Guardian snorted and slowly nodded. "Darkness is gathering faster. For the Heir to accomplish her goals, she must be swift. A single warrior is needed before the next goal can be met."

"And what is that?"

It gave no answer.

"Why can't you tell me?"

"It is not yet your time to know. Here is the token for your final warrior. Claim it. It is yours."

The chest opened, and inside rested a pair of sharpened fist claws. Adwen reached for them, but as her fingers felt the cool metal, they caved in on themselves and turned to liquid. Gasping in shock, she was almost as horrified as Oryn.

"I'm sorry! I didn't mean to!"

"Nothing is wrong, young Andredan. This was meant to be. As the first warrior intended to claim them is no more, the next shall not desire the weapon in its original form. The artifact shall take on the shape of what serves the suitor best."

Jack chuckled. "That's pretty cool."

"No, Jack," Adwen said. "No, it's not."

He and Alex listened intently as the Guardian explained,

"The first warrior to accept a token was Sir Oryn. The second was not reached in time before the darkness ended their life. This human suffered an even worse fate, as their soul was claimed by a Nizaren."

"Who were they?" Jack asked.

"I never knew their name," Adwen replied. "I only saw their face in dreams. Because Sycan had fractured me, my ability to sense certain things was weak. I did not know I was supposed to find them. They paid the price." She hung her head in shame.

The wet, black nose of the Guardian touched her chin and raised her head. Gazing into her eyes, it spoke gently: "What has come to pass was decided without you. You are not at fault. It was meant to be. What happened to the warrior was for a reason. It set the stage for events beyond the reach of your perception. Without this tragedy, a great many things would not be accomplished. Do not doubt, young Andredan. Do not doubt."

Adwen was consoled but still somber. Touching the liquid remnants, they flew up with a life of their own. They started to shine brightly then leaped at her chest, disappearing beneath her armor. Stunned, she took a step back. The sensation of the magical matter coiled around her heart surprised Adwen. Once the sensation settled and the glow died down, she blinked and shook off the odd feeling.

"Now you must go," The Guardian announced. "With my last breath, I can send you to the place where a warrior can be found."

"You're going to die?" Alex was alarmed.

"No. I will simply leave this form and return to another place and time where the Light Spirits command me. As this purpose of mine ends, another begins. Fare you well. Continue to prepare. Prepare for the arrival of the Darkening Time. Good-bye, Adwen Andredan."

The luminous Guardian's body brightened. Then in a stunning display, it burst into countless floating lights. They flew to the companions, circling around them. Faster and faster they went, closing in until it was impossible to see the grotto beyond.

When the bright white light began to die down, a forest

materialized. Wind from the mountains chilled them. Dargadia lay to the southwest and the Lost Roads to the east. Rocky hills and a cave were close by, far from the nearest village or town.

Oryn, Jack and Alex turned to see what Adwen intended to do and found her eyes shining gold. When her normal sight returned, she wore a peculiar expression. She felt surprised but also entertained.

To her suspenseful companions, she said, "It's time you all met an old friend."

Jack chuckled. "How old?"

She rolled her eyes.

"How do we find him?" Oryn asked to cut off another of Jack's remarks.

"We don't. It will take less time if he finds us. Jack, I need you to leave some tracks leading into this cave over here."

He shrugged and started jogging off.

"Not those kind of tracks, Jack!"

Before transforming, he replied, "You need to clarify these things."

When the black Holy Hound was bounding away, she turned to Oryn. "I need you to make your best werewolf howl impression as loudly as you can."

Giving a very confused look, the knight was leery. "What game are you playing at? That is the last request I ever expected from you."

"This warrior is not easy to track, and he is a hunter. It would take less time to get him if we leave a trail rather than try to sniff him out."

Alex became more interested. "How good is this guy?"

"He's the best hunter in Dargadia."

Oryn's expression changed to disturbed. "Wait. Are we seeking the huntsman who traveled with you and Toth once before?"

Adwen had hoped this would not happen. "Yes."

"The hunter, Regorian?"

"Yes."

Staring, he added, "Is he as the rumors tell?"

Recalling the hours spent traveling with the man, Adwen recalled many irritating moments. "I would rather you meet him than explain. My knowledge of him did not come from rumors; it came from actually dealing with him."

Alex wanted to be prepared for whatever was making them act so oddly. "Is he trouble at all?"

Adwen laughed. "That depends on your definition of trouble."

On Jack's return, Adwen led them to the cave entrance. "We can wait inside here. Looks like bandits once used it as a hideout. There's plenty of room."

"I just got done with the fastest mile of my life," Jack grumbled. "What now?"

Tossing Oryn an impatient stare, Adwen sounded exasperated. "Please. Just do it. You're the only one here that knows exactly how they sound."

"As you wish." Transforming into his beastly shape, Oryn towered over his friends and howled, deepening the sound. Several times, he unleashed the loudest, eeriest call possible at the trees.

Jack twisted a finger in one ear afterward. "Think an eardrum burst on that last one."

"Come on," Adwen ordered, "Get inside."

Minutes ticked by while they waited. Less than an hour had passed before Jack and Alex had resorted to games to endure the boredom. They played "I smell" in the place of "I spy," and Oryn sat quietly beside Adwen, trying to ignore the banter.

"I smell with my little nose, something that rhymes with glass."

Jack blandly muttered, "Grass."

"That's not fair. You're reading my mind again."

"No, I'm not. It was too easy. I smell something that rhymes with bed."

Brow furrowed, Alex complained, "There's nothing here that rhymes with bed!"

"Yes, there is, Jarhead."

"You suck."

"No. No I don't."

"Can you guys please shut up?"

"Sorry, Addy."

Adwen groaned. "Don't ever call me that again."

Finally there was quiet for a short time. To everyone's surprise, it was first broken by Oryn.

"I heard many a rumor of Regorian the Hunter. They say he is an honorable slayer of werewolves and beasts, so long as he is not sharing a bed at an inn."

Alex and Jack had been lying down, but both their faces turned up at once.

"In your travels, was there any truth to the claims?"

All eyes turned on Adwen. She sat and said nothing, looking into the distance.

Oryn grimaced. "Was he a lecher?"

At last, she glared back and asked, "If I answer, will you stop looking at me like that?" Oryn continued to wear a look of suspicion.

"Regorian is a gifted hunter with some sixth-sense abilities that are downright frightening. But on the other hand, he is crude, primitive, indecent and absolutely disgusting. Aside from that, he's a good guy. That sums it up."

Jack whistled. "Sounds like a charmer."

She rolled her eyes.

Then the shortest warrior's face changed to stark alertness. "I think he's here. Somebody is following my tracks."

Adwen issued commands: "Jack, Alex, get out of sight. Oryn, take your place there. No one moves unless I say."

The huntsman read the tracks. Not only were they huge, but they were fresh. Judging by the stride and depth, this was likely a powerful werewolf Alpha that had decided to change by day. It would be easy to find his den. Following for a few minutes, a terrible howling came from the hills. Taking out his mahogany crossbow and loading a silver-tipped bolt, the hunt commenced.

After hiking almost a mile, the stride of the tracks shortened, and he became more wary. This beast had slowed down and was probably very close by. The wind blew southward, keeping his own scent from alerting the monster. Then he spied the cave. Forgetting the tracks, it was more important that he be careful of other things. The closer he went, the more he knew something living was inside. He could feel it.

Breaths steady, weapon raised, his footfalls were stealthy as a cat's. Letting his eyes adjust to the gloom, he entered.

The smell inside was musky. Old broken barrels and a cart suggested that this had once been a criminal stash site. Spotting an old set of flints, it became obvious that men had lived here as well. Perhaps this werewolf took the cave for its own. Coming to the larger chamber of the cave dwelling, crumbling stone walls showed this place was far older than he had realized. An ancient ruin hidden in the hills likely originated from before the bandits and the monster.

Movement caught his eye. Not making any sudden moves, the hunter corrected his aim toward a pile of dirt near a wall where light filtered in from a hole above. But when the brown pile moved, he froze, weapon trained. What he had mistaken for rubble was a tall, brown beast in armor. Its jaws were massive. As it did not lunge, he waited, studying this figure. The green eyes glowed in the dark like stars at him. They were intelligent and calculating.

Feeling a presence from behind, he whirled around with his finger on the crossbow's trigger. Shocked to find a woman with white hair and glowing blue eyes, the impulse to shoot disappeared. It was dark, but she was so beautiful he could melt to the floor. As she spoke he held his breath.

"It's been a long time since you pointed that weapon at me."

Lowering the crossbow immediately, Regorian gasped, "Lady Adwen!"

"Come outside. We need to talk."

Bowing deeply with arm side-swept, he declared, "Your wish is my desire."

Adwen gave Oryn a covert look of irritation. "Come on, everyone. Let's go."

Out in the noon sun, she introduced her friends. "This is Alexander, Jack, and Sir Oryn. Everyone, please meet Regorian Lancer."

"How do you do." Regorian dipped his head and nodded.

Jack growled to keep the hunter from understanding. "Okay, when I used the phrase charmer, I was being sarcastic."

Oryn growled under his breath. "A lecher."

"What brings you so far from more lovely places that compliment your beauty, Lady Adwen? This is neither a safe place nor a pleasant one to behold."

Struggling to ignore the compliments, Adwen remained composed. "As the Heir of Darien, I am in search of my final and fourth warrior. You are one who is eligible for the choice."

Regorian put a hand to his head and raked back his black curls, looking as if a breeze could blow him over. A long silence left Adwen stunned. He was never one to take time to react. He remained speechless.

"Is there anything you would like to say?"

Dazed, the hunter's eyes wandered as he thought. Then he returned her gaze and was far more reserved than normal. "Forgive me. I am at a loss. This is something I must think upon."

Worried by the reaction, Adwen nodded. "All right. We can't wait long. The demons are building an army that can wipe out Dargadia. Can we take you back to the Order in Plexus?"

Right away, Regorian returned to his old self. Dropping to one knee at her feet, he gently scooped up her normal hand and caressed it slowly. "But if that is what you want, who am I to deny it? To think on this decision, seeing you safe in the wondrous city would be a blessing."

While Adwen wore a look of astonishment, Oryn came alongside and gave the hunter a deadly, ice-cold glare.

Confused by the looks, Regorian paused to stare back in earnest. Understanding his mistake, he let go and smiled at Oryn. "I am so sorry. I had forgotten in the heat of the moment that she is of noble descent! I must ask permission of her guard to so much as touch her magnificence. May I be granted the chance to express myself by giving her hand a kiss?"

"No."

Gracefully stepping back, the hunter smiled and bowed cordially. "Then I shall pass you one on the breeze." Blowing a big kiss at Adwen, he failed to recognize how close he had come to being ripped to shreds by Oryn's hands.

Adwen shook her head and informed the friendly hunter

of the travel arrangements. "We will carry you ourselves since I know you don't keep a horse. Sir Oryn will be your means."

Held frozen by disgust at the idea, Oryn's eye twitched.

Transforming, Adwen growled and lowered to all fours for the trek. "Well, Jack is carrying Alex. Would you rather I carried him there?"

An image flashed through Oryn's mind of this man clinging to her back, stroking her coat and hugging her neck during the hour long run through the countryside.

Quickly trying to erase the disturbing thought, he turned to address Regorian. "I advise that you hang on firmly to my armor."

The hunter was very fit and able to hold onto his strange mount the whole journey. What he did not know was that Oryn purposefully leaped higher than the others over hills and creeks. Each landing was hard and slammed the man into Oryn's back. Jack and even Alex found it amusing. After passing through the heart of Plexus past people moving back into their homes, they came to a halt at the Order gates.

Regorian slid off and staggered. Bent over with his hands on his knees, he gasped. Beginning to stretch his sore limbs, the first thing he exclaimed was, "Now I recall why I prefer walking."

Alex shook his head, and Jack scoffed. Oryn hid a smirk.

Inside the Hall of Knights, Regorian turned about, in absolute awe. "In all my years, I've never come to this place. It's so beautiful. Lady Adwen? Does the land of the passed on look like this?"

"Regorian?"

"Yes, my Lady?"

Searching him to understand what was making him act strangely, she asked, "Do you still need time to think?"

Taking another bow, he dipped his head low. "Yes, my Lady."

"You can go anywhere you want. When you are ready, return here. I have some errands."

"Of course. I look forward to gazing upon your wondrous form again."

Sighing and shaking her head, Adwen called out to the walls. "Core?"

On cue, the robed figure appeared, startling everyone but her. "What would you ask of me, Lady Adwen?"

"Are the city dwellers moved out?"

"They have returned to their homes of origin, Lady."

"Good. It's time I set up some long-term arrangements. And did you write down any special names for later?"

"Indeed. I have many."

"Then let's get to work."

For the next few hours, using Core's impeccable notes, Adwen used her stone-manipulating power to sculpt the stones in the largest halls. She shaped rock into small homes while creating places for disposal of waste. The displaced villagers were confounded at first by the concept of plumbing, but she was confident they would adjust. Running water was brought up through fountains that she raised from the floor, making the marble ripple and move until a pool formed. All that remained was the issue of rations. Adwen reassured those who asked that the food supply would be provided soon enough. After four hours, the day was coming to an end, and Regorian had not returned. Adwen did not worry. Jack and Alex were busy in the feast hall, eating and entertaining the knights.

Sir Oryn was furious. After checking again to see if the flirtatious Regorian had come to Adwen and did not see him, he resolved to track him down. Picking up the scent, it took him up to the fortress's second level, where fewer visitors wandered. The trail went in many directions but ended up on the far side, facing the mountains. Finding the outrageous human leaning on a stone rail, admiring the view, Oryn's patience had run out.

"Regorian!" he snapped and growled. The hunter did not move, and Oryn stormed over, snarling. There he waited, expecting a response.

After a moment of quiet, Regorian asked, "Isn't that just fantastic to look at?"

Knowing he could break the man's human form with no effort, Oryn refrained from touching him. "We go through all of the trouble to seek you out in the wilds, bring you here, and now you waste time feasting your eyes on sights? There are pressing matters to confront!"

Regorian said nothing.

"Speak! Or do you only speak if a woman interests you?"

As if in a trance, Regorian said, "I am a simple creature, Sir Oryn. All my life, I've sought nothing more than my most basic needs, never seeking more."

Recognizing the deep, contemplative state from past experience, Oryn was stunned and unsettled. Knowing the man would clarify, Oryn fell quiet and listened.

"I can tell that you do not approve of me. Though I am not a clever man, I sense things. Some things I sense are beyond what most are able. You think I may have tried to woo Adwen. I speak to her as I speak to all women; I see women as wondrous creatures due an infinite amount of praise. She had no interest in me, so I've never asked for so much as a kind gesture."

Turning to smile, Regorian looked tired. "My end is upon me, Sir Oryn. I've known it for a short while before you found me. That was what brought me to the hills by the Lost Roads; I was seeking my end. All I've ever wanted was to hunt, eat, sleep and sometimes share warmth with those majestic creatures called women. If I have sired children, I know not. What I do know is that I am not a fit father. So I hunt, teach the art of marksmanship, and take only what I need by earning it. There are no regrets for me. I've lived the life of a bear.

"What Adwen offers is not just a place at her side to serve greater things. To take her token is to extend my life. My senses tell me so. There is no way to know when my end will come after that. This is a difficult question to answer for one as simple as me. This gift is much more than I could ever need."

Finally understanding this stranger, Oryn said, "I find you to be a rather interesting creature."

He chuckled. "Not interesting; only simple. Let me tell you something: I have simple needs. Simple women fulfill me. Adwen is not a simple being."

Oryn quietly thanked him for the remark.

"As I can see it, you are not a simple man with simple needs. My sense tells me exactly where your heart lies."

A skeptical expression returned to the knight.

Stars in his eyes, Regorian the Hunter nodded and said,

"You will be there for her until the end of time."

Skepticism melted and turned to surprise.

"If you insist, now can be the moment I give Lady Adwen my answer."

Oryn escorted Regorian back through less-known passages to save time. When the two arrived, Adwen was waiting with Core at her side. Regorian joined them and listened as she spoke. Some knights passing in the hall stopped to watch as well.

"Regorian, the Light Spirits who command me say that you may become one of my trusted warriors. By joining me, you will be given the strength to fight the powers of darkness that would destroy the living worlds. Will you accept my token, passed on to me by Darien's Guardian of the elf wood?" Holding out an open hand, her palm glowed, ready to summon the amorphous artifact.

Enraptured, Regorian replied, "Your words fill me with pride, Lady Adwen. Truly, I am blessed by the powers. As proud as I would be to take your offering, it is my heart that says this is not mine to take."

Adwen was shocked and stared, astounded.

"I beg of you, dear sweet Lady. Do not think I insult your gift with my refusal. As the man that I am, I want for nothing. My heart is full. This grand thing is meant for a soul grander than mine. Please, keep it safe for the one truly deserving of the honor and privilege."

Giving Oryn a small questioning glance, she took back her hand. "If that is what your heart says, then it cannot be denied. I will save this for another."

"But if I may, dear Lady Adwen, I have a question to ask?"

"Yes?"

"May I have your permission to stay here and serve in the defense of the city?"

Adwen almost laughed at the simplicity of the request. "You do not need my permission, but of course you can stay."

"Thank you a thousand times over, Lady Adwen."

She tossed him a smile and added, "You can take your leave now."

"Thank you. Until the next we meet and I hear your splendorous voice."

Murmurs broke out as the hunter left for the city. Adwen was irritated. Turning to question the knight by her side, she growled to keep the words private.

"What in the worlds was that about? What did you say to him?"

Taking a second to watch the man go, Oryn answered, "I said very little, as he said much. Regorian senses his death. And like a bear, he chooses willingly to charge it."

Chapter 12
THE FOURTH

After Regorian's departure to join the city guard, Adwen had few options aside from trying to sleep. The task she chose to complete involved Core's list.

She sent her adviser to find the men and women with his uncanny speed and memory. They were then sent to a large, empty room on the second floor. It was in a wing of the fortress far from prying eyes, and when she bid the doors closed, not another soul apart from Core was privy to what was said.

Three hundred and fifty-seven people waited, talking amongst themselves. When Adwen entered, they hushed and bowed their heads low. In the silence, her bare feet made no sound on the stone floor.

When she stood before them, she called gently, "Raise your heads, please. I want to see your eyes." They obeyed gradually. None was perfect, as expected, but all were capable.

"Any among you who has too much responsibility to donate time in service, please step to the far side of the room."

After a shuffling of bodies, Adwen told the group, "Everyone, understand me here and now. None of you is under the control of the Order, the knights, the guard or anyone except me while in these halls. Not even the king may interfere with what I am about to ask of you this evening."

Hearing a murmur and smelling fear, she turned and saw a boy near twelve shuddering.

"What is frightening you?"

"I miss my mother, Tame One."

Knowing his mother was just downstairs, she was sympathetic. "You can go back to her in a little while. You won't ever have to come back up here again if you don't want to. Please, listen. This is very important. All right?"

He nodded. Adwen continued her impromptu speech: "I

have asked you here because of two things. The first is that a famine is upon you. Fiery demons ravaged the farms that fed most of the kingdom. Very soon, the food stores will be bare and more people will be coming to stay the winter and until the demons are defeated."

Murmurs and more fear pheromones filled the room.

"The second reason you are here, is because each one of you has magic." Murmurs grew to shrieks of astonishment.

"None of the knights knows anything of this. I had my adviser find you, and no one else but he and I know. Your identities are safe. What I ask is not small. With the combined abilities occupying this room, I know you can help save the kingdom."

Quiet hung suspended by a thread. Then a young man stood, his voice accusatory. "Do you know what you ask at all? If anyone knew, we could be dead in a day! What say you to that?"

"If I could not heal as I do," she said somberly, "my body would be nothing but scars from the things that have been done to me."

He looked torn by the truth she spoke.

"When I first came to Dargadia, I was always in danger. There didn't seem to be anyone to trust. Over time, I met people I could trust. They did not all have magic, but they had hearts. Even when I appeared as a fearsome beast with fangs and claws, some opened their doors to me and shared food. You have my word that if anyone violates you or harms you or those close to you, I will bring down vengeance."

The young man asked with apprehension, "Even your knights or the elders?"

Her eyes burned brightly in rage at the thought. "Especially them. I would not kill them, but I would humble them to their hands and knees like dogs."

He looked around at the assembly to see what they thought.

"What is your name?"

"Balefire Evanston."

Adwen nodded to him. "It is a proud name. I've looked into your heart. You have two gifts. Your most powerful is the strength to lead. I would have you be the first leader of an order of mages."

The declaration took the wind out of Balefire as loud murmurs broke out.

"I would watch you closely. Power can bring great good or great evil. So long as you do not forget humility through service and self-sacrifice, I would see that it brings good. This kingdom's people need you. Your King Lorvan has spoken openly before all the nobility on your behalf, despite the risk of losing their support."

"He truly has?" a woman asked.

Adwen smiled. "I was there to hear it. He said that Dargadia was in disrepair because of the fact that those with magic are downtrodden, threatened and killed. It is his wish that those with gifts not hide, not spread oppression in turn, but share their powers with the world as I do."

Letting the information sink in, the moment came, and she asked, "Are there any among you who can and are willing to serve on my behalf?"

When no one would speak first, Balefire was deep in thought. Then he raised his head and said, "I do not have the magic to give food. My power is with fire and ice. What I can do is what most fear from magic: destruction. If I could, I would be willing to help save Dargadia."

"Can you control it or just create it?"

Confused, he replied, "Well, a little of both, I suppose."

Adwen smiled. "What is good for keeping things fresh, mage?"

When he seemed too shocked to answer, and others became excited, she answered for him. "Ice. And what helps thaw things that are too cold? Fire."

Balefire stared in shock and awe at the revelation.

"Anyone here could be of help in even the smallest way. One of the truths of magic is that anything is possible. If you don't overstep the bounds of pride, a lot of good can be done."

Suddenly, Balefire Evanston blurted, "Where can we start?"

Adwen replied with open arms, "Here in this room. Core is your keeper. For the time being, until I speak with the king, this all must remain secret. After that, whether to come to the aid of the people is up to you. Work together in the security of this room. If you think you can do it, call for Core, and he will let me know. Any other questions before I depart?"

"How do we keep it a secret when any fool could follow us here?"

Turning her gaze to the door, Adwen used her will on it. The wood was absorbed into the wall, and a stone door took its place. A blue seal in the likeness of a firebird was at its center.

"Touch the door, and your magic will be the key to make it open. No ears or prying eyes can get in."

"Thank you, Tame One. We will try whatever we can and report to you what is learned."

"Thank you for being brave enough to stand."

It was just becoming dark when Adwen lay down to rest in her room. A short while later, she could smell Oryn guarding her door. The pleasant, warm scent brought a smile to her face. Feeling very tired, sleep was enticing.

Falling deep into a restful state, dreams tried to form, but the nightmares wouldn't let them. The visions of memories that were not hers began to surface. Screams pierced her ears. Then as they began to escalate in intensity, they vanished.

What replaced them was an image of a small log cabin in the woods. A mutt slept on the porch. Walking from among the trees, a young man with rusty brown hair patted the dog's head before going inside with kindling for the night.

Adwen snapped wide awake knowing it was not a dream. She had seen the next warrior. This time, she knew where to find him. If her instincts were right, there was not much time to get this one out of danger. Stepping into the hall, Adwen only needed to give Oryn a look, and he knew what was happening.

The two darted through the halls to the southeastern-most side of the fortress. Adwen leaped out an open ledge with Oryn close behind. Before they hit the ground, they transformed, and she summoned her power to give their bodies speed. The Holy Hounds shone brightly with light and moved like shooting stars. She led, and he followed.

Each piece of landscape was a blur. It was a little while before Oryn understood that they were flitting through solid objects. He caught up enough to give her an astonished look.

Adwen's growls were distorted but clear. "This comes at a price. Every demon within leagues of us will know we are here. Expect a fight, and be ready for anything."

Trying to answer, he could not. Only she was able to speak while their forms were more magic than solid shapes.

She understood and continued onward.

Crossing the plains, streaking through the woods, dreary castle Gailarien drifted past, and Adwen knew their destination was near. Dismissing the energy, she and Oryn bounded at regular speed, darting between the trees. Detecting demons ahead, they raced into the open and leaped from the top of a ravine. The cabin door was closed, and Wretches were everywhere. Adwen and Oryn came down with jaws bared and weapons ready.

She ripped through her enemies with the black scythe, and Oryn cleaved his way to the porch. When enemies climbed upon the rickety roof, Adwen vaulted over like a gymnast, raking them off as she flew by. Then she rejoined the fight on the ground, twirling and catching overzealous demons that had thought they could reach her. Oryn felled the last attacker.

Hearing the shrill sound of a door creaking open, they quickly changed to their less-frightening forms. Adwen went closer and called, "Tamis? Are you all right?"

Surprised to hear his name, the teen with scruffy, unwashed hair was leery. "How do you know me? Who are you?"

"It's been over a year since you let Toth and me stay the night."

Opening the door enough to get a glimpse of her bright ocean-blue eyes, Tamis blurted, "Tame One! It is good you've come!"

The two went in as he opened the door wide.

He smiled as she entered, then was unsure at the calculating look from her friend and became straight-faced. "I need your help. It is my mother." Closing the wooden door in a rush, the young man directed them into the second room.

Adwen had to take a moment to adjust to the smell. The poor woman had been bedridden for some time. Tamis lacked the means to care for her in this state. Oryn also flinched upon entering.

Going to his mother, Tamis was fearful and pleading. "She's been like this for a fortnight. Can you help her, Tame One?"

Not knowing what she could do, Adwen knelt, resting a hand on the woman. Ignoring her other senses, strange things came to her attention. This woman was worse than sick, though still breathing.

"Can you do anything for my mother?"

"This is dark magic, Tamis. There's nothing I can do."

To their surprise, he replied, "I know. Before I was born, a witch put a curse on her. If she wanted to live, she would have to stay by this cabin. But without the water from the fountain in Deleon below the castle, sickness would take her life."

Tears in his eyes, he wiped them away and clenched his fists. "The whole city is overrun with evil things. When I finally found the fountain again without being seen, it was dry; nothing flowed. She fell ill afterward. Then this sleep claimed her."

Adwen frowned deeply. "I'm sorry."

"When I was little, father left us. Mother said he was lost fishing at sea. She was lying. How would she know if she cannot leave the house? Before you arrived, my sister was off to fetch the water. A day after you had gone, a city guard came, delivering the jar of water and my sister's bloody scarf. A werewolf killed her on the road. Since then, I've been the only one who can help my mother. Please! Is there nothing to be done for this?"

An idea came to Adwen, and she grimly advised, "She is very close to the end, Tamis. I can share my strength with her just to let her speak with you. This cannot be for long. More demons are preparing another attack. Are you ready to say good-bye?"

Cringing and vainly fighting back tears, Tamis sobbed, gazing at his mother. "No."

Oryn put a hand on the young man's shoulder. "A good-bye is seldom granted to most. This offering is not one to shy away from."

Giving Adwen a baleful glance, Tamis nodded.

She bowed her head, closing her eyes as she gripped the back of the woman's neck with light fingertips. Body glowing, some of the power crossed over to the woman lying still in the bed. Thin ragged breaths became easier and deeper. Opening her big, brown eyes, Tamis's mother looked about in surprise.

"Tamis! Tamis?"

He swept around and took up her hand, smiling. "Mother! I'm here."

A beaming smile came to her face. Brushing at his messy hair, she crooned, "My boy! My wonderful, gifted boy. When did you get so grown?"

Tamis turned urgent. "Mother. The Tame One is letting you wake for only a moment. It cannot last long."

Glancing at the being cradling her neck, she replied, "I can feel it. Tamis? I want you to go far away with them. Get out of here. There is nothing left in this little place. When she lets me sleep again, I will die."

He squeezed her hand hard, shaking and gasping with tears streaming down his face. "I'm sorry, mother. I'm sorry."

"No, my boy." Being firm, she said, "This was never your fault. There was no way to break this curse." Wiping some of his tears, the woman explained, "The curse was never that I should perish. It was seeing the sweetest of my children suffer, too afraid to flee the nest and fly. What this does to you is my curse. Death is the end of it. Don't let it keep you looking back. Do you understand?"

Choking and coughing, Tamis nodded.

"When she lets me go, leave. Do not come to bury me until there is nothing but bones. My one wish is that you live. Find your place in the world and shine bright."

He smiled, holding her hand to his wet cheek.

The proud woman's eyes brightened, then they began to close and dimmed.

When Adwen let go and regained consciousness, Tamis was inconsolable. She tried to take his hand from the woman's fingertips. He refused.

Knowing demons were on the approach just outside, Oryn firmly pulled Tamis from the now-lifeless woman's remains.

He screamed and cried, fighting to get back to her side. They darted out the door and dashed into the woods while an army of demons swept over the tiny, secluded cabin like ants.

It was a mad race with the boy. Demons of every type were in pursuit, hunting them while they fled to the vast plains. Once they reached the open lands, the chase intensified. By then, Tamis was of sound mind and clung to Oryn's chest, hanging on with all his might. Face buried in the now-transformed Holy Hound's fur coat, he did not see the hordes of screaming fiends running after them.

Every so often, some pesky hawk-sized Frites would get close until Adwen sliced them to pieces. When several hours passed and they could see the walls of Plexus, they heard an awful roar from above. A giant Dred emerged from the dark clouds overhead. Both Holy Hounds dared not look back. Dawn was coming but would not come soon enough to save them.

Soaring after the pair and their cargo, the Dred locked onto Adwen and spat a black ball of oozy acid. The first shot missed her head by mere feet. If it could blind her, she would be unable to use any of her powers to fight back. Trying again and again, the Dred gained on them, preparing to swoop in and take the white Holy Hound with large, piercing talons.

At the city gate, the guards were rallied around Regorian on the ramparts. Gargoyles were on the way, and he shouted to the other archers.

"Men! In you quivers are silver-tipped arrows! You've used them before, but this time you aim at demons! Only the truest shot can take them down! Help me save the Tame One and her companions! Fire at will! Bring that flying nightmare to the ground!"

Dozens upon dozens of longbows loosed their arrows, most grazing the wings of the tenacious Dred. Regorian shot as well. His crossbow was powerful, and his bolts struck at the wing joints, hitting each time. This did nothing, so he focused his aim on the head, crowned by back-raking horns and tendrils. Shooting again, he struck its jaw, making it scream, but it did not stop.

Regorian reloaded, while the men began to shout louder in desperation. Locking back the mechanism on his gold-inlaid crossbow, he took aim once more, straight for one of the monster's glowing red eyes. When it was about to grab Adwen, a smile curled his lip.

"I've got ya," he whispered and pulled the trigger.

Grabbing Adwen with a talon, it squeezed tight to keep her from fighting free. Then one silver bolt ran through the demon's eye and out the back of its scaly neck. As its grip released Adwen, the Dred flailed and automatically tried to fly higher. Dying as it careened toward the ramparts and shrieking in pain, the monster began to tumble through the air.

Most of the men were able to run and dive out of the way, but those in the Dred's path received the full weight of the five-ton demon. In an explosion of stones, the center of the ramparts broke, crumbling over. Then they fell to the street in a jumbled mess of stone and demon flesh.

Adwen and Oryn were alarmed and ran faster. When they arrived, the Gargoyles came in time to stave off further attacks. Two worked the turnstile and brought up the outer gate for the Holy Hounds. Archers on the wall shouted jubilantly that the monster had fallen as Adwen and Oryn entered the city, skirting over the rubble.

When they reached the other side of the debris, Adwen saw something that made her stop and stare. Oryn looked back as she did. On the cobbled stones before her lay a broken mahogany crossbow, inlaid with gold floral designs. Turning to stare at the mountain of rock, she hung her head, and Oryn lowered his.

After being escorted to the entrance to the Order, Jack and Alex came dashing out. They found Adwen and Oryn walking with a 17-year-old boy.

"Hey, Adwen!" Jack called as he came running up. "We saw the Gargoyles taking off and thought something was wrong. Why didn't you tell us you were going to find a new friend? Who's this?"

Heavy hearted, Adwen spoke softly. "This is Tamis. Tamis, this is Jack and Alexander. Sir Oryn you've already met. Go inside with them. There are things I need to take care of."

Jack knew something was the matter and stopped grinning. "Hey? What's up?"

Looking back, she let him read her mind.

The warrior's face turned white and his eyes wide.

"What happened?" Alex grilled.

Steering the Marine after Sir Oryn and Tamis, Jack patted his shoulder. "I'll explain in a minute. I need to sit down."

Adwen and her Gargoyles took on the task of clearing the path at the gate. Bodies recovered from the rubble were laid aside on the street. When all were accounted for, she made sure that Regorian was brought to the fortress at dawn rather than taken to the city undertaker. With Sir Peregrine and Sir Oryn's help, an assembly was amassed to hold a ceremony in the first morning light. Downcast eyes beneath black hoods, near a hundred came to witness the pyre for the great man.

When it was time to bring the fire, Adwen put her own white flames to wood and set it afire. It burned quickly and brightly. The last thing to be seen of him was the broken weapon on the covering marked with the order's seal. Regorian was never a knight, but as a chosen warrior, he was deemed worthy of the ritual.

Tamis was already in mourning before being brought along to the funeral. For him, two funerals were taking place. Whoever this man was, he hoped his spirit would protect his mother's in the afterlife. Tamis felt a kinship to the man after seeing his face. Though this was not his father, he wished he were so that the hope for his mother would be assured.

His ashes were placed in an urn that would eventually be taken with others to the sea. Adwen said her good-byes along with the others and led Tamis to the central tower. Oryn, Jack and Alex quietly came along, knowing what would happen next.

Filing into a secluded study, as the door closed, Tamis realized everyone was watching him. Looking at the luminous, glowing eyes of the warriors, uncertainty made his words falter. "H-have I done something wrong?"

A smile from Adwen proved otherwise. "I came to find you for a reason, Tamis. I never would have known you were in danger if the Light Spirits had not given me a vision. You are one of the few who are able to become one of my four warriors. I have a magical weapon, and if you accept it, your body and soul will be bound to me and the power of the Light Spirits."

He was quietly astounded.

"It is a lot to take in," she told him. "What are you thinking?"

"Well, what could I do? I only know how to read and hunt rabbits and deer."

Jack chuckled and asked, "Are you a good shot?"

Tamis remained modest. "It's been a long while since I remember missing."

The cop and the Marine exchanged glances.

Looking into the young warrior's eyes, Adwen sensed that he was quite good. A clever smile turned her lips as she realized this. "There's a power in you that I don't think you realize. Your magical gift is amazing, and you can become a legendary warrior."

The boy's face beamed. "It would be an honor. After saving my life, and what you did for my mother, of course I will follow you. I will accept the weapon."

Adwen extended her pure hand, bringing out its essence from her heart. When the light reached the open palm, she encouraged Tamis. "Take it."

With some apprehension, he reached over. In a flash, the liquid-gold material leaped from under her skin, clinging to Tamis's hand. The suddenness frightened him into stumbling backward. When he tried to pull the bright thing from himself it was already taking on a solid shape. Held in his left hand, a majestic golden bow materialized. The string was like a spider silk thread, and the place where an arrow would fly was a strange opening in the body between the arching limbs.

"That bow is going to work well for you. What do you think?"

Befuddled, Tamis shook his head. "This bow is missing much. An arrow can't be fired from it in this state."

Adwen bore a clever smile. "Why don't you see if you can pull it back first?"

Firmly holding the grip, he took the string in his fingers. Light gathered under the tips between his skin and the fine thread. As he drew it to full length, intense magic formed a golden beam out to the body of the bow.

Jack clapped. "Now that is nice."

Holding the string was hard for Tamis. Taking a second to admire the magic arrow that appeared from nowhere, his fingers slipped and he toppled over.

Everyone but Adwen ducked and sidestepped while the magic shaft ricocheted around before crashing through a window.

Picking himself up from the floor, the young man apologized profusely. "Forgive me! I'm sorry! What in blazes was that?"

The others grumbled, and Adwen went to him happily. "That was a magic arrow from your magic bow. It will never run out so long as you wield it."

A big smile brightened his face.

"How about showing the knights a thing or two about archery in the yard?"

"Yes," Oryn said, glowering. "Draw it while outside."

The rest of the day was spent with the knights, shooting targets. Adwen was not surprised when Tamis hit the bullseye without fail. Tamis could not use his bow for the whole time, as the resistance of the string was heavy. When his arms gave out, Adwen had a new surprise.

This strong young warrior needed a bath. Servants swept Tamis away and gave him an intense scrubbing that he would not soon forget. He had never had the opportunity for a heated bath before. When he was pulled from the dirty water, a much-needed haircut came as well. Cut to just over two inches improved his look, though when it dried the front bristled up uncontrollably. Lastly, another donation of dark dragon leather pants and coat was brought for him to try on.

Jack and Alex took it upon themselves to provide a guided tour. They took him to the feasting hall with the knights when he was hungry and showed the best places to find entertainment. Jack's two favorite spots were naturally the feast hall and the armor lockers. There, the knights bickered and joked away from the watchful eyes of the elders or the Elder Guard.

All kinds of trouble were to be found.

When the pair tried to convince him to share some ale, Tamis made it clear he was very tired. The rooms for Adwen and her warriors were in the east wing. Arriving at the hall, he bid them goodnight.

Tamis fell asleep quickly. It had been more than a day since he'd had a chance to lie down to rest. The expensive linens and soft bed felt like sleeping on clouds. He remained still for many hours of the night.

An unearthly scream of horror woke him, and he fell from the bed in a flurry. Landing on unforgiving polished marble made him gasp and groan. Rubbing his sore backside, he hobbled to the hall to see what the matter was.

All was still again, but Sir Oryn stood down the hall, leaning back by a door. His arms were firmly folded over his broad chest, making him look as if he did not want to be disturbed. Still, Tamis's concern outweighed his worry about angering the hero. Padding up to the green-eyed warrior, he took a closer look. Oryn wore an expression of sadness instead of irritation.

"Sir Oryn?"

Glancing over, he stared.

"I thought I heard a scream, Sir."

Oryn sighed and looked over at the closed door. "You are not wrong."

Tamis was alarmed. "That was Lady Adwen I heard?"

Taking the young man aside, he said, "Walk with me. Adwen is not to be disturbed."

"What is happening, Sir Oryn?"

"Nightmares of the worst kind plague her sleep."

"Why?"

He said nothing.

Then Oryn halted abruptly. He looked up and saw three tall women in white. They watched quietly as Oryn and Tamis considered the strangeness of the situation. The black-haired woman, yellow-haired woman and red-haired woman wore serious expressions. These beings gave off no scent, letting Oryn know he was faced with spirits.

"Good evening, Sir Oryn Reynard Conrad and Tamis

Warren Hawk. We are the Horai."

"Why are you here, spirits?"

The redhead inclined an eyebrow. "You have come far since you first spoke to the elf in the city of Deleon."

Oryn gave a calculating glare.

Her black-haired counterpart stepped forward. "We have come for two reasons. One is personal. We wish to thank you for caring for Adwen. You have become who she needs in these dire times. For that, we three are eternally grateful."

"Why do you not visit her yourselves?"

They became slightly sullen. "It would not be wise."

"There was a promise that we could not keep," the blond said.

A growl rumbled in Oryn's throat. "Did you promise to keep her family safe?"

She looked away.

"It was not our place," the black-haired woman said. "We wished to but were forced to be present in a more crucial place instead."

Becoming very angry, he replied, eyes burning, "How crucial?"

Summoning an emerald pendant on a chain, she replied, "As much as this moment here and now."

"This is a safeguard for you," the redhead continued. "Keep it on and out of sight. When the time comes, this token will ensure your escape."

The necklace flashed and was instantly around Oryn's neck. He flinched and growled in surprise. When he angrily tried to remove it, the redhead snapped, making him give pause.

"If you have any love for Adwen, you will keep that where it is!"

Green eyes glowing brightly, he snarled in frustration. It seemed he had no choice but to accept the unwanted gift.

The black-haired woman reassured him kindly, "You will be glad for your choice."

Still vengeful for Adwen's pain, he snarled, "Get out!"

As you wish, she said, still wearing a kind, understanding smile. The woman and her blond counterpart faded from sight, leaving the redhead alone.

When she walked closer, Oryn began to snarl and growl viciously. This did not frighten the spirit. Her attention was on Tamis. Quieting down, he watched as she leaned down to look into the boy's face.

Frightened by the eerie being, Tamis swallowed a lump in his throat.

"Do you know who I am, boy?" she asked.

"I don't, Miss."

She smiled. "I am justice, one of the three spirits of order. There is a fine line between me and vengeance." Looking between them both, she added, "Both of you will have the chance to feel me in your blood very soon. Until that day, farewell."

Chapter 13
WINDS OF CHANGE

In the large meeting chamber Adwen had locked away for the mages, those who decided to hone and explore their abilities did so. Not all were present at once, but a single mage spent every waking moment there. Balefire made sure he was the first to arrive and the last to leave for the three days he worked alongside the others. With his assistance, and due to Adwen's advice, many intriguing solutions were discovered for the famine.

After he finished eating an apple brought by a young mage named Moira, it was time to get to work. Faster than any of his peers, the black-haired young gentleman mastered his skills. But before he resumed training, Balefire called for attention.

"Everyone, hold your powers for a moment." When two younger mages stopped running about with ribbons of light and sparks, silence fell upon the room. "This morning I called upon Core to inform the Tame One that I believe we are ready; we can use our strengths to prevent starvation. She may come at any time. Behave yourselves and look presentable. And Jeromy? Try not to leave anymore marks on the walls with your lightning, please. This is the Tame One's home; that is not respectful. Thank you all, and go back about your work."

An ashamed boy's voice shouted, "Sorry, Bale!"

Shaking his head and smiling, there was nothing he could do to prevent more of the clumsy child's accidents. After three days, it was a wonder no one was harmed yet.

A few paused to observe when their talented leader closed his eyes and held out his hands, taking controlled breaths. Yellow flames came to life in his right hand, and frigid air in his left began to turn deep blue, crystals forming and rotating between his fingertips. This exercise of control over his energies invigorated and calmed the mage. Until being brought to this room, Balefire had struggled daily to subdue his magic. Now he was compelled, not to see how far he could push the world with these powers, but how far he could draw them inward. Each attempt before had ended in loss of concentration or dizziness. Determination swelled in his chest. This would be different.

Relaxing, willing the energy from his body into his hands, both ice and fire turned his palms the same hue as the elements. Then the condensing energies crawled up his limbs, turning the rest of him bright blue and yellow as they went. The closer the sides came to the source at Balefire's heart, the more slowly they progressed. It became strenuous to bring both fire and ice together. Suddenly, he realized what the pairing of them represented, and the energies fused.

The mage's arms remained as the two elements, but his body glowed with washes of green and white, robes fluttering from the raw energy pulsating within. Everyone stared, jaws dropped at the sight of their friend. A sound of stone grinding and slamming closed broke his concentration, sending the fire and ice back to his hands, returning his appearance to normal.

Dozens of faces turned to see Adwen at the door with an astonished old man in rich purple and golden robes, wearing a jeweled crown. Most who realized the king had arrived took a knee, dropping their gaze to the floor. Every mage was terrified. If the king so wished, he could report any of them to the elders and the knights for practicing magic. They were at his mercy, no matter what Adwen had promised. She did not rule the people.

Stunned, Balefire stood still while the bright blue eyes of King Lorvan were firmly fixed on the fire and ice he held. The old man went closer, never meeting his wary gaze. Soon, standing toe to toe with the king of Dargadia, Balefire waited to see what was to become of this meeting.

Finally, King Lorvan looked back at the young man. His old face showed something lost between joy and agony. To Balefire's surprise and everyone but Adwen's amazement, the king gingerly scooped up the flame.

Turning and breathing into the fire, it leaped into the air, soaring around the chamber over their heads in the form of a dragon. Embers rained like stars as it circled before returning to the king, reverting to the form of a harmless little ball of warm energy. Giving the fire back to its master, King Lorvan shed tears that ran past his quaking smile.

Also at a loss, Balefire respectfully knelt to his king, head bowed.

"Stand, please," King Lorvan beckoned.

Confused and startled, the magic users listened, enraptured.

"Hear me, everyone. This is something I've wished for you for generations. Powers that be prevented me from safely granting this freedom to you as well as myself. Now is the time. Fear of you and what I have hidden my whole life must be vanquished. This injustice has gone on far too long. The time for change is now."

A few hours passed, and Adwen called for an Elder Council meeting. She asked that a long feasting table be set but with only one plucked pheasant and a large cut of beef. Whether the request puzzled them, they did not say. When she entered the hall, eight individuals in robes and identical solemn masks filed in behind her. One stood at her side, while the rest waited silently by the meager table setting.

As Adwen formally opened the meeting, the disguised mages remained quiet yet were very nervous. The youngest of them shuddered and stared with glassy eyes behind his mask, watching the stern elders looming over them. Meanwhile, the robed guest with Adwen had no fear at all.

To finish the opening rites, Mamalis announced, "Lady Adwen, the council awaits your words to be presented to their ears."

She nodded and smiled. "Thank you. Elders, I believe I have brought a means of fighting the coming famine. Standing behind this table are seven citizens of Dargadia. Each individual has a gift that may allow them to serve other citizens in ways that even I cannot hope to contribute. Observe."

One by one, the mages took turns demonstrating their abilities. Beginning at the far end, the first mage was of average height. His hands reached out and showed a fist full of seeds.

Firmly pressing them into the table, he concentrated then released a surge of magic, making grain grow up between his fingers, roots drilling into the wood. When he stood back, harvestable grains rustled in the breeze, and the elders held their breaths, dumbfounded. Another mage stepped forward. Taking some grain from the stalks, she crushed it in her hand, letting the finest powder fall to the table linen.

The next summoned a glass of milk from thin air, earning a gasp from his audience. Setting it down, the mage still held a glass of milk while a duplicate remained on the table. This was repeated until a dozen glasses of cold milk stood before them.

Yet another mage took a glass of milk, pouring it out onto his hand. As it fell through his fingers, it became curds. Little lumps tumbled to the table like pebbles.

The following mage waved her hands over the table, concentrating. Clapping them together, the talented teen pulled them apart, opening a small rift. Fish rained out, cascading off the table and onto the floor. The rain of fish ended for a moment. To the mage's shock, as well as the council's, a squid flopped onto the wriggling pile. The mage jumped back from the sight, dismissing the peculiar portal, looking between the frightful thing and the elders anxiously. The smallest mage stepped forward. Approaching the red, raw cut of beef, the little mage cupped both hands to either end. Some elders leaned forward as the small child appeared to be elongating the flesh without stretching it. When he was done, the cut was several lengths larger than before.

The final mage went to the raw pheasant and laid a hand on the breast, almost instantly turning it to a frozen mass. Switching to the other hand, the pheasant rapidly thawed and cooked to golden perfection, steam rising from all its surfaces.

To the flabbergasted council, Adwen explained, "The magic they use is in their control and can be used to great effect in keeping others alive through the winter. The days will not be without hardship, but the people will survive. Without the powers of these mages, untold numbers will perish before the new year whether we defeat the demons or not. I, Adwen Andredan the Tame One, ask for the blessing of the Elder Council."

"The council has heard and seen what you offer. Now the council wishes to speak. Will you hear their words, Lady Adwen?"

"Yes, I will. Thank you."

An elder younger than the rest with black hair flecked with white stood, brow furrowed, hands behind his back. "There is no denying that these ... mages have skills that can aid in supplying food to the needy. What I wish to know is why they wear masks."

"They are afraid," Adwen replied.

"What of? They seek to serve but are unwilling to show their faces. We trust in your judgment, Tame One, but you do not control these free-willed people. What is to stop mages such as the one over here from harming innocents while you are gone? We've had the knights enforce laws against magic for a reason for a very long time."

Adwen's eyes glowed brightly, and her face turned stony. "I was once judged by the knights. They tried to take my head."

He dipped his own head in apology. "Mistakes have been made, Tame One. And yet the knights' justice has protected many."

"At what cost?" asked the eighth masked figure.

Fifty cold looks fell to the masked man. "How dare you interrupt out of turn? This council is not for the likes of you to bring in your quips! Hold your tongue."

Pulling back the hood and removing his mask, King Lorvan glared, making the elders gasp and murmur.

"My apologies, King Lorvan. I did not know it was you."

Brandishing the mask, he frowned. "I knew you would not. How else was I to bypass your cordial rites and discover the truth behind the sincere smiles and bows?" The disguise fell with a clatter to the marble floor as he shed the dark cloak, showing his royal attire.

Mamalis appeared uncomfortable. "King Lorvan, why this deception? The council has served you and the kingdom tirelessly."

Glaring, King Lorvan's voice held a chilling tone. "You may have served me, but how have you served my people?"

After a pause, an elder spoke: "All that we have done was

intended to protect the people."

"Yes. I see that. What I wish to understand is if you intended to protect them from monsters or from each other? The latter is my responsibility, elder."

Murmurs and looks were exchanged until Mamalis replied, "What would you ask of this council and the Order, King Lorvan?"

"Change. The Order was built to defend the innocents from darkness but not from magic. I have found it an insult to my position as king that this Order would see fit to judge and execute my citizens without my consent. For years I watched and listened, unable to act, as the majority of the people saw such practices as just. Now is the time for changes in this hour of need. No more will I leave my people to the Order's judgment. I come here today to reclaim that right. Elder Council, will you relinquish your self-appointed task of passing judgment on mages and other magical citizens of Dargadia and return it to the crown?"

Mamalis thought deeply. If he had made a decision, it was not apparent. Then he looked to the council and replied, "This council hears your words, King Lorvan. Will you hear the council's as well?"

The king remained stern and nodded.

"With the best of intentions, I must ask your majesty," An elder said, "if the knights were bound by law to refrain from passing judgment on mages found in conflicts, who is to apprehend them? Some are quite dangerous. Are your soldiers and guards prepared for the task?"

A clever spark lit the king's eyes. He'd assembled a secret number of magical devotees decades ago. "I've already begun recruiting talented men to deal with the over-ambitious among the populace. A few are rather remarkable."

Fragile silence hung between them, while looks and whispers were exchanged in calm debate. Soon whispers faded to nothing, and all eyes went to the High Elder, wordlessly passing their vote to him.

After meeting the forty-nine gazes, Mamalis proclaimed, "The Elder Council has weighed the choice and made a decision. On the matter of outlawing Order Judgment upon any and all citizens of Dargadia, magical or no, it is impossible to deny the right is the king's alone. From this day forward, no knight may execute people outside the judgment of the crown."

Adwen smiled contentedly, while the king nodded. "Thank you."

Suddenly, a tall mage removed his mask. Setting back the hood, he let the whole assembly see his face.

The younger elder with white-flecked hair and beard stood and gasped.

"Balefire?"

Showing no overt reaction, the powerful mage called, "Hello, father."

Adwen and the king exchanged awkward expressions of surprise amidst a storm of murmurs.

Keeping his voice low, Balefire turned to her. "Might I ask for a turn to speak, Tame One?"

Her clever smile returned. To the elders, she announced, "I present to the council and the Order of the Master Knights, Arc Mage Balefire."

At being dubbed Arc Mage by the Heir of Darien, the young man's breath caught in his chest, and his head swam. Everyone fell quiet and stared as he awkwardly stepped around the table to address the Elder Council. With permission to speak at last, the young Arc Mage drew upon the words he had nearly committed to memory.

"Elder Council, I speak to you as a man and as a mage. Here and now I proclaim my intents, all laid bare. All my life I have tried to hide my magic, as I've known the consequences of being discovered as well as the potential dangers it carried. It was difficult. For as long as I can remember, I've waged war upon myself, resolute in denying the frightening power inside me yet yearning to relinquish the fight. Until now, I could choose neither."

Summoning flame and frost at once to glow in his hands, Arc Mage Balefire noticed each reproachful twinge in the old men. "Look at me. I hold the power of fire and ice. None of the others can contain more than one element, if any. I've pondered as to how I could do so. Today I understand. What I truly hold is what I want more than anything else: life. Fire and ice by design are at odds, but where they meet on equal terms is a place for peace and growth. What is the sun without the sea? What is winter without summer? Both must commune for life to flourish in full.

"I hold no ill will for this council. As my fire and ice have taught me, waging war results in only death. Though I do not wish to wage war or serve the Order, my wish is to stand alongside it. If you would have me, I would be your ally in times of need such as this."

When stunned silence came, he asked, "What say you?"

Balefire's father was as a statue, unable to move, while the other elders pondered and exchanged words.

Mamalis looked about to see the council's consensus. Confounded, he turned back to say, "The Elder Council has heard your words, Arc Mage. As of now, their own words escape them. Your offer is genuine and generous. Gratefully, this council accepts your friendship, Arc Mage Balefire." The woman mage who had summoned the cascade of fish removed her mask. Her eyes were glazed with happy tears as she looked to the High Elder.

Mamalis trembled at the sight of his granddaughter. "Moira."

Pretending not to notice the distraction, Balefire dipped his head and replied, "Thank you, Elder Council. This means more to me than you know. If I may humbly ask, might I take leave of you? There is much to do."

Struggling not to stammer, he regained his composure. "You have the council's leave and blessing, Arc Mage. If there is ever any news, do not hesitate to send word. The Elder Council looks forward to the next time we meet."

Balefire's heart swelled until the magic swirled inside, briefly making his face glow. Taking a bow, stepping back and turning toward the end of the hall, he led his mages out. Exiting through the colossal doors held open by the Elder Guards, more magic coursed through Balefire, brushing at the edges of his control. This felt like a dream; he had done what he thought impossible.

With the giant doors closed again, High Elder Mamalis sighed. The old man rubbed his weary head and asked, "Tame One? Might the council and I speak plainly for a while?"

She heaved a heavy sigh also. "I would like nothing more."

To Elder Liam Evanston, Mamalis shook his head. "That boy is wiser than most men with four decades of life ahead of him. How is it that you are the most surprised by what has happened?"

Battling the shock, Elder Liam asked Adwen pleadingly, "How was this done to him? How did this happen to my son?"

"No one is responsible for his being a mage," she said. "He was born this way. Balefire and his magic were one from the start. The Light Spirits deemed him worthy of these gifts."

"But this changes his standing among the aristocracy. His reputation will be crushed in a single blow. No one will have dealings with him in land or property!"

She raised an eyebrow and gave a calculating look. "Am I not magical, Elder? Are you telling me that even I would not have a chance to live among this kingdom's people based upon my mystical nature?"

"I did not intend to insult you, Tame One. This is different. He is different."

In reply to the frantic elder, Adwen firmly added, "Balefire is still your son."

He stared.

"He is also going to help save the kingdom. Is that not what all Dargadian fathers dream of for their sons?" Leaving the stunned man to sit and ponder, other matters needed her attention. "High Elder, it is time to make our next move now that the enemy knows I have returned."

"What will you do?"

"I would further deprive our enemy of supplies by bringing the remainder of the citizens to the fortress. Without humans to consume or sacrifice, demons struggle to claim territory. For this mission, I will need a number of knights and plan to bring several Gargoyles as well. Carts and horses are important for carrying those who cannot walk or ride the distance."

"When will you need this caravan to be ready, Tame One?"

"As soon as possible."

A stout elder stood and called down, "I can promise fifty

knights and ten carts at dawn tomorrow for your journey. Is there anything else we might provide?"

"Your blessings and patience until my return."

A SPECIAL TREAT

Dawn had come, and the elders were as good as their word in providing knights and provisions. Adwen claimed the head of the procession when it began, passing hopeful commoners in the streets on their way to the gates. Also watching, strumming a crystal ball with cracked, amber finger nails, the ancient sorcerer was bemused. In the dark recesses of a tower, a gradual smirk pushed at folds of skin by his mouth like weathered window drapes. Dead flakes of skin sloughed off, but he paid his bodily condition no mind. He was accustomed to being barely alive. Inside him were bones and dust as well as what remained of his black heart. Finding Adwen alive and not controlled by the sliver pleased this perversity of a man.

Casual footfalls in the stone chamber came closer then ceased. Ozovath's smile widened. "Glad you chose to pay your old man a visit. I might be able to teach you a new trick."

Sycan sneered, and the whites of his eyes turned black, his bleach-pale pupils locked on the frail man with his staff. "I am ageless, and my knowledge is pooled from the centuries before you were an afterthought in your sire's mind. Must you always prod me with the meaningless fact that you summoned me into this world? Other sorcerers from your age were at my master Lord Melanin's disposal, and he happened to use you. It is you who are a child in comparison to me. When you are no longer of use, I will revel in having you taken care of."

Ozovath chuckled. "Time seems to have run your well of knowledge dry. I recall you saying the same thing thirty years ago. Can you not think of a new way to threaten that you have not said before?"

The demon in the shape of a strong young man smashed a fist onto the table at lightning speed. Stone cracked and chipped under the set of gloved knuckled. In the sorcerer's ear, he hissed in the demon language several sinister words.

"Oh, that is good." He chuckled at Sycan's rage.

"I was sent by my master to see that you know how to weaken Adwen and separate her from the others. General Guillot has been dispatched elsewhere to spawn our army. I must oversee my cult's efforts as well, leaving you to deal with the mangy dogs. Capture her and keep her until the general can come and finish what was started in Mortigad. She shall either die in a few days or become one of us. Melanin wants her permanently removed or leashed."

"I am withered, not an idiot; I know what the master wishes."

"Good."

Looking away from the armed caravan in the crystal ball at last, he glanced sidelong, curious and suspicious. "I have heard a whisper in the shadows, child of darkness. A rogue, a powerful one, has surfaced."

Sycan smiled sickeningly.

"Will he be a problem?"

"We crossed paths almost a year back. He is too weak. Besides, he has his own troubles to deal with."

"That is convenient. Then the rogue will be unable to interfere with my next trick. First I will send a friend I summoned: my Nizaren."

Intrigued, Sycan folded his arms, tilting his head. "Nice choice, dust bag, but what if your soul sucker fails you?"

"Then I shall take matters into my own hands. I have a plan that will, at the least, temporarily disable her. Perhaps her pet knight will be erased from existence in the process. Who can know?"

Sycan growled dangerously with a grin that was equal parts rage and thrill. "*Sir Oryn is mine. Leave him to me. I must taste his blood and hear his scream.*"

"Oh-ho! I can see that. I make no promises. My treat for the lovely couple should make for a wonderful show. Adwen has few weaknesses. While blind, she cannot use any of her light powers. Demon steel is needed to kill her, but I know what will take her voice and render her almost useless."

"What? Ah, I see. You have read more of the text I lent you. I would like to have it back, if you don't mind. A little light reading would help pass the time when I'm not disciplining my cult members for mistakes. None who still live has made any, and they bore me."

"I will keep it a while longer."

A terrible growl rumbled in the dimly lit chamber.

"Do not be so put out. As compensation, I have a special treat just for you."

Sycan quieted out of curiosity.

Giving a sinister glance, he said, "They wait in the dungeon."

Ozovath sensed Sycan depart and chuckled.

Two men stood in pitch blackness, starving, afraid and sullied. Wrists chained to the unseen ceiling, it had been two days since being taken captive, but they could not know. The sun was hidden, distorting what little time had passed and what remained until the end. They were going to die here; the strangers conceded to that. The worst part was their longing for freedom, which could not come.

In the absolute dark they heard a rustle. The one with the shred of courage left asked hoarsely, "Who's there?"

A second of quiet instilled the delusion that nothing had made any sound at all. Then a low thunderous growl made the other whine and mumble nonsense. If not for the chains he would have scratched and clawed for an escape through the solid stone. The men shuddered and quaked.

"Hmmm," Sycan whispered to his prey. "What's that I smell?"

Even the braver man was on the verge of panic.

"Defecation? Only babies do that in their trousers."

A feeling like icy death trapped the air in the faltering man's lungs as the demon spoke directly into his ear in the complete darkness.

"I love the taste of babies."

The second man wailed in horror at the morbid sounds and cries as his companion was eaten alive at his side. A symphony of fear and death filled the lower chambers in the depths of the Silver Spire.

Chapter 14
CLOSE

Seldom did demons attack during the caravan's journey westward through the fields. What would have taken a few hours for Adwen and her warriors to traverse took two days with the caravan and cavalry. The knights and their seasoned steeds were strong, but the sluggish carts had to be looked after. Night drew near again, forcing them to set up camp a mile from the northern bridge crossing the river.

The next nearest town was Fort Redu. No one had heard from that fortification in weeks. Fortunately, all but this region had been evacuated. If all went as planned, the last unprotected commoners would be taken to the Order within the week. Everyone on the mission hoped to find more survivors than anticipated.

At first, Adwen resisted riding a horse, but she soon agreed to it. It would have been considered demeaning to her status to walk while the knights rode, but would not have bothered Adwen. Oryn explained that the greater issue would be putting the knights in an awkward situation. If she walked, they would have to as well. It was against their code of conduct for a company to travel more easily than their commander. So Adwen agreed to ride.

Sliding down from the extravagant saddle on the white stallion, she sighed, rolling her eyes while no one saw. The knights had no idea that their gift of a steed was really quite tedious. The whole way he complained of his shoes not being comfortable or having stray hair over his eyes. This was clearly not a knight's horse.

"I trust Ol' Springbuck treated you well, Lady Adwen," said the knight taking the reins for her.

Feigning a pleased expression, she replied, "Of course he did. Thank you."

The fussy beast snorted. "Why lie? You detest me! How many times have you complained of my need to hold conversation?"

Taking advantage of the fact that only she knew the horse had spoken, Adwen completely ignored the comments. Nodding to the bowing knight, she felt relief to be away from Springbuck. Oryn came to escort her to meet with ranking knights and a Gargoyle commander sent by Captain Slate. They discussed plans for safely pressing on, knowing that greater dangers likely awaited them.

Meanwhile, as the camp was set up and guards took their posts, Alex and Tamis found Jack entertaining knights and a few Gargoyles by a fire. Cracking jokes, telling tall tales, the gregarious Holy Hound fed off the laughter.

"Hey, skinny little nubby!" he called to Tamis. "You and my scruffy buddy can share a seat on the warmer side of the fire."

Some chuckled, and others jokingly gave rude gestures from behind the flying embers.

"You know any good stories, Tamis?"

"Yes, but I do not recall enough to tell them, Sir Jack."

He puffed incredulously. "That's when you get to make stuff up! How about you, Fluffy? It's a cloudy night, so you have the time to share soldier stories."

"I have stories, but I suck at sharing," Alex said. "Stop messing around and just tell another one."

"I'm all out! It's your turn anyway. Partying in the feast hall at the Order sucked them out of me!"

Knights nodded, and one called, "It'll do that to ya." Sniggering followed.

Alex had no sympathy. "Well, just make something up."

"Get over yourself, Jarhead." Pondering deeply while others laughed, an idea began to form. Going with the flicker of creativity, Jack hushed his audience.

"Now listen carefully. This is a story of horror."

As he began, Adwen was passing by. Hearing the start of a story, she found it impossible to resist. Adwen let Oryn continue without her, hiding nearby, ears pricked for the campfire tale.

"There was once a young woman. She was beautiful, kind

and very much in love. Her hair was long and shone like bee pollen in the sun. She spoke only sweet words in a voice as soft as her cheek."

With everyone hanging on his words, Jack's tone darkened. "One day, the beautiful woman felt strange. It was as if eyes followed her. Whenever she was alone, it did not matter; the girl knew something stared at her. Voicing these concerns to her lover, he shushed, "Don't be silly, Honey Bee. The only eyes on you are mine. You are safe."

Suddenly Alex's look of curiosity melted. This story had seemed familiar, but now it was too familiar. If Jack was playing a joke, it was not funny.

Adwen also felt strange as she listened. Something in her heart started to ache.

"Comforted, but not convinced, she went out for a walk the next afternoon. Through the forest and back, the unshakable feeling of being followed made her heart race. Reaching home again, afraid for her life, the woman bolted the door and locked every window tight. Finding her lover in the kitchen, she pleaded for him to keep her close and safe."

Adwen remembered the visions she had on her first nights sleeping in the Order fortress. The woman she had seen went for walks in the woods and had long blond hair. The woman also pleaded with someone out of Adwen's sight for protection. Knowing where this was going put a knot in her throat and a lump in her stomach.

What Jack said next made hot rage build in Alex's chest, turning his hands into fists. His pale blue eyes glowed intensely.

"Go upstairs. He told her, Dinner will be done soon. Take a nap, and I will wake you when it is ready. She did go. Too afraid for sleep, the beautiful, sweet girl lay awake with eyes closed, waiting for her protector to come."

"Then there was a small sound, and she smiled, expecting to feel his touch. When there was nothing, she opened her eyes. Confusion and fear gripped the poor girl, holding her still and unable to scream."

Jack paused, watching the audience lean in to hear.

Unnerved, Tamis asked, "What frightened her, Sir Jack?"

Making his mahogany eyes glow, he stared through the fire

at everyone and replied, "A tall, broad shadow ... and a large knife!"

Adwen and Alex knew now that this was not a harmless story spun from thin air. Unfortunately, Jack was unaware that this tall tale was true, having accidentally plucked it from his friends' minds.

When the telling went on into the gory, tragic details, Adwen remembered the terrible final vision of her would-be warrior; this was the one she failed to save. And as Jack told how the woman's lover found her, she recalled what she never could before. It was Alexander Greeves who had come at the end. Grief and shame gripped Adwen in a strangle hold as she darted off in search of Oryn.

With the story concluded, Jack received a few claps. Turning for his friends' approval, he asked, "Scary stuff isn't my shtick, but how was that?"

A big fist slammed his cheek. If Jack were not so powerful, the force would have broken bones. Watching the Marine storm off, opening up his ability to hear thoughts, Jack called after him.

"What did I do? What?" Then he caught a murmur from his companion's head, and his own face blanched. "Oh. Oh, I screwed up bad. That's not good."

A Gargoyle voiced the confusion of the crowd. "How in this wide world do you manage to enrage others with such skill, Sir Jack? This time, we do not even know what it is you have done wrong."

"Are you certain?" Oryn asked, alarmed to find her crying, but even more so by the newest revelation.

"Yes. It was Alex's wife. He was in my visions of her. I was not able to perceive him in those memories until now. The Light Spirits likely hid this from me."

"And for good reason," he sighed ruefully. "Does he know?"

She shook her head, wiping her eyes with her right hand.

"It's best to keep it that way for now."

Turning firm, she snapped, "No."

Alarmed and irritated, Oryn growled. "You cannot be serious. This is not the setting or proper time."

Sapphire eyes blazing, she retorted, "There is never an opportune time to tell these things! Maybe you can hide this, but
I can't. I am accountable for it in the end."

Oryn's growl deepened. "I disagree on many counts of that
claim. How could you have known?"

A tense second passed, and she answered, "I am responsible for my charges, no matter what. I was supposed to find my
warriors as they were presented. At least Regorian had his
chance. She did not. Go back to my tent and wait."

"Where are you going?"

"To take my warrior out for a private conversation."

Growling and shaking his head, the knight disliked this, especially Adwen holding herself responsible for something she
could not have prevented.

Leaning back on the side of a cart, staring into the falling
night, Alex saw only swaying grass and a tree line beneath the
distant mountains and clouded sky. It took great effort to walk
away from Jack and even more to regain control of his emotions. Although he told himself his friend could not have done
this on purpose, smoldering anger remained. He let the rage
burn a little, if only to avoid feelings of loss.

Adwen approached from downwind. Though she moved
soundlessly, Alex sensed her presence. He looked calmer than
before. For a moment she watched him. Nodding to the fields
and trees to make herself clear, she set off at a slow walk with
the warrior close behind.

Neither spoke on the way. She wanted absolute privacy
from prying eyes and ears. Through the trees, with the camp
out of sight, Adwen brought him to the river. By a ledge above
the deep, steady current, she stopped and faced Alex, searching for the right words.

Now that they were far from camp, the Marine had an odd
sense of unease. He waited for Adwen to speak; not knowing
why she brought him here was confounding. Her expression
was solemn, making Alex ponder a variety of possibilities.
None of them was good. No speculation was close to the truth.

"There are some things I need to tell you. I was there for

Jack's story."

A sour grimace formed on his face. "I'm not in the mood to talk."

"Please. This is important."

Seeing no way to refuse her, he huffed, "Fine. Tell me."

"I know who killed your wife."

Sick sensations washed over the warrior as if he were doused in ice water.

"Who? What is their name?"

"Its name ... it is called a Nizaren."

Determination filled the Marine. "Where have I heard that before?"

"The fourth Guardian, the one in the grotto, spoke his name in our meeting."

"I remember. That thing killed a warrior before you could find them."

"Nizaren is a soul stealer, Alex. It consumes the souls of its victims."

Alarmed, he replied, "Then I can still save her."

"She is dead, Alex, but her soul is imprisoned. To set her free, the demon must be destroyed."

"Where can we find it?"

"I don't know. I'm sorry."

A strange feeling came over him, and he became suspicious. "How did you find out that this Nizaren murdered her? Why go through the trouble of taking me all of the way out here for this news?"

"It was Jack's story. Hearing it helped me remember visions from a long time ago. These visions were of the warrior I never found. In them I can only see the warrior; no one else comes into focus. But when I remembered the visions by the fire, I saw the demon. Then I saw you." Alex's suspicion gave way to confusion. Then nauseating horror filled him. Realizing the truth made the Marine shudder and quake with anguish. "No ... no!"

Gazing balefully while he began to pace, clenching fists and restraining tears, Adwen went on: "I failed her, Alexander. I failed you, too. There is nothing I can do to take back my mistake, and I don't expect you to forgive me; not this time. Please, know that I don't believe I can forgive myself either.

With all my heart, I am sorry."

Finally stopping to glare, he felt empty of everything but rage.

Tears in her mismatched eyes, Adwen murmured, "Please, say something."

Before he moved an inch, suppressed regret made him numb. Alex lunged, pushing her over the edge. In a brief moment as she fell backward, a dark void opened over the deep waters. Adwen only had the chance to gasp before it enveloped her. When she disappeared into the black, a hideous demon, its face like poisoned sinuous flesh with multiple eyes, rose up and hovered where the portal had been.

Horrified at what he had done, Alex drew his short sword, prepared for an attack.

Instead, the tall, floating demon opened its gaping mouth. Green light shined in the back of its throat, and the voice he longed to hear again for so long cried out.

"Alex! Help me! It's hurting me!"

"Emily! I'm coming!"

The warrior leaped at the monster as it began to smile deviously. It vanished a second later, leaving him to fall into the river and swim back to shore.

Wet, muddy and near panic, Alex climbed onto the embankment and stood, scanning the forest over the river for the soul eater or any trace of Adwen. He cursed himself loudly in the dark woods.

Running toward the sound of profuse swearing, Oryn and Jack bounded in and changed into their elf-like shapes. "What happened? Where is she?"

As the Marine fell quiet, Jack read enough of his thoughts to understand. Scowling, he growled, "Now you've really screwed up, Jarhead."

"Where is she?"

"The Nizaren took her. There is no trail. It just disappeared into thin air."

"Fine. Cujo and I are going to kill this thing. Get back to camp and try not to do anything else stupid."

Oryn snapped, "No! You must guard Tamis in Adwen's and my absence. If this is a ploy to separate the boy from the Heir and destroy them both, nothing can be left to chance.

This whelp is coming with me."

For a while, Jack rumbled and locked glares with the knight. Finally, summoning a dagger and pointing at the Marine, he snarled, "Don't screw this up. Got it?"

Alex wished he could growl back but settled with returning the harsh expression.

"If we do not return by dawn, lead them back to Plexus."

Jack shook his head ruefully. "No matter which way you slice this, it's a trap. The three of you better come back, because I will send the knights and Gargoyles home before coming in after you." While Oryn prepared a retort, the short warrior dashed back the way he had come.

Every bit as angry as before, the green-eyed Holy Hound growled, "Come along. There are wrongs for you to right."

Through the trees they ran. Like nighthawks, the army of two darted for the nearby bridge and back to the cover of the forest. On their way, the bond that tied them to Adwen drew them to where she lay in great danger. Minutes dragged agonizingly by in their suspense and anticipation. Then the walls of Fort Redu loomed into view.

Coming to a halt at the stone fortifications rising fifty to sixty feet, Oryn judged the height with scrutiny.

Breathless from trying to keep up, Alex panted and gasped, "How far around is the gate?"

"There are two gates. Neither is a risk I am willing to take. We go over from here."

"Outstanding." Alex gasped and restrained a cry of fright when Oryn grabbed hold of the Marine's clothing and lobbed him up to the ramparts. The ledge rushed to meet him, and he reached for the first layer of level stones. Coming down on his chest, he scrambled back to his feet on the main walkway atop the wall.

Oryn stealthily leaped the distance, coming up and over to join Alex like a cat on the prowl, eyes bright and ears pricked for danger. Both pressed onward, alert for the slightest sound or sign of movement. Adwen and the Nizaren were here, hidden in this cramped maze of a town.

Half of Fort Redu was a network of narrow alleys. No windows were lit, and chimneys breathed no streams of smoke. Smells of death wafted upward, extinguishing any question whether humans still lived within. The fort was lost to the demons.

Alex followed without a word. Any instruction from Oryn came in animal speech. It was quieter and less likely to alert enemies. They stalked the rooftops for a few blocks and moved to ground level upon reaching an abandoned market plaza. Remains of the folk who once lived here littered the cobbled square. Doors hung open like gaping mouths, mimicking those who lay in the vacant homes, rotting in the stale air.

The seasoned knight sniffed and scanned the terrain. Then his sights crossed the silhouette of an old town hall, its twin bell towers visible against the horizon. Raindrops gradually started to fall, sprinkling then pouring on their heads.

Summoning his two-handed sword, the Rose Thorne, Oryn followed the alley toward a small plaza and steps that led to the town hall. He growled to Alex. The Marine followed, gripping his own weapon tightly. As they proceeded, Alex watched the knight's back.

Stopping at the top of the stairs, he growled to Alex, resolute in his plan to rescue Adwen. "I will face this thing. While I have it distracted, if Adwen is unconscious, take her and flee."

Alex saw Oryn's luminous emerald eyes burning with a ferocity he had only seen in wild animals. If Alex didn't know better, he would suspect that Oryn had succumbed to his bestial side again. The Marine nodded in acknowledgment.

The powerful knight-turned-Holy Hound faced the towering wooden entrance again and lunged. Sword raised and shoulder lowered, he knocked both doors open wide with the force of a bull's charge. The inside appeared empty at first. Two clouds of dust rose in the wake of the double doors, settling on the floor by the time the warriors entered. Benches cluttered the floor, and withered human remains lay strewn about. Some were impaled through the heart, victims of the soul eater. A wisp of Adwen's scent crossed their noses, leading to a closed door to the mayor's chambers.

A sudden sense of danger froze them where they stood. Both looked around, and Oryn was first to raise his gaze to the rafters. In a flash, the knight instinctively kicked the Marine forward, simultaneously jumping backward. A mass of darkness and streaming green mist slammed down where they once stood, splintering oak planks. The Nizaren straightened up to laugh in amusement.

Alex jumped up as Oryn transformed and rushed the demon, roaring ravenously. But the monster opened its mouth wide and let out a sound like the cries of a thousand souls. The power blasted the Holy Hound off his feet, casting him outside the building into the pouring rain.

The Marine flinched under the demon's vacant stare. Its laugh chilled his blood. To mock how much weaker Alex was in comparison, the Nizaren left to take care of Oryn outside. Alex wanted to follow but resisted. Adwen was in trouble. His sixth sense and his bond with her made it clear that she was not well.

In the open under the brunt of the storm, Oryn's jowls wrinkled into a terrible snarl, streams of rain running along his fur and armor. His opponent faced him, hissing as pained murmurs echoed in streams from behind uneven, jagged teeth. The Nizaren smiled broadly, adding to Oryn's unease. The Holy Hound knew almost nothing of this fiend.

Green mist coiled in the demon's clutching, sinewy hands, growing and overflowing. The Nizaren raised one undulating orb of soul energy and aimed it at Oryn, unleashing several screaming arcs that cut through the raindrops.

Snarling, Oryn dodged the first strikes and slashed the last out of the air, dissipating the arcane projectile like a bad dream. Taking a chance when the demon aimed another orb, Oryn hunkered behind his sword, charging at the levitating monstrosity. His weapon swatted the flying ethereal blades away like insects, prepared to take down the source. When no more green streaks blocked his path, the Holy Hound leaped and raised his sword high, jaws bared.

The demon's mouth opened, and it screamed.

Anticipating the blast, Oryn turned the sword's edge into the force, thinking he could carve an opening. The harsh echoes of misery lashed at his flanks as his quick thinking paid off. The blessed weapon tore a path through the demon's gale, and Oryn closed in.

The Nizaren quickly darted aside, but not soon enough. A

piece of itself was cleaved off. Shrieking in rage, the demon gaped at the oozing stump that once had a hand. It hissed at the warrior who dared to make it bleed.

Oryn took satisfaction at making the Nizaren feel foolish for underestimating him. That satisfaction was soon gone in a flash. Oryn watched in horror as the demon flexed and writhed like a maggot. Curving protrusions on its torso Oryn had mistook for ribs unfurled into four additional arms, summoning more green lights. It laughed loud and hard, the sound of blood lust resounding in Oryn's back-folded ears.

Barrage after barrage cascaded on the Holy Hound, forcing him into the defensive. No source of cover availed him as the soul energy cut through wood and stone alike. Ducking behind the base of a well bought him some time, but it was gradually torn apart by the countless blasts. Stone fragments flew in all directions as Oryn tried to think of a strategy to reclaim the offensive.

For the first time, he noticed he had not gotten to cover unscathed. Pain from numerous cuts, some deep, began to register. Blood welled up, weeping away with the cold deluge. The sight did not frighten him, but it did help him make a decision. His blood drop streams were sand in an hour glass, running faster to the end of the fight. Before his body could turn against him with overwhelming pain, Oryn began the breathing ritual for focus to block out the sensations and to dull them into soreness.

When what little remained of the stone well cracked, he made his move. Rolling aside to avoid being taken down with the last piece of cover, he raised the sword again, charging through the seemingly endless assault. Fragments of green bypassed his weapon, springing up more wells of crimson, leaving nicks in his black and golden armor. He drew closer to the assailant, his strength diminishing with his advance. One of the demon's green beams slashed Oryn's leg, forcing him to falter.

Suddenly the waves of deadly soul blades ceased, and the Holy Hound stood almost within reach of the Nizaren. Fleshy wounds hung open on Oryn's arms, legs and the sides of his head that he was unable to shield with his blade. Unable to feel anything as his limbs quaked and struggling to move, Oryn had to fight just to reclaim control of his severely wounded body. The sight of the demon smiling sparked his determination to override his weaknesses. He pushed beyond the threshold of his limits. Power he only tapped into with his songs of healing turned into an open reservoir. Pale green light radiated over him and made his sword glow bright. Raising it up, with a mighty roar, Oryn swung for the kill.

The demon's mouth opened before Oryn's weapon could block the blast, sending the Holy Hound tumbling backward.

Having lost the focus and the magical energy with it, Oryn staggered to his feet, snarling. Seizing the opportunity, the Nizaren shot a single green blade at the Holy Hound.

Oryn swiftly batted it away, almost toppling over from the strain. A second blade struck Oryn diagonally across the chest, rending flesh and bone. Blood poured down and dribbled from his jaws. He wavered, but his determination did not. His bright, glowing eyes never left the demon. Oryn snarled in defiance, unable to move without falling.

The Nizaren opened its mouth yet again, readying a final scream.

Once the demon went out into the rain in pursuit of Oryn, the door to the mayor's office easily fell to Alex's brute force. After a short search he spotted Adwen lying on a long meeting table. In a rush, the Marine tried to scoop her up but could not touch her. A barrier of evil magic blocked his hands and dealt superficial black burns.

He gasped but quickly ignored the discomfort, desperate to get her free of this strange spell. He scanned the table and her body for any sign of weakness in the barrier. This was beyond his thinking. Magic was completely alien to him still. There were no obvious cues as to what to do.

In the search for a solution, there was a visible incentive to work fast. The demon flesh of Adwen's arm was being empowered by the demonic barrier that kept her unconscious. The black thorny flesh crawled and reached like an amoeba, trying to consume her body. Spiny tendrils like onyx-rose vines spread, wrapping and tangling across her torso.

Instinct kicked in for Alex. After taking a brief glance at his holy blade, remembering the mad chase in the city, he

plunged it through the barrier and into her chest. Adwen was unharmed, but the green force over her shattered. The power of the sword forced the dark flesh into submission. It recoiled as if stung like a frightened mass of tiny snakes and returned to the neutral form of an arm. Right away, he picked her up and bolted out the exit.

Racing past the dry, desiccated remains in the main hall, cold rain showered them both at the door. As he ran down the stairs, he saw Oryn snarling, looking as if he were showered with daggers instead of water drops. The Nizaren screamed and flung Oryn through the wall of a house. The wooden frame cracked, and the home crashed down around the knight, burying him in boards, crossbeams and shingles.

Alex gasped and stopped when the demon turned and saw him holding Adwen. Neither moved, Alex apprehensive and the demon amused.

Seeing that Oryn's plan had failed, Alex saw no options. The more he stared down the demon, the more resolute his heart became. Stealing a glance at his unconscious leader, he regretted having taken his frustration out on her for a second time. Asking forgiveness was futile.

The Nizaren drifted toward Alex slowly, allowing the warrior time to place her on the ground. If he was brave enough to stand his ground, then the demon might give him a moment to prepare for death. Claiming the soul of a proud warrior was much more satisfying than taking that of a coward. A warrior's soul held power it wanted for its collection. When the Marine's was almost ripe, the Nizaren called forth energy into his five remaining hands.

Alex was fearful, though not enough to hesitate. Watching the demon raise its spindly fingers and green orbs, there was just one thought left in his mind: One way or another, he was about to see his wife once more. Familiar strength flowed throughout his body, and he lunged, a feral growl coming from his human throat. In his charge toward certain death, fur, flesh and bone flowed painlessly into his creature form, speeding him faster on his way. Icy-blue eyes aglow, his sword rose to pierce the Nizaren's heart.

Orbs held high and honed on the transforming warrior, the Nizaren's sick grin widened as far as its head could accommodate. This soul eater was ready for its prey.

An explosion of green mist and two severed arms flew, making the demon shriek. Its energies missed their target in the moment of surprise.

Oryn's sword flew past Alex and stuck fast in a building's overhanging support beam. The knight was in his elf-like form, leaning heavily on a lone standing beam amid the wreckage. His body was almost entirely covered in gashes and curtains of red.

Twirling aside and dodging the yellow hound, the Nizaren's side spouted green mist and ooze. It opened its mouth to scream the troublesome Holy Hound into pieces. But it hesitated and gasped. Frozen like a statue, it gagged and looked down to find the tip of Alex's sword protruding from its core. The hound warrior behind it snarled and gave the weapon a hard turn like a stubborn key in a lock.

Screams blasted free from the soul-eater, and it was unable to contain the power it held captive any longer. Green souls broke free, erupting from the demon's form as it crumbled, turning gray as ash and effervescent fragments, drifting off and disappearing in the wind. The freed souls turned blue as they escaped, vanishing on their way to the plane of the hereafter.

The rain slowed. What remained of the demon was gone forever, and a lone green orb hovered where it once was. Turning blue, the soul stretched and grew as if in an invisible mold of a human being. The woman's face beamed back at the stunned expression Alex wore as he lost his hound form, reverting to that of a man.

Trembling, the warrior dropped the sword, and it clattered to the ground. He reached to embrace her. His big strong arms passed through the ethereal body like smoke. The immediate disappointment prompted a look of consoling from his love's lingering soul. His head hung in defeat, and her hands moved to his cheeks, as if to lift it back up.

He looked up in response, sorrow in his expression. The energy of her form warmed his chilled skin. They could not touch, though they were so close.

The familiar spirit's smile returned. Her lips moved, echoing words flowing out. He could not interpret them at first, but his spirit understood, and his mind caught up. Tears that formed and fell were lost in the rain. Alex smiled and did not grieve any longer.

"I know," he choked out in reply. "You always were, Honey Bee."

Emily wanted to cry as she lit up and laughed, joy and love radiating from her. The brighter she shone, the harder it was to discern her transparent shape. When the white glow dissipated, she was gone, crossed over to the other side until the day they were fated to be together again.

With her gone, Alex remembered that Oryn was gravely injured. He had collapsed unconscious by a ruined building. Gathering up and hauling him to the town hall was difficult – not because he was heavy, but because the deep wounds opened in places, his fingers unintentionally taking hold by them. A river of red and bubbles trailed behind and streaked the floorboards inside the main hall.

Laying him near the entrance on a table, which he swept clear of ornaments in one go, the Marine checked for a pulse. It was barely there. Ripping a curtain off a rod to use as a blanket, the dying knight's fluids soaked through. There was nothing Alex could do. He needed Adwen.

Running for the door and outside again, his vision swam. The world around him bent and shifted, distorting. It made him queasy, and he thought he might be sick. Warm energy fluctuated in his chest. Desperation compelled him to keep running. Adwen was just down the stairs. Just as he spotted her, he staggered, tripped and fell. His head smacked onto the cobbled stones, turning distorted surroundings to black.

Alex smelled wet stone and crisp dawn air. His nose and ears siphoned in the surroundings more clearly than ever in his life as he slowly regained consciousness. It felt as if he had only just been born and that the world was brand new. A groggy dog growl vibrated in his throat. The surprise and confusion of it woke him faster. The colors and details were far beyond what was possible before he had managed to knock himself out. It was as if his eyes were that of a hawk.

While lifting himself from the ground, he saw that his hands were human, but also that his dragon leather clothes were gone. Instead, he was covered in thick armor over most of his body. It hung more heavily on his chest, back and neck, rising higher behind his head. Alex took a moment to marvel at the discovery. Then he snapped out of it and looked for Adwen. She was gone.

In his rush back to where he left Oryn, the power newly infused into his body propelled him faster than ever. More useful was the strength to stop on a dime without toppling over when he entered and find Adwen. Her back was to him, gingerly approaching the bloody knight's remains. His razor-sharp hearing picked up her shuddering, hesitant breaths. He did not dare move or break the silence.

Fear held her fluttery heart. She could not sense Oryn. Even before they had become connected through the unwritten pact, Oryn had a presence she could feel. It was gone, and the realization filled her with disbelief on the verge of maddening heartbreak. He was so still. Eyes glazing with tears, Adwen reached to touch the gaping wound across Oryn's chest. There was a hollow hope that she would feel his presence if she placed her hand near his heart.

His hand clutched hers, making her gasp and her heart leap. Tears trailed down her smiling cheeks. Sobs of relief choked a soft laugh.

It took great effort to move and then some more to open his eyes. Each breath was so shallow that his chest did not move. Dim, emerald eyes searched and soon found hers. His expression echoed her joyous relief.

Alex was relieved too. Remembering Jack's warning, it seemed the tender moment needed to be cut short. His voice echoed in the quiet hall.

"It is sunrise," Alex said. "Jack told us he would send the knights back if we did not show by this point."

Watching Oryn succumb and fall into unconsciousness again, Adwen slipped his hand into hers and refused to let go.

More insistently, Alex prompted, "Adwen."

"He would have sensed when I was safe again. The knights are still with him. Call out. Let Jack know to lead them into the fort."

Tempted to ask what she meant, Alex decided that this was not the time to ask for clarification. He would decipher her commands on his own.

Leaving the hall for the cobbled square, the Marine struggled to understand what he was supposed to do. Call out? Then he felt like a true jarhead and was thankful his comedic friend was not here to tell him so.

Alex, now a fully ascended Holy Hound, took a breath and let loose a beastly call. It carried for miles to where their company patiently waited.

Chapter 15
GOOD INTENTIONS

It was funny for Jack, leading a small army on a march. Of the many strange things he had experienced, it felt stranger than anything else. The comparison was what made the instance so amusing. After hearing the call that could only have been Oryn, the roguish Holy Hound took the lead astride Adwen's horse, steadily marching to the gates. Thankfully, the patronizing animal disliked him so much that he refused to speak. That suited Jack just fine. He understood now why Adwen thought her mount was so irritating.

Stopping the company at the closed gate, Jack heard movement in the watchman's post overhead. Merrily, he called out, "Who goes up there! Having a little trouble, Jarhead? I know it's you. Cujo would have had that open a while ago. Take your time. We're in no rush."

Some of the knights chuckled, and others rolled their eyes.

Fumbling and swearing echoed downward. Alex could not figure out how to open the gate.

A knight shouted with a smile, "The lever!"

"Which one?"

"The one that is pointed up!" Raucous laughter rolled amongst the men when the knight demonstrated with a rude gesture that Alex could not see.

The sound of a small thud and rattling chains announced the activation of the mechanism. An outer metal gate rose high as two wooden doors parted inward. Jovial cheers and claps widened Jack's clever grin. It was entertaining to have a jarhead on the team.

As they entered, giving everyone except Jack a shock, the blond warrior jumped from the tower to the nearest rooftop then down beside them. The knights did not recognize him at first. Jack, however, was pleasantly surprised.

Looking over the enhanced appearance and magical armor, Jack could not help but laugh. "Well, look at you! You're a real Holy Hound now! Nice pointy ears, buddy. What do Adwen and Oryn think?"

His friend was especially silent and stared with a stern expression.

Opening his mind in order to read Alex's, Jack froze. Snapping out of the daze, he turned and shouted into the company, "Where are the healers! Get the healers to the town hall right now! Move it!"

When the healers rushed in to find Oryn, Adwen had no choice but to let them do their work. He would live, thanks to their speedy treatment and her advice to take him into the sunshine. Her dearest friend needed rest for a day. They also needed to move on. After having scouts salvage herbs and healing agents from abandoned shops, Adwen climbed back on her horse to continue the mission.

Adwen and her forces passed through the next town. It was small and empty. No demons or humans, living or dead, were to be found. Quickening the pace of their journey, she desperately wanted to find survivors. On the way, the hope steadily faded.

In the next town away from Fort Redu, the dwindling hope renewed tenfold. A gathering of farmers, shopkeepers and many others flooded out to meet them. They poured out their thanks for rescue, some asking for news. Anticipating this bombardment beforehand, Adwen smiled and quietly allowed ranking knights to answer questions on her behalf. This was a great relief.

But her thoughts were with Oryn, lying on a cart at the back of the caravan. The sun shone strong through the day, closing his wounds. When he had briefly awoken before leaving the fort, the knight had said he would only let the healers keep him until nightfall. The hours waned into evening as she sat atop her now quiet stallion, observing as Oryn left the cart beyond the heads of the milling humans.

While Oryn strode closer, she smelled a familiar scent. Upwind, Adwen caught a glimpse of a big man and two small boys. Domus did not see her, as he was too busy discussing important information with one of her leading knights. The urge to call out to Collin and Remy struck her, but Oryn was already at her side. Greeting them could wait till later.

As she nimbly dismounted, Oryn saw that she wore a happy expression, yet he detected an air of gloom. Oryn smiled instead of asking questions.

Adwen asked, "How are you?"

"The healers with us are skilled, and some rarer supplies found in the fort sped my recovery. I am weakened but no longer injured. What of you?"

Maintaining the appearance of relief for as long as possible, she replied, "Alexander did very well when he saved me ... again. I wasn't hurt at all, thanks to his quick thinking."

Oryn frowned. "The valiant act is muddied by the way in which you came into danger. I assume you see no point in retribution?"

"Not really, no."

Smiling, he shook his head.

"The camp is set, and you need a meal," she told him. "There are too many people. Bring some rations to my tent if you want peace and quiet as much as I do."

He nodded. "At your command." His smile never faded.

Tamis found himself lost amidst the crowded village folk and knights. Sunset stained the sky with pleasant warm washes of orange, gold and magenta. Tired after rough travel for three days, the young man tried to find Sir Jack and Sir Alexander. They had told him to use only their names, but it did not seem right.

"Sir Jack!" He shouted, meandering about between tents and carts loaded with essentials. "Sir Alexander!"

"Over here, Tammy! Hurry up while the food is warm!"

Finding them both by a fire with a Gargoyle and some knights, Tamis huffed and puffed from running as he sat down. "Why did you call me that?"

"I thought it was appropriate to give you a nickname like my other friends," Jack chuckled. "Tammy fits you, kid."

His brow furrowed. "But that is a girl's name. It makes me

feel odd."

Tossing a sly glance, the warrior replied, "Now you know how I feel when you call me Sir Jack. We aren't knights. Just our broody green-eyed friend is, or was. Call him Sir all you want."

"I see. My apologies, Sir ... I mean, I'm sorry, Jack."

The Holy Hound ruffled Tamis's rusty-brown hair, making it even messier. "No problem. Cooked a small steak for ya."

When he was handed a wooden plate, the boy finally noticed a piece of meat hovering over the flames like a moth. Staring in astonishment, his wide eyes followed the flying steak on its path to his platter.

Those gathered by the fire to watch Jack's antics chuckled.

Tamis was famished to the point of having shaky hands. Stomach growling, his dull knife barely cut through, forcing out cooked red juices, pooling out from the serving. "This is not cooked, Jack. It is almost raw!"

The two Holy Hounds exchanged entertained looks.

"You will get used to it."

Abashed at first, Tamis suddenly realized what Jack had meant, sending a chill down his spine. "Oh. Well, I suppose you are right."

Alex shook his head. "Jack, just finish cooking it for the kid. He doesn't have to start now. Let him enjoy his normal taste buds while they last."

"All right. I've had my fun anyhow."

Tamis was making a cut into the partially seared flesh when it drifted off lazily into the hottest part of the flames. Fat and fluids snapped and spat in the crackling fire, as if in protest of the steak becoming well done.

Silence hung over the few around the fire, listening to the music of the burning wood and hypnotized by the performance of the dancing heat.

The young warrior was becoming fearful of what he would go through to become Adwen's fourth warrior. To forget for a while, curiosity served as a decent distraction.

"Jack? I heard others say that we will be returning to the Order on the morrow. Are we not going to search the last towns nearby?"

"Don't need to. The leader of these survivors gathered them here to wait for help. These are the last living people on this side of the kingdom. It's time to get back to the fortress safely."

Drawing another question from the many on his mind, Tamis asked, "Do you know why Adwen cannot sleep soundly through the night? She wakes crying out."

It was too late to shush Tamis. Jack wished he had been reading the boy's mind and had stopped him. None of the knights knew about the seriousness of Adwen's condition or what it was, let alone how it came about. If the wrong people knew that her blackened left hand was demon flesh, it could cause panic. Jack puffed in disappointment. "That's complicated, kid. I'll tell that story later."

Suspicious murmurs flashed in the minds of the others, and Jack could hear now that he let his mind open to them. Damage control was necessary. Not being able to sleep soundly was a known sign of dark influence. Only Tamis was naive of that fact.

"Fine. None of you heard this from me. It's really personal." Now that he had the audience's attention, he explained, "Adwen is originally from the other world of the living, where almost no magic exists. Her family is from there; they *were* from there. To hurt Adwen, the demon named Guillot hunted down her entire family line. When this war is over, there will be no one waiting to welcome her home. They killed them all."

This fact laid bare put all concerns to rest.

Tamis turned his somber gaze back to the fire. "I have no one either. My family is gone, too. Nightmares make it very hard to sleep. I wonder what I could have done better to keep my mother alive."

"Cut that out," Jack chided. At seeing Tamis's hurt reaction, he added, "Control is an illusion. No one really has control of anything, least of all someone else's life. None of what happened to you or your mom was your fault. Got it, kid?"

Alex shocked everyone when he spoke up, wearing a wry smile. "Took me a long while to figure that out. Most of us are in the same boat. Jack here is the only one of us who has somebody waiting."

Laughing, Jack shook his head. "Ashley is going to kill me when I finally show up again. She's patient but hates to wait."

Jack finished cooking the steak for Tamis, who ate it with great enthusiasm. For an hour or two, stories circled the campfire, intermittent laughter radiating as much warmth. Though the young man laughed and smiled with the others, a nagging need to do something for Adwen eventually pulled him away. He took a walk to sort out muddled thoughts.

It was an odd feeling, not having his ill mother to care for after a small lifetime doing so. He could not remember not providing for someone. He felt incomplete without that task. Finally an idea struck him: He should give Adwen a gift. Tamis thought that if he could find something to show his appreciation, her heart would surely lighten, as his mother's always had.

Seeking out the refugees, the young man kindly asked if there was anything to spare as a gift for the Tame One. Most people had very little; many had nothing. Those who had an item of value to spare did not have what Tamis deemed appropriate for his new leader. This gift needed to show thanks in an eloquent way that was beyond his taste – something like what he used to spy in shop windows but could never afford.

Huddled by a tiny fire that the wind could blow out if it were strong enough, an old man in rags warmed his gnarled fingers. Tamis doubted that this poor stranger could be of help, but he knew anything was possible. Approaching the lone figure, the eager boy humbly spoke up.

"Pardon me, sir. My name is Tamis, and I need help finding something to give to show my thanks to someone."

The stranger continued to warm himself without as much as a glance. "You are a sweet child. I have few things with me. All of them are precious."

"Please, sir. I have no possessions at all, and my service is already pledged. I must find something else to offer to thank the Tame One."

Somewhat surprised, he thin old man replied, "The Tame One? That would have to be a gift of some value. You say you've already pledged yourself to her service? Then that should be enough, do you not think?"

"No." Tamis was determined. "I must give more. She deserves more."

The stranger pondered. "Then I suppose I can part ways with my most valuable token if it is for the Tame One."

As the old man stood, he did not seem as feeble as he looked. Leaning slightly on a tall walking stick with a dark rock on the top, the stranger faced Tamis at last. His face was weathered and looked almost lifeless. One eye was milky white, probably blind. The faint smile revealed a few rotten teeth.

Tamis secretly thanked the stars that this man had not smiled wider, or he might feel sick. Disguising the discomfort at meeting the vagabond, Tamis pressed, "Thank you, kind sir. What is it?"

After the stranger reached into a ratty satchel, a gleam of glass caught Tamis's attention.

"A bottle?"

Slightly offended, the vagabond corrected the boy. "A bottle? My dear lad, what I hold is a rare bottle of Margierena Blum that is aged more than thirty years! When I lost my fortune, it was one of the few things kept from tax collectors. Take it. My tongue is all shriveled. I could not hope to taste all of the notes in this delicacy."

Tamis was not sure if Adwen liked to drink. For a moment he paused, considering the wine.

"Take it, lad. Quickly before I reconsider. It's worth a small fortune that I'd likely squander."

"Many thanks to you, sir. This is a grand offering. I can never repay your kindness. What is your name so that I can tell her whom to thank?"

"Oh, that's not necessary, lad. Forget me and go. Give the Tame One this fine gift. Is it really that important to say where you got it?"

Perhaps not, Tamis thought. "Thank you. May the Light Spirits watch over you, sir."

The vagabond smiled kindly as Tamis departed. Then the little warmth in the expression chilled to a dead, vacant stare and an insidious sneer. "Light Spirits. They can keep their blighted blessings."

Oryn waited until everyone received rations before claiming a morsel for himself. With a raw cut wrapped in cloth, he was on his way to join Adwen when Tamis found him. He appeared in a hurry.

"Sir Oryn!"

"What is the matter?"

"Where is the Tame One? I have something for her."

Spying the bottle immediately, he inclined an eyebrow. "It would be best to keep it safe for now. Present it to her later when we return to the Order. She is in poor spirits at the moment and undue offerings give her discomfort."

Tamis was becoming anxious. "But I must give it to her sooner. I'm certain it would cheer her at least a little."

Oryn shook his head. "Gifts humble her, Tamis. This is simply not a good time."

Holding it out to the knight, he urged, "Please, sir. Then do me a small service in giving it to her now and end my wait. It will drive me to madness keeping a glass thing from breaking on the road. If it would humble her, then I shall wait to tell her that it was from me. Please, Sir Oryn."

Taking it to inspect the label, the year and origin astonished him. "How did you happen across something rarer than a phoenix? Where did you get it?"

Keeping true to the helpful stranger's wishes, he answered, "One of the kindest villagers gave it to me. I told him the gift was intended for her, and he was glad to help."

Oryn grew suspicious but knew Tamis was sincere. "As you ask, I shall present it to her. Go about your business with the others. I'm certain Jack has more wild tales to tell."

This pleased the teen greatly. "Thank you. Thank you, Sir Oryn. Good evening, sir."

Heaving a sigh and taking another look at the wine label, it occurred to him that even if the wine were poisoned it would not matter. Mortal toxins were of no concern. The only real threat was if the contents turned out not to be authentic. But if it were really the rarest wine in Dargadia, this was a very special treat.

The interior of Adwen's tent was comfortably spacious.

Red cloth shut out the autumn forest, giving her a chance to think. While she waited, she pondered. Possibilities buzzed in her head, weighing on her heart with increasing pressure. The reality of what had almost occurred before dawn lapped at her mind as a tide of worry crashing on a shore of self-doubt. What would she have done if Oryn had never woken up?

His footsteps alerted her before his hand parted the tent flap. From where she sat, Adwen was contented to observe the knight joining her. He took a seat at a table on the other side of the tent, deliberately setting a bottle of wine in clear view before unwrapping a cut of beef.

Neither spoke as he ate. He used a fork and knife for an eloquent change of pace from the normal ripping and tearing with carnivorous jaws. As the last morsels disappeared, she broke the silence.

Her tone was somber. "You almost died today."

Oryn paused before folding the bloody cloth over the utensils.

"I can't stop thinking about that," she said. "It won't get out of my head."

Finally meeting her gaze, he was resolute. "Yet I did not die. This was not the first occasion in which either of us cheated death. You have done so more often than I have. To dwell on these incidents is to distract oneself from the goals ahead."

She was quiet.

Oryn frowned, recognizing where this was leading. "What of this truly bothers you? Speak of it plainly with me."

More than ever the heavy feeling weighed her down. She leaned to the side, head in her good hand. "I thought you were dead. Now I'm asking myself what I would have done if you really were."

After watching her, Oryn deemed it reasonable to uncork the bottle. Twisting the small dinner knife with his powerful fingers into a spiral, he turned it into an acceptable tool. Popping the stopper free, the bittersweet aromas wafted out, and a draft circulated it throughout the tent.

As he poured two glasses and went to give one to Adwen, he replied, "As a knight for the Order, I saw many lives come to an end. Most were great losses. I knew that after each death my purpose would remain the same." Returning to his chair, he added morosely, "The one time that differed was with you."

Adwen looked up from the crimson liquid at him.

"Until you returned to us, all purpose for me had gone. There was nothing else this world held that I wanted. Not even vengeance."

"The vengeance for your twin brother?"

Oryn nodded.

Her gaze parted. "Purpose. My own purpose feels hollow now. I was sent back to the living worlds as a ghost in my living skin. The only thing I exist for is to restore balance. Even if I wanted to, any kind of life worth living is out of reach. I don't have a family anymore, and I can't even start another. After this war is over, and if we succeed, there will just be another. This intended purpose of mine has no conclusion where I have what I want. World peace is a delusion. It's an unobtainable wish, like all of my own dead dreams."

Longing to temper her depression, she imbibed a portion of the glass. The flavor was savory, sweet, and the sensation of liquid silk flowed down her throat with pleasant warmth.

Adwen's words earned Oryn's sympathy. Thinking deeply, he took a sip of wine. The pinnacle of perfection in flavor pleased his senses, helping him in his search for the proper words to say.

"My master was likely the wisest knight to grace the Order's halls. I cast his ashes to the sea myself. While he was alive, the knowledge he imparted did not always influence my choices. In the past year his wisdom has begun to take hold in me. I once made a similar observation as yours: that the struggle against monsters and war was an eternal one with no end; that peace was fictional."

Looking up again, feeling tired, she asked, "What did he tell you?"

"He said that peace was sought by many and seldom found, because too many fools think it exists in the world to be obtained. Strife and peace are first found in the hearts of the people. True peace, regardless of the actions of others, is only ever found within one's heart."

She let his words sink in. A meager smile tugged at the corners of her lips. "Thank you."

He returned the expression as his eyelids became heavy. Rubbing them, Oryn returned his empty glass to the table.

"I'm tired, too," she said. "This time I think I'm going to try staying awake. I'm not in the mood to wake up from the implanted visions again. My heart can't take it."

"No," he insisted. "The sun cannot restore you enough to allow that luxury. Sleep is the only other way for you to replenish strength."

He was correct. She wanted to cry but refused to let herself. "If you say so."

For the journey, a large cot was offered to her. But she accepted only a soft rug on a hard surface. Mattresses remained uncomfortable in comparison. She found a satisfying spot to rest and closed her eyes.

Oryn watched for a time and considered the chair. His usual reason for sleeping in a seat was to be more effective at rising if a threat arrived. Surrounded by many knights, a few Gargoyles as well as two capable warriors, the current threats to Adwen were her nightmares and despair. His sitting at a distance in the past evenings did not provide enough comfort to her. Just this once, he would be within reach when she awoke in tears. Tonight, for her, he would set knightly standards aside.

Joining her side on the wooden bed and plush rug, Oryn lay down. At her back, he was close enough to smell her long silvery white hair. The sound of her breathing indicated that she already had fallen asleep. All the better, he thought. It was not important that she know he slept alongside, so long as she could find him in her panicked waking. He would then pretend to remain asleep and let her draw from his warmth. His final thought before his heavy eyes closed was a wish to take her nightmares away, if he could.

Hours rolled by. Strong light from the four moons shone on the encampment. Knights on watch with Gargoyle companions patrolled in the cool night air. The rest of the residents and travelers barely stirred.

Pale light made the inside of the unlit crimson tent glow in soft shades of violet. Adwen's unfinished glass of wine by her chair sat still, until the contents began to slowly swirl. A maroon glow lit in the liquid, activated by the light of the moons outside. The rich rare wine laced with a flavorless secret ingredient churned faster until the glass itself moved from the mounting force, toppling over. Grass cushioned the fragile cup, but the liquids seeped into the ground and disappeared. Meanwhile, the bottle on the table was far more stable as its glow intensified.

Adwen's eyes opened gradually, awake yet unseeing. A powerful trance held her in both sleep and dreamlike alertness. Unaware of her actions, primal senses guided her moves. The scent of the person beside her grabbed her utmost attention.

Turning to find him, she gazed distantly and unblinkingly, watching as his emerald eyes opened as well. The same powerful trance had trapped him too. There was a brief moment when their stares locked. Neither woke or wavered in their state. Then as she crashed upon him like a tidal wave, both were lost completely to the spell.

In the night, soft breezes came and went. Tree branches brushed, leaves blushed with the season's colors, touching. Yet another breeze came, the edges quivered in a simplistic dance. Limbs like arms folded, grazing each other. The quivering paused only briefly, until the wind instigated further movement.

Crisp air bore dew, like small diamonds on limb and leaf. A chill in the early hour under the moonlit sky made droplets gleam as they ran, dampening surfaces and making them glisten. Over a limpid pool, a crystalline drop tumbled down. Breaking the mirror surface, it vanished, rings of dark and light rushing in its wake, making the moon faces quake and shiver.

In the seclusion of the tent, Oryn leaned lower to kiss her neck again, her face turned away in elation. Before his lips could touch, her body froze and became like a star. Her form disappeared into itself, leaving just a shapeless light.

He stared, motionless under the influence of strong magic, watching vine-like streams of golden light reaching up. The many shining threads bound him, then reached into him. For a moment there was a crushing pain. He gasped as holes were torn into his body and soul over and over again. No blood came from any point where Adwen's light pierced his body, turning his flesh into a transparent emerald green. A rush of power from her struck Oryn and almost shattered him from existence.

Instead, his body became like hers, a celestial nova, floating weightlessly. His green light threatened to flicker out as hers pulsed. But soon, his gained strength, brightening. Seconds later, both pulsed in unison, perfectly in time. A flash from both burst outward, and their physical bodies returned, though both were different than before.

Oryn blinked in the gloom. The spell weakened as it neared its end. His vision began to fade as he gazed down at a slumbering Adwen. Again, he attempted to kiss her neck, but the world turned to black, and he fell unconscious beside her.

Chapter 16
PARTING

Shortly after sunrise, Adwen woke. The first thing she knew was the dull pressure in her head. It ached, pounding as she stirred, blinking blearily. Turning over to pick herself up, the effort resulted in her stumbling off of her sleeping place onto all fours. Confused and distracted by the great discomfort, as the pressure gradually ebbed, Adwen realized why she had failed in the attempt to stand.

Her hands were large paws. Shocked into alertness, she tried to transform into her woman form. When no amount of focus could change her shape, alarm turned to panic, and she yelped loudly.

The high-pitched sound snapped Oryn awake. He sat upright, then clutched his own aching head in his hands, now fitted with intimidating clawed gauntlets. His chest and legs were covered in thick plated armor, though he did not yet take notice. He growled at the throbbing inside his skull and looked to see what was making Adwen yelp and whine.

Through clenched teeth and fangs, he asked, "What is going on?" Oryn disliked this situation more by the second, knowing that this headache was not from a harmless hangover.

Frantically looking herself over and closing her eyes tightly, focusing, she whimpered, "I'm stuck like this! I can't change."

The news stunned him. "What? Why?"

"I don't know," she yelped. "This could happen only if I had done something wrong. I haven't lost my power, but I'm trapped."

Oryn was going to say something but decided to just massage his face, grimacing and waiting for the pain to fade. The pressure in Adwen's head finally went away. As it did, streams of memories flooded in. Detailed recollections of skin, lips and sweat made her heart race madly. Ears folding back, tail tucked in fright and alarm, Adwen's wide, dilated stare locked unblinkingly on the knight.

His headache nearly dispelled after a long, tense silence, Oryn stole a glance at her stunned expression. How she crouched fearfully was confusing.

Wishing she would simply speak up, he muttered, "What? Say what it is and be done with it." Adwen said nothing, so he returned to rubbing his temples. It seemed to do some good.

A flash of a memory struck him, catching the air in his lungs, and he froze. His eyes widened, and the pain in his head was steadily replaced by memories of the evening. He thought to look at Adwen but could not. Shame made Oryn's chest tighten, forcing out a single wheezing cough. How could he have let this happen?

A long whine escaped Adwen in the stillness. "I think I know what happened."

Oryn averted his gaze from hers, mortified. In his mind, he had violated her. Worse still, he had no explanation for his actions in the night.

Adwen began to pace. "This is not good. Why did this happen?"

In the process of looking away from her enormous canine form, his sights fell on the table and his empty glass. No longer feeling lowly and ashamed, seeing the partially full wine bottle made him growl. Suspicious, Oryn got up and went to investigate.

She noticed and followed, watching as he sniffed the open bottle. Filling his glass again to study the contents, a strange substance that had not been there yesterday sank to the bottom. The curdled sediment separated from the beverage, flickering with a bright pink and maroon glow.

The enraged knight worked his jaw and scowled at the expired magic potion.

Oryn firmly set aside the glass and snatched up the bottle, crushing it in his powerful grasp. While he seethed in silence, red dripping from his gauntlet, Adwen waited until he was a bit calmer to speak.

"Where did that wine come from, Oryn?"

His fists clenched. "Tamis."

"What? No. He wouldn't."

"He was obviously an unwitting participant in this trickery."

"Where did he get it?"

"I intend to find out."

Adwen watched him storm off and whimpered, "Good idea."

Once free of the tent and after taking a few paces, Oryn came to a stop and gasped. Free of her gaze, he allowed himself to feel uncertainty, staring frightened at the muddy ground. Never had he thought he could be used in such a way – to cause Adwen harm. Someone had sent this wicked token. That fact aided him in regaining his composure. Standing smartly with hands folded at his back, he let out a sharp and decisive bark, calling Jack and Alex.

By the time both warriors came running, the expression he wore was irritated, but otherwise unreadable.

"What's up, Cujo? Is something happening?"

Keeping his mind blank in Jack's presence, Oryn coolly replied, "Where is Tamis?"

Both companions exchanged glances, and Alex answered. "He's asleep alongside some knights."

"Fetch him."

Pausing to share another confused look with Jack, Alex turned to go. "Roger that."

Moving to stand by the surly knight and wait, the short warrior raised an eyebrow. "So, what's going on? Cat got your tongue?"

Oryn paid no attention to the prompt.

Trying to read Oryn's thoughts proved useless. Jack grew more suspicious. "Where's Adwen?"

"Alone in her quarters."

Staring shrewdly, Jack said, "I'm half tempted to poke you in the head and see what you're hiding up there. Tell me what has you so edgy."

The knight refused to speak.

Rolling his eyes, it did not surprise him in the slightest. "Whatever. I can wait." A moment went by, and a breeze passed under Jack's sensitive nose. An odd odor caught his attention, making him frown. "What's that?"

Taking a split second to watch as Jack sniffed about, Oryn

swiftly realized what the smell was and blanched. Before the fellow Holy Hound could see the shock on his face, he hid it and returned to being stoic.

Jack found his inability to identify the scent frustrating. "What is that smell?"

Oryn tried to change the subject. "Was the night without incident?"

"Huh? Last night was boring. Everybody was tired and hit the hay early and ... What is that smell? I know that smell."

Again, Oryn did not remark.

Tossing an even more suspicious look, Jack was fed up with not knowing. "If you won't tell me what is happening, then I'll ask her."

Faster than a blink, Oryn blocked Jack's path to the tent with an outstretched arm. "She does not wish to be disturbed." Then Jack began to sniff at Oryn, and the knight jerked back, sneering dangerously.

Jack was thoroughly confused at this point. The same unidentified scent that was on his companion also emanated from the tent. Glancing between both sources, Jack's eyes shifted to and fro more quickly as the identity of the odor became clear. When the knight grew angrier, Jack knew.

The thought was too shocking. "Wow! Hold on, now. No, way. You didn't."

Oryn snapped with a snarl, "Keep quiet. This cannot be known."

More stunned to receive a confession, Jack chuckled. "You did. I don't believe this. I have to know what she thinks."

A ravenous snarl burst from inside the tent. "Shut up, Jack!"

He stared in silence. This pleased Oryn, but it was not meant to last.

Jack was confused again and furtively whispered, "Was it really that bad?"

At first the question angered the knight. Then thinking on it quelled his rage and he became contemplative. "Actually ..."

Another angry bark silenced them both. Not even Jack dared to test what she would do at this level of aggravation.

Alex returned with Tamis in tow. "You wished to see me,

Sir Oryn?"

Stern and stony as ever, the knight studied the young man. "When last we spoke, do you recall what you gave me?"

Tamis wondered where this was leading. "Have I done something wrong?"

"What did you present to me, boy? Answer."

"A bottle of wine, sir."

Jack caught wind of Oryn's thoughts. Making the connection between the present conversation and the knight's partial confession, the cop put his hands on his hips and shook his head ruefully. The situation no longer held the entertainment it did before.

"Aw, kid. You've blown it, big time. Who gave you the bottle?" A glimpse into Tamis's surface thoughts presented an image. "Was it the creepy old man?"

Adwen growled as she exited the tent. "What old man?"

The three stared, stunned to see her in her beast form. No one spoke, and Oryn still could not look at her out of self-loathing.

Tamis could only hear animal sounds, unable to decipher the meaning. He did notice a threatening gesture was directed at him. "Tame One! Have I done this? Forgive me. I did not know."

"Why are you like this?" Jack growled in animal speech to be covert.

"Because I'm forbidden from doing certain things. What's happened to me is a punishment, an equivalent of a firm slap on the wrist."

"For how long?"

"A week or so." Adwen paused to throw her youngest warrior a vicious snarl, "Or until I mark him. Whichever comes first will set me free."

Alex barked in annoyance, joining the bestial conversation. "What the hell is going on?"

Everyone stopped to stare and said nothing for different reasons.

Jack, however, approached and spoke in an exaggerated condescending tone. "Calm down. Do as I do and take in a deep breath through the nose. Then slowly exhale." He demonstrated for emphasis.

The Marine was very annoyed but was not above following along. After taking in a big whiff, the same odor that perplexed Jack reached Alex, too. Recognizing it in seconds, he noted the expressions on Adwen's and Oryn's faces.

Eyes wide, he said only, "Oh!"

"Okay, now that you've finally joined us on the issue, we need to find out who gave Tamis the spiked wine."

Alex still was processing the information. "Halt just a minute! Did you two do what I think you did?"

"They were drugged, Jarhead."

"Wow!"

"That's what I said. Anyway, we need to find a super creepy stranger giving out goodies to unsuspecting kids. Right, Tammy?"

Tamis hung his head, feeling as big as a thimble.

"Where did you meet him?" Oryn demanded.

He pointed north. "At the edge of the people's camp by the trees, sir."

"What would you have us do, Adwen? I advise that Jack, Alex and I take Tamis to seek out this insidious beggar."

"Go. I will stay here. For now, I'm practically useless. I have my light powers but can't use any of them."

"If we find nothing, our return shall be swift. If we uncover who is behind this, it shall take as long as necessary."

"Be careful out there, you guys. I don't like the way this smells."

From the point where Tamis showed them the small smoldered campfire, Oryn took the lead. The scent trail left by the stranger was disconcerting. The knight hid his unease from the boy, as did the others. The strong smell was of dead skin, but much stronger was the scent of dark magic.

Jack was not as concerned, confident in their combined strength. "Why isn't she allowed to do it? That makes no sense to me, Cujo. She isn't hurting anyone."

"She is simply forbidden, Jack. Keep quiet. We could be heard by whomever we are tracking."

"Think about this: What if there's a little one of you running around about nine months from now? Imagine you as a father."

Oryn stopped cold. Resentment for himself and remorse for Adwen swelled in his chest. "It can never be."

"Why not?"

"When she traveled alone into the mountains she learned of her nature. Her one purpose is to serve and protect. She also confided in me that when the Light Spirits transformed her into a spirit, they had also stricken her barren in the process. No amount of hoping or wishing can change that fact."

Jack sensed how much this hurt him. It seemed the right time to try to cheer Oryn up a bit. "Well, at least you got to have a good time, at least once."

Outrage flared within the knight, making him roar and transform.

Alex instinctively grabbed hold of Tamis and brought him along as he flattened to the ground. Jack's eyes bulged at seeing Oryn change in a split second into an enhanced hound form. Now two feet taller and his sword broader with a spiny hand guard, the enormous Holy Hound twirled and lashed out, narrowly missing Jack by inches. The blade slashed through a nearby tree, felling it in one swing.

As it crashed down just behind, Jack shouted. "Hey! Get a grip on yourself! You almost killed us, not to mention Tamis!"

Oryn's wrinkled jowls gnashed overhead, giving Jack pause. "Do you not understand? I was used as a weapon against her! I take no joy from that knowledge. The memories are too tainted to relish."

Recovering his nerve, Jack stared down the titanic beast twice his height. "That wasn't your fault, but it's also no secret to me that what happened last night was something both of you have wanted for a while. Forget the bad and salvage what you can. What's driving you crazy right now is that you can't reconcile between the cause and the result! You did not do anything wrong. Forgive yourself already!"

The words sunk in but did not faze Oryn. Bringing in his sword, which was now a hand-and-a-half blade, the tip grazed Jack's leather breastplate.

The cop remained unflinching. "Okay, let me just add one more thing: What happened between you two gave you a huge amount of power and made you very angry at the same time.

Whoever is responsible has made a big mistake."

Reverting to his elf-like form, Oryn leaned in until his nose almost touched Jack's. He sneered, "No truer words have ever escaped your oversized mouth."

Nearby clapping ended the confrontation, drawing their attention to an opening amid a dead stand of trees. Tamis recognized the old man, his staff rested in the crook of his arm, smiling.

"That's him," Tamis murmured.

Even from downwind, dark magic wafted over, putting the group on full alert.

Taking up his staff, the stranger spoke, clearly entertained. "You Conrads have always had strange tastes in women." Something more than anger was in Oryn's gaze. "You know who I am, don't you, Sir Oryn Reynard Conrad?"

"Who is this creep?" Jack growled.

"He is supposed to be dead. This is a sorcerer; the same who forged the first werewolves, including Sycan himself."

As a shiver ran up their spines, a chortle came in reply. "Oh, ho! An astute historian. Rather charming to see you know of me by that accomplishment. My name is Ozovath. But did you know that I am the reason you are so alone? Your family is cursed – cursed to fail and fade away. You will be the last of your family line."

Oryn sneered. The vile shadow of a man was baiting. He whispered to Tamis, "Flee back to camp. Do not linger. Go."

The young man took a last glance at the evil man and began to run. When he was out of sight, Tamis stopped and stayed to see if they would defeat the sorcerer.

"Shall I tell you what's happened to you, Oryn?"

Jack retorted, "No, but you can tell us what you want and get it over with, dirt-bag."

Ozovath scoffed. "I've heard better slanders over the centuries. Fortunately, my mood is gracious today. What transpired after you tasted of the wine was no mere incident of copulation. To a spirit such as Adwen, it is a ritual. If the soul of one is not strong enough or is impure, they will be rent apart. But if they survive, the souls are forever bound. In your case, your soul was put through her fire and emerged whole. In return for passing such a measure, you have been granted as much power as your living form can bear to carry." The wicked, withered sorcerer chuckled darkly.

"Then why are you still laughing?" Alex asked guardedly.

"Because it does not matter. I have come for her, and nothing you can do will stop me."

Jack snarled at Oryn. "What are you waiting for? Kill him!'

"It's a trap," he rumbled back. "He's attempting to goad us."

Then Ozovath called out sadistically, "Oh, Jack? Look what I have here." Summoning a sphere of smoke, the sorcerer waved his wrinkly fingers about, melodically speaking. "Where, oh, where can Ashley be? Where, oh, where has she gone? Ah. There she is."

The cop's face flushed white at seeing his wife unpacking their pickup. She was nearly finished taking her belongings into a hotel.

"Oh! So she did go north, just as you asked. A pity she will be so easy to find."

In a flash, Jack transformed and lunged, daggers out. "Bastard!"

Oryn tried to stop him. "Jack, no!"

Using the ancient staff, Ozovath shot a black orb that crackled and sparked. It hit the black-and-white Holy Hound square in the muzzle. A burst of darkness swallowed the warrior, and he disappeared into thin air with a loud crack like thunder.

The two remaining warriors flinched and recoiled, summoning their weapons.

Right away, a second spell orb flew, and it was aimed for the Marine. Oryn and Alex dove aside to avoid the dark magic, but the mysterious ball arched after him. The blond warrior turned in time to be struck in the chest and yelped before disappearing as well.

Panting and snarling, Oryn's gaze snapped from where his companion had vanished and toward the smiling sorcerer. Retreat was not a viable option. After seeing Alex's attempt to elude the magic, he knew there was no escape. Ready to test his new strength and the power of his blade, he roared and leaped. When the next spell came flying in, his sword edge caught the dark orb. For an instant, the spell was held back, but it burst and enveloped him just the same.

With the three Holy Hounds captured, Ozovath sighed contentedly and turned to go. Humming merrily to himself, using the staff to open a dark portal, it took him back to his humble abode. There he would wait.

Tamis gasped and bolted back to camp, fear driving his steps.

The air of Adwen's tent was taut as she paced, waiting for silence to be broken. Her patience wore thin not long after her warriors had begun their pursuit of the old man, leaving her to tormenting thoughts. She was over the initial shock of what had happened, but two things bothered her: She could not speak and therefore could not lead the knights; and Oryn would not look at her. Right away, he had distanced himself, and she felt so alone. Perhaps, she thought, Jack could tell her what Oryn obviously could not.

Then the scent of the wine caused her gaze to drift over to the remaining glass. Growling, she lunged and batted the contaminated drink to the dirt. The act gave her some relief. It was a mild distraction from the fear that Oryn would remain distant. In her heart she knew that without his comfort, her state could weaken. What the others did not know was that the Nizaren had awoken the dark sliver. If her will weakened, the infection could begin to grow again.

The sound of Tamis's voice caught her ear, and she forgot her blackened appendage and the wine. Brushing past the tent flap, Adwen went out to meet the frantic teen. Knights and Gargoyles saw him go by shouting for her and followed. As he stumbled to a stop before her, a small gathering listened and pondered why Adwen had changed.

Tamis panted heavily, scarce of breath. "A sorcerer. He took them. They are gone. The man who gave me the bottle was evil. He has them."

She and the onlookers were alarmed.

A knight took a step closer. "Tame One? What has happened to you?"

Unable to answer, Adwen stared at her warrior, ears

pinned back angrily.

Tamis hung his head. "I was tricked into giving her a potion by a wicked sorcerer. The very same now has captured Sir Oryn, Jack and Alexander. Where he has taken them, I do not know. I am sorry."

The knights glared but did not make a move. Then a high-ranking Gargoyle spoke. "What is your command, Lady Adwen? I am able to interpret your speech."

Relief washed over her, and she took advantage of the small blessing. "I'm taking Tamis with me to get them back. Everyone else must return quickly to the Order. If possible, go without stopping. This was likely a trap from the beginning – to lure me in and crush all others. Get them to the fortress quickly and safely."

"As you command. It will be done, Lady Adwen."

"Thank you."

Tamis listened as she made a series of barks and growls, then turned to growl at him and dipped down low. He stared, perplexed.

The Gargoyle chided, "You had better climb on and hold tight. She is as large as your pony, but I doubt she is as forgiving to ride. Farewell and remain in the eyes of the Light Spirits."

No sooner was Tamis on board than she took him to reclaim his bow, and they departed. The forces left behind would have to fend for themselves until they reached the gates of Plexus in the east. It would be a miracle if everyone survived the trek. Even graver still was the journey ahead for Adwen and her new archer.

"He's waking up," Alex barked.

Jack panted heavily in reply, "About time. We need to get out of here. Hey? Cujo? Wakie-wakie, eggs and bakie."

Raising his jaws from the stone floor of a prison, faint light from a high, barred opening filtered down. The first things Oryn saw were the bars of the cell and the two others sharing it. One was a yellow dog with pale eyes who stood as tall as a deer. The second was black and white with a curled tail, panting eagerly now that Oryn was awake. There was no question in his mind that he was looking at Jack and Alex.

Getting up, he found that he too was trapped in a canine form, but much bigger. Quickly deciding that the unusual shape did not matter, gauging the situation was more important.

"Where are we, do you think?" Alex asked.

Oryn tested the air from overhead through the bars. "I smell slime, mud and death. We are close to a marsh. It is my belief that we are many leagues to the north. It is possible we are inside a fortification called the Silver Spire."

"That's not good, is it?" Jack growled.

"It is decidedly not." As he studied the cage for weaknesses, he pondered. "Have either of you tried to break free?"

Jack replied, "Yeah, I fiddled with the lock using my claws, but they're too short and not narrow enough."

Both looked on as Oryn lunged without warning, attacking a wooden chair by an empty bucket. He easily shattered the thing to splinters and did not stop until nothing remained.

"Calm down! Eating the furniture won't help us!" When Oryn approached, dropping a few salvaged iron nails, Jack fell quiet.

"Try again," rumbled the enormous brown hound with strange black markings.

Adwen ran for hours. Tamis was well rested but very hungry and weak. Nothing sustaining for the young man lived in this place of dark water, muck and decomposing weeds. After traveling through the day, taking several breaks for Tamis to rest, sunset arrived, and a rare plot of higher ground came in sight. A meager shelf of stone jutted out at an angle, providing a small shelter.

The boy looked at the dry patch of ground then glance back. "Do you not think you deserved the better place to rest?" He gasped as he was roughly nudged by her nose toward the tiny shelter.

She growled to him even though he could not understand. "It's not about deserving it. You need to stay dry." Then she huffed and curled up alongside, avoiding prickly thorns and foul-smelling slicks.

Tamis remained where he fell, turning over to rub his freshly bruised knees. "As you wish, Tame One." The ground was slanted, providing a perfect place to recline. He learned right away that it held no comfort. Sleeping here would be a challenge.

Time passed slowly. Guilt kept Tamis awake in the dark, and he was only just beginning to drift off when he heard Adwen crying. Her subtle whimpers put a knot in the pit of his empty stomach. Feeling guiltier, there was one more thing he thought to do and reached into a small sack holding his water flask and tokens. Perhaps, he thought, this should have been his gift to her.

She was so frightened. Adwen feared for her fate and that of her assembled companions. She was terrified of what had or may happen to Oryn. The uncertainty squeezed her fragile heart.

Then the sound of a flute filled her ears. She did not move to look, knowing it was Tamis playing.

He played the beautiful tune for a long time. It clearly helped to put her at ease. At least, Tamis thought to himself, he had gotten this right.

Chapter 17
DUST

Dense fog hid the sun from view. On the marsh, their little island of rock and weeds seemed cut off and adrift from the world. When Tamis woke, it was to Adwen's damp nose prodding his forehead. She repeatedly nudged until he stirred and peered up from his dirt and stone bed.

Lying on the ground, Tamis could not perceive her mood. She made a soft bark, which held no more meaning than her stare. Rubbing his now moist face, it felt as if he had not slept at all. "Is it much farther to go to find them?"

Soundlessly, the white creature with a black, thorny left paw slunk out of sight around the boulder shelf.

He thought this was her way of reminding him she was still cross. Picking up the bow and traveling bag, it appeared to be time to set out. Adwen waited a short distance away, gazing out into the murky haze. As he joined her side, she growled and a faint silhouette caught his eye as it gained definition. Across another stretch of bog rested a small fortress and an immense tower against a mountainside.

"That must be where they are. Is that right?"

Adwen growled louder, hunkering low to let him climb on. In their approach to the looming structure, an indescribable sense of danger made Tamis cringe. His grasp on Adwen's soft snowy coat tightened.

At the fortress threshold, she stopped by the wall to let him off. He was nervous. The memories of his home overrun with shrieking demons compelled Tamis to take the bow from his back and grip the string. Taking a few stealthy steps toward the gate, he gasped as he was caught by his belt.

Adwen quietly growled, the leather strap held between her small front teeth.

"What is it?"

Letting go, she came alongside to stand shoulder to shoulder. A simple glance made her intent clear.

"You wish me to stay close?"

Adwen nodded.

Tamis took a deep breath. "I'm ready, Tame One. Lead on."

Loud banging of metal being struck echoed over and over. Alex sat beside Jack, who was lying on some straw, licking his burnt paws. After working all day and into the night, the curly tailed hound wore out every nail trying to pick the lock. The mechanism was heavily enchanted. Most of the iron picks snapped in half, but Jack nearly unlocked their cell twice and received a nasty shot of black magic.

Unwilling to sit by, Oryn tirelessly tackled the door. His immense weight and size did nothing more than jostle the door in its frame. This was not enough to deter him from trying. Again and again, the giant beast threw himself at the bars to no avail.

"Take a break, already!" Jack growled. He was annoyed by his stinging paws and now the incessant noise. "Those bars must be enchanted, too. You can't break them down."

Pausing in his wild battering of the door, Oryn turned and snarled. "You would have me submit to failure? Go back to tending to your burns. Adwen is coming to walk into Ozovath's trap, and we are the bait."

"You don't think we know that?" he growled in return. "Of course she's coming. We need to get out, but how about using your tactical brain for a change? Slamming the metal barrier is obviously not working. You've been at it for hours."

Oryn growled dangerously.

Then the three sensed Adwen at once and froze, raising their heads and ears.

"She has arrived."

"You know what? Never mind. Go back to what you were doing, Cujo."

"Gladly!"

Before he could lunge again, Jack saw a glimmer of metal

on the brown and black hound's neck. "Hold up! What is that?"

"What now?"

He limped closer to get a better look. "We can't summon anything, so how do you have that around your neck? Is it a fancy collar?"

The fur was much thicker than his usual Holy Hound form – so thick that he had not noticed the thin chain. Oryn lowered his head, shaking rigorously until the thing fell free. Once it came off, clattering to the ground, he recognized the pendant given by the Horai.

Jack cocked his head. "Wow. I wonder why it didn't get taken away like everything else. Let me check it out."

No sooner did Jack reach out a seared paw to investigate the glistening emerald than Oryn pinned it with his own padded toes.

"It's not for the likes of you, blathering lock-picker."

Jack prepared a clever retort, but the pendant suddenly shone bright under Oryn's claws.

The three recoiled and observed as it floated up and began to spin. As it shone even brighter, a beam of white-hot energy shot out, cutting through the lock on the door. Then the jewel exploded into nothingness, blasting the door open with a resounding clang of steel on steel.

A short silence was broken by Jack's entertained panting. "Whatever that was, I want one. Where did you get it?"

Oryn did not reply. He crouched low and prowled off with Jack and Alex close behind.

Tamis went up to the great door first and pushed as hard as he could. It hardly moved until Adwen lowered her head and joined in. When there was an opening big enough, they entered through a big cloud of dust. Tamis coughed loudly, earning a hushed growl from her.

Tears blurring his vision further, it felt like he had swallowed a dry dirt clod. Coughing and sputtering, he managed to wheeze out an apology. "Sorry. Did not think to hold my breath." He saw Adwen roll her big blue eyes and shake her head.

A tremor shook the ground beneath them, and the sound of crumbling rocks made them freeze and look about.

"What was that?" Tamis murmured, gripping his bow firmly.

Adwen sniffed, but did not make a sound in reply. She did not seem to know either and continued onward. Her long ears stood tall on her head, alert for the slightest noise.

Frightened, Tamis's heart pounded against his ribs. He could barely see a thing aside from the end of the hall, where faint sunlight spilled in from high overhead. At the entry to what was once a grand hall, now a ruin, Adwen stopped. She did not want to go in just yet.

When she growled, he looked about the vast chamber. It was impossible to see through the dark shadows beyond the filtering sunlight. Broken chains hung, swaying slightly from a breeze and the recent shaking of the structure. A wretched stink passed under his human nose, and he gagged for the second time since entering this vile place.

Adwen glanced at him and pinned back her hears, wrinkling her jowls.

"Sorry," he whispered.

Moving on through the gloom amidst rocks and ancient debris, they both tiptoed. It was important not to attract attention from whatever was making that smell. The nasty thing was hidden somewhere close by. The white hound slunk around in the poor lighting with ease.

Tamis held his golden bow firmly and the silken string by the bends of his fingers. Realizing Adwen was a bit farther ahead, he sidled past a broken feast table to catch up. Free of the narrow gap, his foot found a stray timber plank. It snagged his boot and he tripped, crunching onto rotten wood beside his weapon.

The racket shocked Adwen into freezing on the spot. When Tamis raised his head from the mess, he was going to say sorry again.

Another much greater tremor shook the ground, followed by a monstrous snort and a gravelly groan. Tamis saw two beady eyes glinting from high in the shadows across the great hall, but Adwen could see the entire hulking creature, a giant dragging a crude hammer made from a fallen tree. The head of the weapon was a square stone, secured to the roots by a steel chain.

When the thirty-foot brute came into the open, it spotted Tamis and his shiny bow. It wanted the weapon for its horde of trophies.

Adwen rushed forward, barking and snapping her jaws.

Her ploy to distract the dumb beast started to work. The sound of her incessant barking annoyed the giant, making him scowl and drool. He quickly swung the hammer down, and when she leaped aside just in time, the giant bellowed in outrage.

The hammer came much closer than she was comfortable with, and the chain was easier to see. Each link glinted black and barely caught the light. The giant's weapon had demon steel links strapped across every surface. As the giant raised the huge hammer again, Adwen knew there could be no room for error. To be struck by that would be a devastating end to this confrontation.

With that in mind, she continuously snapped and lunged, dodging each titanic blow. Each miss from the giant left a rectangular crater in the stone floor. Luring her adversary about the wide-open hall, Adwen struggled to form a plan. She wanted to get in close and chip away at its ankles. If the giant were thrown off balance, that could leave an opening for attacking the head or throat. The giant's hammer made another impression on the floor, and the white hound darted for its legs. She sunk her fangs in deep and thrashed hard, snarling.

It was no use. The skin was too thick, and the giant seemed to feel no pain. It grunted in surprise, trying to kick her off. As it raised the hammer for another swing, a shining arrow took out one of its piggish eyes. A terrible holler filled the halls, blood spurting.

Surprise caused Adwen to release. Landing on level ground, the thrashing giant stood between them, flailing blindly in a mad fit.

When the hammer in the giant's grasp began to fall once more, Adwen no longer had control over her actions. Eyes blazing solid gold in the gloom, her form streaked toward Tamis, racing against the hammer to reach him.

Across the hall, from a partially collapsed passage, Oryn

arrived in time to see her snatch the boy by the leg. Her jaws swung, and he was cast aside out of harm's way, tumbling across the stones and debris. Then the hammer came down.

A sick sensation sank the warriors' stomachs as Adwen's sudden weakness diminished their strength in kind. Stunned, they stared in disbelief as the weapon withdrew, and they heard her gasp for air.

Seeing Adwen's human hand reaching out for anything to pull her from the crater of cracked stones sent Oryn into a rage. He roared and leaped into action.

The noise gained the brute's attention while the boy with the shiny bow was hidden behind some rubble. All of the barking and the loss of an eye had put the giant in a vengeful state. It swung to crush the enormous dog just like it had the white one.

But Oryn was far more enraged, fast and cunning. The hammerhead smashed down, and Oryn jumped back just enough. He then ran up along the tree trunk handle and up the hairy, grayish arm. Jaws wide, he latched onto the giant's throat.

Jack and Alex tried to join in, but once Oryn got hold of the giant's throat there was no opening to assist. The colossal figure wailed, swinging its arms, dropping the weapon before toppling over. It punched at the black and brown hound, but it did not matter. Oryn was too angry. He only stopped when two putrid, callused hands pried him off and lobbed him a great distance.

Gaining control of the descent, the hound deftly landed upright and dashed to Adwen. He could see her, weakly crawling out of the hole, silver blood streaking from chain-like impressions on her woman's body. She collapsed at the edge but could see him coming, her face desperate as she reached out her soft hand, shaking.

As he went close she touched his face. Her power over him shed the spell that trapped him as a dog, and he became his more human self. Kneeling low, he held her head up, gently supporting the weight she no longer could.

While the giant continued to struggle back to its feet, there was a moment for them to share. As weak as she was, Adwen's heart warmed at seeing him again. His gentle look let her know that he would not abandon her to this fate or anything else. At that, she smiled.

He did as well, until the giant's bellow made him frown. Once he gently let her back down, Oryn stood and turned to finish was he had started. Summoning the enhanced holy sword to confront the creature, his emerald eyes burned.

Jack and Alex lunged and jumped about, drawing the monster's attention. As its hairy back turned to the knight, Oryn rushed in and swiftly sliced through thick skin and tendon. His strike to the ankle made it wail, forcing it to kneel. One enormous arm swung round to bat him aside, but Oryn lifted the sword, letting the strength of the stupid thing impale itself.

The arm soon withdrew from the sting, and the giant writhed, trying to stop the bleeding in futility. Alex and Jack moved back as their friend twirled around and below the slouched figure. Transforming into his new true form for a longer reach, Oryn stood beneath the giant's downturned face. He drove the sword tip deep between its eyes and gave a smart twist. Gradually, it toppled over on its side with an almighty crash of stone and wood, its wailing silenced.

Reverting to his smaller shape, he turned to the others. "Find Tamis."

Alex barked, "Roger that."

While they worked to uncover the boy from the debris, Adwen had Oryn's undivided attention. As he knelt by her again, sword in hand, he swept the hair from her face, caressing her cheek. The knight ignored the noise made by the others and Jack's praise for the masterful kill. She had fallen unconscious but woke, her eyes fluttering, trying to remain open. The deep sapphire blue enraptured him.

Adwen was very weak and could not get enough air to warn him. Instead, she used what little strength she had to show fear, darting her eyes to the side.

Oryn was confounded. Then his nose caught a trace of thick dust and dark magic. He looked where her glance indicated to see Ozovath walking nearer.

Coming to a stop at a safe distance, the sorcerer struck the ground with his staff, hitting the stones with cool finality. His smirk was chilling. "Now who let you out of your kennel? It appears that I shall just have to put you back and use a better lock."

Everyone was quiet, watching the crafty old villain size them up. Oryn stole a glance back at Adwen. She was not worried anymore and gave a tiny nod.

Oryn's warm look hardened as he stood to face Ozovath for the second time. His expression did not give any indication of confidence. Only contempt was clearly etched.

"I said that I would have her, Sir Oryn, last of the house of Conrad. Are you prepared to die for her?"

Taking a deep breath, energy ignited inside him as he focused. Eyeing the ancient man, his body felt like lightning, barely contained. For the first time, the power Oryn nearly had hold of in Fort Redu was at his command. Keeping the pale green energy hidden, the magical knight bided his time like a card player, withholding his hand.

Ozovath raked a yellow fingernail through his thin beard, contemplating what spell to use. It needed to be as powerful as the last spell to confront the holy sword.

Tensions increased as each combatant could tell the other was almost ready to make a move. Oryn's sword began to rise, and Ozovath focused his magic via the honed staff. The dark stone at its tip glinted.

That was the cue Oryn needed. He rushed in, sword up to strike.

Ozovath suddenly pointed the staff, unleashing a pillar of black fire. The stones in its path were scorched, turning molten red.

The knight was ready. He drew forth his deep wellspring of long-buried magic, casting a large shield ahead of his weapon. It deflected the blast of flames, allowing his charge to go unhindered, and he sped closer to the sorcerer.

Surprised to find out Oryn was a mage, he cursed himself for not remembering the ancient Conrad lineage. The sorcerer set up a black shield of his own, making himself almost invisible. From behind the mirror-like wall, Ozovath fired a barrage of purple missiles.

The storm of spells cracked and shattered the green barrier. This did not matter. Oryn was prepared. A second shield formed over his left hand, which he used to swat the rest of the projectiles away like flies. Taking another deep breath on the final approach, he raked the dark wall with his shield-coated gauntlet, cutting through it like a curtain. Diving into the thick cloud of mist on the other side, he knifed the sword at its heart and continued through. On the other side, he turned back, taking another stand to wait as the sorcerer's false fog dissipated.

Oryn sneered and growled at seeing no one. The sorcerer had vanished. A raspy cough from nearby drew his attention, and he raised his sword in anticipation.

Stepping out of the shadow of a pillar, Ozovath grinned. Holding out a hand, he let a fistful of dust fall. Going closer, even more dust poured from a hole in his chest where his heart should be, leaving a trail behind. Coming to stand before Oryn, the vile being said, "I should have known you had magic in you, Conrad. That was my mistake. It's been in your family line, appearing at random from generation to generation since the time of Darien."

Oryn lowered his sword and summoned a shield to his other hand, flexing his fingers, making the energy snap and crackle like green electricity. "This was never of my family. Keegan Conrad did not possess magic enough to pass down to his kin."

Holes formed in the sorcerer's visage, his dead body fading like his spirit, turning to even more dust. Uncaring, Ozovath was fixated on Oryn. "You are right; he did not. However, his bride did."

The sorcerer smiled sickeningly at seeing the knight tormented, having gotten one last moment of pleasure before he was gone. The particles that were once Ozovath scattered, swept off by subtle drafts, lost to all but terrible memory.

Chapter 18
THICKER THAN WATER

The wooden beam pinning Tamis across the chest behind some rubble hurt, and breathing was difficult. Where Adwen had bitten his leg was even more painful. After he heard the battle with the sorcerer end, Jack and Alex disappeared from sight. When they returned to dig him out, both had regained their more human shapes.

"Hold on, kid! We'll have this off of you in a sec."

Transforming into his hound form, the black and -white Holy Hound used his claws to grip the broken beam. He lobbed it aside, sending a cloud of more dust flying elsewhere, and changed back again to hold out a hand to Tamis.

Taking it, the boy coughed. "That could have crushed me. My thanks, Jack." Taking a step, pain shot up his thigh, causing him to stagger and limp, gasping. Thin trails of blood wept, glistening wet in the dim ambiance.

Observing from nearby, Oryn cradled Adwen close to his chest. "Carry him. That wound will close within the hour. We must leave this place."

They all agreed. Alex grabbed Tamis around the waist and transformed, hoisting him up to sit on his armored shoulders. Jack obliged in stowing the golden bow for later. The exit was not far, and bright sunlight showed the way to the door.

The three unharmed warriors bore their friends out into the fresh air and toward the main gate. As they left the grounds below the Silver Spire, their path started southward. They had hardly gone a few yards when Adwen gasped. Her black arm cracked, shifting and bending. It burned Adwen, drawing tears and more gasps while she tried to reclaim control of the appendage.

Unwilling to stand by, Oryn set her propped against the stone wall. Using his newly awakened magic abilities, crackling green electricity danced over both hands. The warm energy radiated from his fingers, tiny streams touching Adwen's injuries, rapidly closing them. With that finished, he placed a hand on her chest, transferring some of his own strength to her body. When she was strong enough to resist the infection, the knight continued to siphon his power.

Adwen was able to move again but weakly. She pulled his hand away. When he frowned, she shook her head. "That's enough. You're going to need all the strength you can get. I'm okay now."

"What is happening to you?"

"The Nizaren reactivated the dark infection when it captured me. I need to keep my strength up to hold it in check."

This upset the devoted knight. "Why have you said nothing before now?"

She grimaced in defiance and remorse. "You wouldn't have been able to do anything. It wasn't necessary until this point. I'm sorry."

Knowing it was true, Oryn remained silent and contained the argument to his thoughts. There was no point in being critical over hurt feelings.

Jack pointed southward beyond the marsh. "What the heck is that?"

Their heads turned, and they saw a deep black mist building on the horizon. The blackness grew slowly, rising higher and drifting closer. In a few hours, the ground on which they stood would be enveloped.

Adwen shuddered, and the others felt her fear. "It's him; Guillot's coming. He's searching for us."

Oryn snarled at the deep shadows. "Let him come."

She was frightened but firm. "No. Even together, the three of you can't beat him. No matter what, he can't be allowed to touch me."

Jack glanced over, horrified at what he heard from her mind. "Think that again?"

Losing patience under the tension, the knight asked, "What would happen then?"

"The infection is a fragment of Guillot; it is a part of his essence. If he touches me for even a second, I will be completely consumed."

Alex growled; his yellow and white muzzle wrinkled at the ominous sight. "Where do we go? We're completely cut off."

Oryn scooped Adwen back into his arms and turned to face them. "Not entirely. To the north and south is danger, and west is the sea, where we would be cornered. We must go east, into the mountain passes. That is the one way to escape. The weather will be foul because winter is near, but it shall hopefully cover our tracks."

"Can't the demons pick up on the scent of magic like we can?" Jack asked.

This received a scowl. "Yes. Magic leaves a trail, but a weak one. Because of this we must move swiftly and let the tracks fade behind us. We must go now."

True to Oryn's claim before setting out, the bite wound on Tamis's leg healed rapidly. It seemed surreal for such an injury to be gone so soon. They were far into the mountains, steadily climbing higher on an old path. By evening it started to snow.

Tamis shivered. His teeth chattered ceaselessly in the dark. A whiteout filled the sky, completing the darkness of night. He had to climb atop Alex again when he could not see, getting what little sleep he could. There was no place to camp and no time to lose with a demon general in pursuit.

Clinging to Alex's furry neck and head for warmth, Tamis shuddered like a leaf in the cold, biting wind.

Jack remarked from close by. "Just think, kid: If the moons had come out instead of the storm, you would have a fur coat."

He thought to agree but said nothing. Remembering the occasions a few days ago when he witnessed Alex transform, Tamis had reservations. Judging from the amount of pain that appeared to be involved, he decided that being in a snowstorm without a coat did not seem so bad anymore.

Jack read his mind and chuckled. "Good point, kid, but would three minutes of that be worth being warm the rest of the night?"

"Leave him be," Oryn called back from the lead. "His time will come. Be quiet."

"I have been quiet all day till just now. I think I've earned the right to say something."

Alex rumbled, "What about when you tried to start a game of 'I smell' halfway up the first mountain pass?"

Oryn added to the argument, "Not to mention the irritating tune you carried for several hours about a womanizing man named Henry the Eighth."

Adwen murmured over his shoulder at the warrior as well. "Did you forget that you also sang 'Ninety-nine Bottles of Beer', too?"

The warrior heaved a sigh. "All in a day's work. Don't thank me. It's not necessary. I love what I do."

Tamis decided it was high time he spoke up. "What you do is pester everyone until they want to throw you off a mountain."

This earned gales of laughter from Jack and soft chortles from Adwen.

"I was wondering if you were ever going to speak up for yourself!" Jack said. "Good job, Tamis. Very good job. I approve."

Cold, tired and very hungry, Tamis replied, "Please, shut up, Sir Jack."

"Since you were first to ask so nicely, it would be my pleasure."

Everyone rolled their eyes. Jack relished the reaction and became silent.

A faint call that sounded like a woman reached them from ahead. "Who's there? Name yourselves!"

They stopped dead, staring into the dense snowfall. No one spoke.

A small figure trudged through the deepening white powder, crunching closer. Oryn took a step back at the sight of the old woman in rags. Jack and Alex summoned their weapons, studying the elderly woman with suspicion.

A round scar was visible on the side of her brow. She had no cane or staff. Her shoulders hunkered in the cold, though she did not seem to feel it. The black clothes on her emaciated form fluttered in the wind, shredded and partially faded. When the withered hag halted before the small company, her bright eyes flashed with many colors and returned to a silvery hue. The magic in her body was easy for the travelers to detect; it was old and very great. Her expression was one of uncertain curiosity. Somehow, her eyes could cut through the dark just as easily as theirs.

Oryn snapped in warning when she tried to come closer, holding Adwen tight. "Keep your distance, witch! You still draw breath only because your intent is unclear. Why do you block our path?"

Unafraid, the old woman said nothing. Then as Adwen's glowing blue eyes turned to fix on her, she shuddered and gasped.

Adwen asked, "What is your name?"

Her wispy white hair and dark rags fluttered like loose feathers as she fell to her knees. Breathlessly, she murmured to herself on the brink of tears. "Through it all, I had thought I was cursed. Now I see, I've been blind. I am blessed. Darien's child has come at last."

Oryn snarled and shouted, "What do you want with her, hag?"

Jack answered for the woman, surprised and in awe as he lowered his daggers. "She wants to help us."

Looking over the stranger with no less suspicion that before, the knight glared. "Why? What purpose do you have for aiding us?"

Strength filled the woman's bones, letting her stand with the solidity of a statue. Face set in a firm stare, she replied, "The demon, Guillot, is hunting you. My name is Gren'Gedar. In your language, I am Frost Tongue. It would give me great satisfaction to see the Terrible Sliver fail and even more when he falls. I know these mountains better than any other. The swifter, safer paths are clear. I can show the way."

As much as Oryn disliked the eerie stranger, he looked to Adwen.

She smiled kindly at Frost Tongue and nodded. "Thank you."

"We must hurry," Frost Tongue said. "The demon gains on you in the night. Come."

Their guide took them through many passes. Her spry step made Oryn uncomfortable. Even for a magical being, it would be a challenge to move as fast as the Holy Hounds. Frost Tongue effortlessly maintained their pace, following alongside to be close to Adwen. After such a long wait alone, she did not dare to stray far.

Eventually, she noticed Adwen's arm and grimaced. "I know what that is, Child of Darien. You are fortunate not to have suffered the same as I have at the hands of Guillot." Brandishing the ovular scar on wrinkled skin, her pointed nails gently caressed the old wound. "I have suffered his gift as well."

Adwen was surprised but then was hopeful. "How did you get rid of it?"

Frost Tongue was somber. "I did not. It was broken off. A piece remains inside. But when it broke, so did his hold over my will. That allowed me to undermine the demon and later save my sister. When he was cast from this world, I fell in sleep through the centuries. I awoke again many months ago, and I knew; I knew he had returned as well. We may be connected, but he holds no sway over me any longer."

The admission to being connected to Guillot put a bitter taste in Oryn's mouth. He glared, using his most icy stare.

When the old woman saw, she stared back. Then her eyes widened in shock. "I know those eyes. That look is hers, but the eyes are his. You are sired from the line of the great dragon slayer."

Disgusted to hear this creature speak of his forbear, he looked away, hoping for silence. His wish was not granted.

Eager and excited, Frost Tongue carried on as she walked at his side. "She earned that look from our adopted mother. You wear it well. Such a cold look always hid how warm her heart was. Keegan Conrad did need to try to win her affections. Even though I was controlled by the demon, I saw glimpses of their hearts drawing closer. My twin sister, Winter Maw, had a pair of fang-shaped daggers, imbued with light magic by Darien himself. She was always good with a knife. She could be vicious with the daggers one moment and merciful the next. You have the dragon slayer's visage, but your spirit is so much like hers. It is as if I have found her again. They called her the White Sorceress from the mountains."

Realizing that not one, but two, of the Master Knight's chosen were family to him left Oryn's head spinning. He was descended from both the great dragon slayer as well as the white sorceress? It could not be. If what this rambling old sorceress said was true, then they shared blood. The thought made his stomach churn. Learning that he was a repressed mage the whole time he was a knight before ever meeting Adwen meant he had ill-treated his kind for a lifetime. Meeting this ancestor made the matter even more upsetting. Regret and contempt for himself and the woman causing this pain weighed him down.

"I've heard enough," he stated, hiding the emotional anguish.

Frost Tongue almost pleaded. "Are you not a Conrad? If you are, you must believe me. We are kin. The magic I sense in you is from my twin, Winter Maw."

He shouted, pain evident in his voice, "Enough!" When everyone stopped to stare, he hung his head and murmured, "That is enough."

Their now-silent guide nodded, saddened that she somehow had hurt her distant nephew. Frost Tongue led on.

The winds that howled through the pass picked up, gusting strongly at their backs. Flurries were blinding. If not for their guide, one of them surely would have slipped and fallen a bone-shattering distance and become lost. Sure as a constant star, Frost Tongue never wavered on her course amid the intense blizzard.

On their way, Jack realized the weapons in his possession were the same ones she described to Oryn. If not for the lack of visibility, it would have been interesting to show them to Frost Tongue and hear some stories. The path had been narrow but widened, and they came upon a pocket of shelter by the side of the mountain, holding back the snowflakes. Before he could go closer, everyone stood stark still, a terrible fear flooding their bodies with the cold. Everyone turned to look back blindly along the passes.

Adwen was frightened, but Frost Tongue became resolute. "Do not be afraid, child. He has caught up, but not for long. I knew he would be the faster." A clever smile spread on her pale face, and her eyes flashed. "He is too late. It is here that I leave you. Follow the abandoned Dwarven road until its end.

Run wherever possible, and the demon will be hard-pressed to catch you by dawn." Their brilliant stares followed as she walked past to go stand behind, gazing deep through the impenetrable storm of white.

"Where is the entrance?" Oryn asked, becoming worried. He could not tell yet if the concern he felt was for him and his companions or more for this distant relation.

She chuckled. "There is none. I will open a way. Guillot will be unable to follow, but might head you off if he knows of the exit. If I can hold him back long enough, you will be too far gone and your tracks too cold to follow."

Now truly worried for Frost Tongue, the knight replied, "You cannot defeat him alone. How do you intend to hold him off?"

Her voice was calm and amused. "Have you never heard the tales?" Frost Tongue's smile was sly, and the pupils of her eyes became slits like a cat's. "My sister and I were raised by dragons."

To their surprise, the sorceress's black and gray rags swirled, covering her body as she stretched upward and outward. Talons on the bend of a wing grasped the high wall overhead, and the other wing's talons gripped the opposing side of the path, venous membranes furling in the wind. A long, pointed tail whipped out, barely visible in the falling snow as Frost Tongue's slender neck bent down low. Her pointed, angular head hung before them in the air pocket formed by the mountainside.

Oryn stood transfixed by the pair of silvery dragon eyes amid onyx scales. Only now could he sense the blood that they shared. Then as she turned to open her maw at the stones, a mysterious and calming series of sounds poured from her throat. Like him, Frost Tongue was able to use song as a focus to project magic and channel the power. They truly were blood kin.

The magic in the transfigured sorceress's voice formed a portal through the mountain, revealing a path lit by glowing sunstones. Jack and Alex entered straight away, eager to escape the freezing cold, but Oryn hesitated. He stole one last look at Frost Tongue, knowing it would be the very last. Her reptilian stare was not cold. Only he could tell, past the pair of dragon eyes, she was beaming warmth as she nodded, encouraging him to go. He had no choice. The knight departed from his powerful ancestor's presence, and she closed the portal behind them.

Inside on the passage steps, silence was absolute aside from the knight's heavy breathing. His heart raced as he stared out at nothing. He hoped against all hope that Frost Tongue would survive. Finally noticing the many expectant looks on him, Oryn took a breath to steady his nerve and regain composure.

Firmly, he nodded to assure them. "We travel swiftly until dawn. This way."

Their steps were fleet. The halls were intact after the hundreds of years since their abandonment. The Dwarves had migrated farther north to unknown territories, away from interfering nations and in pursuit of more sun crystals. After a few minutes of running through the hushed passages lit like an autumn festival, the mountain began to shudder. Again and again, quakes caused by a titanic battle outside sent down small tremors to their feet. An occasional trill was loud enough to echo through the rocks and into the passages. The sound of Frost Tongue casting immense magic spells served as an added motivation to move faster. In their retreat, for nearly an hour, the tremors and shrieks continued.

A final tremor and a long, terrible cry echoed through to them in the halls, stopping Oryn in his tracks. The breath lodged in his throat, and his heart skipped a beat. They all stopped to watch the knight and listen. No more pounding or dragon calls came after. The battle in the passes was over.

Adwen looked up into his eyes. "It's okay. She's free, Oryn. It's what she wanted."

His jaw clenched as he restrained tears, bright green eyes glassy from holding them at bay. Blinking hard to dispel them, Oryn nodded. "I know."

They moved onward and did not stop again. Several passages came to diverging paths, but crisp drafts alerted their noses to the right way. Many more miles of stone passed under their feet. Hours went by, and the exit eventually came in sight with faint dawn light.

The company of five came out by way of a high-arched

tunnel entrance, hidden by a natural fold of the mountain. Sky overhead appeared navy and gray as the night came to an end. The final few passes to the valleys below lay just ahead over a frozen land bridge.

Oryn pretended to be intent on their escape, but Adwen knew his thoughts were still lost back on the mountainside. She whispered soothingly, "When this is all over we can find her and give her proper burial rites."

The gesture got a small smile from him. "It would be good to grant her that for all her suffering on our behalf. Thank you."

Crossing the bridge, they looked southward. Beyond a few more leagues of mountains, Dargadia waited for them. The sky was clear, and a deep blanket of white covered everything in sight. Going would be slowed by the drifts of snow.

A sudden gust of icy cold blew in their faces from across the bridge. Realizing it was an unnatural chill, the Holy Hounds gasped, and Jack summoned his daggers snarling, "Are you serious? He still caught up with us?"

Rising from a dark pool of shadow, a conglomerate of many black shards rose. Coming to stand atop the ice and snow, General Guillot stared, sinister green lights for eyes glinting in the dark of the mountain. He summoned a sword made of the same spikes that made his towering body and pointed it at Adwen, who was cringing in Oryn's arms.

The demon's voice was sonorous and echoing. "Come to me. Come and join with me, Heir of the Neverborn."

She shuddered, and Oryn snarled.

Alex set Tamis down to summon his short sword, and Jack returned the golden bow to its master. Going to stand at the front, the two friends prepared to hold back the fiend and let the others make a run for it if possible.

Guillot laughed, pouring green fire over his sword. There was time before the sun was high enough to interfere. Adwen would be under his control long before then.

A bright glint flashed over them from a ledge. The light crossed the demon, causing his form to smoke and burn momentarily, and he hissed in anger.

All gazes turned to the mass of magic forming into a figure. A beautiful young woman with yellow dragon eyes glared down at General Guillot.

Adwen and Oryn exchanged astonished glances.

Frost Tongue's magic was so great that her spirit lingered, anchored by the unfinished task: preventing Guillot from catching the companions. Her ghost pointed an accusing finger, making the evil figure take a step back.

"By the grace of the Light Spirits, I have remained, and it is their command that I stop you, spawn of the void! You will not have the Heir, and you will not claim the life of the child descended from my sister." Her white robes furled with her long white hair, and she cried out, sending a huge blast of magic to banish the demon from the mountain.

Guillot tried to block the spell but crumpled to his spiky knees, shrieking in outrage. As the demon tried to resist being transported, the Holy Hounds looked to the ghost of Frost Tongue. She smiled back, then faded from the world.

The demon general roared, using all his might to fight the spell. He could not, and the force shook the ground. The quaking grew as he resisted. A groaning emitted from everywhere until the building mass of dark energy and light exploded, sending a powerful tremor in all directions. Guillot disappeared amid the flash.

Adwen gasped, and Oryn knew it was not from relief. With a roar, a vast wave of ice and snow came ripping down the northern slope. The force from the demon attempting to stave off the spell of banishment unleashed a deadly avalanche. In seconds the white wall swallowed the crossing, picking up and burying everyone caught upon it. Crushing darkness and ice carried them far down the steep mountainside, leaving each of them alone without air, far from any warmth.

Chapter 19
THEN AND NOW

The avalanche poured down the slopes, across rocks and ledges, covering everything in its path for miles. When the white clouds of powder finally settled, Tamis was very alone, trapped deep in the snow. He struggled to move and dig out. More clumps came down on his face, making him rethink the situation. If he tried to dig, he would just suffocate faster by collapsing the small pocket of air.

Panic set in, and he cried out. "Help! Oryn, Jack, Alex. Help me! Somebody!"

No answer came. Minutes passed, and his head began to throb. His eyes grew heavy. After fifteen minutes his air had run out. If Adwen had not marked him, he would not have survived much longer, but he clung to life in and out of consciousness. Every few hours he would revive long enough to shout once before blacking out again. No one heard his calls.

Night set in. Tamis's body had grown cold. His skin was like ice and turning blue. The boy's heart was beating weakly, barely keeping him alive. With the boy encased in a hill of hardened snow, the moons began to emerge. One was full. The further the circle in the sky moved into view, the faster Tamis's heart pounded. His body warmed at first, then became hot. Blood vessels split, swelling beneath the skin in anticipation of his first transformation into hound form.

The burning sensation in his veins spread like ravenous roots, awakening him. The pounding in the boy's head was unbearable. Barely conscious, the waves of building pressure overwhelmed his oxygen-deprived brain. When the full moon reached high in the sky, Tamis writhed, gasping. His form contorted and flexed in response to the excruciating sensations.

Through the combined thrashing and intense body heat,

the side of the snow pack gave way atop a high stone ledge. He was blinded by the transformation, unable to prevent himself from falling. Slipping from the breach in the mound, Tamis plummeted to the unforgiving earth below. The impact rendered him unconscious. His body continued to roll down a steep, rocky side of the mountain.

Battered and bloody from the tumble down the slope, a terrible injury on his brow oozed red. He picked himself up, unconsciously aware of his surroundings, and staggered through a forest. The dazed warrior wobbled on all fours, and eventually he became partially aware that he was standing upright, swaying precariously.

A sturdy tree interrupted his stagger. Tamis leaned against it heavily, panting, studying the terrain. In every direction he saw tall pines, old oaks and evergreen shrubs. He smelled blood and reached to feel the sore place on his scalp. Checking for subsequent fluids, thick crimson coated his unsteady hand. Staring long, his hand did not look the way it should. Pitch-black claws sat on the tips of his fingers, and what appeared to be course fur grew like a thin carpet over his skin. Confounded by the injury, his sight wavered, and his inhuman fingers seemed to double in number.

When he collapsed in a heap, an arrow meant for his head stuck fast in the bark of the tree. The one who had fired it stared. It was unusual for him to miss and even more unusual to find a werewolf wandering this far north. The beast was down, so he reloaded his crossbow on the way to investigate.

Going near, his pace slowed as he spotted a long metal weapon slung on the creature's back. Up close, the object turned out to be a golden bow. Unafraid of the unconscious rusty-brown creature, his hand reached to touch the weapon. Dawn came at that moment, and the man withdrew as the creature shrank into a heavily bruised boy.

Pulling down the scarf that covered his mouth, the hunter stood, jaw dropped. Only now did he realize that this was no werewolf. Stories had been coming in from Dargadia with trade caravans until the traders mysteriously stopped coming a few weeks ago. This was one of the warriors of light.

Incredible smells were smothering. Stinks from hidden mold, dust and unwashed animals filled Tamis's nostrils. When he woke up, noon sun streamed through a window across the room. Coughing from the dust, he turned over and stared at the light source, confused by the unfamiliar location. Once the young warrior registered that he was in a strange home with an unknown man sitting by the window, Tamis became alert.

Sitting up fast, looking about, he gasped, "Where am I? Where is my bow?"

The hunter had a thick mane of black hair and a well-trimmed beard. Wearing red linens and heavy leathers for travel, his smile was one of entertainment. Puffing on a pipe, smoke churned out the corners of his mouth. After looking Tamis over now that he was awake, he smiled and reassured him.

"You're bow is fine. I've stowed it beneath that bed you're on." The hunter observed the relieved reaction, as the boy pulled the weapon out, admiring the ornate designs. "You are very far north, leagues from Dargadia's borders. Welcome to Jenkirk, pearl of the mountains, known for trade between your kingdom and, occasionally, Keirnendale to the east."

Concern and worry formed a frown on Tamis's face. "How did I get here?"

The hunter continued to puff on his pipe, enjoying the simple conversation. "I found you in the woods. It looked as though you had been in quite a fight. Did you stumble across a troll or a rabid bear?"

Some of the bruises remained on his arms and hidden beneath his dragon-leather clothes. The boots he had worn the day before were now gone, destroyed.

"What are you?"

Tamis looked up from his bare toes, shocked at the candidness of the question. Unsure if it was wise to openly discuss the topic, he played coy. "What do you mean?"

Chuckling, smoke shot from both nostrils, and the hunter replied, "If you want to play games, I can tell you that this is one you shall lose. When I came across you in the forest just south of here, you did not look as you do now."

He had wondered if the fuzzy recollections from last night

were real. Learning that they were made Tamis a bit nauseous. Judging by the stranger's expression, none of this bothered the man in the slightest. Finding the nerve to answer was not easy.

"There are those who call what I am a Holy Hound. Was there no one else where you found me?"

The hunter shrugged. "Afraid not. I would know if there was. I am part of an elite group charged with culling dangerous pests such as werewolves. What is a Holy Hound? You are not a man or a beast or an abomination. It is a curious dilemma. Do you even know?"

The new question puzzled Tamis greatly. After briefly trying to think, he knew very little. "There are only five of us. Four of us are warriors in service to Adwen the Tame One, Heir of Darien the Master Knight."

A cloud of smoke shot from the hunter's broad grin as he suddenly rocked forward, pointing with his pipe. "Ha! I knew it was so! This is a grand meeting indeed! What brings one of the chosen warriors this far from the Order?"

"We were fleeing through the mountain passes, chased by a powerful demon."

"Fascinating."

"It nearly caught us, but a spell sent it far away. The blast shook the earth, and so much snow fell from the cliffs it was like an ocean of white swallowed us. Somehow I broke free from where it buried me. Now I am here."

Considering what the boy had described, the hunter tilted his head, lost in thought. "It is a good story, but the way you tell it could use some embellishment."

Tamis was abashed. "You do not believe me?"

"Oh, make no mistake: I believe you. I simply think such a tale is deserving of more flavor for the listener. Pursued by a demon in the mountains, only to escape and be eaten up by the wild nature of the ice! That is how to tell a story, lad."

This stranger seemed odd to Tamis. For a moment he considered the chance that he was completely mad. "If you say so."

"Perhaps you have heard of one of my lot. He is most popular among the women of Dargadia: Regorian Lancer. I would send a letter to him if the daft fool could read."

Somberly, Tamis remembered the near-meeting. "I know

of him. He saved my life and the Tame One's life."

"That is so like him – finding all of the action. How is the brothel-loving man?"

Tamis wet his lips before replying. "I was at his pyre in the Order."

The vivacity drained from the hunter. "Oh. I see. How did he go?"

"He shot down a demon. It was large and collapsed the ramparts he was on."

"Was it with that bow or with his own and a silver arrow?"

The question was peculiar, but Tamis answered. "Silver, I think."

Gales of laughter erupted from the hunter. "And I bet you anything it was a single shot! What a glorious end for king and country. Of course, that sugary-tongued fool managed to fell a demon with a lesser weapon. What a triumph!"

More worried than before about this man's sanity, Tamis failed to hide the hesitance in his voice. "Why are you not sad? Your friend has died."

Calming himself, the hunter could see that this young man was not aware. With an air of fatherly love, he explained, "Of course I feel sad, boy. I shall greatly miss him, but all who serve the lands and the people do so with their lives. The single most honorable thing a real man can do is give his life protecting what is important and much bigger than himself. Regorian achieved this, and that is cause for much jubilation. Has your father not taught you these things?"

Tamis looked away. "No, he did not."

Right away, the meaning was understood. "Then I say it is his loss and not yours. When you first woke, I could tell you have the makings of a great man. Also, I can tell you are not a true man."

With an uncomfortable sidelong glance, he replied. "You already know I am not a human?"

"That's not what I'm getting at. You are a boy, a child who has yet to grow into his own. It has little to do with what is in your blood."

Tamis pondered, not quite understanding.

The hunter cleared his throat and indicated the world outside the window. "And while you are here waiting for your companions, it would be best to keep your little secret to yourself. These folk take pride in having a magic-free and monster-free city and farmland. Many come here to escape those things. If the wrong folk found you out, there would be good reason for you to flee back to the forest."

"Then I should leave and not take the risk." Going to look outside, sunshine warmed his skin. The feeling was different from before, like subtle fingers caressing, comforting his hurts. He stood and studied the city below their abandoned manor atop a hill. Wild dogs on the grounds began to bark at a figure walking up the road.

"If you were hunted in the mountains by demons, then going out there alone would be an even greater risk. Hide yourself here. Demons have not bothered to reach for this quaint little valley. As for those mangy mutts, don't worry about them. That motley pack of random strays did not mind me bringing you in. Everyone else is kept out."

"Why do they only let you inside?"

"Do you like badger? Those beasts sure do. They love to chew on them and tenderize the meat before feeding. Have you never had a badger for a meal?"

Tamis was too distracted. "Um. Who is that?" The figure had arrived close to the gates, but came no further, as the dogs went close and kept barking.

Joining his side, smoke trailed behind as he went to have a look. "Ah. The road here is in the dog's territory. If anyone wants to pass, the dogs accept a sort of toll as compensation. Most everyone avoids it, but some take pleasure in feeding the mongrels. I know I do. So do you or do you not like badger?"

The woman on the road held Tamis's interest. Watching her offer a piece of cured meat, it did not surprise him when the biggest dog with a missing leg lunged. As the hungry animal snapped, taking the morsel, she jumped back, and the large straw hat fell off. The girl with rusty-brown hair quickly reclaimed it before one of the dogs could snatch it up as well.

Tamis's stomach clenched. Eyes wide and mouth agape, everything felt unreal in that instant. "This cannot be true. Is this a dream? That is my sister!"

Brow furrowed, the hunter replied, "I am sure that I am real. That means she must be just as real, lad. Your sister is a lovely looking woman. What is her name?"

"It is Olivia, but I thought she's dead!"

The hunter had an inclination of where this was going and wore a suspicious frown, pipe firmly in his teeth. "She is clearly alive and well. How is it that she is supposedly dead?"

"A year ago, my sister went to Deleon to get a remedy for mother and never came home. The next day, a guard delivered the remedy and said he found it on the road with her scarf. When he gave it to us, it was covered in blood. Why is she here?"

Becoming very serious, the hunter's tone darkened. "Listen to me, lad, and take my advice: Do not approach her. She seems to be here of her own free will. Whatever the truth of this matter is, I'm certain that you do not want to know it. Remain within the manor grounds. It's much better that way."

Watching Olivia walking away, Tamis's heart raced. "I can't."

The hunter chuckled, shaking his head. "I thought so. Take my cape. If you do go out in the streets, be sure not to let anyone see your face. They don't trust outsiders. I have to get back to hunting, so tell me, do you want a badger for your dinner tonight or not?"

With his sister out of sight and the question posed to him for the third time, Tamis turned and gave an uncomfortable look. "I don't know. I guess so."

At first, the hunter was perplexed. Then an epiphany struck him, and the smoke in his mouth slowly leaked out in thin streams. Sensitive to the boy's unsettled disposition, he remarked in concern and surprise. "You used to be human."

Tamis avoided eye contact.

"Last night must have been the first you've spent as a creature." When the young warrior remained silent, it seemed appropriate to help as best he could with zest and care. Cheerfully, he declared, "Then tonight you shall try your first badger! What is your name, warrior? What may I call you?"

He noticed after the pause that the hunter was extending a hand to shake. Taking the firm grip with his own, Tamis tried to smile. "Tamis, sir."

"I am Virgil. Virgil Gaspard. I'm known here as the Ranger of the North. Tonight's weather is going to be clear, so don't tarry in the city after dusk. It will be hard to resist, as to-day and through the night is Seasons Bounty."

"What's that?"

"It's the local harvest festival. Be careful, but do try to have some fun. Perhaps it shall help distract you from your troubles and your estranged sister."

The city streets were packed with locals trading goods, grown or crafted. Laughter and loud music filled the air. The smells that were not human were tolerable, and some were pleasant. Other odors challenged Tamis's gag reflex to its lim-it. These new senses were going to take some getting used to.

He soon felt free to take in the sights, sounds and smells without much worry. Everyone was so busy shopping or pre-paring for the evening's festivities that he was nearly invisible. As fun as it was to watch and listen to everyone, the keen sens-es and Virgil's warnings reminded him not to drop his guard. This relative invisibility would only last as long as nobody took notice. Thankfully, he was so new to being a Holy Hound that his eyes did not hold a glow. His small fangs had yet to grow in as well. The bow was safe on the second floor of the manor, so almost everything about his appearance was normal.

For a while, as he had no coins, his time was spent in the crowds watching rope walkers high in the air. Jugglers and rib-bon dancers performed on platforms, dressed in bright cos-tumes and decorated with mask-like face paint. It was not mag-ic, but Tamis thought the displays of skill were on equal foot-ing with the wondrous talents of mages.

The people watching alongside and all around were dressed in their best attire. A wide variety of hats and bonnets made from straw in celebration of the harvest was everywhere. Eventually, he caught a glimpse of a unique hat. The one be-longing to Olivia was weaving through the crowd, leaving the town square.

Tamis could not keep himself from following. No matter what Virgil had said, this was something he had to do. He had to know why and how she came to be here.

For a moment he lost sight of her hat but quickly found it again, going down another street. He followed and maintained a safe distance when the throng became less dense. Olivia came into full view on quieter streets. Coming to the other side of the city in the rural district, Tamis watched her enter a home.

When the door closed behind his sister, only he and a handful of others walked that street. Most everyone was at the festival. Going closer, the young warrior peeked through the window. The wooden shutters were open wide, and the interior of the house glowed with orange sunlight from another window. Tamis stood enraptured as Olivia greeted an old man, smiling happily. She kissed his cheek, and he chuckled, patting her hand.

For a while he observed as they talked, indifferent to the setting of the sun. It felt impossible to be seeing her smile again, and he remained stunned. There were no emotions. Tamis felt numb.

He was still numb when a silhouette joined with his in the reflection on the window. Before he could move, a hand gripped his shoulder and something rock solid smacked the top of his head. The world around him turned black.

A bucket of freezing cold water drenched him from head to toe, making Tamis gasp and wake with a start. He coughed and looked about. It was dark in the storage shed where he was bound tightly to a wooden chair. A lantern hung on a hook intended for curing beef, swinging slightly. The bright glow from the flame cast hard shadows on the man who had hit him with the water. The angry stranger was tall, at least five years older than Tamis and strong. He worked his jaw, covered in a thin beard.

Lobbing the empty bucket at a wall, the man shouted, "You think you can peep into my home and not be caught? What did you think to steal?"

Tamis said nothing, studying the familiar stranger. As the man took hold of the boy's hair and sneered into his face, he recognized him. This was the guard who had delivered Olivia's scarf and flask over a year ago. The eyes were savage but recognizable.

"I don't suffer thieves," he warned. "Who are you? I don't

know your face. Are you mute? Speak."

By now it was becoming clear: Olivia had eloped with the guard from Deleon. His sister, his flesh and blood, had abandoned him to care for their dying mother alone. The numbness of his mind and heart gave way, and rage burned hot in its place.

He glared back, and the words came from his lips as if they were not his own. "I am not the thief here. It is you who is the thief."

The man was initially surprised to hear him speak at all, then became irritated by the accusation. "Am I? What have I taken?"

Tamis's reply was an accusing glare.

Having had enough, the man's anger got the best of him, and he slammed a fist into Tamis's gut. It knocked the wind from the young warrior's lungs. While he was gasping for air, another swing connected with Tamis's cheek. His head rocked to the side, and stars blinked in his sight momentarily.

Taking up the lantern, the man spat on the ground and sneered, "I will be back with the guards. Tomorrow, they will hang you upside down for all to see in place of the festival ornaments. That is the punishment for thieves in this city."

The door slammed and locked as his captor left. Alone in the dark of the storage building, Tamis's stomach hurt terribly. He wondered where he had been taken. Using his nose without thinking, the smells from a high window let him know that this place was far from the city center. A faint scent of pines and soil told Tamis that he was close to the outskirts. Even if he called for help, it was not likely to be heard or heeded. The door was locked. No one could get in without a key or lock pick.

This certainly was a mess, he thought to himself. Virgil was right; he did not want to know why Olivia was alive. She had betrayed him and their mother, leaving her to die. It had proved impossible for Tamis to care for their mother alone. He could get plenty of food with his talents in hunting, but that was never enough. Feeling solemn, he thought perhaps his mother had weakened because Olivia was gone. The cruel trick may have broken her heart, killing her slowly with sorrow. Whether that was true, Tamis decided he didn't wish to know.

An aching in his head made Tamis wonder how hard the man had hit him. But when he could feel the veins bulging under the skin on his arms and face, fear gripped him. A full moon was rising. This was not a good place for that to happen. Olivia's lover was fetching the city guards and would be back soon.

He struggled against the ropes on his wrists and ankles. As he tried to break free, the pressure and heat inside him increased, making the task much more difficult. When he felt like a kettle about to rupture, he completely forgot about escaping.

Sweat poured down his face, and he thrashed, crying out in agony. His eyes glowed brilliantly in the dark. He could see into the shadows now, but the pain was blinding. Bones crunched, ground on each other and stretched, forcing a scream from his expanding chest. The sound was inhuman, frightening Tamis further. Claws sprouted from his fingertips, and his toes scratched at wood. His lengthening jaws snapped and clenched between loud outcries and ragged gasps. The ropes grew tighter as his body expanded, pressing against the sides of the chair.

Through his thrashing and expanding, one of the ropes on his ankles snapped, and his leg jerked free. He toppled over. The impact on his shifting body made his bones feel like glass, and he yelped. With the changes nearly complete, every muscle locked as if cramping, holding him paralyzed, straining for breath. A long moment of this passed, and Tamis slumped, huffing and puffing, cool air soothing his stretched lungs.

A soft growl vibrated in his throat as he turned over, ears tilted back. The ropes were broken, and the chair was barely intact. Using a nearby shelf for balance, he stood on wobbly legs, looking about. Nocturnal vision was new to him. It made some things almost glow, and the contrast of light and dark was beautiful even though nothing cast a shadow.

Snapping out of the daze, he remembered he needed to escape. Tamis eyed the overhead window where the stars blinked through. This body felt very different than he had expected, and he was unsure how much effort a ten-foot leap required. Quickly crouching then springing toward the opening, Tamis found out. Using all his strength, he sailed straight through the window and onto the rooftop.

He slid a short ways before panicking and gripping the shingles with sharp claws. Tamis panted rapidly, alarmed by the experience and the near fall to the cobbled streets. Eyeing the gutter by his feet and tail, he found the hound portions of his appendages disconcerting at first. Having padded paws was a bit shocking.

A real shock came when footsteps from a nearby street reached his long ears. The clank of the key in the lock made him freeze and hold his breath, waiting. The man had returned, and Tamis could hear two guards speaking. Then he listened closer as they entered the storage house. Light flickered through the roof window by Tamis's head. From inside, he heard one of the guards.

"Well? Where is this thief? I see nothing."

"He was just here! I had him tied to the chair."

There was a pause. "Looks to me like the blighter was more resourceful than you thought. I see nothing but a toppled chair and some ropes. Doubtful that the pest was a werewolf. The hunter is too good at his job, and it would have laid waste to the inside of this storage. Are you sure you tied him properly?"

"Yes. He was strung tight as a drum."

The other guard laughed. "Go back to the festival. Everyone in town is there. Forget this blighter. If you happen across him again, let us take care of things."

"I can't promise anything," Olivia's lover grumbled.

"Come along now. Let's not miss the bonfires. It is going to be cold tonight."

Tamis held still until they locked the door and departed. Once the sound of their footsteps disappeared, he stood up.

The city looked completely different in the night. He could not tell where he was or where the manor stood. Leaping across to the next block, the rusty brown hound climbed to a higher roof for a better vantage point. The claws and immense strength made it easy to reach the top without a ladder.

Wind whipped at the coarse fur on his neck as he craned his head. Right away, the bright town center and bonfires by the fields stood out. The rest of the city was unlit. Eventually, he spied the abandoned manor and the walls encompassing its grounds. It sat on a hill a few miles away.

Stealthily, Tamis hopped from block to block, skirting over wooden shingles, hoping none would give way. The roofs were old but in good shape. His weight was supported well enough. The guards' claim that the whole population was attending the festival was correct and thankfully so, Tamis thought. Sneaking back to the sanctuary of the manor would be much more precarious if people were in their homes.

Dropping down from the final roof at the city's edge, Tamis saw that the manor's gates were open wide, just as when he had left. Running upright proved too much of a challenge, and he was contented to drop to all fours. Tamis bounded under the moonlight, eager for the security of the walls.

Loud barking and baying announced the presence of a pack of wild dogs. The large leader with a missing leg ran for Tamis, growling and making him stop cold.

"Who and what are you? You aren't welcome here. This is my territory!"

"Please," Tamis whined, "I was here this morning with Virgil, the hunter. I need to get back inside. If anyone sees me like this, I don't know what will happen."

"What?" The dogs ceased yapping, and their leader sniffed. Biting his lip with a sharp fang, he cocked his head. "Blow a whistle and call me a sheep dog. You're that boy. Fine. Get in before I change my mind. Don't cause any trouble."

"Thank you." Relief washed over Tamis once he was beyond the gates.

Going into the manor while the elderly wild dogs patrolled outside, Tamis went back upstairs. Reaching the guest room, he found Virgil sitting by a table with a candle. The young warrior froze in place when the hunter glanced over and stared.

Virgil was not afraid. Giving another puff of smoke from his pipe, he raised an eyebrow. "What did I tell you about getting back by sunset?" He chuckled. "It's quiet out, so it seems your little moonlight stroll went unnoticed."

"I hope so."

"I haven't the foggiest idea what you said, but I do have that badger I promised." He indicated a sack by the foot of

Tamis's guest bed. "Freshly killed, and I'll bet all of the excitement out there made you hungry."

It had been days since Tamis last ate. Opening the bag, a large gray carcass with black and white on its head lay balled up at the bottom. After hesitating, Tamis reached and brought it up by the nape of the neck. He gave it a sniff. The musky animal was repelling, but it disturbed him that the scent of blood made saliva pool in his jaws.

"If you don't want to make a mess of the place, the kitchen is on the bottom floor in the east wing. The dogs tend to eat what they will and bury the rest outside."

Perhaps he was right, Tamis thought. The dusty kitchen was not far. Going to the carving table, away from witnesses, he set the carcass down and gazed at it. The badger lay there, eyes glazed over and dilated.

Tamis had cleaned and cured his share of animals, but the idea of feeding on a fresh kill had his mind and stomach in knots. Turning the thing over, belly up, there did not seem to be an obvious means of starting. The smell of the blood filled his senses.

Though hesitant, Tamis tried to think of how to eat this badger. He felt silly for holding back, knowing Jack, Alex and even Oryn would be ridiculing him at this moment. On the other hand, he did not feel quite like he was enough of an animal to commit such a gory act.

For several minutes he debated with himself. He could feel a part of his mind wanting to feed. It scared him a little. Closing his eyes a moment, Tamis weighed the options. He could consciously go about this or let the growing instincts do the dirty work.

His heart began to race, and his toes twitched at the prospect; the fear and the hunger divided him. For now, he decided, it was time to let the animal free. Forgetting his human reservations, the hound sunk its fangs into the limp, furry body. He gripped with claws, ripping open skin and exposing flesh, sinew and bone. The blood leaked from severed veins onto the wooden table, adding to older stains. Bite after bite, Tamis tore into the dead creature, swallowing chunks whole. Slowly his belly began to fill, satisfying his primal needs.

Chapter 20
LYING LOW

"Well, it seems you got as much enjoyment out of that badger as there was to get."

Virgil's voice woke Tamis with a start where he had fallen asleep at the table. The hunter's footfalls were light. Trying to wake his mind enough to form a response, Tamis rubbed his eyes with human hands.

Virgil picked up the dried, bloody remains and bones. "You picked it almost clean, but the dogs would love to have this. Do you wish to save it for later?"

Looking up at the shredded carcass, surprise struck him at seeing what he had done to the dead thing. After submerging himself into the instincts, they proved much stronger than anticipated. He could hardly recall finishing and falling asleep. This disturbed him greatly.

He shook his head and replied. "No thank you. I don't want it anymore."

The pleasant smile left Virgil's face, and he studied the sullen warrior. Setting the remains aside on a forgotten cutting board, he took up a seat beside him. "Is it the act of feeding that bothers you, or is it possible you regret seeking out this Olivia yesterday?"

Tamis's brow furrowed. "I'm not sure. Both, I think."

"Let us begin with the easier of the two: What bothers you about the badger?"

Giving a frightened look, he restrained a shudder. "I was told of animal instincts that would take the place of my human ones. Last night I was quite hungry, but not at all glad to eat the thing. It was far easier to let the animal in me do so instead. When I did let that side of me take control, I was lost; I seemed to have disappeared. I was not me."

Virgil gave an encouraging smile. "Even the tamest beast

experiences such occurrences. Dogs in a frenzy become slaves to their drives. Until their inner spell is spent, they are not themselves. It is the nature of certain creatures. Some humans are prey to primal instincts and find trouble when they cannot keep these motives in check."

Tamis did not appear consoled.

"Take my old friend Regorian Lancer: The man had a love for women that was unquenchable. In his many encounters, most ended in conflict because he could not keep his blasted trousers strapped on. That is as feral an instinct as it gets. You said yourself that you were quite hungry, did you not? You did no wrong, so there is no cause for you to fear these instincts. Understand, boy? Make no mistake: If I thought you were a threat, I would not have brought you to this place so close to humans."

Feeling better, a small smile turned up his cheeks.

Pointing at the mangled mess of skin and bones, Virgil scoffed. "If you were hungry enough to pick that thing as clean as this, then it is no surprise to me that you experienced a feeding frenzy."

At this, Tamis finally laughed.

"It is about time you were light-hearted. Laughter is one of the best remedies."

"I don't even know why it is funny to me."

"Does it matter?"

"I suppose not."

"Now, not to dampen your rare cheery mood, but what exactly happened with Olivia?"

He fell quiet and stared long at the blood-stained table covered in dust and claw marks.

"What did she have to say for herself?"

"I found her but did not get near enough to ask. She did not see me. I was knocked over the head and taken captive by the man she is staying with. When the moon came out I broke the ropes and escaped."

Virgil was startled. "He saw you change?"

"No. He had gone off to fetch the guards. I was out of sight before they returned."

The hunter smiled. "You had a masterful spirit of luck on your side then."

A familiar flame of anger lit in Tamis's stomach again. "Remember the guard I mentioned before?"

"The one from your tale about how your sister deceived you to think her dead?"

"The man Olivia lives with is the same. He did not remember me, but I know his face. I never forgot. He was the one who delivered her bloody scarf and flask."

Virgil became serious. "You must know what this means?"

He nodded. "My sister eloped with him. She really abandoned us."

"Not so fast, boy. There is the chance that the trick was planned by her lover and she simply went along. Don't be too quick to lay all of the blame on your sister. There is always more to know."

Angry, Tamis looked back, and his eyes glowed for a moment. "Does it matter?"

Considering the look in the young man's stare, Virgil raised an eyebrow. "That depends. She is most likely not the only one at fault in this instance of deceit. Times like these are hard. Choices must be made, and not easy ones. You must walk the razor's edge and think how you wish this story to end. How would you see the chapter of your life involving Olivia to conclude?"

Still heated, he replied, "I don't know."

"I advise that you make a decision. Believe me when I say that you do not want this choice to be made without you. For now, follow my suggestion from yesterday and remain within the manor grounds. The man with your sister may spot you on the streets. I've seen your eyes spark with light once already. If he were to catch you in a moment of rage, your secret would be known. Lie low for a time."

As much as Tamis wanted to get more answers, he was in no mood to meet that man again. He nodded. "Yes, sir."

Virgil chuckled. "Thank you for the compliment, but call me by my name. We are friends, are we not?"

Tamis's heart warmed, and the anger subsided. "Yes. I suppose so."

While the Ranger of the North went out to patrol the passes and keep the roads safe, the abandoned estate was much quieter. To escape the musty odors, Tamis walked the overgrown garden. Ivy consumed most everything. Stubborn roses peered out between the stifling vines. These rare blossoms were known for blooming late and long at the end of summer. They defied the cold until the first snowfall. Only then would the red petals wilt.

They smelled wondrous. There was no need to put his nose to them. From arm's length, the scent was strong enough. His keen senses also alerted him to a squirrel living in the garden and several bird nests. The smells that upset his sensitive sinuses were all of the markings left by the dogs near their leavings. Several times he avoided treading barefoot on an old pile. Tamis promised himself that this was something he would never allow any instincts to drive him to. Human or not, some sensibilities needed to be maintained.

When no more of the vast garden was left to explore, a cold wind compelled him to go indoors. For the remainder of the day, Tamis napped in the guest room warmed by the brilliant sunshine. He woke as it began to set. Gazing out at the dying light, he realized that the cause for his waking were the instincts. Night was time to be alert, for better or worse.

He took the bow from under the bed. Testing the taunt string, he realized it had been two days since he last drew it back. Right away, he noticed that his strength was either much greater or the bow was slack. Tamis pulled the string far with almost no resistance, light focused on the string in the form of a ready arrow, notched for flight. It would take a little practice to adjust to the lack of resistance.

Carefully letting the string straighten, Tamis watched the light arrow dissipate, and he looked at the darkening glass window. Where were the others, he pondered? Would Adwen find him in this place? For all he knew, they were still trapped in the snow like a frozen tomb. There was no way he could know, and Virgil was right. Setting out in an unfamiliar forest alone with demons looking for him would be foolish. He had no alternative but to wait and hope.

The downstairs entrance opened on squeaky hinges, and a draft brought Virgil's scent. Smells of the elderly dogs wafted along with it as he left the door open for them and ascended the stairs. Virgil entered the bedroom and chuckled upon seeing the young warrior on the bedside. "I am glad to see you took my advice. No badger tonight, I'm afraid. You aren't hungry are you?"

Tamis shook his head. "No. I'm actually not hungry at all."

"Good," Virgil replied as he sat at the table and took up his pipe and tobacco. "No need to disappoint your appetite with the stroke of bad luck. The feisty buggers seem to be catching on and hiding from me. All the better. When they multiply in spring, there will be good hunting in the autumn again. For now, I shall hunt rabbit and the occasional sheep or deer."

Setting the bow aside, Tamis looked outside, growing anxious. "It is night."

Unconcerned, Virgil nodded, packing tobacco into the pipe. "Yes. It is."

Tamis fidgeted, searching for the words. "The sky is clear, isn't it?"

Virgil paused and stared.

"Perhaps I should move to another room for the night," Tamis offered.

"Whatever for?" the hunter scoffed and carried on. "I see no point in it. Stay. Help keep this room warm. Another body helps stave off the chill."

Tamis was unsure if he was being clear. "I'm going to change soon."

Virgil chuckled, tossing a clever smile. "You are rather bashful, boy."

"You are not bothered?"

He rolled his eyes. "Do I appear bothered? Come now. I've seen werewolf transformations enough to not find a shifting body so unsightly anymore. And after stumbling across a few harmless shape shifters living in the wilds, my tolerance for witnessing such things is unrivaled. Stay. I am intrigued to see the comparison of your change to that of a shape shifter."

"True-blooded shape shifters still exist?"

"Some of them are friends of mine. I help keep them safe from outsiders." A sly glint was in his eye, and he held a finger to his lips. "Don't tell anyone." He chuckled.

Tamis was surprised and intrigued. "A shape shifter change is different from that of a werewolf?"

Nearly finished stuffing the pipe, he tested it and talked through his teeth in between puffs. "Night and day of difference." Finally lighting it, he took a few drags until he was satisfied and blew a large ring. Looking through it at the stunned look on Tamis's face, Virgil added, "The change of an abomination is as unsightly as it gets. Their bones don't stretch; they bend and break. If that's not bad enough, the skin on their faces melts off. That is why their wolfish faces are mottled shades of red; it is dried blood and sinew."

The mental image sent a shiver down the young warrior's spine.

Virgil noticed. "Are you more comfortable hiding alone in a vacant room for the experience?"

After thinking it over, Tamis shook his head. "I would not be. I thank you for your company. It distracts me from unpleasant thoughts."

"You are very welcome, my friend." The hunter puffed another ring.

Minutes went by while they waited. Remembering what it felt like to fall while in mid-transformation led Tamis to choose to sit on the floor. His back rested against the wooden bed frame as he watched Virgil light candles and put on a show with his smoke. In the moments leading up to the gripping fever, the skilled smoker managed to blow smoke in squares. When Tamis began to sweat and rub his head, it was Virgil's turn to observe. The hunter saw how the young man's skin blushed, pumped thick with rushing blood. His interest was placid, as if this were no different from watching passersby on a road.

But once the changes began, Tamis hollered, and the volume made the man wince and plug his ears. He carried on puffing on the pipe, holding it in place precariously with his lips and teeth. With the exception of the pain the boy went through, this transformation was very much like a shape shifter's. Face, hands, feet and ribs were first to noticeably extend, swiftly followed by the rest of the bones. Muscles and tissues gradually filled in as bare skin was overgrown by a fur coat. The dragon leathers held together perfectly, fitting to Tamis's altering form.

The commotion got the attention of the dogs downstairs. They all barked, but the leader came up and stopped at the door, growling as the warrior finished changing.

Crouched low on all fours, quaking and gripping the floorboards with sharp claws, Tamis panted. The pain faded, letting him relax at last. Now quiet and no longer shuddering, he heard and understood the dog at the door.

"If I thought for a second that you had control of your shape, I would teach you a lesson for upsetting the old ones. They're not long for this cold world, and the last thing they need is being startled to death. You're lucky I didn't just attack."

Ears low, Tamis gave an apologetic whine. "I thank you for not doing so."

Virgil unknowingly interrupted. "That change was not so bad. Be thankful you are in the service of the Heir. You will never know what it is to be under the curse of the werewolf. If you don't mind, it is time for me to get some sleep. Good evening to you, boy." Virgil pulled the hood of the cloak Tamis had borrowed down, covering his eyes. The hunter forgot to clean out his pipe and attempted to sleep with it smoldering in his grasp. Wisps of smoke trailed upwards, dissipating before his lazy breaths.

The big dog departed downstairs, mumbling to himself. "Mangy human. He's lucky we need him."

For a moment Tamis thought of trying to sleep as well, but he was wide awake. So not to disturb his friend, he followed after the gruff pack leader.

He came down to the bottom of the stairs and stopped to watch. The dog was busy checking over the old strays of various sizes. All had dirty matted fur. Tired and hungry, they licked their jowls and achy paws, and curled up for the night. Finished with his rounds, the pack leader ambled over to sit at the open door, standing guard.

Tamis quietly came within a short distance. "May I join you?"

After looking him over and sniffing, a low growl came in answer. "So long as you don't make any loud howling."

"Sorry."

The dog said nothing and turned back to look at the city firelights beyond the gate and the field. He was alert and unreadable to the warrior.

Tamis abandoned the support of the handrail, barely accustomed to walking on his new legs and feet. The door frame became his next source for balance, and he sat on the steps beside the dog in silence. They observed the smells and flickering candlelight and torchlight from distant homes, which were much warmer than theirs. By midnight, most were doused. Two or three taverns remained lit.

Over the course of unmarked hours, Tamis found himself glancing over at the dog. One of his hind legs was severed at the second knee, leaving the shaggy haunch. He could sit upright, and after so many times of doing so, the hairless nub at the end was heavily scarred. The warrior found it difficult to look away for reasons he could not perceive.

Several times he looked, until the dog remarked blandly. "Looking won't make it sprout back."

Tamis swiftly looked away. "I didn't mean to offend."

The dog scoffed. "Look all you like. You have a little magic in you. I can smell it. Maybe I'm wrong and your stare will return it to me."

The statement caught him off guard. "If I have magic, it is not much."

"Any amount is a lot. Yours is in your eyes, and it is spreading to the rest of you as we speak."

Both were quiet. Then Tamis's curiosity won over his caution.

"What happened? To your leg, I mean."

The dog did not answer right away. When he did, he was somber. "Do you know what betrayal is, strange boy creature?" Catching the scent of Tamis's aggravation about his sister, the dog went on: "Ah. You know. I can smell it on you. To a dog, betrayal is almost impossible to contemplate. There are challenges for pack status, but betrayal is unspeakable. I hate the human breed for that weakness of nature. They can betray."

He began with a growl. "I was devoted to my master. There were only him, my mate and me hunting in the forest. He was not a hunter of whatever sort the human upstairs is. I have heard him called ranger. My old master was not one of them, but just as proud; maybe more so. I did not know at the time, but my master was foolish. He led us off after prey, and we lost the tracks in the snow. We were deep in the mountains when a sudden blizzard came, trapping us in the wilds. We found a cave and took shelter there, but our master was unprepared for this. After the first day, the storm continued, and he became desperate. He was desperate for warmth, and no wood was available for burning.

"That was when he looked at us. To try to escape the cold, he used my mate's carcass, fitting himself in her gutted chest. I feared him then, and I hate myself for not trying to stop him. That made me a fool as well, and I was made a greater fool when I stayed at his side. The next day, the storm still had not ended. My master's bags were empty, and so was his belly. I barely escaped."

The dog sniffed his stump and looked up at Tamis. "The storm went on for several more days. Cold and ice sealed my wound, saving my life. My master did not survive, and I was without a master or a pack. That ranger found me, and he was bold enough to bandage my wound and guide me to this empty human dwelling. He did not demand anything of me, nor I of him. Over time, I found other strays with different stories and brought them to this place. There are ten of us now. Without that mangy ranger, they would perish of empty bellies. That is a slow and painful death."

Tamis looked back at the unlit hearth where the old dogs lay, some snoring. "What happened to them?"

"Some had good masters who died. A few were throwbacks – they were born unwanted by their mother's masters. One I pulled from a river as a pup where a human had thrown her, intending her to drown. She helps me patrol and is my second in command. When I am gone, she will replace me as pack leader." He chuckled to himself at the thought. "Even though I am missing a leg, she cannot best me for my rank."

The hound warrior's ears dipped low, and he whined. "I could never betray you or your pack. That would be terrible."

The big alpha dog scoffed again. "You may not be human, but the nature that makes you more human than beast can make matters complicated. In a pack, there is only service to the others and the alpha. In human packs, their complicated set of loyalties muddies the water. Even by accident, betrayal can happen."

Tamis heaved a heavy sigh. "I suppose I should just count myself lucky that I was left whole in the end."

"You are wrong, pup boy." The dog rumbled, "No one escapes betrayal whole. A piece of who you are is broken off and lost, leaving a scar and a callus behind."

Chapter 21
ONE SHOT

Tamis found sleep beside the dogs before the empty hearth. A few curled up against and on top of him, undisturbed when his body shrank with the passing of the full moon. The creatures that found his body had shrunken away merely got up and moved closer. They clustered by the slumbering warrior, drawing from his strong warmth.

Just before sunrise, when the first people in the city went out to work, a bell tower chimed. The ringing reached for miles around.

The barking of the alpha woke the older dogs, causing them to gingerly get up on arthritic hips and legs. They trotted out into the early-morning air, barking ceaselessly. Going after them, Tamis was groggy, but becoming more alert. He found Virgil already standing at the gate across the lawn.

He joined the hunter, following his gaze up to the clouds over Jenkirk. A black shape glided and circled like a vulture with a long, serpentine neck looking back and forth.

"What's happened?"

Cleaning the pipe he had neglected in the evening, the ranger was brooding. "That demon showed up about an hour ago. I think it is searching for you. The town's people just sounded the alarm."

Anxious, Tamis turned to him. "Well? What is your advice?"

"I'm not sure it knows you are here. If no one antagonizes it, and it does not attack, it may leave. Keep your head down. Killing it would let all of the other demons know you are in this valley. The people also would discover your presence. That would not bode well, even if you could destroy the fiend."

The dogs continued to bark at the sky, and the two companions watched more people cluster in the streets as others closed their windows and doors tight. Archers began to line rooftops. Two longbow men tested the demon's range, and the pair of arrows fell short by a vast distance.

A few more minutes passed as the people were baffled, every eye watching the Dred riding the wind. Then it appeared to be irritated by the squabbling below and at not finding its prey. The monster's throat swelled, and it spat a black mass of flesh-dissolving acid that stuck like glue. Screams of fear and wails of agony echoed to the hilltop manor.

Virgil was knocking the pipe against the stone wall, empty-ing it when the first attack landed. Clenching his jaw, he sneered as Tamis was already headed inside. "Damn bugger!"

The warrior came back with the golden bow, ready to dash into the streets, but the ranger stopped him. "Hold up a mo-ment, boy."

"You said to lie low unless it attacked!"

"Calm yourself! I'm only giving you my cloak again. Here." While Tamis donned it and drew the hood over his head, Virgil warned, "Keep to the shadows. Stay out of sight. If you actually can strike it down, be ready to disappear right away. Do not linger. If you are seen, you will be followed. Mark my words, if you are found out, I may not be able to protect you. Monsters and dangerous beasts are my game, not mobs of common folk."

Tamis nodded and bolted, moving quickly as a frightened hare. He secretly marveled at the speed with which he went down the hill. A horse would be hard-pressed to keep the pace. Coming to the first building, he remembered the times the other warriors jumped great distances.

With the agility and guile of a stag, Tamis left the cobbled ground and sailed up to the rooftop. He ducked beneath an overhang, avoiding the line of sight from the demon and the archers. The Dred circled farther away over other districts, forcing Tamis to continue in search of a better place to take aim.

As he dashed and vaulted, hidden from sight, the Dred spat again and again at the scrambling humans. The thing hissed and shrieked, its bloodlust aroused by a symphony of screams. It did not notice the warrior moving deeper into the city.

In his approach to an ideal position, Tamis felt almost as he did when he hunted in the southern forests. Olivia had taught him how to shoot so that she could tend to other matters such as washing and cooking. She had told him once that his accuracy was unnatural. In his life, only three times had he missed a target. He prepared himself, taking a steady breath and drawing back the string.

When he turned out from his hiding place and took aim, what the alpha dog had noticed in the night proved true: Powerful magic was in his eyes. Sighting along the shimmering shaft of the light arrow, his magical vision closed the gap to the demon. It appeared as if it were thirty yards away, gliding slowly by. Tamis blinked in shock, flinching at the terrible sight of the demon.

Swallowing the fear, the young warrior became stern, and his grasp on the bow relaxed. His aim steadied as a result. Following the demon's travel with his arrow, Tamis aimed for where a heart should be, if the fiend had one. Once he sensed the time was right, he released the silken string.

The unsuspecting Dred felt invincible, soaring near a mile over the helpless city. A glimmer caught its eye just before the shard of light ran it through. A spray of purple slime burst out the exit wound with the shining arrow before it vanished. The demon shrieked in surprise and pain, buckling in midflight.

In the street, countless people saw the demon struck then begin to flail and fall. Some looked for who could have done the feat. Among them, Olivia and her lover. The initial flash before the arrow flew had grabbed her attention. The moment the missile hit the demon, she gasped, and her eyes became wide. Looking back to the isolated shadow on the far away roof, Olivia knew.

Her lover soon followed her gaze. He recognized the cloak that the mysterious archer wore. Instead of being thankful for the boy's return, fresh anger came over him. Magical or not, the would-be thief still had to answer for the other day. Having already asked around only to find no one who knew the boy, he had an idea where his hiding place might be.

Right after Tamis's arrow left the string, his sight returned to normal. He jumped from the roof after briefly plotting a safe course to avoid detection. Hiding the shiny weapon as best he could beneath the cloak, his path took him to the out-skirts. Along the forest's edge, the cover of the greenery served him well. Few sticks found the undersides of his bare feet. His experience as a woodland hunter saved his skin the additional punishment. To ensure no one saw him, the warrior returned to the manor by circumnavigating Jenkirk.

Leaving the forest for open fields, Tamis slowed to a walk. He was winded, and people were dispersing. His inhuman speed would blow his cover, even from a distance. Panting and gasping for air, the rest of the way back to the manor was pleasant. Walking up the final hill and approaching the gate, Tamis felt good to have killed the demon, but more were like-ly searching as well. The Dred was gone, but real dread re-mained.

Tamis realized too late that the dogs were hiding in the house, the alpha snarled from the open threshold.

By a long stretch of stone wall, downwind, a familiar man's voice chided, "Where do you think you are going?"

Tamis whirled around and froze in the dirt road.

Olivia's lover stalked closer, accompanied by three com-panions with a club and two bows. "Magic of any kind is not welcome here. I should have known you were worse than a common burglar. You are a freak, a blight on nature."

Anger made Tamis's eye glow brightly, hidden under the hood, and he snapped back, "Says the man who deserted his place as a guard in Deleon and left his honor behind as well."

The three friends stared at the man, who was now out-raged. "Why you little prat!"

Tamis was roughly grabbed and thrust back, falling to the ground. The cloak hood folded away, and he glared up at them, clenching his teeth. The warrior was unaware that his eyes glowed and that his small fangs had grown in. Though not as long as the other Holy Hounds' fangs, they were noticeable.

The four men were stunned, and one pointed his empty bow. "Hey, Garret? You didn't say this thief was a monster, too!"

Garret's face twisted into a deadly sneer, and he spat at the ground. Then he shouted, "Kill it!"

Tamis scrambled back a short ways as the dogs barked

louder and the men set their arrows. As they were taking aim, something hit the dirt at their toes. They all stopped to gape at a crossbow bolt stuck in the ground.

The ranger had already reloaded as he came out from hiding behind the manor wall. Pointing the deadly weapon at the men, his voice was cold and calm.

"I would put those down if I were you. The first one to touch him gets a second stick knocking between his knees."

The men stared, motionless and silent.

Virgil's glare deepened, and he added slyly, "You boys know I won't miss."

One gulped.

"Put those toys away before someone gets hurt. Away with you now. Go back and tend to the wounded."

While the three lowered their weapons and prepared to go, Garret pointed at Tamis and shouted, "I found this thing staring into my home, and then it had the nerve to insult me by calling me a thief!"

"Is that so? It seems both of you have been offended. There is just one way to settle this then." Stalking to where Tamis lay on the ground, Virgil warned the men, "I shall lower my weapon, but know this: I serve and protect the people. This does not mean I would not defend myself. Raise your weapons at me and you die. Am I clear?"

Nervous nods from the trio of goons answered from behind their surly friend.

The ranger extended a hand to help Tamis to his feet. Pulling the boy up, Virgil whispered in his ear, "You are not a boy, and you are not an animal. He's challenging you. A real man stands before his enemies and defends his honor."

"Let's get on with it!" snapped Garret, balling his fists.

Rushing out from her hiding place in the bushes by the wall, Olivia cried, "No, don't!"

Everyone paused to see the woman go to her lover, and Garret sighed, shaking his head. "I said to stay away. Go home. This will be taken care of soon enough."

"No," she pleaded. "Let him go. Please come back with me. Leave him alone."

He glanced between her and the warrior. "You know this creature? Wait. This is your brother! You said you would not tell him we were here."

"Tamis? Tamis, look at me. What are you doing here?"

Ignoring Olivia's pleas, the warrior turned to Virgil.

"Show them," the ranger murmured assuredly. "Show them you are a man."

As Tamis stepped forward, Garret shushed Olivia and made certain she was at a safe distance. "This is why you call me thief? For rescuing your sister from that witch of a mother? If that woman had her way, Olivia would have wasted her youth staying cooped up in that pathetic excuse for a house."

Olivia gasped and snapped at him, "Garret, stop! That's enough. Let's go."

Anger made the now-permanent light in Tamis's eyes brighten, focusing on Garrett as he spoke: "You are nothing more than a thief because you took without asking. Now you insult my mother. You are a venomous monster like that flying demon lying dead in the fields."

Garret huffed and came close, sneering into Tamis's face. "You think you are a man, little beast? I heard what that filthy huntsman said. Do you think yourself a man?" Swiftly, he smacked Tamis, making him flinch and glare in defiance. "Do you think you are a man?" Smacking him again and again, he kept asking the same question as Tamis's face became redder from the abuse.

Olivia cried out, beginning to cry, "Garret! Stop it! Stop it, please!"

After taking several insulting raps about the face and head, the rage that first came to be in the dark of the storage shed rekindled. Without thinking, instincts both human and inhuman, drove him to move. When the next open hand swatted for his cheek, his own came up in the blink of an eye, taking an unbreakable death grip on Garret's wrist.

Shocked, the assailant paused.

Tamis's other hand swung over, striking Garret on the temple. The sheer power behind the open palm nearly flipped the man, his head finding the dirt before the rest of him landed in a heap.

Virgil slowly applauded as the others gasped, watching Garret struggle to regain consciousness, fidgeting as his world spun round.

Olivia was quick to go to her lover's side as he groaned, touching him with comforting hands. She looked up at her younger brother. Emotional and angry, the woman scolded, "Go away, Tamis! Go home! Tell mother I'm staying here!"

"She's dead!"

The face of his sister flushed white. "What did you say?"

"She's dead, Olivia! I couldn't take care of her on my own, and she died! The curse killed her!"

"There is no curse, Tamis," she retorted. "There couldn't have been!"

Tamis glared back, his voice cold. "The Heir of Darien saved me from demons and tried to help her. The Heir of the Master Knight cannot lie, and she said it was true, that dark magic was sapping her life. You were wrong, Olivia. Your doubts poisoned your heart against your own flesh and blood. I used to be too trusting but not anymore. But not you. You, Olivia, did not trust enough."

Sobbing, she cried out, helping Garret to his feet, "I did what I had to! I wanted to live my own life! Mother never would have let me go!"

Tamis's eyes glazed with tears that threatened to fall. Yet coldly, Tamis replied, "She let me go. In the end, I learned that she wanted more for me. Mother would have let you go too. You forgot how much she loved us, and then you broke her heart."

Olivia sobbed harder, and Garret steadily regained some balance. Embracing the crying woman, he shot Tamis a deadly look. "Leave her be, animal. You've done enough."

"So have you," Tamis snapped. "You drove her to hurt our mother with lies! She tricked our mother to think she was dead! You gave us her bloody scarf!"

"That was my doing, not hers! Leave Olivia out of this! It was my idea!"

After thinking it over, the warrior shook his head. "It doesn't matter. Olivia allowed it. That makes her as guilty." To her, he said, "I will stay until the Heir comes to find me. Then I will go." Tamis picked up his bow and was about to go to the manor.

Virgil stopped him. The ranger's tone was serious, "Have you made a decision? What of your sister?"

His back turned, without a final glance, he stated, "My sister is dead. She died on the road to Deleon a year ago."

Olivia gasped and wailed, watching Tamis stalk back onto the manor grounds and disappear into the estate.

After observing the encounter and the sister's wailing of anguish, Virgil addressed the other four at the gate. "Your welcome has worn out. Young lady, make sure these boys toddle off back to their homes. Run along now. There is nothing for any of you here."

As the humans departed, only Garret gave a backward glance. The malice was gone as he tried to comfort Olivia. He did not know exactly what Tamis was and considered for the first time that perhaps this was his fault.

Virgil recognized the look of reconsideration. Taking out the pipe, he went inside to find Tamis in the upstairs guest room. Leaning against the door frame, Virgil packed in a pinch of tobacco as his warrior friend paced nearby.

Tamis still felt angry and in knots that he could not untangle. Glancing out the window at the dwindling figures on the road, the sense of contempt for Olivia was strong. Finally acknowledging the ranger at the door, he snapped, "She abandoned us! She left us just like father did." Spotting the solemn expression Virgil wore, Tamis was frustrated. "You think I've done wrong, don't you?"

The silent ranger worked his pipe.

Scratching at an itch on the side of his neck for a moment, Tamis glowered and continued pacing. "How could she do it? How could she? What she did to mother and to me is unforgivable. Don't you think what she did was unforgivable?"

Virgil took a slow, deliberate draw and exhaled a vast plume of smoke.

When the ranger remained silent, Tamis went to lean on the window sill, gazing at the city. What he could not understand was if his sister was so wrong, then why did he feel this way? Why did he feel so bad? Tamis could not find a reason and heaved a heavy sigh.

At last, Virgil spoke. "Which do you think shall knock on your door first? The people or the hordes of demons hunting you?"

Tamis was calmer and somberly replied, "They won't tell

anyone. The city people won't come. I'm not human, but I am her brother. The people would blame her for my presence here, just as they would blame me for the demon that arrived this morning. They would not take the risk."

The ranger was pleased. "Very clever. Very clever indeed. You are a smart man."

Irritated, Tamis rounded on him. "What is it that makes me a man? Being angry? Being smart? Fighting back? What is the point?"

Virgil was unperturbed and understanding. "That you would ask that question is what makes you a man more than them. I was born a son to a noble. We did not see eye to eye. Regardless of birth or status, good men are strong of will and mind. It takes years of experience and age to learn the answers to it all. You lack both age and experience, but you are learning faster than most. Then again, many never learn the difference from a man and a narrow-sighted brute."

Tamis lost his anger and saddened. "Why won't you tell me if I was wrong to cast my sister aside?"

"It is not for me to say, young man. This is your affair; it is your story. The choice cannot be made by me."

Frustrated with himself more that the ranger, he replied, "You think I should forgive her. I know it. Why won't you say it?"

"I see the turmoil in your eyes. It is you who wants to forgive. That is the source of your aggravation now, not Olivia. You must recognize that."

"But I can't!"

Virgil's look was comforting. For a while he watched Tamis wrestle with his emotions. "Let me ask a question then: Does it matter if what she has done is forgivable?"

"I don't understand."

Blowing smoke from his nostrils before answering, he sighed. "Let us suppose you do not choose to forgive Olivia. What is to gain and what is the purpose? To keep her from hurting you again? Life does not work that way. As long as you hold this over her head, it hangs over yours even more. The weight of your grudge will wear you down, bit by bit, changing who you are, and not for the better. To forgive is not to forget or to relinquish control over Olivia. You do not control her;

control is an illusion. Choosing to forgive is for the benefit of yourself. I can see how your heart already strains under the weight of it, like a mountain on your shoulders."

More torn that ever, Tamis wanted to rip his hair out at the roots. "How can I? I don't know how?"

"You must think about it. Once more, this is a riddle only you can answer."

Chapter 22
ANOTHER STORM

Tamis wandered the garden. It felt like a contemplative place with its twists and turns that led back to the beginning. The little green labyrinth was simpler than the tangled mess in his head. A secluded corner had a stone bench, and he sat there, despite its coldness chilling his legs.

The sound he heard Olivia make when he walked away still filled his ears. That cry of pain had struck him, but Tamis only pretended not to listen. She deserved it, he thought. That was hardly close to the pain he felt being ripped from his mother's side. He had to be carried off, but Olivia left willingly. Even if she believed the curse was a lie, how could she be so callous? How could his sister be so selfish?

Smelling the alpha dog and hearing his footfalls, it did not surprise the warrior when the crippled creature appeared. Going close, he growled, and Tamis understood.

"What have you done? You skulk like a pup who's soiled a carpet."

Stunned at first, Tamis marveled for a moment. "I what?"

"So you can hear me. I thought that your ears were only open when your less-human shape allowed you that luxury. All the better; we need to talk."

Tamis looked away. "I don't feel much like talking."

"I want to tell you how much I respect how you dealt with that man. It is well within your strength to kill him with little effort. Those hands of yours can bend a sword. What you did to his head was like a firm spanking. Even angered, you showed restraint. For that, I respect you."

Thinking back, the dog was right. He had held back a bit, just a little.

"However, you should give your sister another chance."

Tamis's eyes gleamed dangerously. "Why? Virgil already

let me know in his way that he thinks I should. What is your reasoning? You, most of all, understand betrayal."

"I may not have understood part of their human speech, but I heard you very clearly. It sounds as if Olivia was lured. And her actions, once you made her see the truth, make me believe she grasps the error."

"And so?"

"If she did not care, it would not have made her howl like a banshee."

"But she betrayed me."

"My master betrayed me and my mate. Let me tell you a secret: I still have a feeling of devotion to that man for his desperation. Yet I have not forgotten, and I would never trust him again even if he lived."

As the wind rustled in the vines, a long silence ensued as Tamis pondered.

"I smell it on you; you hurt because of what you said, because you are still devoted to your family. Olivia is your sister, so you cannot forget, and you struggle to forgive. It is a double-edged sword in your heart."

He grumbled, "One I wish would be removed."

"What I suggest is to give Olivia what you must, rather than what she does or does not deserve. Withhold trust, and give her what is necessary to ease your suffering. What must you give her, even if not forgiveness, to stop this hurt?"

Confused, he asked, "A compromise of sorts?"

"Yes, a compromise, with yourself. That should allow you time to decide whether or not to forgive. Pain and anger cloud judgment, man pup."

"Time." Tamis felt uneasy. "I feel strange. It feels like time is slipping from under me, like ice cracking beneath my feet on a pond."

The big dog with a missing leg put his nose to the air and sniffed. "A storm is coming. Better get inside before it rains. Escort me there, if you please."

"No, thank you."

"I'll not leave you. As far as I am concerned, I count you among my pack."

Finally making eye contact, Tamis saw the subtle warmth in the beast's stare.

"Are you getting up, or are we getting a cold bath?"

He smiled and almost laughed. "Okay. I'll come inside."

The dog was right. Rain did come. A steady shower covered the valley until blasting winds shook trees, bringing sheet after sheet of sleet. The dirt road turned muddy, and tiny rivers of brown ran down the hill to Jenkirk. With the last of the old dogs inside, the alpha made sure that his second in command was not left out. It was too wet to smell trespassers. The tan colored dog shook her soaked fur at the door, misting the walls with her musky scent.

Virgil remarked as he came down with his lit pipe and a candle, "The smell of dog is rather strong once it rains." He chuckled, while a few of the mutts licked the rain from their coats. "If there were any dry kindling I would light a fire."

"What of the kitchen stools? No one uses them."

"Ah, but what if guests arrive?"

Tamis could not help but laugh a little.

"You are a guest, aren't you? There is always a chance."

Tamis shook his head, chuckling. "How is it that you are so strange?"

A clever smile made Virgil's eyes sparkle in the deepening dusk. "I'm well-traveled. The more interesting experiences one has, the stranger they become. I take it as a compliment."

Instead of retreating to the guest room, the friends shared the quiet with the pack of strays. They listened to the storm raging outside as wind rattled shutters on their hinges, as if it wanted to enter. Doors and windows were shut tight, keeping out the cold.

At the start of their peaceful silence, while Virgil played with the pipe smoke again, an intangible itch bothered Tamis. No amount of scratching at his neck and back would alleviate. It increased until the ranger thought it was strange.

Making another square to entertain the warrior, he saw that his performance went unnoticed. "Oh, don't tell me you've acquired flees. They are damned hard to get rid of for this lot."

One of the dogs whined in protest.

Tamis was perplexed. "I don't itch, but I can't help it.

When I try to keep still it gets worse."

The alpha dog's head rose and his ears pricked. Rising to his three legs, he turned and growled at the window facing Jenkirk. "I smell something."

Glancing between the two creatures, Virgil became serious. "Something has you all nervous. That's why you are scratching at nothing, my friend. Those instincts of yours are keener than even mine. What's the cause for concern, do you think?"

Following the alpha's lead in staring at the closed window, the storm raged on and his itch was gone. Fear crawled up his back, making the fine human hair on his arms and neck stand on end. Gazing at the rattling shutters, he murmured, "I'm not certain, but I don't like it. This feels like when I was being stalked by a wild mountain cat and heard it growl from behind. I can't see what frightens me, but I know it is there."

"What did you do then, when you heard the big beast?"

Getting up in a rush, he went up the stairs by twos and threes to get his bow. When he came back down, Virgil was by the door waiting.

"If demons have come, you will be near helpless. This dreadful night is too dark. They would see you long before you see them."

Tamis was afraid, but strangely calm in his reply. "Do you see how my eyes glow?"

"Yes, and it has been intriguing me all day."

"The dark is like day to me now, no matter my form. It would be better if you stayed."

"But who will have your back?"

He gave a questioning glance, although he was not surprised.

A daring look lit the ranger's face as he put out his pipe.

They went together, the ranger having donned his cloak and loaded the crossbow as Tamis led the way.

"What can you tell me of these creatures? Is there a way to spot them more easily?"

Hair now soaked and matted on his head, Tamis answered, "Of sorts. Their eyes glow red in the dark like vile fireflies. Some can spring from your own shadow if you are not careful."

"Good to know," Virgil chuckled. "Then I must not dawdle in one place for very long."

Despite the danger they were about to face, the remark got a laugh from Tamis.

"That's the spirit," the ranger added. "Meet the deadly things with a grin before feeding them an arrow. To business now."

Below the eaves of homes and stores was darkness. Water ran off the lips of shingles like wispy cascades, pounding the cobbled stones. The pair's footfalls were seldom louder than that of the pouring runoff everywhere in the city. Though the demons' presence made their skin crawl, they were nowhere in sight. All of the streets were quiet and still, aside from the rain and flickering candles in windows. They came to a stop by a shaded corner overlooking the city center. The emptiness of the plaza puzzled them. Everything was quiet.

While Virgil kept a sharp watch from behind, Tamis scanned the area, certain the demons were very close. He could feel it. Then he heard a noise too subtle for the human's ears. Amid the noise of rain battering wood, thatch and stone, a swift scratching came and went.

That was when Tamis finally looked up. His eyes widened at seeing Wretch demons darting overhead from one roof to the next like a plague of rats. It was an endless fluctuation of demons scouring the city from above.

After giving the ranger a soft prod in the arm, both held their breaths as they observed the frightening numbers. Each of them was eight feet tall and more than twice the weight of a man. Thankfully, the rain dulled their sense of smell, or else they would have already found the warrior and his human friend.

Tamis slowly began to draw his bow when Virgil stopped him. "Not yet. They would swarm in the blink of an eye. We cannot defeat them in a little nook." Nodding toward the other side of the plaza, he continued. "The bell must be rung. I will see to that while you take care of these monsters."

"If you ring it, the people will wake up, and it would be a bloodbath."

"You think they would leave if you were killed? Whether we ring the warning bell or not, there will be innocent blood shed tonight. Get to the top of the highest roof on this side without being seen, and ready your bow."

The idea of what demons would do afterward alarmed Tamis. "Wait. When you ring it, they will swarm. They will kill you!"

Virgil put a hand on his shoulder. "That is why I need you to be ready. I will wake the people and draw the blighters in for you to shoot. Ever since I found you lying in the woods, I have had your back. Tonight, I must have you watch mine. The Light Spirits deemed you worthy of being in the Heir's company. There is no doubt in my mind that you can do this. Besides, your bow is powerful enough to slay each fiend in a single hit. Also, don't tell anyone, but you are a better shot than I am."

Tamis wanted to laugh but could not. He smiled instead, afraid of losing his mentor to the demons. They parted. Virgil used his experience in going undetected to reach the town hall, leaving Tamis to his goal of getting up high enough to protect him. Shortly after reaching the lowest roof, it became clear that Virgil had the safer task.

The large, spiked demons prowled, jumping and sniffing everywhere. These things knew to look for him on higher ground, and that realization made Tamis sick. One fact that gave the boy a fighting chance was his inhuman agility. He had almost forgotten.

Slipping from one hiding place to another, Tamis worked his way around corners and up to other levels. His bare feet made no sounds, and the demons could not smell him at all. The warrior's heart raced, banging in his chest frantically as he dashed or froze in place as needed. If the act were not so dangerous, it would have been exhilarating or even fun.

As he neared the top of the highest building, he darted into a shallow recess to avoid being spotted by the nearest Wretch. When he thought it was about to leave, it began to sniff under the eaves. Tamis held his breath, looking out at the silent bell tower. Had Virgil made it inside yet? He was not sure. If this demon found him and sounded a warning call of its own, the plan would be useless. The wail of a Wretch could be heard for miles. He had not forgotten the ones that attacked his home.

The demon sniffed, raising its head to get a better whiff. It

had found Tamis's scent in the drier space by the walls. Listening to the monster close by and eyeing the distant bell, his hand on the bow fidgeted for a more comfortable grip. It seemed likely that he would have to shoot sooner than planned. The flash would blow his cover, again ruining the plan. His predicament was precarious.

It was beside the corner, just out of sight, about to discover him. Tamis took hold of the string on his holy weapon. In the second that he drew back and stepped out, the bell began to ring. The Wretch looked away from the hiding place and never saw the light arrow fly. Its blood spattered shingles as it fell, and the small flash of light from the weapon went unnoticed. The sonorous ringing worked as a perfect distraction.

Right away, demons flooded to the sound. Tamis went straight to work, taking down those that were closest to the tower. The magic of his sight made aiming easy, and the energy of the arrows went unhindered by wind. Each one flew true and fast as a lighting strike, hitting almost immediately after the string was released. Dozens and dozens were killed long before they realized where their enemy was.

Regardless of Tamis's efforts, some Wretches got inside the tower as the rest turned and wailed, alerting others to target the warrior. People flooded into the streets and started to scream. Chaos descended on Jenkirk in a mess of humans and fiends shrieking everywhere.

Demons climbed to reach the warrior, blasted away by raw light energy at random. In seconds, the monsters flooded the town, and most scaled the buildings, covering Tamis's perch like angry ants. There were too many, despite his arrows culling several demons at once. The waves of Wretches kept coming. His location was no longer defendable.

The next lowest rooftop was very far down. Knowing that the long drop would be kinder than the monsters baying for his blood, Tamis turned and dashed off the edge. He controlled the fall, and the raindrops seemed to stand still as he plummeted amidst them. His bare feet hit hard on the far side of a slanted roof, his body absorbing the impact with some effort. The slippery stone shingles made for poor footing. Just as he landed, he slid, stumbled and tumbled off toward the streets. Demons were in pursuit, and he saw them coming as he turned over to find his bearings before hitting the cobble-stones.

Seeing how close the Wretches were made Tamis welcome the help of gravity in drawing him off the roof. Reaching the ground first, he swiftly shot the closest pursuers and bolted. Even more demons filled the street as he went. Headed for the plaza, he hoped to join Virgil in facing this horde.

Humans and demons were running in all directions wailing and roaring. For a moment Tamis was lost in the throng, his animal senses bombarded by so much noise and movement. He could barely tell how close a monster was at his heels. Then his focus returned as an arrow flew past his head, making him gasp at hearing the fletching whistle by.

One Wretch was in hot pursuit, chasing him amongst the terrified humans. An arrow caught the wretch in the eye. It writhed until Tamis finished it off with a quick shot. As it melted in death, Tamis turned to look for Virgil.

Instead he saw Garret. A quiver of hawk feathered arrows set on his back and a sturdy longbow in hand, he shouted, "Tamis! They took her! They took Olivia! The fiends have her."

Forgetting the ranger completely, the boy felt as if he had swallowed a rock. Tamis ran to Garrett's side, and both pushed through droves of panic-stricken villagers. The humans fled from different directions, but more heavily from the south. That was the direction Garret led Tamis to find his sister. After leaving the chaotic plaza, travel was easier, and they ran.

Both sopping wet, the archers raced along the streets. The majority of the screaming came from behind, but Tamis took the lead once a single set of cries met his ears. It served as a guide farther to the edge of town. Where they found her was already evacuated. The only human in the southern district was a frantic Olivia, the demon gently holding her neck.

A towering demon with a broad outline and pale eyes stood silent. It watched the warrior and the man approaching. At its hip was a long sword, and its armor was like weathered steel painted black. The fiend had no mouth, and its face was unreadable and featureless. It had the telltale features of a fallen king, warped beyond recognition. A troop of Wretches stood behind, awaiting instruction from their patient captain.

Tamis was desperate to free Olivia. Coming to a halt at a safe distance, he fired an arrow for the demon's core above his sister's head. To his horror, the light met with the gleaming armor and glanced off before dissipating. He and Garret stared, dumbstruck.

The demon gave a subtle look to show it was unimpressed. Olivia, held between its long, bladelike fingers, continued to sob. The sharp edges rested along her exposed throat, grazing her skin.

While they glared at each other in silence, Garret urged, "Try it again!"

"It's no good. I'm not strong enough."

Then the demon raised a hand and beckoned with its mouthless voice as cold as ice, "Come to me, warrior of light. Come to me."

Tamis clenched his jaw, knowing better than to simply obey this nightmare figure.

"If you come willingly, she will be spared. When this place is hollowed out and dead, Olivia shall be the sole survivor, left to tell the tale. Come. There is no hope." Tamis stood his ground, trying to think.

"Do you not love your treacherous sister?"

Not understanding how the dark thing could know, the blood in Tamis's veins ran seemed to freeze. How could it know? He was too stunned to answer. As the dark chill subsided, his eyes went back to Olivia's. Tears glazed them. His sister did not expect mercy from him or the demon. She anticipated imminent death.

The answer to the demon's question was clear: Of course he loved Olivia. He was not sure he could forgive her, but he did love her. Did it matter if he could forgive her, he wondered? The answer to that thought was clear as well. It fortified his heart, making him resolute.

Wretch demons had them surrounded, crouching low on rooftops and blocking escape routes. Hissing and screeching, their red eyes shone in the downpour.

Garret realized that they were likely to die here in this street. Fear gripped the human. Tamis was far less afraid. He thought, does it matter now if he is afraid? No. Just like it does not matter if he could forgive Olivia for what she had done. Here and now, very few things mattered. Waves of energy swelled in his chest upon his next breath.

The demon inclined its head mockingly. "Have you made a decision?"

Tamis felt strange, but his attention was with his sister in the demon captain's clutches. Eyes blazing brighter than ever, a vicious growl came out of him as he replied with a sneer, "Yes. I have."

In the blink of an eye, he took a shooting stance. As he swept one foot back and drew the string, his body erupted into its true form. Garret stumbled back, startled at seeing his form expand. As the warrior pulled on the string and changed, his bow glowed, transforming as well. The metallic limbs sprouted several layers, growing in detail and power. A blindingly brilliant arrow appeared, aimed for the demon's chest once again.

The fiend tilted its head, unsure, and tightened its hold on the woman. A fine cut drew beads of blood meant to warn the warrior not to make a move.

Then the Wretches behind the dark captain began to shriek and cry at a nearby alley. A roaring mass bigger than a bull charged in, running them over and smashing a few through a building. Purple blood sprayed over the walls and window panes. The demon captain glanced toward the mighty crash.

Tamis loosed the honed arrow in that moment. The force from it repelled raindrops in its wake before it found the demon and pierced its armor.

The fiend staggered, releasing Olivia, who ran for cover, screaming. Garret ran out to fetch her, while Tamis fired again and again, punching holes through the monster.

Slammed over and over, the demonic captain shouted and drew his sword, growing weaker with each arrow. When it finally found balance and charged, Tamis snarled, firing one more time for the wicked visage. Long before the demon could reach him, the bolt of light struck between its pale eyes, rending its head inside out.

Raindrops shredded what remained of the dissipating shadow, washing it from the air and away to the gutters. The last of the demon flowed out of sight with the rest of the street filth."

All around Tamis and the pair of humans, Wretch demons shrieked and wailed as they were ripped apart. Alex emerged from the wreckage of the house where he had crushed the demons with his armored bulk and short sword. Adwen and the others assaulted the numbers atop the city roofs. At last, demons that were not close enough to attack retreated, diving into shadows and vanishing. The dark forces knew that this was not a fight they could win and chose to save their strength for later – for the day of the coming battle.

Adwen and the others joined Tamis as he shrank back into his human form. He was overjoyed to see them. "How did you find me? How did you escape the snow?"

She smiled, dismissing her dark scythe and replied, "It took a lot of digging."

Then Jack chuckled and patted him on the shoulder. "And finding you was easy. We just had to listen for the demons and follow their trail."

Alex slugged Jack's arm. "Shut up. We found him because we could sense he was in danger and followed our instincts."

After rolling her eyes, Adwen gestured toward the humans huddled together in the rain. "Who is this, Tamis? Friends of yours?"

He took a moment to watch his sister sobbing with relief in Garret's arms. She was safe. Then he thought of his other friend and became frantic. Setting the bow over his back, he turned for the city center and ran as fast as he could.

His breathing was labored from all of the dashing and jumping, but he could not rest until he knew Virgil was all right. The city folk were calming down when he found the plaza. Going for the city hall and its tall bell tower, his progress went ignored in the dark of night. No one was a witness to his search. Quickly, Tamis rushed past the threshold.

Once inside, he stopped and stared around, looking. "Virgil? Are you here?"

No answer came, and he saw purple blood on the floor. Several humans lay dead inside, their red blood splattering the floor among the demon remains. By the mangled bodies Tamis found a broken oak crossbow. Crimson fluids stained its sides.

"No," he murmured as he picked it up. One of the bodies was a man, or had been. It was hard to tell from how shredded the corpse was. Tamis thought he might be sick. He could have been pushed over by a slight breeze, trapped in disbelief.

"Well, my friend," said a voice beside him, "it seems you weren't as good a shot as I thought."

Tamis dropped the broken weapon and hugged Virgil so tightly it was difficult for the ranger to breathe. He managed to gasp, "Take it easy! Don't kill me after I just scraped away with my life! You didn't really think they would catch me, did you?"

"But who is this? I thought that was you!"

"Ah." The ranger became serious. "The mayor and a few ladies were enjoying themselves and did not take kindly to my entry. This sorry sod and lady companions would not heed my warnings and called me a liar when I said demons were attacking. The mayor will not be missed, but as I said, the deaths of innocents such as these women were inevitable tonight."

Adwen and the others joined them. While Jack marveled at the bloody corpses, Tamis introduced his friends. "Tame One, this is Virgil. He took me in while I was separated from your company. Virgil, this is Adwen, Heir of the Master Knight."

"The pleasure is mine, your grace," he said and bowed deeply.

Oryn frowned and noticed the broken crossbow. Judging by the elaborate design, he realized they were in the company of one of the rangers of Dargadia. "Tell me, hunter. Are all of your order given to inflamed flattery?"

Virgil laughed. "You must mean Regorian. Perhaps not flattery, but I can only hope I am as good a man as he was. I wish I could have been there to see his triumphant end in your service."

At this, Oryn gave a friendly look of approval.

"Lady Adwen," Virgil asked, "might we adjourn to a more private place for the night? When the sun rises, the confused locals are likely to take out their frustrations on you and yours. It would be best if you are not seen before you depart."

The sun shone bright the following morning. Warm rays purged the last of the demon remains, leaving the damage they had created. There were not as many casualties as there could have been. The citizens of Jenkirk were alarmed and confounded by the sudden appearance of demons. Rumors were beginning to circulate of the mysterious archer and the lightning bow, but Tamis and the others were already preparing to leave. Just before dawn, the young warrior underwent the same experience Alex did less than a week before in Fort Redu. His dragon leather garments were replaced by enchanted hunter garb. Jack had laughed when the discovery of the longer fangs and pointed ears startled him. For this, both his arms were slugged by Alex and Oryn from either side.

Outside at the gate, Virgil and the pack of strays wished them well on their journey back to the Green Kingdom of Dargadia.

"It was a pleasure to meet you all, and especially you, my young friend," Virgil said.

Tamis nodded and a soft growl accompanied his smile.

The dogs panted at Adwen. They had adored her since she arrived at the manor grounds and never left her side. Most of all, the alpha acted as escort, treating her as a guest of honor.

He made a small gruff bark. "We hope you will return someday. Thank you for staying with us and sharing your warmth."

"You are all very welcome. I hope I can see you again too." She beamed at the strong beast. "You are a very special creature."

The alpha became bashful and looked away.

Then the second in command chimed in. "Can you not bless him? I heard the Heir of Darien can give powerful blessings."

He tried to shush the beta. "Don't pester her. She does not need to waste a blessing on a beast."

Adwen shrugged. "I don't see why not."

All eyes were on her as she knelt down before the crippled dog. When her face came close to his muzzle, he bowed his head in polite submission, humbled.

Touching his scruffy coat, there was a pause, and she

leaned in to kiss his head. For a moment they were frozen. As she pulled away, energy made the ground beneath the animal glow. Grass and clover sprouted between the stones at his paws. Strong magic from the surroundings surged to that place and siphoned into his body. When the dog could move again and the light was gone, the alpha felt strange.

"My leg!" he barked in ecstatic glee. "My leg is back! I can hunt again! I can hunt!" The dog and his pack barked and frolicked, licking him. "We won't starve any longer! Thank you, Adwen! Thank you into infinity!" With that, the dog and his pack went for a run in celebration of the miracle.

Virgil began to pack his pipe with tobacco. "Now I must say, I have never seen that animal as happy as that. Then again, I never thought I'd hear him speak!"

The others were shocked to know Virgil had understood the dog, but Adwen sighed. "Can you help him stay out of trouble? He doesn't know that his body is infused with powerful magic now. He is no longer just a dog. I blessed him, but the magic of this world decided to use that to make him into something more. I don't know for what purpose, but he is meant to become an entity of pure magic. Over time, he will realize this. Please be a guide for him as you were for Tamis."

"The moment I heard him shouting about his leg I knew he would need some looking after - more than usual. I will keep him honorable, Lady Adwen. You have my word."

Before they could leave, Tamis turned and asked, "Where did you get that pipe?"

Virgil lit it and raised an eyebrow. "Why?"

"I want to know where I might get one of my own someday."

The ranger chuckled. "That is a story for another day, friend."

Tamis was undeterred. "But I may not get the chance to hear it."

Eyeing the Holy Hound with the magic bow, Virgil sighed and admired his old pipe. His expression softened, revealing nostalgia. "Recall how I mentioned my father and I did not get on? Well ... we found we could set aside our differences in the end."

A warmth lifted the warrior's spirits. Time was the answer;

with time he could forgive his sister. Already he felt relief at the knowledge. "Thank you, Virgil Gaspard, for everything."

With a clever glint in his eye, the ranger puffed a perfect circle and nodded. "Farewell my friend. Until we meet again."

Chapter 23
THE CURE

Early the next morning, after running throughout the day and resting at night, they reached Plexus and the Order. The halls were alive with new arrivals and mages escorted by knights. While the Holy Hounds were away, the orders of knights and mages had bonded, setting aside differences. Plenty of resistance was put up by groups of citizens to this open acceptance of magical beings, but the knights and some of the king's guards provided support. With time and peaceful efforts, a mutual understanding began to form. This developing trust made it easier for the mages to provide rations for the refugees.

Adwen was pleased. "Thank goodness. I thought once or twice I would return to find this place on fire."

"Or frozen solid," Arc Mage Balefire said as he approached, smiling. "It is good to see you returned to us. You just missed the king and the High Elder. They will wish to meet with you as well. What was told to us by the company that returned was quite upsetting. Were you captured?"

She heaved a heavy sigh. "Not for long, but yes. For a while we were separated but managed to regroup. Has anything changed aside from lessened hostility to you and the other mages?"

He smiled. "More good news: Your phoenix has brought a parcel for you. It waits in the topmost tower on the war table."

King Lorvan, High Elder Mamalis, Captain Sir Peregrine and Captain Slate were gathered at the war table with Core and Arc Mage Balefire. Arriving at the war table, Adwen and her warriors reviewed the four scrolls bearing the seals of the alliance. The messages had some differences but meant the same: All the armies were mustered and armed for battle. Only the matter of bringing them to the battlefield in the north beyond the marshes remained.

Captain Slate's rough, hard voice boomed as he pointed at the castle in the northern region of the map. "Castle Sax is where Darien fought and defeated Melanin before my kind began to slumber in wait for the Heir's arrival. Darien's power was great, but not sufficient to banish or destroy the demon. Instead it was cut off from the void and sealed into the castle itself, unable to leave and crippled. Now is the time for you to use your ability to purge the castle and finish the task."

Growing secretly anxious, Adwen asked, "How do I move four armies across these land barriers and a bog? I can't march them through small portals into the other world and back, or through the kingdom gates. None of them open on the far side of the marshes. No gates of light open up in that region."

Glances were exchanged, and the huge Gargoyle inclined his head, unconcerned. "Darien opened gates as he pleased and closed them as well. I would know. I was there. You should have this power, as you are the Heir and inherited this gift. With all of your warriors fully ascended, that should be available to you now."

Jack had his telepathy open and heard her thoughts. He did not like what was in her head, and he grimaced while others waited curiously.

Feeling defeated, Adwen decided it was time to tell her secret to the assembled leaders. "When Sycan captured me and took me to Mortigad, he tortured me and implanted images from the slaughter of my family. He did this by fusing a sliver from General Guillot within my body. I could neither expel nor destroy the infection, and it took hold. The only thing I could do, with the help of my friends, was force it as far from my heart as possible. Since it was already a part of me, it became my arm and part of my eye."

A chill swept the leaders, and Sir Peregrine was shocked. "The rumors are true? Your darkened flesh is indeed demonic?"

She gave a solemn nod. "It has capped my strength. As long as I am infected, I will not be able to obtain the last of

Darien's powers."

The human knight cursed the fiends under his breath as King Lorvan spoke up. "Perhaps you should visit your old friend in the tower library. Since just before you set out, he has worked tirelessly but would not tell me what he was looking for. I am certain he has been seeking the cure for your condition. We will keep your secret. In the meantime, find a way to cleanse yourself. It is the only way to beat back this enemy before he arrives on our doorstep. His forces surely are ready as well."

Toth never cursed much, but his tongue had learned quickly over the course of the fruitless search. By the time Adwen and Oryn came into the library, anger and frustration had long festered. When the door swung open, Toth was in mid-swear, shouting at another book, slamming the cover excessively.

Suddenly noticing them, he cleared his throat and regained a more calm composure. "Oh! Forgive me. I did not hear you enter."

Oryn gave Adwen a sardonic glance and pointed out, "You did not knock."

"Sorry. Toth? Are you okay?"

Giving up the act, he slumped back into a chair. "Forgive me, Adwen. I tried. I've looked high and low, skimming scrolls, turning pages till my fingertips were stained with ink. I cannot find a way to rid you of the sliver. And neither can I find the location of Darien's fabled sword."

She went to console him, already knowing the answer would not be here. "It's okay. I didn't think you would. The answers were never going to be in this library."

Looking up balefully with his remaining eye, the king's adviser was surprised. "Why would it not be? Everything the Order knows of demons is in this place."

"You forgot," she added. "For a long time, members of the Elder Council, some of the few with access to this collection, were hosts to demon parasites. I'm sure that this plan to infect me was something they had set up for a long while. Anything having to do with extracting the sliver would have been destroyed. The demons make mistakes, but their plans are very intricate. It's really not your fault."

Toth felt less critical of himself and more foolish for not considering this. "Of course. I should have known. And the location of Darien's sword is lost as well. That surely would have been here too. The demons need to keep you from the one weapon that can channel your strength enough to kill the Demon Lord Melanin. Dreadful, indeed, but as you said, they spin their webs intricately."

Pulling him by the hand, she coaxed, "Come on. You need to get out of here and get some rest. You've done enough. Thank you for trying so hard."

The half-elf carried on describing what he had managed to learn that was useful. He rambled on, and as they left the library, she and Oryn exchanged dark looks. Without a way to rid her of the sliver or find the Gray Blade, their world was ripe for the taking.

Adwen went to her private chambers for peace and quiet. Oryn thought to discuss this issue but decided that after foul rumors had spread before and what had happened at camp, this was not advisable. Sharing a private space with her was sure to be noticed once again. He went to oversee training of the knights. That would be enough of a distraction.

Fresh air flowed through the veranda of Adwen's room. For a while she paced, wondering if she had access to the knowledge about how to get rid of the dark infection. Hours passed while she explored her connection to the Light Spirits, but no answers came. They also did not tell her where to find Darien's sword.

At dusk, a cold autumn breeze began to cycle through, ruffling her silver and gold hair. Sitting at a table with a mirror, brushes and a wash basin, Adwen studied herself. Looking deep into her own eyes, she felt lost in the reflected emotion of despair. It was the sliver's doing. The darkness infecting her body made it difficult to feel hopeful. She began to wonder whether the sliver dulled her ability to receive guidance from her masters.

Touching her cheek with a razor-sharp sliver-spawned fingernail, she could not burn herself with it. The sensation of the demon finger on her skin was a black icicle, sharpened to a point. She tried to will it to leave, pull it from her so that she could burn it away. With her right hand, she summoned a bit of light to a finger. And as a test, tried to pierce the stony, black exoskeleton of her other arm.

Purple blood welled up from the puncture, and she gasped in pain. Dismissing the light, she clenched her teeth at the self-inflicted injury. A mingled growl and whine escaped her. More than before, Adwen felt despondent. Cutting it from herself could kill her, or, like an aggressive cancer, it could take over if she were weakened.

She wanted to cry. Her eyes filled with tears. A small flash of gold light in the depths of her gaze lit her reflection for an instant. It left behind a simple direction: She must look out the veranda. In a mixture of obedience and curiosity, she left the lavish woman's vanity. The wind gusted strongly beyond the wall by the rail. Her quarters were located on the opposite side of the fortress from the city. Just plains and distant forests lay before her. Scents from the wilds beyond the fields to the north soothed some of her anxieties. A moment passed as she stood there before she noticed a fire at the base of the wall.

The white and yellow flames flickered far below. Finally, she recognized the creature as Auburn. The spectral fire horse tossed his head, kicking the dirt, beckoning.

Before she could leave, Core materialized beside her.

"Lady Adwen?"

Her gaze remained on Darien's steed, and she did not answer.

"Where are you going?"

Dismally returning his stare at last, Adwen wondered what to say.

With the rest of the warriors in the feast hall, Oryn remained lost in thought. Training knights did not work well in keeping his mind off of Adwen's troubles. Despite the needs of the worlds, he worried for her instead. What was to become of her? How was she to be cured? It was foretold that she would be sent to fight on behalf of the living and the dead alike. Never did the prophesy say that she would succeed or even survive. If this were the fabled Darkening Time, the title seemed appropriate.

Jack eavesdropped on Oryn's thoughts and frowned. "Cujo, relax. She's going to be okay. Don't start doubting now. It's too late for that, wouldn't you say?"

The magical knight shook his head. "Again, it is a miracle: We agree on something. But tell me, how do you foresee this venture coming to a close? There is the chance that, among your powers of the mind, you can foretell future events."

"Sorry. I don't think I can, but I can make good guesses."

After a long pause, Oryn replied, "Humor me."

"She's a prophesied Heir sent to kill demons. In most stories that are like this, there is a last-second discovery that no one sees coming. I think she will find a way to purge herself and get the Gray Blade when we least expect it."

Jack's assumption seemed strangely reasonable considering past experiences with Adwen. The word "purge" stuck in his mind along with thoughts of Darien's Gray Blade. He suddenly felt sick with fear. He knew how Adwen needed to eliminate the infection, and the idea made him blanch.

The thoughts naturally passed to the psychic rogue whose face also flushed with pale colors. "I don't like that. I don't like that at all. Should we stop her?"

Alex and Tamis waited in confusion. The Marine snarled, "Just tell us what is going on!"

Core appeared out of thin air, giving them a shock as always. Only Adwen could tell when he was about to show himself. "Sir Oryn."

Rounding on the unique entity, Oryn growled, "Where is she?"

Frowning, Adwen's adviser said, "She told me to deliver a message to you specifically. She says it shall be all right. She knows where to find the sword."

The knight and the speechless rogue exchanged terrified looks.

Alex shouted, "What?"

"I'll explain on the way," Jack snapped back. "We have to move! Come on! She's got a big lead on us and can run fast-er."

Transforming in a feral fit, Oryn roared, "Move it!"

Chapter 24
THE GRAY BLADE

Adwen's speed was far greater than any of her pursuing warriors could achieve. Alongside the white stallion bathed in flames, she raced northward to the highest of the mountains. The white Holy Hound and the fire horse traveled with haste through the darkened passes and valleys, never stopping or slowing. Hours went by, as did many leagues.

The way up the mountainside began as a rocky incline and steadily transformed into a frozen, snow-covered slope. No matter the thickness of the frigid blankets on the mountain's face, their claws and hooves bore them up so swiftly that it was like flight. Faint traces of tracks lay in their wake. Like two comets, they ascended King's Peak until the long-forgotten stairs began.

It took most of the night to reach the destination. Only a little tired, Adwen shifted into her woman form, laying a hand on the stallion's mane. She smiled a little, nervous of what was to come.

"Thank you for staying with me for the journey, Auburn. It means a lot."

He flicked his ears. "I was there in the beginning. It is fitting that I be here for this."

Her look brightened. "You're right. You were there. Thank you for that, too." She patted his neck before continuing alone to the mouth of the cavernous alcove.

Walking past the threshold and the pair of pedestal-mounted sun crystals, the wind ceased. Within was calm and yet resistant to the natural staleness that normally would result. Standing amongst the pedestals and crystals, her predecessor awaited. He turned to watch her approach, and she stopped to return his gaze. It felt like an eternity since her last visit, and it had not been a kind one.

Darien was more transparent than before, but this time he was in armor. A spectral bastard-style sword hung from his hip. She noticed it but ignored the weapon for now. The spirit of her ancient ancestor approached silently, studying her appearance and the morose feeling in her stare. It made it easier to explain by saying nothing. Words failed Adwen in this moment of reunion. Tears swelled and fell.

His hand held her left cheek as she quietly cried. The pain Adwen carried was familiar to him, and he pitied her. Looking at her darkened eye, Darien ruefully sighed. "I had hoped this would not come to pass. The Light Spirits showed me what was likely to occur and the purpose for my lingering so long. Do you know why you have returned to this hallowed place?"

Adwen shuddered and simply nodded.

The Master Knight embraced her. "There is a little time to wait. We can spend it quietly alone or together if you wish. It is your choice."

As they parted from each other's arms, she wiped some tears. "It would be best if we did this soon. I had to leave my warriors behind because they would try to stop me."

They strode to a place to sit at the back by a smooth wall of raw stone. Darien was perplexed. "They would stop you?"

"Well, the others might have gone along with it, but Oryn would try to stop me."

Sitting at her side, he asked, "Why would he do such a thing?"

Averting her gaze, bashfully, she replied, "He's a bit protective."

Darien understood. "Ah, I see. Then I am glad for you. You have been fortunate to gather such caring companions. I suppose it is only natural for them to oppose this necessary step. This will lead to the defeat of the evil forces from the void. However, we must wait. This can work only with the first light of dawn. That is the moment when your golden heart is most open."

Adwen turned sorrowful again. "The light doesn't dance on my skin anymore in the morning light. Are you sure it will work?"

His warm hand on her shoulder brought with it much-needed assurance. "I have known for a long time that it will work. My spirit was not sealed in this secret temple simply to give guidance; I was placed here for your purging."

She stared back, trying to be less afraid.

Darien beamed. "It is my duty to remove the demonic sliver. This will be our final meeting. Is there anything else you would wish to come from this?"

"Yes. I want Guillot."

He chuckled. "Then I shall give him to you. Let me tell you how it must be done."

Adwen's tracks led the transformed Holy Hound warriors from her lofty veranda and deep into the wilds. The trail was fresh, and so was the trail left by something made of fire with hooves. Oryn had no guesses while his mind was turned upside down by the feral state. Emotions steeped the beastly knight in the base primal drive to protect what mattered most to him.

She needed the Gray Blade for its power to purge body and soul, leaving nothing behind. If she used it on herself to eliminate the infection, there would no longer be an Heir of Darien. Of the light or not, that weapon would destroy her. That was the last thing he would allow to happen. The night steadily neared its end, and her tracks took them far up a mountain named King's Peak, due to its unmatched height.

Each of them panted, tongues lolling. The snow deepened, slowing their urgent climb. Clouds enveloped the slopes and veiled the distance they must travel.

Alex slowed, and when his bulk sank into a pocket of soft snow, he yelped and barked, "Go on without me! I can dig myself out and catch up."

Turning back, Jack growled to Oryn, "You're big enough to outrun us in this mess! Go without us while we pull Jarhead out of his sink hole!"

The feral knight did not need encouragement. He bolted off through the mist without hesitation. His long legs carried him much faster in the deep snow. Wind whipped at his face and jaws, the cold moisture freezing to his fur and armor, falling off as he went. When he burst out of the descended clouds, the crystalline fragments trailed in his wake like tiny stars.

Clear skies glowed with an eerie haze in the east that heralded the dawn. The snow under claw and foot turned to ice at this elevation, making Oryn's climb swifter. A fire ahead caught his eye, and intrigue dispelled the madness that had taken him. Recognizing the fiery horse, he went close to see if it was an illusion of dawn's first light.

Approaching the magical steed, Oryn's ears perked, and his stare became wide. Panting heavily, he growled. "Why are you here? Where is she?"

"It is good to see you again, descendant of Conrad and Winter Maw. Now that you know your true lineage, perhaps you are ready to know more. Do you wish to know who sired Keegan Conrad?"

Oryn was impatient and snarled irritably. "Tell me where she is!"

The horse pinned his ears back, and the flames on his body roared in swaths of bright gold and orange tongues. "Calm yourself! She is ahead. Do not interfere with the ritual that is taking place."

"What? No!"

"It is time," Darien said with a comforting look. "A new day is about to dawn on the horizon. Come to the center of the circles, where you stood to reawaken me."

They walked in silence, broken only by the sound of her kneeling. An inlaid crystal beneath her radiated with warmth as the sun prepared to rise outside.

Looking up into the blue eyes of Darien, she watched his short white hair and gold bangs move as if he were under water. The warm smile he had was as assuring as ever, but she remained afraid. Glancing at the entrance behind the ghostly form of the Master Knight, sunshine washed over the crystals at the edge of the formation of twenty-four pedestals. The energy filled them and overflowed to the others as golden beams, continuing to interlink the ritual circle.

As the streams of flowing light completed the network, seven beams connected with her heart. It glowed hot in her chest, pulsing energy around her with each frightened, fluttery beat.

Watching Darien draw the Gray Blade, the beat quickened.

Quivering and closing her eyes, she asked, "Will it hurt?"

"I do not know. It was good to have spent time with you, Adwen. The Light Spirits made you their magnum opus."

Her smile was weak and her reply timid. "Thank you, Darien. I'm going to miss you. And good-bye."

He took aim with the sword tip. "Farewell, Adwen Andredan."

The ghostly sword of Darien drove deep into Adwen's heart. Silvery flames poured out from the elaborate hilt guard like a torch. Light drew up along the weapon, filling the sword. When the blade became solid, the effect carried on to its master. The brighter Adwen's body shone, the more solid Darien's became. A final flash burst from her chest and shot up the now living Master Knight's arm. It settled in his chest, making his sapphire eyes glow.

What remained of Adwen had turned to stone, while the dark infection writhed. Like a ball of spiny snakes, the arm broke apart to try to manifest, reaching and intertwining. It consumed most of her torso, sprouting higher, enveloping her head. When the unrelenting shadow formed a face on the feminine statue, it hissed and glared with blood-red eyes.

In one swipe, Darien slew the demon as it fought desperately to materialize. It burst into fading pieces like embers, and the stone figure crumbled.

Then a terrible roar broke the silence. Oryn shifted into his smaller shape, raising the awakened Rose Thorne high and leaped. When he came down with the sword to cut the unknown offender in half, his blade struck another sword, which held it at bay.

Both swordsmen stared past their touching weapons, the knight panting and shaking with horror and rage. The longer Oryn glared, the more he calmed. His anger was not sated, but his mind cleared of the feral drives, letting him think. Those blue eyes and strange hair color were blatantly familiar. He held his pose, not yet willing to yield after seeing Adwen destroyed.

Darien coolly observed his opponent. This was clearly one of the warriors. His eyes were filled with defiance to hide anguish. He watched for a reaction as he asked, "I know your eyes. Are you a Conrad?"

A more aggressive look was the only reply amid his panting breaths.

"Do you know who I am?" Darien asked.

Oryn's glare intensified, and he tried not to snap. Taking control of his anger, he replied, "Yes. You are Darien."

The Master Knight glanced at the crossed swords, raising an eyebrow.

After a pause, Oryn growled angrily and withdrew his blade, as did Darien.

"What have you done to her? What have you done to ..."

Darien raised a hand, and his power over the warrior closed his mouth, freezing his tongue in place. When the knight was frustrated, Darien kindly advised him.

"Do not speak her name. It would undo what she has done. Wait for when the time is right. Not here. Be patient. You shall have her back soon."

"Why?" Oryn snapped at last, barely containing his outrage. "Why?"

Sheathing the Gray Blade, Darien was unperturbed. As he explained, Jack and the others arrived. "The same reason as before: A mortal body has two traits that make it impossible to hold enough light to slay the ultimate enemy. Firstly, living flesh can heal, but holding that much energy would slowly rend the body from within over time. They would die a slow, yet painless death by bleeding out."

With a gathered audience, he added, "Secondly, only a pure vessel can contain the greater powers of light. Even if she tried, her form would break, same as a living one. This was the only way for her to be rid of the dark sliver."

Jack spoke on behalf of the others: "So when is she coming back? There's an army to move and a battle to fight."

Getting a brief look into Jack's heart, the Master Knight found him entertaining. "So long as Sir Oryn Conrad can refrain from speaking her name too soon, I will remain until the moment that she asked to be brought back. As a consequence, she wishes that I be the one to muster the armies and begin the battle. Are you ready for travel?"

They followed him as he strode past and out into the sunshine. Auburn came trotting up the steps to meet him, whinnying. He patted his old friend's muzzle and chuckled. "It's good to see you, too. What do you say to one final ride?"

The snorting beast tossed his head, kicking the ground with anticipation.

This made Darien laugh as he climbed on, a saddle and reins manifesting as he did. Adwen's warriors gathered near, and Alex was confused.

"Permission to speak, sir?"

To the polite soldier, the Master Knight smiled and replied, "Granted."

"If that battle is today, we'll be too late. It took all night for us to get here."

Jack rolled his eyes. "Seriously? You already forgot that this guy can open gates and go wherever he wants?"

There was a pause, followed by an embarrassed, "Oh. Roger that."

"Yes, that." Darien chuckled at the two friends. "But first, there is unfinished business that both Adwen and I have deemed ready for our attention. Do you wish to come along or return to the fortress to wait? It will only be an hour at most."

"What unfinished business?" Oryn asked, brow furrowed.

Jack read Darien's mind and grinned. "Oh, yes! I'm coming along for this one."

"In that case, we're all coming," Alex added.

Tamis and Oryn gave agreeing nods.

Waving the silvery sword awash in blue flames, a portal unlike any they had seen before opened up beside the steps. A wreath of the same blue fire appeared to part time and space. The other side was entirely devoid of light. Darien rode Auburn through, and the four Holy Hounds summoned their weapons. A few weeks were not enough to forget what lay in wait in Mortigad.

The ring of lapping flames converged and extinguished at their backs. Auburn's hooves clicked rhythmically on polished stone atop the stairway, passing under the ragged banners. Below and beyond rested the undead city, hidden from the sun and sky. Before them stood the pillars and ancient throne room waiting for the company to enter. It was as dreary and desolate as Jack remembered.

Then the familiarly grotesque sight of Nasogus Vard, the undead king, appeared ahead. As usual, the oozing, pustule-covered figure had yet to leave his marble throne. Coming to a halt before the horrific figure, the four warriors winced at the stench.

After a moment of staring, Nasogus stirred. The mostly blind gaze traveled about them, and his expression twisted into a vengeful sneer. Finally, he hissed, "You."

Mockingly, Darien replied, "Yes, me."

"Are you back to make more idle threats, like your waste of an Heir? Where has she wandered off to, Neverborn scum?"

Oryn snarled at the insult, but Darien did not care.

"There are no more threats; only promises fulfilled. I have not forgotten what this place used to be. This was once a paradise aglow, a sanctuary for healing."

Nasogus spat back. "It did not heal me! They lied."

"So you destroyed it? You speak of wastes; that is a waste." Darien raised his flaming sword, pointing at the rotting figure dressed as a king. "I'll waste no more time or words on you. There is no redemption in your stilled heart."

Beginning to laugh and cough uncontrollably, the first undead cried out. "Kill me and you will be buried alive! Have you forgotten I am bound to this throne and the whole of this black kingdom? Strike if you dare, fool pariah prince!"

Darien smiled while the fire grew larger on the blade. "Time must have robbed you of all sense. Did you truly forget that I can summon gates?"

Nasogus's laughing ceased, but his coughing became worse, choking his words. He became furious as he tried to curse the Master Knight. It was no use. He could hardly keep enough breath to speak.

Like from a dragon's maw, a pillar of flames shot out, enveloping the stone, flesh and silks. While Nasogus burned and writhed, unable to scream, the halls began to crumble and the ground shook. Darien turned and opened another portal. Sunshine blazed through, beckoning the warriors and horse. The five went through, the magical exit closed, and the quaking only worsened as the vast range of blackened stones crumbled.

The other side of the gate opened to many acres of dead trees, rotting stumps and fog. A few rusted swords stood among ragged weeds, marking where men had fallen long ago. The mist parted to the north, showing the top of a distant castle tower. They stood together looking at the ominous shape.

Darien nodded to it and added wryly, "I wish I had the power to purge as Adwen does, so all of you would be spared this burden. The princess Eyrie is kept in the tower. She is alive but not well. As strong as the forces are, the only way to stop the endless waves of demons is to charge through the ranks. Adwen already knows the plan: While the armies keep the vast numbers busy and hold the front, you are to enter the fortress and kill the demon Melanin. The army will eventually break and wither on the field. With haste, some casualties will be prevented. Do you understand?"

He received four proud and prepared nods.

The Master Knight beamed. "It is my great pleasure and honor to ride into battle with you all. My company was strong and fearless, but you are even more so. Be proud of your accomplishments and your stumblings as well. They forged you each into the warriors necessary to win this battle. Shall I open the gates, good friends of Adwen?"

Jack laughed, twirling his daggers in the air with his mind. "If you're ready, we sure are. Let her rip!"

Darien laughed. "As you wish, Master Jack. As you wish."

Chapter 25
RETRIBUTION

Pointing the Gray Blade to the south, three tongues of fire shot out. A trio of vast gates opened, and an army waited on the other side of each. They marched out from the desert far in the southeast. King Loggias of the Lorisans headed his troops and collection of trained fire drakes. Heavily armored Minotaur tribes stood with the men, brandishing battle axes. Astride his giant three-headed dog, the powerful man laughed heartily as his forces arrived on the edge of the dead marsh.

The Bebidin King, Isban Leshano, came on the shoulder of one of the thousand jade statues. Their weapons were of the same stone set in bronze hafts and shafts. Behind the formation of living statues rode in his finest cavalry of purebred stallions, the envy of the White Sea Desert.

Then came Queen Xenorithia. The matriarch of the Zsu nation wore ruby robes and armor that caught the light in the same way as her golden spear. Intimidating war makeup transformed her fierce face into that of a deadly warrior. She seemed to glide across the ground without walking until she tapped something beneath the soil. Rising up beneath her came a spiny sail fin followed by a striped, scaly mass. It looked like a reptilian fish with dragon eyes as well as row upon row of serrated teeth forming a jagged grin. Behind the queen and her enormous sand shark came hundreds of men and women armed with spears and bows. Several carts rolled in as well with extra weapons should the need arise.

Letting the portals remain open in the case of a retreat, Darien called to the armies and their leaders. "Adwen the Tame One will join the battle to come and sent me in her stead to rally your spirits! Before you is the battlefield of ancient times past. Here was where the first leaders of your kind stood and where others fell. Beyond is Castle Sax! Within is the sealed enemy, reawakened to condemn the living worlds!" Pointing his fiery blade at the castle in the parting mist, he bellowed, and his voice magically carried across the barren wastes. "Today, Melanin will cease to be!"

Many voices and beastly cries filled the air, and a plume of unnatural pitch-black clouds billowed out from above the castle tower. While it expanded, reaching and rolling outward to blot out the sun, the ground shivered a moment. None of this dampened the rallied forces and their fearsome call.

"Steel yourselves!" The Master Knight cried out with his magical voice, further bolstering their resolve. "It begins and ends here. They conjure. Be ready for my commands in the moments to come!"

While they watched the darkness creep steadily closer, a smooth voice spoke up beside Darien and the others: "You have not lost your touch, blood-brother."

The four warriors stared in surprise, and Darien chuckled. "Arianwyn. I am glad to see you here of all places. It is like old times, is it not?"

Adorned in the armor of an elven king, his sharpened sword glinted at his hip. "It is, in a way. I am glad to get one more meeting with you, Darien, at the end of our roles in this grand dance." Smiling at Adwen's Holy Hounds, he added, "After we are gone, what comes next is left to you and her. We have played our parts to the fullest. Well done, each of you. Well done indeed."

Darien sighed. "Once more, three lines of royal blood stand at the front."

Confused, Jack forgot the dark clouds overhead. "Three?"

"Oryn. Before I am gone, I will tell you what was never written. This castle was once the home of a great king. His throne, land and people were conquered by an invader who settled his own rule over Dargadia from the south. When he was beaten in a duel and his queen perished in the streets, homeless, Keegan Conrad was orphaned."

Jack, Alex and Tamis marveled and looked to see Oryn's stunned expression.

"Your blood is from a royal line older than any other in this world of magic."

"Why tell me this now?"

"Because you have a right to know the gravity of what you are about to do. That castle is your birthright desiccated beyond repair. Today is the day that the Conrad line returns to take part in its destruction. You are the last of your family, doomed by a curse of ruin from Ozovath and blessed by me in turn. My blessing has granted unforeseen things. These blessings, Oryn, are yet to be realized. Be patient. One day, what the elf told to you in that shop will come to pass."

At first Oryn was glad to hear these words, but then he became fearful. "I thought the future she promised had already come to pass. My previous life ended. I have gained power from your Heir. With the exception of my vengeance, all she told was done."

The smile faded from the Master Knight on his magical steed. "No. Only a little has been done. Her warnings remain as do the promises of blessings while in Adwen's presence. Do not worry for the future, long lost Prince of the Magical Realm. Rarely is anything as it seems. Take heart. Amazing things await you."

Arianwyn added darkly, "As do horrors beyond count on this battlefield. Be ready. They are coming at last."

The dark clouds thickened and churned. Far across the acres of leeched soil, cracks in the ground flashed with red flames. Out from the earth crawled near one hundred Hell Hounds; volcanic bones and lava flesh emerged and howled. The sounds echoed all around as they formed a line and started bounding closer.

King Loggias looked to Darien. "My drakes are ready, Master Knight!"

The rows of fidgety reptiles snapped and clawed the ground, eager to attack.

"Hold," Darien commanded. "Hold steady!"

Meanwhile, the demonic elementals ran faster. The tracks they left sizzled and smoked, dirt and weeds scorched.

"Hold!"

The ranks behind him tensed, watching the deadly things closing in.

When the monsters were within a mile, he raised his sword skyward, blue flames flying high. A gate opened wide, releasing a wave of giant moths and their riders.

Queen Xenorithia grinned deviously as her swarm went to work.

Sweeping low, the moths hovered before the Hell Hounds, fluttering their wings with fervor. Fine dust swirled about the enemies, causing them to slow. With each second, the heat of their bodies died, chilled, slowing them to a crawl.

Then a terrible shrieking came from the clouds and a flight of Dreds swooped down from hiding. They spat acid at the moths, hitting a few before the riders could take evasive maneuvers.

Darien raised his sword again just as the flying demons emerged, opening a final gate. A storm of shrill cries came out.

Hearing the eerie sounds, the demons paused to look up, and sonic booms knocked them back. More blasts came through as the Eskrani army from across the sea arrived astride their flocks of sonic Griffins. The Griffins' gold-plated talons were made for shredding demon flesh, same as their serrated eagle beaks.

While the aerial battle intensified, the open fields burst and churned. Purple light flickered underground with the arrival of the demon army: Wretches, Creepers, Felons and a swath of other nightmarish forms never seen before. The twisted hordes rose up like a tide, flooding the land between the living beings and Castle Sax.

Darien gave King Loggias a nod.

Blowing a ruby-encrusted battle horn, Loggias unleashed the drakes to finish off the Hell Hounds. Impervious to fire, the stone-armored beasts rushed out.

Darien was about to issue another command, but the ground shook as a demon with the shape of a dragon burst free. It roared, crawling from the crater it created. Before long the black and green abomination belched a series of fire balls, aimed for the leaders of the alliance.

"Brace yourselves!" Darien cried in horror, unprepared for the resurrected enemy to rise from the grave.

King Loggias, Isban and Queen Xenorithia could not avoid the enormous volleys without trampling their own soldiers. The three glared defiantly at the ghastly flames.

One of the tarp-covered carts brought by the Zsu nation ripped open, and a slew of goblins gave a vicious battle cry as they leaped out, waving crude weapons. Still in the cart, two of the toothy creatures cackled on either side of a giant sun crystal fitted with an intricate apparatus. Their taller leader shrieked in their primitive language, pointing to the sky with his bone scepter. Both remaining goblins touched the crystal, focusing the magic within.

As the fireballs came down they struck an immense barrier and dissipated. The goblins cheered while their chief cackled wildly, grinning at the thousands of astonished faces. No one was more shocked by the rescue than the queen. The demons and the demon dragon were bombarded by concussive Griffin attacks, giving the leaders time to marvel.

King Loggias gave a loud guffaw and asked, "Queen of the Zsu, it looks as if you have found that crystal you accused us of murdering your king for."

She continued to stare in astonishment at the tribal creatures, speechless.

Both of her allies observed her, and the king on his three-headed dog curiously asked with a sly tone, "Is this the end of your bloody feud with our peoples, Mighty Fighting Queen of the Zsu?"

Recovered from the extreme surprise, she inclined her head and glared over at the Lorisan King. "I here by decree the war against you both is concluded. Be careful not to let this moment of my embarrassment go to your heads. I am still watching you."

Darien laughed, shaking his head. "This is a pleasant surprise, Goblin Chief!"

The green, gangly creature shouted back with his raspy voice, "What you want, Pretty-man?"

This got a chuckle from the Master Knight. "Thank you for your help. Can you shield the kings and the queen? Keep them safe until that dragon is slain."

Another devious giggle and a thumbs up was given. "You got it." Turning to his minions, the chief shouted translated instructions, pointing at the royal figures.

"Well, my friends, it is time to join the fray. The four of you shall assist me in killing that foul abomination spawned from a dragon's corpse. Arianwyn?"

The elf king smiled. "Yes, blood-brother?"

"Thank you. Thank you for all you have done for me and my dear Adwen. None of this would be possible without your involvement. I shall miss you when I am gone."

"The very same to you, Darien Andredan."

To the whole of the allied armies, Darien cried out like thunder, "This is for all who came before and who will come after! For the living and the glorious dead! Charge!"

The armies roared in reply. All four Holy Hounds transformed and bounded at Darien's sides with three nations coming from behind. While the soldiers, riders and trained beasts collided with the closest demons, they continued on. Their enormous foe was still distracted by the aggressive Griffin assault.

A few of the Griffins fell from deadly bites and burns before Darien and the Holy Hounds arrived at the dragon's feet. Darien shouted, "Tamis! Get his attention and keep him on you. Jack, carve off one of his wings to keep him down while Oryn and Alex follow me to flank!"

One well-placed light arrow was all it took to take out one of the demon's eyes. It roared and swiped at him with a set of claws the size of a small house. Tamis was the quicker, leaping out of harm's way to shoot again, doing heavy damage and providing Jack a distraction.

Summoning the tooth-shaped daggers, the curly-tailed Holy Hound sent the blades flying and whirling. Using intense focus, he swiftly carved through scales, black flesh and bone in the blink of an eye. Then, for good measure, cut the length of the membrane as the demon dragon began to roar in agony and rage. Jack was forced to dash away to dodge the falling severed appendage. The daggers returned to his hands just in time to escape.

The titanic enemy forgot Tamis to exact vengeance on the telekinetic warrior, leaving the remaining three undetected. On the demon's other flank, Darien gave further instructions.

"Oryn, throw your heavy armored friend up to carve a hole in that thick hide. Be ready to leap free and run for your life, Alex! Once it is done, everyone stand clear!"

Unhappy with the plan, the yellow and white Holy Hound held his short sword tightly. One moment, he was lifted off his feet; the next he sailed through the air at the heaving sides of a demonic dragon. Roaring in fright and excitement, the warrior held up his weapon and sharp claws, using them to catch the rough scales. His body slammed hard against the monstrosity. In a few unforgiving slices, he slashed a bloody, gushing hole between a set of long ribs.

Gasping and shrieking, the dragon buckled and stood upright, flailing. Alex let go, kicking off to remove the sword and jump clear. He landed, tumbled and bounded off, narrowly avoiding being stepped on. The ground shook under the weight of the creature as it hit the ground.

Oryn stood by Darien's side snarling as the Master Knight took aim at the open wound. Just as the dragon reared his head, taking a breath to blow flames, blue and white fire shot from the end of the Gray Blade. The ethereal flames entered corrupted flesh, striking at the monster's heart. The dragon gasped, mortally wounded. Roaring, flailing and collapsing, the dragon's insides erupted with the blue energy. In moments, the whole of the corrupt dragon was engulfed. Dead on its feet, the beast fell to the soil with a mighty crash of fire, flesh and bones, melting into putrid filth.

The Master Knight and the Holy Hounds felt relief. It was not to last. A sickly wind swept the battle field, making the hair on their backs stand on end. Darien looked to the north, where a deep shadow opened into a narrow portal.

"Oryn, keep within earshot of me, but do not come close. Wait for my signal. It is time. Go." The enormous Holy Hound nodded and dashed away, leaving Darien to dismount and dismiss Auburn, and stare down the evil general.

Guillot stepped out, his black, fragmented form glinting and his green lights for eyes burning. A huge, jagged sword stretched from his left hand, sprouting green flames on its edges. Glaring at the Master Knight, the Sliver of Darkness bellowed long and loud, chilling the blood of all but Darien.

The Master Knight smiled with a clever light in his blue glowing eyes.

The talon feet of the general dug into the dirt, launching him into a fearsome charge. He bellowed again, needle teeth bared in his skull-like head.

Darien waved the sword high, pointing at the veiled sky. "Good-bye, Conrad! Do it now!"

The towering Holy Hound took a deep breath and howled out Adwen's name at the top of his lungs.

A column of noon sun cut through the false clouds, illuminating Darien and the ground he stood upon. Pebbles floated, caught in the flux of energies. He smiled at the angry demon coming closer as his form glowed hot white, losing all definition. A flash burst from where he stood just before General Guillot leaped, swinging his sword to cut the Master Knight in half. The demon collided with a solid form, and they both slid across the ground to a gradual stop, still on their feet.

The Gray Blade blocked the demon's blow and held them with their swords locked. Blue flames from the Gray Blade scrawled higher, cloaking Adwen's long arms. As the spirit fire spread to the rest of her body, adorned silver armor and pieces of blue cloth, the snow-white Holy Hound glanced sidelong into the demon's eyes. The golden emblem on her forehead shone like her sapphire stare.

In Darien's place, shoulder to shoulder with Guillot, she quietly said, "Hello."

In a single leap, he roared and retreated to a safer distance, enraged that Darien had escaped for the last time. Not only that, but Adwen was at her full, raw potential.

Swinging the Gray Blade, she lobbed a ball of energy straight for him.

Guillot barely dodge it, allowing the blue mass to incinerate a distant Felon in an instant. His glare deepened.

She snarled, baring her fangs. With her most basic abilities restored, Adwen lunged forward and disappeared amid a bright flash. A split second later, she reappeared leaping down through the air, swinging the holy sword, commencing the duel.

Guillot was surprised at her ability to transport in a blink and only just raised his weapon to stop the blow and return one. She seemed to dance to and fro, blinking back and forth from either side, testing his strength. Several strikes and blocks later, his temper flared. Guillot roared, and an explosion of demon splinters launched from his body to force her back.

Adwen blinked to avoid the pulse of deadly darts. Taking a fighting stance she obtained from the last of Darien's combat knowledge, she rushed in again. The white and blue flames on her and the sword served as additional armor in her duel against the general. Back and forth, they exchanged strike after strike, and she dodged using her agility and powers.

A second shower of splinters flew, but Adwen evaded them again with a swiftly timed blink. One or two clipped her arms, drawing silver blood. The stinging sparked anger, igniting her fire into an inferno. Its intensity made it painful for Guillot to remain in close combat, shying away from the pure light powers that burned.

To end the fight, Adwen vanished in a flash to appear from behind, but Guillot anticipated the move. He stomped the ground, summoning huge black spikes.

Razor sharp points and edges clamped onto her limbs and cut the white being. Snarling, she was nearly impaled, grasping the sword while the dark masses caged her between them.

Guillot laughed at her, caught in his trap. While Adwen writhed, trying to free herself, he hefted his weapon up to drive it down into her exposed chest. A terrible grin spread under his burning, triumphant stare.

Adwen gnashed her jaws, her body shone, and the black spikes cracked. In a brilliant flash she vanished. Another crunch followed and she reappeared far behind the demon.

Lost in a blind fury at her escape, he turned and glared, roaring in outrage. For a moment they stared each other down. When Adwen did not make a move, Guillot noticed blue flames forming a ring around his midsection. The fire gradually spread, making the ring broader. He struck his sword in the ground at his side, sneering at the Holy Hound in realization of his defeat.

She watched his body shake and shudder, then he wailed. The sound echoed all around. The blue fire poured from his mouth as it burned from within. General Guillot's body turned pale, becoming like ash and dust, disintegrating into nothingness.

As he died at last, Adwen howled, calling the four warriors to her side. Together, they began the final charge to the castle. She, Jack and Tamis ran on the backs of countless demons, striking at random, while Alex and Oryn barreled through. Their bodies bashed past, knocking enemies aside on their way. At the steps they stopped and shifted into their smaller forms.

Adwen and Oryn were about to go inside when three enemies came riding in on their mounts. The demons from the
plains rushed to stop them, brandishing their weapons.

"We can take care of these goons," Jack barked. "We'll
cover the front! Go on!"

The two darted for the entrance, swords in hand. Meanwhile, the three hounds snarled, eyes aglow. When the fiends
came closer, Tamis loosed an arrow, Alex ran out to meet
them, and Jack's daggers danced in a cyclone of flashing metal.

The castle interior appeared deserted. Adwen's and Oryn's
sixth sense gave them certainty that a powerful presence
lurked. Hidden in the monstrous castle, a demon darkened
every corner, preserving the structure despite the deterioration
time normally brings. If the elements had their way, this place
would have become a ruin long ago.

Adwen's feet and Oryn's boots made little sound, leaving
prints in the dust as they ran. Rounding a few corners in
search of the way to the highest tower, the duo raced through
many halls. Noxious incense burned, its vapor irritating their
lungs until they learned to hold their breath as they passed.

Dashing into a cavernous main hall large enough to contain a cathedral, a figure waited for them at its center. Both
Holy Hounds came to a halt, growling, eyes shining brightly in
the near-complete darkness.

Sycan stood with his side to them, taking a deep breath
and slowly sighing. Glancing sidelong with a subtle glint in his
stare, he smiled contentedly at them. "So it comes to this.
Adwen, you are looking well."

She growled, and Oryn snarled.

"Now that the general is out of the way, I look forward to
our rematch, child of light. It should be a closer battle, would-
n't you say?"

Adwen and the pale-eyed demon watched the knight step
forward, gripping the Rose Thorne with purpose. His glare
was fierce.

She looked between them both as the ancient werewolf
started to grin.

Realizing right away who his opponent would be, Sycan chuckled, his voice compounding like a raspy choir. He liked this change of plans very much.

The powers Sycan held were easier for her to gauge than for Oryn. He did not know how dangerous this fight would be. As strong as her knight had become, this would be his ultimate test, and in ways beyond combat. Her heart told her so. Before leaving him behind, she murmured, worriedly, "Be careful."

Oryn nodded, never looking away from Sycan as she bolted for the end of the hall. When she vanished down another corridor, Sycan approached his opponent, sizing him up.

Facing the knight, the Last of the First Six tilted his head, summoning his own sword. The sickly smile remained as he spoke softly: "I prefer it this way. Sir Oryn Reynard Conrad, this has been on my mind ever since our meeting in Mortigad. Your scream is exquisite. It is my favorite by far. So much rage and pain. I've never forgotten it, and I look forward to hearing it again."

The knight took a stance he deemed appropriate for this fight.

Sycan chuckled. "Is there nothing you wish to say before you die?"

"Shut up and fight."

An inhuman voice from behind shark-like teeth replied, "As you wish."

They collided in a flurry of metal and immense force.

Adwen climbed a spiral staircase higher and higher. The farther she went up the stairs, the colder it became. Close to the top, her breaths came out as steam clouds. In the dark her sword acted as a torch, though she did not need it in order to see. Blue light splashed across stone walls that steadily became less and less like stones. True darkness coated every surface, retreating when the glow of her sword came near and where her feet landed.

At the top she slowed to a cautious walk, approaching a black door. It soundlessly opened to invite her inside, giving her an even greater feeling of foreboding. Beyond the threshold was a secluded plane apart from the living worlds. Past the open door was a piece of the void. Leery, Adwen mustered her determination and entered, not flinching as that door closed behind, cutting off any retreat.

A haze hung suspended in the air. It defied her nocturnal vision, obscuring most of the surroundings. If she weren't so sure, this place would pass easily for an ordinary castle chamber. Going a bit farther inward, a large shape caught her attention. On closer inspection, her sight deciphered the outline of a throne atop a small flight of stone steps. Finally, Adwen could smell her amid the murk.

Breathless and staring in disbelief at a solitary figure on the throne, she whispered, "Eyrie?"

Suddenly the haze and blackness veiling the walls retracted and shrank. It withdrew to vanish behind the ornate chair designed for royalty. With the air clear, the princess became clearly visible, seated and seemingly asleep. Her long pale-blond hair flowed down as her head rested lazily on her chest. The form of the still young human girl was dressed in black, and she had no obvious signs of harm.

Adwen knew something was terribly wrong as she gingerly approached the bottom step. Her distant cousin remained silent and unmoving. Becoming very aware of a presence nearby, she called more urgently, "Eyrie, can you hear me?"

The face of the princess looked up, and her eyes opened. They were black as onyx marbles. Then a pair of white specks in the depths of a shadow peered out from behind the throne. The two gazes blinked in unison, watching Adwen with growing intrigue.

A layering of voices, including the one belonging to the princess, crooned, "I knew you would not be fooled once you saw her. She can hear you but can say nothing. I chose to spare the fair human when it came to my attention that her body could be of great use. You see, Bastard Heir of Darien, a little of his blood fortifies her flesh. With that small amount and without the direct touch of light, she can become my vessel and not die from the strain of containing my wondrous majesty. Before I forget, thank you for interfering with the Bloody Brothers. I never would have had the chance if they had killed her that night. In time, I will leave this prison and walk the worlds in her skin as you do in yours. Would that not be a beautiful sight?"

"I'm not here to stand by and watch, Melanin. And I'm not here to listen to your delusions of grandeur."

"Ah, but you are here to take my prize." The possessed body of the princess stood, smiling.

Adwen glared back. "By destroying you, I will finish what Darien started. Today."

"You are alone, dear child of light. No one can come to your aid. And I have a question to ask." A long, thin sword made of what looked like black glass formed in the hand of Princess Eyrie. "How will you kill me without killing her as well?"

Transforming into her true form, cloaking herself in flames, Adwen snarled. The answer to the deadly riddle was far from clear.

The girl floated into the air, brandishing the evil weapon, laughing in unison with the demon puppeteer. In a flash, the shadow hovering behind her formed into a torso and arms with long, spindly talons. A head with many horns and layers of dragon-like and wolfish shapes held recognizable features of a human face, grinning broadly. "Cower and despair, Andredan. I am Melanin, the bender, the breaker! *I am the demon maker!*"

Melanin flew with Eyrie, laughing louder, swooping in to kill the Holy Hound.

Minutes of back-and-forth battle between Oryn and Sycan carried on, each matching the other blow for blow. They knew each other's style, could read subtle body language to anticipate a move. A twitch of the foot or a small shrug was enough of a hint for what would come. Both loathed each other and reveled in the fight, but Sycan grew bored. He could see that the knight was not putting emotion into the match. Something would need to change that. After waiting so long for this day, the demon was ready to stoke the flames of the warrior's rage.

To create a window of opportunity, the demon lunged to bash the knight. As Oryn blocked him, Sycan stuck out his long blue forked tongue and licked the knight's face. Then the monster in human form tilted his weapon and pushed at an angle.

The distraction shocked Oryn, and the feeling of more force from his enemy drove him to leap back. After almost losing his arm and retreating to a safe distance, he felt a stinging sensation. A cut bled on his arm where the armor did not reach. Looking up, the demon with wine-red hair tasted the fresh blood on his blade.

After considering the flavor, he smiled, pleasantly satisfied. "It is not as sweet as that of your brother, but it will do." Seeing the color flush from Oryn's stunned expression, Sycan gave a mocking laugh, shaking his head. "You did not know? You never guessed? That was when I first heard your scream! It was perfect! Equal parts anguish and rage! It is your cry that has always been my most savored in all the centuries. A young child had never been marked before, and I was curious how things would unfold. That night was remarkable, especially the moment you took off his head."

A feral roar erupted from Oryn as he lunged, transforming to tower over the demon. He tried to cut Sycan down the middle, but the demon blocked the blow with his own blade. Snarling and gnashing jaws to bite his head, the raging warrior pressed down hard with the holy sword, to end the one responsible for his pain and Sycan's laughter.

"That's more like it!" the demon crowed and pushed back, transforming and then towering over the Holy Hound. At thirteen feet, the monstrous werewolf with white eyes stood three feet taller than Oryn. The set of enormous jaws seemed to split in a grin with an additional pair of incisors, reminding Oryn of the dragon slain outside. Echoing, croaking guffaws puffed hot breath in Oryn's face before he was knocked farther away. The beast roared in delight, ready for more blood.

Adwen fended off Melanin's sword, careful to avoid harming Eyrie. She tried to flash jump and reappear behind to strike the demon lord, but the darkness of this place would not let her. With that ability no longer an option, she remained defensive, straining to think while no time was afforded to do so. The attacks were unrelenting, picking up in pace.

Evading another stroke of the shadow sword, Adwen dashed away and whirled around. She shot a plume of blue fire at the demon's head over the shoulder of the princess. But Melanin raised Eyrie higher, smiling wider when the Heir gasped, redirecting the shot just enough to miss the girl. Yet the blue fire singed Eyrie's shoulder and a few strands of hair. Red blisters glistened on the girl's fair skin, making Adwen feel sick as the demon laughed.

"You surprise me, Adwen. Do you hate your kin so much you would finish off this one? What comes next? Setting the king of Dargadia aflame?"

She snarled, wrinkling her jowls in frustration.

Again, the unfair fight commenced. Melanin hissed and cackled, enjoying Adwen's growing despair. The emissary of the Light Spirits could not defeat him.

It became difficult to block every attack, leading her to dodge the strikes. Adwen yelped when the sword clipped her ear and then her forearm. Silver trickles began to saturate her fur, running like liquid metal. She had to ignore the small injuries as more came. Keeping her eye on Eyrie, Adwen noticed that Melanin's form always hovered behind the girl's shoulders and over her head. He smiled all the time. Adwen needed to reach the demon past the princess, and she could not see an opening. Even more cuts from the shadow sword bled, helping her come to a conclusion. There would be only one chance to save Princess Eyrie. The move would need to be precise.

Letting herself be driven back to the steps of the throne, Adwen carefully defended herself. Repeatedly, she blocked and deflected, letting Melanin gain ground. Then, when the moment was right, Adwen feigned a fall, toppling backward onto the steps with a loud yelp.

Melanin could not resist, roaring as he pounced with the princess. Adwen shifted into her woman form to become a smaller target, but the demon did not care. This time his sword found her ethereal flesh, pinning her to the floor like a fly.

Oryn had trouble guarding against the full strength that

Sycan wielded with his large, crude sword. He resorted to tumbling and dodging some strikes, knowing it was useless to block. It was not easy to forget the first time that the demon's weapon rent his body open. Though that took place in the magical mirror, it felt as real as this attack. No mistakes could be made, or death would be certain.

Bashing the talented warrior about with his brutal power gave Sycan flashbacks to wondrous fights with Darien and Keegan. This was like dueling both at once. It was too much fun to let it end too soon. Lost in reminiscing, he began to toy with Oryn, looking for the perfect times to whittle him down, piece by piece. This kill needed to be slow; it needed to be savored.

As another cut from Sycan's sword appeared on Oryn's other arm, the knight recognized the look on the werewolf lord; he was leisurely. This meant he would begin the end of the fight, and that also meant that he was becoming lazy. Oryn had to act now, or risk losing.

When Sycan moved to strike low, Oryn jumped up, dodging the critical blow. Then as the swing carried back to cut his side. In the blink of an eye, the knightly Holy Hound formed strong protective magic over his free gauntlet. He blocked, grabbing a hold of the dark weapon with the shielded hand. Keeping a tight grip as he spun in close, he slashed with all his might. Just after dealing the blow, Oryn jumped back out of reach, growling.

Sycan was not ready for that. He did not know that Oryn could do such a thing. Frozen in astonishment, the wretched beast hung his head to watch as blood and a few lengths of intestines tumbled out. Then he began to laugh. His laughter mounted, escalating to maddening croaks that filled the grand hall.

Oryn growled. Blood dripped from his sword. "For my brother, you die here. You will claim no more victims."

Slumping to his knees, taking up the exposed organs in his claws, presenting them, Sycan tilted his head. A sickening snap came as his neck seemed to break and his head landed on a muscular, fur-covered shoulder. He rumbled, chuckling darkly, "What was his name? I never did catch wind of it. No matter. The simpering little boy is dead and gone, forever."

The knight flinched as one of Sycan's arms burst, blood flying as muscles and veins protruded, too large for his skin to contain. Shuddering and twitching as if wracked by a seizure, the monster cried out in excitement, "Bravo! Well, done, Conrad! You have proved yourself worthy. Behold! My true form put into flesh by my maker, Lord Melanin!"

A sickening crack and a splashing was made when the flesh and bones of Sycan burst out from the mass. His fleshy body turned inside out, his black fur coat swallowed by the bulbous mass that continued to grow. Oryn retreated backward, watching in horror as two arterial claws reach out of the bloody folds, gripping the stone floor. What he thought were several additional arms reached upward while the body grew outward, but mismatching heads with bone spikes opened wide. Their jaws were misshapen, armed with rows of uneven fangs. A serpentine tail whipped around, convulsing until spikes protruded all along it like a quilled whip. Last, a broad mouth with razor-sharp teeth opened where the chest should be on the bloody, fleshy form. It smiled wide.

The twisted perversion of a hydra shrieked with its many heads that brushed the ceiling, and Oryn's ears flattened in distress. He had guessed Sycan would be hideous but never imagined this. Seeing the spiked tail swinging at him, he leaped back, only to feel blasts of fire from the several heads. Oryn stood his ground, using a magical barrier to hold back the flames. Heat radiated through, forcing him to avert his gaze as his hand and armor grew hot.

Once Sycan ceased his fire breathing, the powerful Holy Hound watched the oversized mouth on the belly open. It laughed with a thousand voices, the breath reeking of decay. That was when Oryn saw it. At the back of the throat was a pulsing object the size of a broad shield.

While it laughed, Oryn ran straight for Sycan. The tail swatted, but he bounded over, tucking and rolling back to his feet. The mouth still laughed as the warrior continued the charge. When Oryn jumped, leaping high toward the gaping, guffawing mouth full of pointed teeth, he took a deep breath. Then it closed him in with a loud slamming of jaws. A moment passed. Sycan's many heads trilled amongst themselves in victory.

Suddenly, a shudder swept his horrendous body. The many heads wailed like sirens. Pained and weakened, the monster began to writhe. He collapsed, the giant mouth retching and gagging. When Sycan began to wither, turning inside out as he changed, Oryn tumbled free, gasping for air.

Shifting into his smaller form covered in slimy saliva, he held his sword up, watching the heads disintegrate. Bleeding, pulsating flesh shrank. The claws receded, and the tail retracted, leaving a round, pink ball of veins, skin and fatty tissues. Once it was not much larger than Oryn, the egg-like mass popped. Liquids splashed in all directions, and a body with black fur writhed, struggling to its four paws.

A black wolf, starved and driven to madness, bore a single scar across its face. The scar reverted to a bleeding wound, and the pathetic animal snapped and snarled. He trembled before Oryn, the demon gone. Seconds passed, and the mad wolf froze in place. His body turned to stone from within, suspending him in perpetual rage. The knight pitied the dead creature left behind. At last, he answered the demon's final question.

"His name... was Kai."

With an easy swing of his sword, Oryn destroyed the remains. A long sigh later, silence filled his heart with closure. Then it was rudely interrupted. The castle shook, stones cracking, showering pebbles and dust from overhead.

Dismissing the sword, he felt a stabbing pain in his chest. It filled him with fear. Following Adwen's scent, the castle began to quake as he raced to find her.

Adwen shivered, panting with the shadow blade through her chest, staring up at the princess and the demon.

Eyrie's face and the fiend's expression mirrored each other in surprise as Adwen's sword reached beneath the girl's arm. The fire only lit the end, avoiding the princess' unarmored side, penetrating the core of Melanin.

The demon set the girl on her feet, gazing in disbelief until Adwen grimaced, surging more fire to the end of the Gray Blade. Melanin wailed in many voices, and the princess screamed before collapsing. Eyrie landed at Adwen's side, and the blue flames engulfed the terrible entity, purging him. The floor and walls began to shake as the wailing of anger and pain died with the shadow.

Dismissing her weapon, Adwen bled around the blade left in her torso. She no longer had the strength to take it out. Quivering, everything started to fade.

Princess Eyrie awoke to the sound of stones falling and found Adwen close by. The woman shrieked and cried out, "Adwen! Adwen! Don't die! Not now!"

As Adwen's eyes closed, the princess pulled the sword out, tossing it aside. When she knelt and tried to stop the flow of silver blood, the door burst open.

Oryn darted inside while in human form, scooping Adwen into his arms. "We must run!" he shouted. "This way, Princess!"

The foundations began to crumble, and stone began to fall all around. Eventually, Oryn had no choice but to carry Eyrie around the middle and run at full speed. He dodged many falling pieces of rubble. Each block was larger than the last. Castle Sax rained down on their heads, as if to keep them from escape. Clouds of dust and flying pebbles enveloped them as the light of day appeared at the broad entryway.

Leaping free of the falling castle, flying down the stairs, Oryn set the princess down. Both coughed, running away as the walls continued to fall.

All demons on the battlefield lay dead or withering, their master destroyed. Combatants from the armies gathered and stared at the figures emerging from the billowing clouds of dust. Jack, Alex and Tamis went to meet them, along with Arianwyn riding on Auburn's saddle. Many faces, some covered in purple and red smears, waited to see who had survived.

A stillness settled over the land in the wake of the storm. Sunlight steadily shredded the darkness, fading it away. Oryn cradled Adwen's limp body in his arms yet again. Warm light touched them as he studied her face, waiting.

Ever so slowly, she stirred. When she looked back into the eyes of her devoted knight, he strained against shedding tears again. He gave the others a beaming smile to let them know she lived.

Jack succumbed to the thrill and pumped his fists in the

air, shouting as loudly as he could, while Alex and Tamis laughed. The diversity of soldiers cheered, raising weapons, banging chest plates and roaring triumphantly.

Glad for the good fortune while the sun shone on them, Oryn did not withhold his feelings. He touched his brow to hers, holding her close. The sun warmed them both before the cheering masses.

Chapter 26
TILL THEN

The following day, Adwen and her warriors met with the kings and queen in the Order's Elder Hall. Smiling proudly, the goblin chief studied their looks, waiting for them to make a decision. Things were going his way for a change.

"Absolutely not!" Queen Xenorithia snapped. "This little beast is responsible for the killing of my husband! I will not reconsider this. He is my enemy."

Fully healed, Adwen sighed. "I understand. The trouble is that the crystal he killed him for was used to save us all, including yourself."

The goblin giggled.

"See! He goads me to slay him even now! You feed his pride, Tame One."

He said a few things in his own language, sniggering, shaking his head. The long bat-like ears flapped.

"Give back the crystal!" she sneered, "It is not yours to own."

"Goblins do not own the pretty rock, dumb human. After we stole pretty rock it told us goblins what to do!"

They exchanged looks, and Adwen asked, "Can you please explain?"

"We wanted pretty rock to fight Vampies. Vampies call goblins food! But pretty rock said it dies if it kills. Pretty rock showed us what to do. It helped us to hide and find yummy fishes. Then pretty rock told goblins that you crazy humans have plan to kill Vampies! Goblins had to leave the dark and make things. Goblins could help win!"

More looks were exchanged.

Adwen pondered then continued to investigate. "What does the crystal want you to do now?"

Looking up at the queen with his lamp-like eyes, he

smiled. "Pretty rock wants goblins to stay in the sun. It says we live good by the lake. It says goblins are smart if they put pretty rock in the water. Make lots of fishes and trees."

The queen was dumbstruck. That was her initial plan for the sun crystal.

Adwen turned to her. "You owe him your life, and he wants the same thing you do."

Glaring fiercely at the green-skinned creature in rags, she hissed, "So long as you keep your word and place it in the lake, I will spare you and your kind. But if any of my people are attacked by goblins in the future, I will feed you to my sand shark."

The goblin chief cackled, entertained by the honest threat.

King Loggias chuckled, nudging a frowning King Zulo. "I'm learning to like goblins."

Oryn rolled his eyes when no one was looking.

Adwen was relieved. "It's agreed then: The goblins will be allowed some territory by the lake in repayment for their deeds."

Everyone nodded, even the suspicious queen.

"What of you, Lady Adwen?" asked King Lorvan. "Will you remain in the halls of the Order?"

She shook her head, smiling. "I thought about it. Eventually I will, but for a while I'd like to go back to the other world, where I was born."

"And what of your warriors?"

She looked at them, wondering what they would answer.

Jack scoffed, "I have to go find my wife and take her home! If the demons are dead, I might get my old job back. There's going to be a big house cleaning, that's for sure."

"I should probably stay here," Alex said.

"Absolutely not!" Jack told his friend. "You are coming with me! After all we've been through, I think I can help you start fresh. Wanted for murder or not, we're partners, and I'm not leaving you behind."

The blond warrior smiled. "Roger that, Scruff McGraw."

"Zip it, Lassie."

Tamis sheepishly said, "This world is the only home I've ever known. It would be best if I found my place in it."

King Lorvan beamed. "You shall accompany me when I

return to my castle in Deleon when the time comes. It will be your new home outside of the Order. And what will you do, Sir Oryn? Where will you go?" A clever glint in the old man's eyes let on that he knew the answer.

Oryn smiled and shared a brief look with Adwen, who returned the expression. "I serve Adwen. I will never leave her side."

In the courtyard they met after she and her friends said their goodbyes. The foreign leaders passed through portals Adwen provided, sending them to their respective kingdoms. Then she opened one more gate ringed in blue fire. On the other side was a forest and the non-magical world. The blue tongues of flame swayed, beckoning.

Jack and Alex went through, returning salutes from the knights. Then Sir Peregrine blocked the shorter warrior's path. He snared the mouthy comrade in a bear hug before letting him go on. The friends passed through and continued between the trees on the other side.

Adwen and Oryn looked back at the Order one more time. Hundreds of Gargoyles and knights waved and whooped, bidding them good tidings on their way. Balefire and the mages called from the ramparts along with many commoners.

Finally looking at each other, their eyes shone brightly, and they followed Jack and Alex. The fire portal closed, and Malik the phoenix trilled. The firebird's call was unlike anything the gathering had heard before. The song of the phoenix signaled the end and the beginning, same as its never-ending cycle so many speak of.

LATER…

Winter passed, and spring thawed the land into new life. Many more months passed, and songs continued to be sung of Adwen's and the Holy Hounds' victory. The demon who had darkened the land was dead. The king of Dargadia and his people gradually returned to their homes, beginning anew.

As farms the demons had set aflame were rebuilt, and the more fertile soil was worked and sown, the singing carried on. In taverns bards told of the Tame One with her blue fire, as well as the faithful few who followed her into unspeakable dangers.

In one tavern, as the song was sung long and loud, people cheered, toasting repeatedly till they swayed in their seats. A man sat alone, unshaven, unbathed and seething. He hated the song. After being cast out of the Order by Adwen, Jacques never forgave and never forgot the embarrassment and disgrace. The mead was cheap enough for him to buy, but not strong enough to drown out the hatred.

Taking another swig, he belched and scowled at the revelers. "Curse the Tame One. Curse her into the void." The filthy man took another drink.

A different song reached his ears over the throng. It made him pause. All else seemed muted. In moments there was only the sweet song. The sound called to the angry man, distracting him from the things that put the fury in him in the first place. Dropping the mug to the ground, Jacques left the boisterous tavern without paying.

Outside, the call was stronger and lovelier. It was haunting like an incantation and as soothing as a lullaby. Leaving the town for the wilds, he wandered in search of the source. It grew louder, bringing him deep into the woods, far from all else.

Coming to a clearing with a hollow tree bearing few leaves, the song was at its loudest. He approached the nearly dead trunk, unafraid. The song was so enchanting. It began to say his name. The voice was so sweet that he could taste sugar on his tongue. Then as he leaned his head into the dark space, it said his name once more. The song was gone, and the new voice was deep, like the shadows inside the hollow.

Many thin arms of darkness grabbed Jacques, pulling him down, out of sight.